CHRISTMAS WHERE THEY BELONG

BY
MARION LENNOX

Published in Great Britain 2014
by Mills & Boon, an imprint of Harlequin (UK) Limited,
Eton House, 18-24 Paradise Road, Richmond, Surrey, TW9 1SR

ISBN: 978-0-263-91340-8

23-1214

Harlequin (UK) Limited's policy is to use papers that are natural, renewable and recyclable products and made from wood grown in sustainable forests. The logging and manufacturing processes conform to the legal environmental regulations of the country of origin.

Printed and bound in Spain
by CPI, Barcelona

Marion Lennox is a country girl, born on an Australian dairy farm. She moved on—mostly because the cows just weren't interested in her stories! Married to a "very special doctor", Marion writes for the Mills & Boon® Medical Romance™ and Mills & Boon® Cherish™ lines. (She used a different name for each category for a while—readers looking for her past romance titles should search for author Trisha David as well). She's now had well over ninety novels accepted for publication.

In her non-writing life Marion cares for kids, cats, dogs, chooks and goldfish. She travels, she fights her rampant garden (she's losing) and her house dust (she's lost). Having spun in circles for the first part of her life, she's now stepped back from her 'other' career, which was teaching statistics at her local university. Finally she's reprioritised her life, figured out what's important and discovered the joys of deep baths, romance and chocolate. Preferably all at the same time!

This book is dedicated to Lorna May Dickins.
Her kindness, her humour and her love
are an inspiration for always.

CHAPTER ONE

'DIDN'T YOU ONCE own a house in the Blue Mountains?'

'Um…yes.'

'Crikey, Jules, you wouldn't want to be there now. The whole range looks about to burn.'

It was two days before Christmas. The Australian world of finance shut down between Christmas and New Year, but the deal Julie McDowell was working on was international. The legal issues were urgent.

But the Blue Mountains… Fire.

She dumped her armload of contracts and headed for Chris's desk. At thirty-two, Chris was the same age as Julie, but her colleague's work ethic was as different from hers as it was possible to be. Chris worked from nine to five and not a moment more before he was off home to his wife and kids in the suburbs. Sometimes he even surfed the Web during business hours.

Sure enough, his computer was open at the Web browser now. She came up behind him and saw a fire map. The Blue Mountains. A line of red asterisks.

Her focus went straight to Mount Bundoon, a tiny hamlet right in the centre of the asterisks. The hamlet she'd once lived in.

'Is it on fire?' she gasped. She'd been so busy she hadn't been near a news broadcast for hours. Days?

'Not yet.' Chris zoomed in on a few of the asterisks. 'These are alerts, not evacuation orders. A storm came through last night, with lighting strikes but not much rain. The bush is tinder dry after the drought, and most of these asterisks show spot fires in inaccessible bushland. But strong winds and high temperatures are forecast for tomorrow. They're already closing roads, saying she could be a killer.'

A killer.

The Blue Mountains.

You wouldn't want to be there now.

She went back to her desk and pulled up the next contract. This was important. She needed to concentrate, but the words blurred before her eyes. All she could see was a house—long, low, every detail architecturally designed, built to withstand the fiercest bush fires.

In her mind she walked through the empty house to a bedroom with two small beds in the shape of racing cars. Teddies sitting against the pillows. Toys. A wall-hanging of a steam train her mother had made.

She hadn't been there for four years. It should have been sold. Why hadn't it?

She fought to keep her mind on her work. This had to be dealt with before Christmas.

Teddies. A wardrobe full of small boys' clothes.

She closed her eyes and she was there again, tucking two little boys into bed, watching Rob read them their bedtime story.

It was history, long past, but she couldn't open her eyes. She couldn't.

'Julie? Are you okay?' Her boss was standing over her, sounding concerned. Bob Marsh was a financial wizard but he looked after his staff, especially those who brought as much business to the firm as Julie.

She forced herself to open her eyes and tried for a smile. It didn't work.

'What's up?'

'The fire.' She took a deep breath, knowing what she was facing. Knowing she had no choice.

'I *do* have a house in the Blue Mountains,' she managed. 'If it's going to burn there are things I need to save.' She gathered her pile of contracts and did what she'd never done in all her years working for Opal, Harbison and Marsh. She handed the pile to Bob. 'You'll need to deal with this,' she told him. 'I'm sorry, but…'

She couldn't finish the sentence. She grabbed her purse and went.

Rob McDowell was watching the fire's progress on his phone. He'd downloaded an app to track it by, and he'd been checking it on and off for hours.

He was in Adelaide, working. His clients had wanted to be in the house by Christmas and he'd bent over backwards to make it happen. Their house was brilliant and there were only a few decorative touches left to be made. Rob was no longer needed, but Sir Cliff and Lady Claudia had requested their architect to stay on until tomorrow.

He should. They were having a housewarming on Christmas Eve, and socialising at the end of a job was important. The *Who's Who* of Adelaide, maybe even the *Who's Who* of the entire country would be here. There weren't many people who could beckon the cream of society on Christmas Eve but Sir Cliff and Lady Claudia had that power. As the architect of their stunning home, Rob could expect scores of professional approaches afterwards.

But it wasn't just professional need that was driving him. For the last few years he'd flown overseas to the ski fields for Christmas but somehow this year they'd lost their appeal. Christmas had been a nightmare for years but finally he was beginning to accept that running away didn't help. He might as well stay for the party, he'd decided, but now he checked the phone app again and felt worse. The house he and Julie had built was right in the line of fire.

The house would be safe, he told himself. He'd designed it himself and it had been built with fires like this one in mind.

But no house could withstand the worst of Australia's bush fires. He knew that. To make its occupants safe he'd built a bunker into the hill behind the house, but the house itself could go up in flames.

It was insured. No one was living there. It shouldn't matter.

But the contents…

The contents.

He should have cleared it out by now, he thought savagely. He shouldn't have left everything there. The tricycles. The two red fire engines he'd chosen himself that last Christmas.

Julie might have taken them.

She hadn't. She would have told him.

Both of them had walked away from their house four years ago. It should have been on the market, but…but…

But he'd paid a housekeeping service to clean it once a month, and to clear the grounds. He was learning to move on, but selling the house, taking this last step, still seemed…too hard.

So what state was it in now? he wondered. Had the bushland encroached again? If there was bushland growing against the house…

It didn't matter. The house was insured, he told himself again. What did it matter if it burned? Wouldn't that just be the final step in moving on with his life?

But two fire engines…

This was ridiculous. He was thinking of forgoing the social event of the season, a career-building triumph, steps to the future, to save two toy fire engines?

But…

'Sarah…' He didn't know what he intended to say until the words were in his mouth, but the moment he said it he knew his decision was right.

'Yeah?' The interior decorator was balancing on a ladder, her arms full of crimson tulle. The enormous drawing room was going to look stunning. 'Could you hand me those ribbons?'

'I can't, Sarah,' he said, in a voice he scarcely recognised. 'I own a house in the Blue Mountains and they're saying the fire threat's getting worse. Could you make my excuses? I need to go…home.'

At the headquarters of the Blue Mountains Fire Service, things looked grim and were about to get worse. Every time a report came in, more asterisks appeared on the map. The fire chief had been staring at it for most of the day, watching spot fires erupt, while the weather forecast grew more and more forbidding.

'We won't be able to contain this,' he eventually said, heavily. 'It's going to break out.'

'Evacuate?' His second-in-command was looking even more worried than he was.

'If we get one worse report from the weather guys, yes. We'll put out a pre-evacuation warning tonight. Anyone not prepared to stay and firefight should leave now.' He looked again at the map and raked his thinning hair. 'Okay, people, let's put the next step of fire warnings into place. Like it or not, we're about to mess with a whole lot of people's Christmases.'

CHAPTER TWO

THE HOUSE LOOKED just as she'd left it. The garden had grown, of course. A couple of trees had grown up close to the house. Rob wouldn't be pleased. He'd say it was a fire risk.

It was a fire risk.

She was sitting in the driveway in her little red coupé, staring at the front door. Searching for the courage to go inside.

It was three years, eleven months, ten days since she'd been here.

Rob had brought her home from hospital. She'd wandered into the empty house; she'd looked around and it was almost as if the walls were taunting her.

You're here and they're not. What sort of parents are you? What sort of parents were you?

She hadn't even stayed the night. She couldn't. She'd thrown what she most needed into a suitcase and told Rob to take her to a hotel.

'Julie, we can do this.' She still heard Rob's voice; she still saw his face. 'We can face this together.'

'It wasn't you who slept while they died.' She'd thrown that at him, he hadn't answered and she'd known right then that the final link had snapped.

She hadn't been back since.

Go in, she told herself now. *Get this over.*

She opened the car door and the heat hit her with such force that she gasped.

It was dusk. It shouldn't be this hot, this late.

The tiny hamlet of Mount Bundoon had looked almost deserted as she'd driven through. Low-lying smoke and the lack of wind was giving it a weird, eerie feeling. She'd stopped at the general store and bought milk and bread and butter, and the lady had been surprised to see her.

'We're about to close, love,' she said. 'Most people are packing to get out or have already left. You're not evacuating?'

'The latest warning is watch and wait.'

'They've upgraded it. Unless you plan on defending your home, they're advising you get out, if not now, then at least by nine in the morning. That's when the wind's due to rise, but most residents have chosen to leave straight away.'

Julie had hesitated at that. The road up here had been packed with laden cars, trailers, horse floats, all the accoutrements people treasured. That was why she was here. To take things she treasured.

But now she thought: *it wasn't.* She sat in the driveway and stared at the house where she'd once lived, and she thought, even though the house was full of the boys' belongings, it wasn't possessions she wanted.

Was it just to be here? One last time?

It wasn't going to burn, she told herself. It'd still be here…for ever. But that was a dumb thought. They'd have to sell eventually.

That'd mean contacting Rob.

Don't go there.

Go in, she told herself. *Hunker down. This house is fire-safe. In the morning you can walk away but just for tonight... Just for tonight you can let yourself remember.*

Even if it hurt so much it nearly killed her.

* * *

Eleven o'clock. The plane had been delayed, because of smoke haze surrounding Sydney. 'There's quite a fire down there, ladies and gentlemen,' the pilot had said as they skirted the Blue Mountains. 'Just be thankful you're up here and not down there.'

But he'd wanted to be down there. By the time he'd landed the fire warnings for Mount Bundoon had been upgraded. *Leave if safe to do so.* Still, the weather forecast was saying the winds weren't likely to pick up until early morning. Right now there was little wind. The house would be safe.

So he'd hired a car and driven into the mountains, along roads where most of the traffic was going in the other direction. When he'd reached the outskirts of Mount Bundoon he'd hit a road block.

'Your business, sir?' he was asked.

'I live here.' How true was that? He didn't live anywhere, he conceded, but maybe here was still…home. 'I just need to check all my fire prevention measures are in place and operational.'

'You're aware of the warnings?'

'I am, but my house is pretty much fire-safe and I'll be out first thing in the morning.'

'You're not planning on defending?'

'Not my style.'

'Not mine either,' the cop said. 'They're saying the wind'll be up by nine, turning to the north-west, bringing the fire straight down here. The smoke's already making the road hazardous. We're about to close it now, allowing no one else in. I shouldn't let you pass.'

'I'll be safe. I'm on my own and I'll be in and out in no time.'

'Be out by the time the wind changes, if not before,' he said grudgingly.

'I will be.'

'Goodnight, then, sir,' the cop said. 'Stay safe.'

'Same to you, in spades.'

He drove on. The smoke wasn't thick, just a haze like a winter fog. The house was on the other side of town, tucked into a valley overlooking the Bundoon Creek. The ridges would be the most dangerous places, Rob thought, not the valley. He and Julie had thought about bush fire when they'd built. If you were planning to build in the Australian bush, you were stupid if you didn't.

Maybe they'd been stupid anyway. Building so far out of town. Maybe that was why…

No. Don't think why. That was the way of madness.

Nearly home. That was a dumb thing to think, too, but he turned the last bend and thought of all the times he'd come home, with kids, noise, chaos, all the stuff associated with twins. Sometimes he and Julie would manage the trip back together and that was the best. *'Mummy, Daddy—you're both here…'*

Cut it out, he told himself fiercely. *You were dumb to come. Don't make it any worse by thinking of the past.*

But the past was all around him, even if it was shrouded in smoke.

'I'll take their toys and get out of here,' he told himself, and then he pulled into the driveway… and the lights were on.

She'd turned on all the lights to scare the ghosts.

No. If there were any ghosts here she'd welcome them with open arms—it wasn't ghosts she was scared of. It was the dark. It was trying to sleep in this house, and remembering.

She lay on the king-sized bed she and Rob had bought the week before their wedding and she knew sleep was out of the question. She should leave.

But leaving seemed wrong, too. Not when the kids were here.

The kids weren't here. Only memories of them.

This was crazy. She was a legal financier, a good one, specialising in international monetary negotiations. No one messed with her. No one questioned her sanity.

So why was she lying in bed hoping for ghosts?

She lay completely still, listening to the small sounds of the night. The scratching of a possum in the tree outside the window. A night owl calling.

This house had never been quiet. She found herself aching for noise, for voices, for…something.

She got something. She heard a car pull into the driveway. She saw the glimmer of headlights through the window.

The front door opened, and she knew part of her past had just returned. The ghost she was most afraid of.

'Julie?' He'd guessed it must be her before he even opened the door. Firstly the car. It was a single woman's car, expensive, a display of status.

Rob normally drove a Land Rover. Okay, maybe that was a status thing as well, he conceded. He liked the idea that he might spend a lot of time on rural properties but in truth most of his clients were city based. But still, he couldn't drive a car like the one in the driveway. No one here could. No one who commuted from here to the city. No one who taxied kids.

Every light was on in the house. Warning off ghosts?

It had to be Julie.

If she was here the last thing he wanted was to scare

her, so the moment he opened the door he called, 'Julie, are you here? It's Rob.'

And she emerged from their bedroom.

Julie.

The sight of her made him feel… No. He couldn't begin to define how he felt seeing her.

It had been nearly four years. She'd refused to see him since.

'I slept while they died and I can't forgive myself. Ever. I can't even think about what I've lost. If I hadn't slept...'

She'd thrown it at him the day he'd brought her home from hospital. He'd spent weeks sick with self-blame, sick with emptiness, not knowing how to cope with his own grief, much less hers. The thought that she blamed herself hadn't even occurred to him. It should have, but in those crucial seconds after she'd said it he hadn't had a response. He'd stared at her, numb with shock and grief, as she'd limped into the bedroom on her crutches, thrown things into a suitcase and demanded he take her to a hotel.

And that had pretty much been that. One marriage, one family, finished.

He'd written to her. Of course he had, and he'd tried to phone. *'Jules, it was no one's fault. That you were asleep didn't make any difference. I was awake and alert. The landslip came from nowhere. There's nothing anyone can do when the road gives way.'* Did he believe it himself? He tried to. Sometimes he had flashes when he almost did.

And apparently, Julie had shared his doubts. She'd written back, brief and harsh.

I was asleep when my babies died. I wasn't there for them, or for you. I can barely live with myself, much less face you every day for the rest of my life. I'm sorry, Rob, but however we manage to face the future, we need to do it alone.

And he couldn't help her to forgive herself. He was too busy living with his *own* guilt. The mountain road to the house had been eroded by heavy spring rains and the collapse was catastrophic. They'd spent the weeks before Christmas in the city apartment because there'd been so much on it had just been too hard to commute. They were exhausted but Julie had been desperate to get up to the mountains for the weekend before Christmas, to make everything perfect for the next week. To let the twins set up their Christmas tree. So Santa wouldn't find one speck of dust, one thing out of place.

He'd gone along with it. Maybe he'd also agreed. Perfection was in both their blood; they were driven personalities. They'd given their nanny the weekend off and they'd driven up here late.

But if they'd just relaxed… If they'd simply said there wasn't time, they could have spent that last weekend playing with the boys in the city, just stopping. But stopping wasn't in their vocabulary and the boys were dead because of it.

Enough. The past needed to be put aside. Julie was standing in their bedroom door.

She looked…beautiful.

He'd thought this woman was gorgeous the moment he'd met her. Tall, willow-slim, blonde hair with just a touch of curl, brown eyes a man could drown in, lips a man wanted to taste…

It was four years since he'd last seen her, and she was just the same but…tighter. It was like her skin was stretched to fit. She was thinner. Paler. She was wearing a simple cotton nightgown, her hair was tousled and her eyes were wide with…wariness.

Why should she be wary of him?

'Julie.' He repeated her name and she stopped dead.

She might have known he'd come.

Dear heaven, he was beautiful. He was tall—she'd forgotten how tall—and still boyish, even though he must be—what, thirty-six?—by now.

He had the same blond-brown hair that looked perpetually like he spent too much time in the sun. He had the same flop of cowlick that hung a bit too long—no hairdresser believed it wouldn't stay where it was put. He was wearing his casual clothes, clothes he might have worn four years ago: moleskins with a soft linen shirt, rolled up at the sleeves and open at the throat.

He was wearing the same smile, a smile which reached the caramel-brown eyes she remembered. He was smiling at her now. A bit hesitant. Not sure of his reception.

She hadn't seen him for four years and he was wary. What did he think she'd do, throw him out?

But she didn't know where to start. Where to begin after all this time.

Why not say it like it was?

'I don't think I am Julie,' she said slowly, feeling lost. 'At least, I'm not sure I'm the Julie you know.'

There was a moment's pause. He'd figure it out, or she hoped he would. She couldn't go straight back to the point where they'd left off. *How are you, Rob? How have you coped with the last four years?*

The void of four long years made her feel ill.

But he got it. There was a moment's silence and then his smile changed a little. She knew that smile. It reflected his intelligence, his appreciation of a problem. If there was a puzzle, Rob dived straight in. Somehow she'd set him one and he had it sorted.

'Then I'm probably not the guy you know, either,' he told her. 'So can we start from the beginning? Allow me to introduce myself. I'm Rob McDowell, architect, based in Adelaide. I have an interest in this house, ma'am, and the contents. I'm here to put the most…put a few things of special value in a secure place. And you?'

She could do this. She felt herself relax, just a little, and she even managed to smile back.

'Julie McDowell. Legal financier from Sydney. I, too, have an interest in this house.'

'McDowell?' He was caught. 'You still use…'

'It was too much trouble to change it back,' she said and he knew she was having trouble keeping her voice light.

'You're staying despite the fire warnings?'

'The wind's not due to get up until tomorrow morning. I'll be gone at dawn.'

'You've just arrived?'

'Yes.'

'You don't want to take what you want and go?'

'I don't know what I want.' She hesitated. 'I think… there's a wall-hanging… But it seems wrong to just…leave.'

'I had two fire engines in mind,' he admitted. 'But I feel the same.'

'So you'll stay until ordered out?'

'If it doesn't get any worse, maybe I can clear any debris, check the pumps and sprinkler system, fill the spouts, keep any stray spark from catching. At first light I'll go right round the house and eliminate every fire risk I can. I can't do it now. It's too dark. For the sake of a few hours, I'll stay. I don't want this place to burn.'

Why? she wanted to say. *What does this house mean to you?*

What did it mean to her? A time capsule? Maybe it was. This house was what it was like when…

But *when* was unthinkable. And if Rob was here, then surely she could go.

But she couldn't. The threat was still here, even if she wasn't quite sure what was being threatened.

'If you need to stay,' she ventured, 'there's a guest room.'

'Excellent.' They were like two wary dogs, circling each other, she thought. But they'd started this sort of game. She could do this.

'Would you like supper?'

'I don't want to keep you up.'

'I wasn't sleeping. The pantry's stocked and the freezer's full. Things may well be slightly out of date…'

'Slightly!'

'But I'm not dictated to by use-by dates,' she continued. 'I have fresh milk and bread. For anything else, I'm game if you are.'

His brown eyes creased a little, amused. 'A risk-taker, Jules?'

'No!'

'Sorry.' Jules was a nickname and that was against the rules. He realised it and backtracked. 'I meant: have you tried any of the food?'

'I haven't tried,' she conceded.

'You came and went straight to bed?'

'I…yes.'

'Then maybe we both need supper.' He checked his watch. 'It's almost too late for a midnight feast but I could eat two horses. Maybe we could get to know each other over a meal? If you dare, that is?'

And she gazed at him for a long moment and came to a decision.

'I dare,' she said. 'Why not?'

* * *

He put the cars in the garage and then they checked the fire situation. 'We'd be fools not to,' Rob said as they headed out to the back veranda to see what they could see.

They could see nothing. The whole valley seemed to be shrouded in smoke. It blocked the moon and the stars. It seemed ominous but there was no glow from any fire. 'And the smoke would be thicker if it was closer,' Rob decreed. 'We're safe enough for now.'

'There are branches overhanging the house.'

'I saw them as I came in but there's no way I'm using a chainsaw in the dark.'

'There's no way you're using a chainsaw,' she snapped and he grinned.

'Don't you trust me?'

'Do I trust any man with a chainsaw? No.'

He grinned, that same smile... *Dear heaven, that smile...*

Play the game. For tonight, she did *not* know this man.

'We havc neighbours,' Rob said, motioning to a light in the house next door.

'I saw a child in the window earlier, just as it was getting dark.'

'A child... They should have evacuated.'

'Maybe they still think there's time. There should still be time.'

'Let me check again.' He flicked to the fire app on his phone. 'Same warnings. Evacuate by nine if you haven't already done so. Unless you're planning on staying to defend.'

'Would you?' she asked diffidently. 'Stay and defend?'

'I'd have to be trustworthy with a chainsaw to do that.'

'And are you?' The Rob she knew couldn't be trusted within twenty paces of a power tool.

'No,' he admitted and she was forced to smile back. Same Rob, then. Same, but different? The Rob of *after.*

This was weird. She should be dressed, she decided, as she padded barefoot back to the kitchen behind him. If he really was a stranger…

He really is a stranger, she told herself. Power tool knowledge or not, four years was a lifetime.

'Right.' In the kitchen, he was all efficiency. 'Food.' He pushed his sleeves high over his elbows and looked as if he meant business. 'I'd kill for a steak. What do you suppose the freezer holds?'

'Who knows what's buried in there?'

'Want to help me find out?'

'Men do the hunting.'

'And women do the cooking?' He had the chest freezer open and was delving among the labelled packages. 'Julie, Julie, Julie. How out of the ark is that?'

'I can microwave a mean TV dinner.'

'Ugh.'

But Rob did cook. She remembered him enjoying cooking. Not often because they'd been far too busy for almost everything domestic but when she'd first met him he'd cooked her some awesome meals.

She'd tried to return the favour, but had only cooked disasters.

'What sort of people occupied this planet?' Rob was demanding answers from the depths of the freezer. 'Packets, packets and packets. Someone here likes Diet Cuisine. Liked,' he amended. 'Use-by dates of three years ago.'

She used to eat them when Rob was away. She'd cooked for the boys, or their nanny had, but Diet Cuisine was her go-to.

'There must be something more…' He was hauling out

packet after packet, tossing them onto the floor behind him. She was starting to feel mortified. Her fault again?

'You'll need to put that stuff back or it'll turn into stinking sog,' she warned.

'Of course.' His voice was muffled. 'So in a thousand years an archaeological dig can find Diet Cuisine and think we were all nuts. And stinking sog? For a stink it'd have to contain substance. Two servings of veggies and four freezer-burned cubes of diced meat do not substance make. But hey, here's a whole beef fillet.' He emerged, waving his find in triumph. 'This is seriously thick. I'm hoping freezer burn might only go halfway in or less. I can thaw it in the microwave, chop off the burn and produce steak fit for a king. I hope. Hang on a minute.'

Fascinated, she watched as he grabbed a torch from the pantry and headed for the back door. That was a flaw in this mock play; he shouldn't have known where a torch was. But in two minutes he was back, brandishing a handful of greens.

'Chives,' he said triumphantly and then glanced dubiously at the enormous green fronds. 'Or they might have been chives some time ago. These guys are mutant onions.'

Clarissa had planted vegetables, she remembered. Their last nanny…

But Rob was taking all her attention. The Rob of now.

She'd expected…

Actually, she hadn't expected. She'd thought she'd never see this man again. She'd vaguely thought she'd be served with divorce papers at some stage, but she hadn't had the courage or the impetus to organise it herself. To have him here now, slicing steak, washing dirt from mutant chives, took a bit of getting used to.

'You do want some?' he asked and she thought *no*. And then she thought: *when did I last eat?*

If he had been a stranger she'd eat with him.

'Yes, please,' she said and was inordinately pleased with herself for getting the words out.

So they ate. The condiments in the pantry still seemed fine, though Rob dared to tackle the bottled horseradish and she wasn't game. He'd fried hunks of bread in the pan juices. They ate steak and chives and fried bread, washed down by mugs of milky tea. All were accompanied by Rob's small talk. He really did act as if they were strangers, thrust together by chance.

Wasn't that the truth?

'So, Julie,' he said finally, as he washed and she wiped. There was a dishwasher but, as neither intended sticking round past breakfast, it wasn't worth the effort. 'If you're planning on leaving at dawn, what would you like to do now? You were sleeping when I got here?'

'Trying to sleep.'

'It doesn't come on demand,' he said, and she caught an edge to his voice that said he lay awake, as she did. 'But you can try. I'll keep watch.'

'What—stand sentry in case the fire comes?'

'Something like that.'

'It won't come until morning.'

'I don't trust forecasts. I'll stay on the veranda with the radio. Snooze a little.'

'I won't sleep.'

'So…you want to join me on fire watch?'

'I…okay.'

'You might want to put something on besides your nightie.'

'What's wrong with the nightie? It's sensible.'

'It's not sensible.'

'It's light.'

'Jules,' he said, and suddenly there was strain in his voice. 'Julie. I know we don't know each other very well.

I know we're practically strangers, but there is only a settee on the veranda, and if you sit there looking like that…'

She caught her breath and the play-acting stopped, just like that. She stared at him in disbelief.

'You can't…want me.'

'I've never stopped wanting you,' he said simply. 'I've tried every way I know, but it's not working. Just because we destroyed ourselves… Just because we gave away the idea of family for the rest of our lives, it doesn't stop the wanting. Not everything ended the night our boys died, Julie, though sometimes…often…I wish it had.'

'You still feel…'

'I have no idea what I feel,' he told her. 'I've been trying my best to move on. My shrink says I need to put it all in the background, like a book I can open at leisure and close again when it gets too hard to read. But, for now, all I know is that your nightie is way too skimpy and your eyes are too big and your hair is too tousled and our bed is too close. So I suggest you either head to the bedroom and close the door or go get some clothes on. Because what I want has nothing to do with reality, and everything to do with ghosts. Shrink's advice or not, I can't close the book. Go and get dressed, Julie. Please.'

She stared at him for a long moment. Rob. Her husband. Her ex-husband. Her ex-life.

She'd closed the door on him four years ago. If she was to survive, that door had to stay firmly closed. Behind that door were emotions she couldn't handle.

She turned away and headed inside. Away from him. Away from the way he tugged her heart.

He sat out on the veranda, thinking he might have scared her right off. She didn't emerge.

Well, what was new? He'd watched the way she'd closed

down after the boys' deaths. He was struggling to get free of those emotions but it seemed Julie was holding them close. Behind locked doors.

That was her right.

He sat for an hour and watched the night close in around him. The heat seemed to be getting more oppressive. The smoke hung low over everything, black and thick and stinking of burned forest, threatening enough all by itself, even without flames.

It's because there's no wind, he told himself. Without wind, smoke could hang around for weeks. There was no telling how close the fire was. There was no telling what the risks were if the wind got up.

He should leave. He should make Julie leave, but then… But then…

Her decision to come had been hers alone. She had the right to stay. He wasn't sure what he was protecting, but sitting out on the veranda, with Julie in the house behind him, felt okay. He wasn't sure why, but he did know that, at some level, the decision to come had been the right one.

Maybe it was stupid, he conceded, but maybe they both needed this night. Maybe they both needed to stand sentinel over a piece of their past that needed to be put aside.

And it really did need to be put aside. He'd watched Julie's face when he'd confessed that he wanted her and he'd seen the absolute denial. Even if she was ever to want him again, he'd known then that she wouldn't admit it.

Families were for the past.

He sat on. A light was still on next door. Once he saw a woman walk past the lighted window. Pregnant? Was she keeping the same vigil he was keeping?

If he had kids, he'd have them out of here by now. Hopefully, his neighbour had her car packed and would be gone at dawn, taking her family with her.

Just as he and Julie would be gone at dawn, too.

The moments ticked on. He checked the fire app again. No change.

There were sounds coming from indoors. Suddenly he was conscious of Christmas music. Carols, tinkling out on…a music box?

He remembered that box. It had belonged to one of his aunts. It was a box full of Santa and his elves. You wound the key, opened the box and they all danced.

That box…

Memories were all around him. Childhood Christmases. The day his aunt had given it to them—the Christmas Julie was pregnant. 'It needs a family,' his aunt had said. 'I'd love you to have it.'

His aunt was still going strong. He should give the box back to her, he thought, but meanwhile… Meanwhile, he headed in and Julie was sitting in the middle of the living room floor, attaching baubles to a Christmas tree. She was still dressed in the nightgown. She was totally intent on what she was doing.

What...?

'It's Christmas Eve tomorrow,' she said simply, as if this was a no-brainer. 'This should be up. And don't look at the nightgown, Rob McDowell. Get over it. It's hot, my nightie's cool and I'm working.'

She'd hauled the artificial tree from the storeroom. He stared at it, remembering the Christmas when they'd conceded getting a real tree was too much hassle. It'd take hours to buy it and set it up, and one thing neither of them had was hours.

That last Christmas, that last weekend, the tree was one of the reasons they'd come up here.

'We can decorate the tree for Christmas,' Julie had said. 'When we go up next week we can walk straight in and it'll be Santa-ready.'

Now Julie was sitting under the tree, sorting decorations as if she had all the time in the world. As if nothing had happened. As if time had simply skipped a few years.

'Remember this one?' She held up a very tubby angel with floppy, sparkly wings and a cute little halo. 'I bought this the year I was trying to diet. Every time I looked at a mince pie I was supposed to march in here and discuss it with my angel. It didn't work. She'd look straight back at me and say: "Look at me—I might be tubby but not only am I cute, I grew wings. Go ahead and eat."'

He grinned, recognising the cute little angel with affection.

'And these.' Smiling fondly, he knelt among the ornaments and produced three reindeer, one slightly chewed. 'We had six of these. Boris ate the other three.'

'And threw them up when your partners came for Christmas drinks.'

'Not a good moment. I miss Boris.' He'd had Boris the Bloodhound well before they were married. He'd died of old age just before the twins were born. Before memories had to be put aside.

They'd never had time for another dog. Maybe now they never would?

Forget it. Bauble therapy. Julie had obviously immersed herself in it and maybe he could, too. He started looping tinsel around the tree and found it oddly soothing.

They worked in silence but the silence wasn't strained. It was strangely okay. Come dawn they'd walk away from this house. Maybe it would burn, but somehow, however strange, the idea that it'd burn looking lived in was comforting.

'How long do Christmas puddings last?' Julie asked at last, as she hung odd little angels made of spray-painted macaroni. Carefully not mentioning who'd made them. The twins with their nanny. The twins…

Concentrate on pudding, he told himself. Concentrate on the practical. *How long do Christmas puddings last?* 'I have no idea,' he conceded. 'I know fruitcakes are supposed to last for ever. My great-grandma cooked them for her brothers during the War. Great-Uncle Henry once told me he used to chop 'em up and lob 'em over to the enemy side. Grandma Ethel's cakes were never great at the best of times but after a few months on the Western Front they could have been lethal.'

'Death by fruitcake...'

'Do you remember the Temperance song?' he asked, grinning at another memory. His great-aunt's singing. He raised his voice and tried it out. *'We never eat fruitcake because it has rum. And one little bite turns a man to a...'*

'Yeah, right.' She smiled back at him and he felt strangely triumphant.

Why did it feel so important to make this woman smile? Because he'd lost her smile along with everything else? Because he'd loved her smile?

'Clarissa made one that's still in the fridge,' she told him. Nanny Clarissa had been so domestic she'd made up for both of them. Or almost. 'And it does contain rum. Half a bottle of over-proof, if I remember. She demanded I put it on the shopping list that last... Anyway, I'm thinking of frying slices for breakfast.'

'Breakfast is what...' he checked his watch '...three hours away? Four-year-old Christmas pudding. That'll be living on the edge.'

'A risk worth taking?' she said tightly and went back to bauble-hanging. 'What's to lose?'

'Pudding at dawn. Bring it on.'

They worked on. There were so many tensions zooming round the room. So many things unsaid. All they could do was concentrate on the tree.

Finished, it looked magnificent. They stood back, Rob flicked the light switch and the tree flooded into colour. He opened the curtains and the light streamed out into the darkness. Almost every house in the valley was in darkness. Apart from a solitary light in the house next door they were alone. Either everyone had evacuated or they were all sleeping. Preparing for the danger which lay ahead.

Sleep. Bed.

It seemed a good idea. In theory.

Julie was standing beside him. She had her arms folded in front of her, instinctive defence. She was still in that dratted nightgown. Hadn't he asked her to take it off? Hadn't he warned her?

But she never had been a woman who followed orders, he thought. She'd always been self-contained, sure, confident of her place in the world. He'd fallen in love with that containment, with her fierce intelligence, with the humour that matched his, a biting wit that made him break into laughter at the most inappropriate moments. He'd loved her drive to be the best at her job. He'd understood and admired it because he was like that, too. It was only when the twins arrived that they'd realised two parents with driving ambition was a recipe for disaster.

Still they'd managed it. They'd juggled it. They'd loved…

Loved. He looked at her now, shivering despite the oppressive heat. She looked younger, he thought suddenly.

Vulnerable.

She'd never been vulnerable and neither had he.

But they'd loved.

'Julie?'

'Yes?' She looked at him and she looked scared. And he knew it was nothing to do with the fires.

'Mmm.'

'Let's go to bed,' he said, but she hugged her arms even tighter.

'I don't...know.'

'There's no one else?'

'No.'

'Nor for me,' he said gently. He was treading on egg-shells here. He should back off, go and sleep in the spare room, but there was something about this woman... This woman who was still his wife.

'We can't...at least...I can't move forward,' he told her, struggling to think things through as he spoke. 'Relationships are for other people now, not for me. But tonight... For me, tonight is all about goodbye and I suspect it's goodbye for you as well.'

'The house won't burn.'

'No,' he said, even more gently. 'It probably won't. At dawn I'll go out and cut down the overhanging branches—and even with my limited skill with power tools, I should get them cleared before the wind changes. Then we'll turn on every piece of fire-safe technology we built into this house. And after that, no matter what the outcome, we'll walk away. We must. It's time it was over, Jules, but for tonight...' He hesitated but he had to say it. It was a gut-deep need and it couldn't be put aside. 'Tonight, we need each other.'

'So much for being strangers,' she whispered. She was still hugging herself, still contained. Sort of.

'I guess we are,' he conceded. 'I guess the people we've turned into don't know each other. But for now...for this night I'd like to take to bed the woman who's still my wife.'

'In name only.' She was shivering.

'So you don't want me? Not tonight? Never again?'

And she looked up at him with those eyes he remembered so well, but with every bit of the confidence, humour, wit and courage blasted right out of them.

'I *do* want you,' she whispered. 'That's what terrifies me.'

'Same here.'

'Rob…'

'Mmm.'

'Do you have condoms? I mean, the last thing…'

'I have condoms.'

'So when you said relationships are for other people…'

'Hey, I'm a guy.' He was trying again to make her smile. 'I live in hope. Hope that one morning I'll wake up and find the old hormones rushing back. Hope that one evening I'll look across a crowded room and see a woman laughing at the same dumb thing I'm laughing at.'

That had been what happened that night, the first time they'd met. It had been a boring evening: a company she worked for announcing a major interest in a new dockland precinct; a bright young architect on the fringes; Julie with her arms full of contracts ready to be signed by investors. A boring speech, a stupid pun missed by everyone, including the guy making the speech, and then eyes meeting…

Contracts handed to a junior. Excuses made fast. Dinner. Then…

'So I'm prepared,' Rob said gently and tilted her chin. Gently, though. Forcing her gaze to meet his. 'One last time, my Jules?'

'I'm not…your Jules.'

'Can you pretend…for tonight?'

And, amazingly, she nodded. 'I think…maybe,' she managed, and at last her arms uncrossed. At last she abandoned the defensive. 'Maybe because I need to drive the ghosts away. And maybe because I want to.'

'I need more than *maybe*, Jules,' he said gently. 'I need you to want me as much as I want you.'

And there was the heart of what she was up against. She wanted him.

She always had.

Once upon a time she'd stood before an altar, the perfect bride. She remembered walking down the aisle on her father's arm, seeing Rob waiting for her, knowing it was right. She'd felt like the luckiest woman in the world. He'd held her heart in his hand, and she'd known that he'd treat it with care and love and honour.

She'd said I do, and she'd meant it.

Until death do us part…

Death had parted them, she thought and it would go on keeping them apart. There was no way they could pick up the pieces that had been their lives before the boys.

But somehow they'd been given tonight.

One night. A weird window of space and time. Tomorrow the echoes of their past could well disappear, and maybe it was right that they should.

But tonight he was here.

Tonight he was gazing at her with a tenderness that told her he needed this night as well. He wanted that sliver of the past as much as she did.

For tonight he wanted her and she ached for him back. But he wasn't pushing. It had to be her decision.

Maybe I can do this, she thought. *Maybe, just for tonight, I can put my armour aside…*

Her everyday life was now orchestrated, rigidly contained. It held no room for emotional attachment. Even coming here was an aberration. Once the fire was over, she'd return to her job, return to her life, return to her containment.

But for now…that ache… The way Rob talked to her… That he asked her to his bed…

It was like a siren call, she thought helplessly. She'd loved this man; she'd loved everything about him. Love had almost destroyed her and she couldn't go there again, but for tonight… Tonight was an anomaly—time out of frame.

For tonight, she was in her home with her husband. He wasn't pushing. He never had. He was simply waiting for her to make her decision.

Lie with her husband…or not?

Have one night as the Julie of old…or not?

'Because once we loved,' he said lightly, as if this wasn't a major leap, and maybe it wasn't. Maybe she could love again—just for the night. One night of Rob and then she'd get on with her life. One night…

'But not if you see it as scary.'

His gaze was locked on hers. 'It's for pleasure only, my Jules,' he said softly. 'No threats. No promises. No future. Just for this night. Just for us. Just for now. Maybe or yes? I need a yes, Jules. You have to be sure.'

And suddenly she was. 'Yes,' she said, because there was nothing else to say. 'Yes, please, Rob. For tonight, there's no maybe about it. Crazy or not, scary or not, I want you.'

'Hey, what's scary about me?' And he was laughing down at her, his lovely eyes dancing. Teasing. Just as he once had.

'That's just the problem,' she whispered. 'There's nothing crazy about the way I feel about you. *That's* what makes it so scary. But, scary or not, for tonight, Rob, for the last time, I want to be your wife.'

For those tense few minutes when they'd first seen each other, when they'd come together in the house for the first time in years, they'd made believe it was the first time. They were strangers. They'd relived that first connection.

Now…it was as if they'd pressed the fast forward on the replay button, Rob thought, and suddenly it was the first time he was to take her to bed.

But this was no make-believe, and it wasn't the first time. He knew everything there was to know about this woman. His wife.

But maybe that was wrong. Yes, he knew everything there was to know about the Julie of years ago, the Julie who'd married him, but there was a gaping hole of years. How had she filled it? He didn't know. He hardly knew how he'd filled it himself.

But for now, by mutual and unspoken consent, those four years didn't exist. Only the fierce magnetic attraction existed—the attraction that had him wanting her the moment he'd set eyes on her.

They hadn't ended up in bed on their first date, but it had nearly killed them not to. They'd lasted half an hour into their second date. He'd gone to her apartment to pick her up…they hadn't even reached the bedroom.

And now, here, the desire was the same. He'd seen her in her flimsy nightgown and he wanted her with every fibre of his being. And even if it was with caveats—*for the last time*—he tugged her into his arms and she melted. Fused.

'You're sure?' he asked and she nodded and the sound she made was almost a purr. Memories had been set aside—the hurtful ones had, anyway.

'I'm sure,' she whispered and tugged his face close and her whisper was a breath on his mouth.

He lifted her and she curled against him. She looped her arms around his neck and twisted, so she could kiss him.

Somehow he made it to the bedroom door. The bed lay,

invitingly, not ten feet away, but he had to stop and let himself be kissed. And kiss back.

Their mouths fused. It was like electricity, a fierce jolt on touching, then a force so great that neither could pull away. Neither could think of pulling away.

He had his wife in his arms. He couldn't think past that. He had his Julie and his mind blocked out everything else.

His wife. His love.

She'd forgotten how her body melted. She'd forgotten how her body merged into his. How the outside world disappeared. How every sense centred on him. Or on *them*, for that was how it was. Years ago, the moment he'd first touched her, she'd known what marriage was. She'd felt married the first time they'd kissed.

She'd abandoned herself to him then, as simple as that. She'd surrendered and he'd done the same. His lovely strong body, virile, heavy with the scent of aroused male, wanting her, taking her, demanding everything, but in such a way that she knew that if she pulled away he'd let her go.

Only she knew she'd never pull away. She couldn't and neither could he.

Their bodies were made for each other.

And now…now her mouth was plundering his, and his hers, and the sensations of years ago were flooding back. Oh, the taste of him. The feel… Her body was on fire with wanting, with the knowledge that somehow he was hers again, for however long…

Until morning?

No. She wasn't thinking that. It didn't matter how long. All that mattered was now.

Somehow, some way, they reached the bed, but even before they were on top of it she was fighting with the buttons of his shirt. She wanted this man's body. She wanted to feel the strength of him, the hardness of his ribs, the tightness of his chest. She wanted to taste the salt of him.

Oh, his body… It was hers; it still felt like hers.

Four years ago…

No. Forget four years. Just think about now.

His kiss deepened. Her nightgown was slipping away and suddenly it was easy. Memories were gone. All she could think of was him. All she wanted was him.

Oh, the feel of him. The taste of him.

Rob.

The years had gone. Everything had gone. There was only this man, this body, this moment.

'Welcome home, my love,' he whispered as their clothes disappeared, as skin met skin, as the night disappeared in a haze of heat and desire.

Home… There was so much unsaid in that word. It was a word of longing, a word of hope, a word of peace.

It meant nothing, she thought. It couldn't.

But her arms held him. Her mouth held him. Her whole body held him.

For this moment he was hers.

For this moment he was right. She was home.

He'd forgotten a woman could feel this good.

He'd forgotten…Julie?

But of course he hadn't. He'd simply put her in a place in his mind that was inaccessible. But now she was here, his, welcoming him, loving him.

She tasted fabulous. She still smelled like…like… He didn't know what she smelled like.

Had he ever asked her what perfume she wore? Maybe it was only soap. Fresh, citrus, it was in her hair.

He'd forgotten how erotic it was, to lie with his face in her tumbled hair, to feel the wisps around his face, to finger and twist and feel her body shudder as she responded to his touch.

The room was in darkness and that was good. If he could see her…her eyes might get that dead look, the look that said there was nothing left, for her or for him.

It was a look that had almost killed him.

But he wouldn't think of that. He couldn't, for her fingers were curved around his thighs, tugging him closer, closer…

His wife. His Julie. His own.

They loved and loved again. They melted into each other as if they'd never parted.

They loved.

He loved.

She was *his*.

The possessive word resonated in his mind, primeval as time itself. She was crying. He felt her tears, slipping from her face to his shoulder.

He gathered her to him and held, simply held, and he thought that at this moment if any man tried to take her his response would be primitive.

His.

Tomorrow he'd walk away. He'd accepted by now that their marriage was over, that Julie could never emerge from the thick armour she'd shielded herself with. In order to survive he needed to move on. He knew it. His shrink had said it. He knew it for the truth.

So he would walk away. But first…here was a gift he'd long stopped hoping for. Here was a crack in that appalling armour. For tonight she'd shed it.

'For tonight I'm loving you,' he whispered and she kissed him, fiercely, possessively, as if those vows they'd made so long ago still held.

And they did hold—for tonight—and that was all he was focusing on. There was no tomorrow. There was nothing but now.

He kissed her back. He loved her back.

'For tonight I'm loving you, too,' she whispered and she held him closer, and there was nothing in the world but his wife.

CHAPTER THREE

NOTE: IF A bush fire's heading your way, maybe you should set the alarm.

He woke and filtered sunlight was streaming through the east windows. Filtered? That'd be smoke. It registered but only just, for Julie was in his arms, spooned against his body, naked, beautiful and sated with loving. It was hard to get his mind past that.

Past her.

But the world was edging in. The wind had risen. He could hear the sound of the gums outside creaking under the weight of it.

Wind. Smoke. Morning.

'Jules?'

'Mmm.' She stirred, stretched like a kitten and the sensation of her naked skin against his had him wanting her all over again. He could…

He couldn't. Wind. Smoke. Morning.

Somehow he hauled his watch from under his woman.

Eight-thirty.

Eight-thirty!

Get out by nine at the latest, the authorities had warned. Keep listening to emergency radio in case of updates.

Eight-thirty.

Somehow he managed to roll away and flick on the

bedside radio. But even now, even realising what was at stake, he didn't want to leave her.

The radio sounded into life. Nothing had changed in this house. He'd paid to have a housekeeper come in weekly. The clock was still set to the right time.

There was a book beside the radio. He'd been halfway through it when…when…

Maybe this house should burn, he thought, memories surging back. Maybe he wanted it to.

'We should sell this house.' She still sounded sleepy. The implication of sleeping in hadn't sunk in yet, he thought, flicking through the channels to find the one devoted to emergency transmissions.

'So why did you come back?' he asked, abandoning the radio and turning back to her. The fire was important, but somehow…somehow he knew that words might be said now that could be said at no other time. Certainly not four years ago. Maybe not in the future either, when this house was sold or burned.

Maybe now…

'The teddies,' she told him, still sleepy. 'The wall-hanging my mum made. I…wanted them.'

'I was thinking of the fire engines.'

'That's appropriate.' Amazingly, she was smiling.

He'd never thought he'd see this woman smile again.

And then he thought of those last words. The words that had hung between them for years.

'Julie, it wasn't our fault,' he said and he watched her smile die.

'I…'

'I know. You said *you* killed them, but I believed it was me. That day I brought you home from hospital. You stood here and you said it was because you were sleeping and I said no, it wasn't anyone's fault, but there was such a big part of me that was blaming myself that I couldn't go any further. It was like…I was dead. I couldn't even speak. I've thought about it for four years. I've tried to write it down.'

'I got your letters.'

'You didn't reply.'

'I thought…the sooner you stopped writing the sooner you'd forget me. Get on with your life.'

'You know the road collapsed,' he said. 'You know the lawyers told us we could sue. You know it was the storm the week before that eroded the bitumen.'

'But that I was asleep…'

'We should have stayed in the city that night. We shouldn't have tried to bring the boys home. That's the source of our greatest regret, but it shouldn't be guilt. It put us in the wrong place at the wrong time. I've been back to the site. It was a blind curve. I rounded it and the road just wasn't there.'

'If we'd come up in broad daylight, when we were both alert…'

How often had he thought about this? How often had he screamed it to himself in the middle of troubled sleep?

He had to say it. He had to believe it.

'Jules, I manoeuvred a blind bend first. A tight curve. I wasn't speeding. I hit the brakes the moment I rounded the bend but the road was gone. If you'd been awake it wouldn't have made one whit of difference. Julie, it's not only me who's saying this. It was the police, the paramedics, the guys from the accident assessment scene.'

'But I can't remember.' It was a wail, and he tugged her back into his arms and thought it nearly killed him.

He was reassuring her but regardless of reason, the guilt was still there. *What if...? What if, what if, what if?*

Guilt had killed them both. Was killing them still.

He held her but her body had stiffened. The events of four years ago were right there. One night of passion couldn't wash them away.

He couldn't fix it. How could it be fixed, when two small beds lay empty in the room next door?

He kissed her on the lips, searching for an echo of the night before. She kissed him back but he could feel that she'd withdrawn.

Same dead Julie…

He turned again and went back to searching the radio channels. Finally he found the station he was looking for—the emergency channel.

'…evacuation orders are in place now for Rowbethon, Carnarvon, Dewey's Creek… Leave now. Forecast is for forty-six degrees, with winds up to seventy kilometres an hour, gusting to over a hundred. The fire fronts are merging…'

And all his attention was suddenly on the fire. It had to be. Rowbethon, Carnarvon, Dewey's Creek… They were all south of Mount Bundoon.

The wind was coming from the north.

'Fire is expected to impact on the Mount Bundoon area within the hour,' the voice went on. *'Bundoon Creek Bridge is closed. Anyone not evacuated, do not attempt it now. Repeat, do not attempt to evacuate. Roads are cut to the south. Fire is already impacting to the east. Implement your fire plans but, repeat, evacuation is no longer an option.'*

'We need to get to a refuge centre.' Julie was sitting bolt upright, wide-eyed with horror.

'There isn't one this side of the creek.' He glanced out of the window. 'We're not driving in this smoke. Besides, we have the bunker.' Thank God, they had the bunker.

'But…'

'We can do this, Jules.'

And she settled, just like that. Same old Jules. In a crisis, there was no one he'd rather have by his side.

'The fire plan,' she said. 'I have it.'

Of course she did. Julie was one of the most controlled people he knew. Efficient. Organised. A list-maker extraordinaire.

The moment they'd moved into this place she'd downloaded a Fire Authority Emergency Plan and made him go through it, step by step, making dot-points for every eventuality.

They were better off than most. Bush fire was always a risk in Australian summers and he'd thought about it carefully when he'd designed this place. The house had been built to withstand a furnace—though not an inferno. There'd been fires in Australia where even the most fireproof buildings had burned. But he'd designed the house with every precaution. The house was made of stone, with no garden close to the house. They had solar power, backup generators, underground water tanks, pumps and sprinkler systems. The tool shed doubled as a bunker and could be cleared in minutes, double-doored and built into earth. But still there was risk. He imagined everyone else in the gully would be well away by now and for good reason. Safe house or not, they were crazy to still be here.

But Julie wasn't remonstrating. She was simply moving on.

'I'll close the shutters and tape the windows while you clear the yard,' she said. Taping the windows was important. Heat could blast them inwards. Tape gave them an extra degree of strength and they wouldn't shatter if they broke.

'Wool clothes first, though,' she said, hauling a pile out of her bottom bedroom drawer, along with torches, wool caps and water bottles. Also a small fire extinguisher. The drawer had been set up years ago for the contingency of waking to fire. Efficiency plus.

Was it possible to still love a woman for her plan-making?

'I hope these extinguishers haven't perished,' she said, pulling a wool cap on her head and shoving her hair up into it. It was made of thick wool, way too big. 'Ugh. What do you think?'

'Cute.'

'Oi, we're not thinking cute.' But her eyes smiled at him.

'Hard not to. Woolly caps have always been a turn-on.'

'And I love a man in flannels.' She tossed him a shirt. 'You've been working out.'

'You noticed?'

'I noticed all night.' She even managed a grin. 'But it's time to stop noticing. Cover that six-pack, boy.'

'Yes, ma'am.' But he'd fielded the shirt while he was checking the fire map app on his phone, and what he saw made any thought of smiling back impossible.

She saw his face, grabbed the phone and her eyes widened. 'Rob...' And, for the first time, he saw fear. 'Oh, my...Rob, it's all around us. With this wind...'

'We can do this,' he said. 'We have the bunker.' His hands gripped her shoulders. Steadied her. 'Julie, you came up here for the teddies and the wall-hanging. Anything else?'

'Their...clothes. At least...at least some. And...'

She faltered, but he knew what she wanted to say. Their smell. Their presence. The last place they'd been.

He might not be able to save that for her, but he'd sure as hell try.

'And their fire engines,' he added, reverting, with difficulty, to the practical. 'Let's make that priority one. Hopefully, the pits are still clear.'

The pits were a fallback position, as well as the bunker. They'd built this house with love, but with clear acceptance that the Australian bush was designed to burn. Many native trees didn't regenerate without fire to crack their seeds. Fire was natural, and over generations even inevitable, so if you lived in the bush you hoped for the best and prepared for the worst. Accordingly, they'd built with care, insured the house to the hilt and didn't keep precious things here.

Except the memories of their boys. How did you keep something like that safe? How did you keep memories in fire pits?

They'd do their best. The pits were a series of holes behind the house, fenced off but easily accessed. Dirt dug from them was still heaped beside them, a method used by those who'd lived in the bush for generations. If you wanted to keep something safe, you buried it: put belongings inside watertight cases; put the cases in the pit; piled the dirt on top.

'Get that shirt on,' Julie growled, moving on with the efficiency she'd been born with. She cast a long regretful look at Rob's six-pack and then sighed and hauled on her sensible pants. 'Moving on… We knew we'd have to, Rob, and now's the time. Clearing the yard's the biggie. Let's go.'

The moment they walked out of the house they knew they were in desperate trouble. The heat took their breath away. It hurt to breathe.

The wind was frightening. It was full of dry leaf litter, blasting against their faces—a portent of things to come. If these leaves were filled with fire… She felt fear deep in her gut. The maps she'd just seen were explicit. This place was going to burn.

She wanted to bury her face in Rob's shoulder and block this out. She wanted to forget, like last night, amazingly, had let her forget.

But last night was last night. Over.

Concentrate on the list. On her dot-points.

'Windows, pits, shovel, go,' Rob said and seized her firmly by the shoulders and kissed her, hard and fast. Making a mockery of her determination that last night was over. 'We can do this, Jules. You've put a lot of work into that fire plan. It'd be a shame if we didn't make it work.'

They could, she thought as she headed for the shutters. They could make the fire plan work.

And maybe, after last night… Maybe…

Too soon. Think of it later. Fire first.

She fixed the windows—fast—then checked the pits. They were overgrown but the mounds of dirt were still loose enough for her to shovel. She could bury things with ease.

She headed inside, grabbed a couple of cases and headed into the boys' room.

And she lost her breath all over again.

She'd figured yesterday that Rob must have hired someone to clean this place on a regular basis. If it had been left solely to her, this house would be a dusty mess. She'd walked away and actively tried to forget.

But now, standing at their bedroom door, it was as if she'd just walked in for the first time. Rob would be carrying the boys behind her. Jiggling them, making them laugh.

Two and a half years old. Blond and blue-eyed scamps. Miniature versions of Rob himself.

They'd been sound asleep when the road gave way, then

killed in an instant, the back of the car crushed as it rolled to the bottom of a gully. The doctors had told her death would have been instant.

But they were right here. She could just tug back the bedding and Rob would carry them in.

Or not.

'Aiden,' she murmured. 'Christopher.'

Grief was all around her, an aching, searing loss. She hadn't let herself feel this for years. She hadn't dared to. It was hidden so far inside her she thought she'd grown armour that could surely protect her.

But the armour was nothing. It was dust, blown away at the sight of one neat bedroom.

It shouldn't be neat. It nearly killed her that it was neat. She wanted those beds to be rumpled. She wanted…

She couldn't want.

She should be thinking about fire, she thought desperately. The warnings were that it'd be on them in less than an hour. She had to move.

She couldn't.

The wind blasted on the windowpanes. She needed to tape them. She needed to bury memories.

Aiden. Christopher.

What had she been thinking, wondering if she could move on? What had she been doing, exposing herself to Rob again? Imagining she could still love.

She couldn't. Peeling back the armour, even a tiny part, allowed in a hurt so great she couldn't bear it.

'Julie?' It was a yell from just outside the window.

She couldn't answer.

'Julie!' Rob's second yell pierced her grief, loud and demanding her attention. 'Jules! If you're standing in that bedroom thinking of black you might want to look outside instead.'

How had he known what she was doing? Because he felt the same?

Still she didn't move.

'Look!' he yelled, even more insistent, and she had to look. She had to move across to the window and pull back the curtains.

She could just see Rob through the smoke haze. He was standing under a ladder, not ten feet from her. He had the ladder propped against the house.

He was carrying a chainsaw.

As she watched in horror he pulled the cord and it roared into life.

'What's an overhanging branch between friends?' he yelled across the roar and she thought: *He'll be killed. He'll be...*

'Mine's the easier job,' he yelled as he took his first step up the ladder. 'But if I can do this, you can shove a teddy into a suitcase. Put the past behind you, Julie. Fire. Now. Go.'

He was climbing a ladder with a chainsaw. Rob and power tools…

He was an architect, not a builder.

She thought suddenly of Rob, just after she'd agreed to marry him. He'd brought her to the mountains and shown her this block, for sale at a price they could afford.

'This can be our retreat,' he'd told her. 'Commute when we can, have an apartment in the city for when we can't.' And then he'd produced his trump card. A tool belt. Gleaming leather, full of bright shiny tools, it was a he-man's tool belt waiting for a he-man. He'd strapped it on and flexed his muscles. 'What do you think?'

'You're never thinking of building yourself?' she'd gasped and he'd grinned and held up a vicious-looking… she didn't have a clue what.

'I might need help,' he admitted. 'These things look scary. I was sort of thinking of a registered builder, with maybe a team of registered builder's assistants on the side. But I could help.'

And he'd grinned at her and she'd known there was nothing she could refuse this man.

Man with tool belt.

Man with ladder and chainsaw.

And it hit her then, with a clarity that was almost frightening. Yesterday when she'd woken up it had been just like the day before and the day before that. She'd got up, she'd functioned for the day, she'd gone to bed. She'd survived.

Life went on around her, but she didn't care.

Yesterday, when she'd told her secretary she was heading up to the Blue Mountains, Maddie had been appalled. 'It's dangerous. They're saying evacuate. Don't go there.'

The thing was, though, for Julie danger no longer existed. The worst thing possible had already happened. There was nothing else to fear.

But now, standing at the window, staring at Rob and his chainsaw, she realised that, like it or not, she still cared. She could still be frightened for someone. For Rob.

But fear hurt. Caring hurt. She didn't want to care. She couldn't. Somehow she had to rebuild the armour. But meanwhile…

Meanwhile Rob was right. She had to move. She had to bury teddies.

He managed to get the branches clear and drag them into the gully, well away from the house.

He raked the loose leaves away from the house, too, easier said than done when the wind was blasting them back. He blocked the gutters and set up the generator so they could use the pump and access the water in the tanks even if they lost the solar power.

He worked his way round the house, checking, rechecking and he almost ran into Julie round the other side.

The smoke was building. It was harder and harder to see. Even with a mask it hurt to breathe.

The heat was intense and the wind was frightening.

How far away was the fire? There was no way to tell. The fire map on his phone was of little use. It showed broad districts. What he wanted was a map of what was happening down the road. He couldn't see by looking. It was starting to be hard to see as far as the end of his arm.

'We've done enough.' Julie's voice was hoarse from the smoke. 'I've done inside and cleared the back porch. I've filled the pits and cleared the bunker. All the dot-points on the plan are complete.'

'Really?' It was weird to feel inordinately pleased that she'd remembered dot-points. Julie and her dot-points… weird that they turned him on.

'So what now?' she asked. 'Oh, Rob, I can't bear it in these clothes. All I want is to take them off and lie under the hose.'

It gave him pause for thought. *Jules, naked under water...* 'Is that included on our dots?' Impossible not to sound hopeful.

'Um…no,' she said, and he heard rather than saw her smile.

'Pity.'

'We could go inside and sit under the air-conditioning while it's still safe to have the air vents open.'

'You go in.' He wouldn't. How to tell what was happening outside if he was inside? 'But, Jules, the vents stay closed. We don't know where the fire is.'

'How can we tell where it is? How close...?' The smile had gone from her voice.

'It's not threatening. Not yet. We have thick smoke and wind and leaf litter but I can reach out my hand and still—sort of—see my fingers. The fire maps tell us the fire's cut the access road, but how long it takes to reach this gully is anyone's guess. It might fly over the top of us. It might miss us completely.' There was a hope.

'So...why not air-conditioning?'

'There's still fire. You can taste it and you can smell it. Even if the house isn't in the firing line, there'll be burning leaf litter swirling in the updraught. On Black Saturday they reckoned there were ember attacks five miles from the fire front. We'd look stupid if embers were sucked in through the vents. But you go in. I'll keep checking.'

'For...how long?' she faltered. 'I mean...'

'For as long as it takes.' He glanced upward, hearing the wind blasting the treetops, but there was no way he could see that far. The smoke was making his throat hurt, but still he felt the need to try and make her smile. 'It looks like we're stuck here for Christmas,' he managed. 'But I'm sure Santa will find a way through. What's his motto? *Neither snow nor rain nor heat nor gloom of night shall stay St Nicholas from the swift completion of his appointed rounds.*'

'Isn't that postmen?' And amazingly he heard the smile again and was inordinately pleased.

'Maybe it is,' he said, picking up his hose and checking pressure. They still had the solar power but he'd already swapped to the generators. There wouldn't be time to do it when...if...the fire hit. 'But I reckon we're all in the same union. Postmen, Santa and us. We'll work through whatever's thrown at us.' And then he set down his hose.

'It's okay, Jules,' he said, taking her shoulders. 'We've

been through worse than this. We both know...that things aren't worth crying over. But our lives are worth something and maybe this house is worth something as well. It used to be a home. I know the teddies and fire engines and wall-hanging are safe but let's see this as a challenge. Let's see if we can save...what's left of the rest of us.'

They sat on the veranda and faced the wind. It was the dumbest place to sit, Julie thought, but it was also sensible. The wind seared their faces, the heat parched their throats but ember attacks would come from the north.

Their phones had stopped working. 'That'll be the transmission tower on Mount Woorndoo,' Rob said matter-of-factly, like it didn't matter that a tower not ten miles away had been put out of action.

He brought the battery radio outside and they listened. All they could figure was that the valley was cut off. All they could work out was that the authorities were no longer in control. There were so many fronts to this fire that no one could keep track.

Most bush fires could be fought. Choppers dropped vast loads of water, fire trucks came in behind the swathes the choppers cleared; communities could be saved.

Here, though, there were so many communities...

'It's like we're the last people in the world,' Julie whispered.

'Yeah. Pretty silly to be here.'

'I wanted to be here.'

'Me, too,' he said and he took her hand and held.

And somehow it felt okay. Scary but right.

They sat on. Surely the fire must arrive soon. The waiting was almost killing her, and yet, in a strange way, she felt almost calm. Maybe she even would have stayed if Rob hadn't come, she thought. Maybe this was...

'We're going to get through this,' Rob said grimly and she hauled her thoughts back from where they'd been taking her.

'You know, those weeks after the boys were killed, they were the worst weeks of my life.' He said it almost conversationally, and she thought: *don't. Don't go there.* They hadn't talked about it. They couldn't.

But he wasn't stopping. She should get up, go inside, move away, but he was waiting for ember attacks, determined to fight this fire, and she couldn't walk away.

Even if he was intent on talking about what she didn't want to hear.

'You were so close to death yourself,' he said, almost as if this had been chatted about before. 'You had smashed ribs, a punctured lung, a shattered pelvis. But that bang on the head… For the first few days they couldn't tell me how you'd wake up. For the first twenty-four hours they didn't even know whether you'd wake up at all. And there I was, almost scot-free. I had a laceration on my arm and nothing more. There were people everywhere—my parents, your parents, our friends. I was surrounded yet I'd never felt so alone. And at the funeral…'

'Don't.' She put a hand on his arm to stop him but he didn't stop. But maybe she had to hear this, she thought numbly. Maybe he had to say it.

'I had to bury them alone,' he said. 'Okay, not alone in the physical sense. The church was packed. My parents were holding me up but you weren't there… It nearly killed me. And then, when you got out of hospital and I asked if you'd go to the cemetery…'

'I couldn't.' She remembered how she'd felt. Where were her boys? To go to the cemetery…to see two tiny graves…

She'd blocked it out. It wasn't real. If she didn't see the

graves, then maybe the nightmare would be just that. An endless dream.

'It was like our family ended right there,' Rob said, staring sightlessly out into the smoke. 'It didn't end when our boys died. It ended…when we couldn't face their death together.'

'Rob…'

'I don't know why I'm saying this now,' he said, almost savagely. 'But hell, Julie, I'm fighting this. Our family doesn't exist any more. I can't get back…any of it. But once upon a time we loved each other and that still means something. So if you're sitting here thinking it doesn't matter much if you go up in flames, then think again. Because, even though I'm not part of your life any more, if I lose you completely, then what's left of my sanity goes, too. So prepare to be protected, Jules. No fire is going to get what's left of what I once loved. Of what I still love. So I'm heading off to do a fast survey of the boundary, looking for embers. It'd be good if you checked closer to the house but you don't need to. I'll do it for both of us. This fire…I'll fight it with everything I have. Enough of our past has been destroyed. This is my line in the sand.'

CHAPTER FOUR

THE SOUND CAME before the fire. Before the embers. Before hell.

It was a thousand freight trains roaring across the mountains, and it was so sudden that they were working separately when it hit. It was a sweeping updraught which felt as if it was sucking all the air from her lungs. It was a mass of burning embers, not small spot fires they could cope with but a mass of burning rain.

Stand and fight… They knew as the rumble built to a roar that no man alive could stay and fight this onslaught.

Julie was fighting to get a last gush of water onto the veranda. A branch had blasted in against the wall and Rob had been dragging it away from the building. She couldn't see him.

He was somewhere out in the smoke, heading back to her. Please, she pleaded. Please let him be heading back to her.

She had the drill in her head. *When the fire hits, take cover in your designated refuge and wait for the front to pass. As soon as the worst has passed, you can emerge to fight for your home, but don't try and fight as the front hits. Take cover.*

Now.

'Rob…' Where was he? She was screaming for him but she couldn't even hear herself above the roar. The heat was blasting in front of the fire, taking the temperature to unbearable levels. She'd have to head for the shelter without him…

Unthinkable!

But suddenly he was with her. Grabbing her, hauling her off the veranda. But, instead of heading towards the bunker, he was hauling her forward, into the heat. 'Jules, help me.'

'Help?' They had to get to the bunker. What else could they do?

'Jules, there are people next door.' He was yelling into her ear. 'There's a woman—pregnant, a mum. She was trying to back her car out of the driveway and she's hit a post. Jules, she won't come with me. We need to make her see sense. Forcibly if need be, and I can't do it by myself.'

And, like it or not, sensible or not, he had her arm. He was hauling her with him, stumbling across their yard, a yard which seemed so unfamiliar now that it was terrifying.

There were burning embers, burning leaves hitting her face. They shouldn't be here. They had to seek refuge. But…

'She's lost…a kid…' Rob was struggling to get enough breath to yell over the roar of impending fire. 'When the car hit, the dog got out. The kid's four years old, chasing his dog and she can't find him. I have to…' But then a blast of heat hit them, so intense he couldn't keep yelling. He just held onto her and ran.

But she wanted to be safe. She wanted this to be over. Why was Rob dragging her away from the bunker?

A child… Four years old? She tried to take it in but her mind wouldn't go there.

And then they were past the boundary post, not even visible now, only recognised because she brushed it as they passed. Then onto the gravel of the next-door neighbour's house. There was a car in the driveway, visible only as they almost ran into it.

She didn't know the neighbours. This house had been owned by an elderly couple when they'd built theirs. The woman had since died, her husband had left to live with his daughter and the house had stood empty and neglected for almost the entire time they'd lived here.

Last night she'd been surprised to see the lights. She and Rob had both registered that there'd been someone there, but then they'd both been so caught up…

And then her thoughts stopped. Through the wall of smoke, there was a woman. Slight. Shorter than she was.

Very, very pregnant.

Rob reached to grab her and held.

'I can't find him.' The woman was screaming. 'Help me! Help me!' The scream pierced even the roar of the fire and it held all the agony in the world. It was a wail of loss and desperation and horror.

'We will.' Rob grabbed Julie's arm, thrust the woman's hand into hers and clamped his own hand on top. 'Julie, don't let go and that's an order. Consider it a dot-point, the biggest one there is. Julie, Amina; Amina, Julie. Amina, Julie's taking you to safety. You need to go with her now. Julie, go.'

'But Danny…' The woman was still screaming.

'I'll find him. Julie, the bunker…'

'But you have to come, too.' Julie was screaming as well. Already they were cutting things so close they mightn't make it. The blackness was now tinged with burning orange, flashes looming out of the blasting heat. Dear God, they had to go—but they had to go together.

But Rob was backing away, yelling back at her over the roar of the fire. 'Jules, there's a little boy.' His voice held a desperation that matched hers. 'He ran to find his dog. I won't let this one die. I won't. Go!'

And his words stopped her screaming. They stopped her even wanting to scream.

She checked for a moment, fought for air, fought for sanity. A wave of wind and heat smashed into her, almost knocking her from her feet. Burning embers were smashing against their clothes.

The woman was wearing a bulky black dress but it didn't hide her late pregnancy. Another child. Dear God…

And they didn't have to wait until the fire front hit them; the fire was here now.

'Jules, go!' Rob was yelling, pushing.

But still… 'I can't…leave you.'

'Danny…' The woman's scream was beyond terror, beyond reason, almost drowning Julie's, but Rob had heard her.

'Jules.' He touched her once, briefly, a hand on her cheek. A touch of reassurance where there was no reassurance to be had. A touch for courage. Then he pushed her again.

'Keep her and her little one safe. You can do this,' he said fiercely. 'But stay safe. I won't lose…more. I'll find him,' he said fiercely. 'Go!'

The woman had to be almost dragged to the bunker. Somewhere out there was her son, and Julie could feel her terror, could almost taste it, and it was nearly enough to drown her own fear.

Left on her own she'd be with Rob, no question. Did it matter if she died? Not much. But she was gripping her neighbour's hand and the woman looked almost to term. Two lives depended on her and Rob had told her what he expected.

And she expected it of herself. That one touch and she knew what she was doing couldn't be questioned.

But by now it was almost impossible to move. She hardly knew where the bunker was. The world was a swirling blast of madness. Trees loomed from nowhere. She could see nothing. How could she be lost in her own front yard?

She couldn't. She wouldn't. She had the woman's hand in a grip of iron and she kept on going, tugging the woman behind her.

Finally she reached the side of the house. There was no vision left at all now. The last of the light had gone. The world was all heat and smoke and fear.

She touched the house and kept touching as she hauled the woman along behind her. The woman had ceased fighting, but she could feel her heaving sobs. There was nothing she could do about that, though. Her only thought was to get to the rear yard, then keep going without deviation and the bunker would be right there.

But Rob…

Don't think of Rob.

There was so much smoke. How could they breathe?

And then the bunker was right in front of her groping arm. She'd been here earlier, checked it was clear. She should have left the door open. Now it was all she could do to haul it wide. She had to let Amina go and she was fearful she'd run.

If it was her little boy out there she'd run.

Christopher. Aiden…

Don't think it. That was the way of madness.

But Amina had obviously made a choice. She was no longer pulling back. Her maternal instincts must be tearing her apart. Her son was in the fire but she had to keep her baby safe. She was trusting in Rob.

Do not think of Rob.

Somehow she managed to haul open the great iron door Rob had built as the entrance to the bunker. The bunker itself was dug into the side of the hill, with reinforced earth on the sides and floor and roof, with one thick door facing the elements and a thinner one inside.

She got the outer door open, shoving the woman inside, fighting to keep out embers.

She slammed it shut behind her and it felt as if she was condemning Rob to death.

Inside the inner door was designed to keep out heat. She couldn't shut that. No way. The outer door would have to buckle before she'd consider it. One sheet of iron between Rob and safety was more than she could bear; two was unthinkable.

The woman was sobbing, crumpling downward. There were lamps by the door. She flicked one on, took a deep, clean breath of air that hardly had any smoke in it and took stock.

She was safe here. They were safe.

She wasn't sure what was driving her, what was stopping her crumbling as well, but she knew what she had to do. The drill. Her dot-points. Rob would laugh at her, say she'd be efficient to the point where she organised her own funeral.

He loved her dot-points.

She allowed herself one tiny sob of fear, then swallowed it and knelt beside the woman, putting her arm around the woman's shoulders.

'We're safe,' she told her, fighting to keep her voice steady. 'You and your baby are safe. This place is fireproof. Rob's designed it so we have ventilation. We have air, water, even food if we need. We can stay here until it's all over.'

'D...Danny.'

'Rob is with Danny,' she said with a certainty she had to assume. But suddenly it wasn't assumed. Rob had to be with Danny and Rob had to be safe. Anything else was unthinkable.

'Rob will have him,' she whispered. 'My…my husband will keep him safe.'

'Danny! Luka!' Why was he yelling? Nothing could be heard above the roar of the fire. He could see nothing. To stay out here and search for a child in these conditions was like searching in hot, blasting sludge. A child would be swallowed, as he was being swallowed.

He'd asked for the dog's name. 'Luka,' Amina had told him through sobs. 'A great big golden retriever my husband bought to keep us safe. Danny loves him.'

So now he added Luka to his yelling. But where in this inferno…?

He stopped and made himself think. The boy had followed the dog. Where would the dog go?

Back to the house, surely. He'd escaped from the car. He'd be terrified. If Danny had managed to follow him…

The heat was burning. He'd shoved a wool cap over his head. Now he pulled it right down over his eyes. He couldn't see anyway and it stopped the pain as embers hit. He had his hands out, blundering his way to the front door.

At least Julie was safe. It was the one thing that kept him sane, but if there was another tragedy out of this day…

He knew, none better, how close to the edge of sanity Julie had been. He knew how tightly she held herself together. How controlled…

He hadn't been able to get past that control and in the end he'd had to respect it. He'd had to walk away, to preserve them both.

If he died now maybe Julie's control would grow even

deeper. The barriers could become impenetrable—or maybe the barriers would crumble completely.

Either option was unthinkable.

Last night he'd seen a glimmer of what they'd once had. Only a glimmer; the barriers had been up again this morning. But he'd seen underneath. How vulnerable…

He could go to her now. Save himself.

And sit in the bunker while another child died?

He had his own armour, his own barriers, and they were vulnerable, too. Another child's death…

'Danny! Luka!' He was screaming, and his screams were mixing with the fire.

'Please…'

Please.

She said it over and over again. She'd found water bottles. She'd given one to Amina, and watched her slump against the back wall, her face expressionless.

Her face looked dead.

Her face would look like that too, Julie thought. Maybe it had looked like that for four years?

She slumped down on the floor beside her. Fought to make her mind work.

What was safety when others weren't safe? When Rob was out there?

'Do you think…?' Amina whispered.

'I can't think,' Julie told her. She took a long gulp of water and realised just how parched she'd been. How much worse for Rob…

'So…so what do we do?' Amina whispered.

'Wait for Rob.'

'Your husband.'

'Yes.' He still was, after all. It was a dead marriage but the legalities still held.

'My…my husband will be trying to reach us,' Amina whispered. 'He's a fly in, fly out miner. He was flying back in last night. He rang from the airport and told us not to move until he got here. I'm not very good in the car but in the end I couldn't wait. But then I crashed.'

'What's his name?' She was trying so hard to focus on anything but Rob.

'Henry,' Amina said. 'He'll come. I know he will. I…I need him.'

You need Rob, Julie thought, but she didn't say it.

And she didn't say how much her life depended on Rob pushing through that door.

Amina's house had caught fire. Dear God, he could see flames through the blackness. The heat was almost unbearable. No, make that past unbearable.

He had to go. He was doing nothing staying here. He was killing himself in a useless hunt.

But still… His hand had caught the veranda rail. He steadied. One last try…

He hauled himself onto the veranda and gave one last yell.

'Danny! Luka!'

And a great heavy body shoved itself at his legs, almost pushing him over.

Dog. He couldn't see him. He could only crouch and hold.

He searched for his collar and found…a hand. A kid, holding the dog.

'Danny!' There was nothing of him, a sliver of gasping fear. He couldn't see. He hauled him into his arms and hugged, steadying for a moment, taking as well as giving comfort. Taking strength.

God, the heat...

'Mama...' the little boy whimpered, burying his face in Rob's chest, not because he trusted him, but to stop the heat.

Rob was holding him with one arm, unbuttoning his wool flannel shirt with the other. Thank God the shirt was oversized. The kid was in shorts and sandals!

He buttoned up again, kid inside, and the kid didn't move. He was past moving, Rob thought. He could feel his chest heaving as he fought for breath. His own breathing hurt.

He had him. Them. The dog was hard at his side, not going anywhere.

He had to get to the bunker. It was way past a safe time for them to get there but there was nowhere else.

Julie would be at the bunker. If she'd made it.

And he had something to fight for. For Rob, the last four years had passed in a mist of grey. He'd tried to get on with his life, he'd built his career, he'd tried to enjoy life again but, in truth, every sense had seemed dulled. Yet now, when the world around him truly was grey and thick with smoke, every one of his senses was alert, intent, focused.

He would make it to the bunker. He would save this kid.

He would make it back to Julie.

Please...

'Hold on,' he managed to yell to the kid, though whether the little boy could hear him over the roar of the flames was impossible to tell. 'Hold your breath, Danny. We're going to run.'

Amina was crying, not sobbing, not hysterical, but tears were running unchecked down her face.

Julie was past crying. She was past feeling. If Rob was safe he'd be here by now. The creek at the bottom of the gully was dry. Even if it had been running it was overhung with dense bush. There was no safe place except here.

She was the last, she thought numbly. Her boys had gone. Now Rob, too?

Last night had been amazing. Last night it had felt as if she was waking up from a nightmare, as if slivers of light were finally breaking through the fog.

She hadn't deserved the light. She might have known…

'Your husband…' Amina managed, and she knew the woman was making a Herculean effort to talk. 'He's… great.'

'I…yeah.' What to say? There was nothing to say.

'How long have you been married?'

She had to think. Was she still married? Sort of. Sort of not.

'Seven years,' she managed.

'No kids?'

'I…no.'

'I'm sorry,' Amina whispered, and the dead feeling inside Julie turned into the hard, tight knot she knew so well. The knot that threatened to choke her. The knot that had ended her life.

'It's too late, isn't it?' Amina whispered. 'They would have been here by now. It's too…'

'I don't know…'

And then she stopped.

A bang. She was sure…

It was embers crashing against the door. Surely.

She should have closed the inner door. It was the last of her dot-points.

Another bang.

She was up, scrambling to reach the door. But then she paused, forcing herself to be logical. She was trying desperately to think and somehow she managed to make her mind see sense. To open the outer door mid-fire would suck every trace of oxygen from the bunker, even if the fire didn't blast right in. She couldn't do that to Amina.

Follow the dot-points. Follow the rules.

The banging must have been flying embers. It must. But if not…

She was already in the outer chamber, hauling the inner door closed behind her, closing herself off from the inner sanctuary. 'Stay!' she yelled at Amina and Amina had the sense to obey.

With the inner door closed it was pitch-dark, but she didn't need to see. She was at the outer door. She could feel the heat.

She hauled up the latch and tugged, then hauled.

The door swung wide with a vicious blast of heat and smoke.

And a body. A great solid body, holding something. Almost falling in.

A huge, furry creature lunging against her legs.

'Get it…get it sh—'

Rob. He was beyond speech. He was beyond anything. He crumpled to his knees, gasping for air.

She knew what he'd been trying to say. She had to get the door shut. She did it but afterwards she never knew how. It felt as if she herself was being sucked out. She fought with the door, fought with everything she had, and finally the great latch Rob had designed with such foresight fell into place.

But still…the smoke… There was no air. She couldn't breathe.

It took effort, will, concentration to find the latch on the inner door but somehow she did. She tugged and Amina was on the other side. As soon as the latch lifted she had it open.

'Danny…' It was a quavering sob.

'He's here,' Rob managed and then slumped sideways into the inner chamber, giving way to the all-consuming black.

Rob surfaced to water. Cool, wondrous water, washing his face. Someone was letting water run over him. There was water on his head. The wool cap was nowhere. There was just water.

He shifted a little and tasted it, and heard a sob of relief.

'Rob…'

'Julie.' The word didn't quite come out, though. His mouth felt thick and swollen. He heard a grunt that must have been him but he couldn't do better.

'Let me hold you while you drink.' And she had him. Her arm was supporting his shoulders, and magically there was a bottle of water at his lips. He drank, gloriously grateful for the water, even more grateful that it was Julie who had him. He could see her by the dim light of the torch lamp. Julie…

'The…the boy…' Maybe it came out, maybe it didn't, but she seemed to understand what he said.

'Danny's safe; not even burned. His mother has him. They're pouring water over Luka's pads. His pads look like your face. You both look scorched, but okay. It's okay, Rob.' Her voice broke. 'You'll live. We'll all live, thanks to you.'

CHAPTER FIVE

HOW LONG DID they stay in the shelter? Afterwards they tried to figure it out, but at the time they had no clue. Time simply stopped.

The roar from outside built to a crescendo, a sound where nothing could be said, nothing heard. Maybe they should have been terrified, but for Julie and for Amina too, they'd gone past terror. Terror was when the people they loved were outside, missing. Now they were all present and accounted for, and if hell itself broke loose, if their shelter disintegrated, somehow it didn't matter because they were there.

Rob was there.

He roused himself after a while and pushed himself back against the wall. Julie wasn't sure where the black soot ended and burns began. None of his clothes were burned. His eyes seemed swollen and bloodshot, but maybe hers did too. There were no mirrors here.

Amina was cuddling Danny, but she was also cuddling the dog.

The dog had almost cost her son his life, Julie thought wonderingly, but as Amina poured water over Luca's paws and his tail gave a feeble wag of thanks, she thought: *this dog is part of their family.*

No wonder Danny ran after him. He was loved.

Love...

It was a weird concept. Four years ago, love had died. It had shrivelled inside her, leaving her a dried out husk. She'd thought she could never feel pain again.

But when she'd thought she'd lost Rob… The pain was still with her. It was like she'd been under anaesthetic for years, and now the drug had worn off. Leaving her exposed…

The noise...

She was sitting beside the dirt wall, next to Rob.

His hand came out and took hers, and held. Taking comfort?

Her heart twisted, and the remembered pain came flooding back. Family…

She didn't have family. Her family was dead.

But Rob was holding her hand and she couldn't pull away.

She stirred at some stage, found cartons of juice, packets of crackers and tinned tuna. The others didn't speak while she prepared a sort of lunch.

Danny was the first to eat, accepting her offering with pleasure.

'We didn't have breakfast,' he told her. 'Mama was too scared. She was trying to pack the car; trying to ring Papa. I wanted toast but Mama said when we got away from the fire.'

'We're away from the fire now,' she told him, glancing sideways at Rob. She wasn't sure if his throat was burned. She wasn't sure…of anything. But he cautiously sipped the juice and then tucked into the crackers like there was no tomorrow.

The food did them all good. It settled them. *Nothing like a good cup of tea*—Julie's Gran used to say that, and she grinned. There was no way she could attempt to boil water. Juice would have to do as a substitute, but it seemed to be working just as well.

The roaring had muted. She was scarcely daring to hope, but maybe the front had passed.

'It's still too loud and too hot,' Rob croaked. 'We can't open the door yet.'

'My Henry will be looking for us,' Amina said. 'He'll be frantic.'

'He won't have been allowed through,' Rob told her. 'I came up last night and they were closing the road blocks then.'

'You were an idiot for coming,' Julie said.

'Yep.' But he didn't sound like he thought he was an idiot. 'How long have you lived here?' he asked Amina, and Julie thought he was trying hard to sound like things were normal. Like this was just a brief couple of hours of enforced stay and then they'd get on with their lives.

Maybe she would, she thought. After all, what had changed for her? Maybe their house had burned, but she didn't live here anyway.

Maybe more traces of their past were gone, but they'd been doomed to vanish one day. Things were just…things.

'Nearly four years,' Amina said. 'We came just after Danny was born. But this place…it's always been empty. The guy who mows the lawns said there was a tragedy. Kids…' And then her hand flew to her mouth. 'Your kids,' she whispered in horror. 'You're the parents of the twins who died.'

'It was a long time ago,' Rob said quietly. 'It's been a very long time since we were parents.'

'But you're together?' She seemed almost frantic, overwhelmed by past tragedy when recent tragedy had just been avoided.

'For now we are,' Rob told her.

'But you don't live here.'

'Too many ghosts,' Julie said.

'Why don't you sell?' She seemed dazed beyond belief. Horror piled upon horror…

'Because of the ghosts,' Julie whispered.

Amina glanced from Julie to Rob and back again, her expression showing her sheer incomprehension of what they must have gone through. Or maybe it wasn't incomprehension. She'd been so close herself…

'If you hadn't saved Danny…' she whispered.

'We did,' Rob told her.

'But it can't bring your boys back.'

'No.' Rob's voice was harsh.

'There's nothing…' Amina was crying now, hugging Danny to her, looking from Julie to Rob and back again. 'You've saved us and there's nothing I can do to thank you. No way… I wish…'

'We all wish,' Rob said grimly, glancing at Julie. 'But at least today we have less to wish for. A bit of ointment and the odd bandage for Luka's sore paws and we'll be ready to carry on where we left off.'

Where we left off yesterday, though, Julie thought bleakly. *Not where we left off four years ago.*

What had she been about, clinging to this man last night? The ghosts were still all around them.

The ghosts would never let them go.

'We're okay,' Rob said and suddenly he'd tugged her to him and he was holding. Just holding. Taking comfort or giving it, it didn't matter. His body was black and filthy and big and hard and infinitely comforting and she had a huge urge to turn and kiss him, smoke and all. She didn't. She couldn't and it wasn't just that they were with Amina and Danny.

The ghosts still held the power to hold them apart.

* * *

An hour later, Rob finally decreed they might open the bunker doors. The sounds had died to little more than high wind, with the occasional crack of falling timber. The battery-operated radio Rob had dug up from beneath a pile of blankets told them the front had moved south. Messages were confused. There was chaos and destruction throughout the mountains. All roads were closed. The advice was not to move from where they were.

They had no intention of moving from where they were, but they might look outside.

The normal advice during a bush fire was to take shelter while the front passed, and then emerge as soon as possible and fight to keep the house from burning. That'd be okay in a fast-moving grass fire but down in the valley the bush had caught and burned with an intensity that was never going to blow through. There'd been an hour of heat so intense they could feel it through the double doors. Now…she thought they'd emerge to nothing.

'What about staying here while we do a reconnaissance?' Rob asked Amina and the woman gave a grim nod.

'Our house'll be gone anyway; I know that. What's there to see? Danny, can you pass me another drink? We'll stay here until Rob and Julie tell us it's safe.'

'I want to see the burned,' Danny said, and Julie thought this was becoming an adventure to the little boy. He had no idea how close he'd come.

'You'll see it soon enough.' Rob managed to keep the grimness from his voice. 'But, for now, Julie and I are the fearless forward scouts. You're the captain minding the fort. Take care of everyone here, Danny. You're in charge.'

And he held out his hand to Julie. 'Come on, love,' he said. 'Let's go face the music.'

She hesitated. There was so much behind those words.

Sadness, tenderness, and…caring? How many years had they been apart and yet he could still call her *love*.

It twisted her heart. It made her feel vulnerable in a way she couldn't define.

'I'm coming,' she said, but she didn't take his hand. 'Let's go.'

First impression was black and smoke and heat. The wash of heat was so intense it took her breath away.

Second impression was desolation. The once glorious bushland that had surrounded their home was now a blackened, ash-filled landscape, still smouldering, flickers of flame still orange through the haze of smoke.

Third impression was that their house was still standing.

'My God,' Rob breathed. 'It's withstood… Julie, Plan D now.'

And she got it. Their fire plan had been formed years before but it was typed up and laminated, pasted to their bathroom door so they couldn't help but learn it.

Plan A: leave the area before the house was threatened. When they'd had the boys, this was the most sensible course of action. Maybe it was the most sensible course of action anyway. Their independent decision to come into a fire zone had been dumb. But okay, moving on.

Plan B: stay in the house and defend. They'd abandon that plan if the threat was dire, the fire intense.

Plan C: head to the bunker and stay there until the front passed. And then implement Plan D.

Plan D: get out of the bunker as soon as possible and try to stop remnants of fire destroying the house.

The fire had been so intense that Julie had never dreamed she'd be faced with Plan D but now it had happened, and the list with its dot-points was so ingrained in her head that she moved into automatic action.

The generator was under the house. The pump was under there too. If they were safe they could pump water from the underground tanks.

'You do the water, spray the roof,' Rob snapped. 'I'll check inside, then head round the foundations and put out spot fires.' It was still impossibly hard to speak. Even breathing hurt, but somehow Rob managed it. 'We can do this, Julie. With this level of fire, we might be stuck here for hours, if not days. We need to keep the house safe.'

Why? There was a tiny part of her that demanded it. *Why bother?*

For the same reason she'd come back, she thought. This house had been home. It no longer was, or she'd thought it no longer was. But Rob was already heading for the bricked-in cavity under the house where they'd find tools to defend.

Rob thought this place was worth fighting for—the remnants of her home?

Who knew the truth of it? Who knew the logic? All she knew was that Rob thought this house was worth defending and, for now, all she could do was follow.

They worked solidly for two hours. After the initial checks they worked together, side by side. Rob's design genius had paid off. The house was intact but the smouldering fires after the front were insidious. A tiny spark in leaf litter hard by the house could be enough to turn the house into flames hours after the main fire. So Julie sprayed while Rob ran along the base of the house with a mop and bucket.

The underground water tank was a lifesaver. The water flowing out seemed unbelievably precious. Heaven knew how people managed without such tanks.

They didn't, she thought grimly as finally Rob left her

to sentry duty and determinedly made his way through the ash and smoke to check Amina's house.

He came back looking even grimmer than he had when he'd left.

'Gone,' he said. 'And their car… God help them if they'd stayed in that car, or even if they'd made it out onto the road. Our cars are still safe in the garage, but a tree's fallen over the track leading into the house. It's big and it's burning. We're going nowhere.'

There was no more to be said. They worked on. Maybe someone should go back to Amina to tell her about her house, but the highest priority had to be making sure this house was safe. Not because of emotional ties, though. This was all about current need.

Mount Bundoon was a tiny hamlet and this house and Amina's were two miles out of town. Thick bush lay between them and the township. There'd be more fallen logs—who knew what else—between them and civilisation.

'We'll be stuck here till Christmas,' Julie said as they worked, and her voice came out strained. Her throat was so sore from the smoke.

'Seeing as Christmas is tomorrow, yes, we will,' Rob told her. 'Did you have any plans?'

'I…no.'

'Do we have a turkey in the freezer?'

'I should have left it out,' she said unsteadily. 'It would have been roasted by now. Oh, Rob…' She heard her voice shake and Rob's arms came round her shoulders.

'No matter. We've done it. We're almost on the other side, Jules, love.'

But they weren't, she thought, and suddenly bleakness was all around her. What had changed? She could cling to Rob now but she knew that, long-term, they'd destroy each other. How could you help ease someone else's pain when you were withered inside by your own?

'Another half hour and we might be able to liberate Amina,' Rob said and something about the way he spoke told her he was feeling pretty much the same sensations she was feeling. 'The embers are getting less and Luka must be just about busting to find a tree by now.'

'Well, good luck to him finding one,' she said, pausing with her wet mop to stare bleakly round at the moonscape destruction.

'We can help them,' Rob said gently. 'They've lost their house. We can help them get through it. I don't know about you, Jules, but putting my head down and working's been the only thing between me and madness for the last four years. So keeping Amina's little family secure—that's something we can focus on. And we can focus on it together.'

'Just for the next twenty-four hours.'

'That's all I ever think about,' Rob told her, and the bleakness was back in his voice full force. 'One day at a time. One hour at a time. That's survival, Jules. We both know all about it so let's put it into action now.'

One day at a time? Rob worked on, the hard physical work almost a welcome relief from the emotions of the last twenty-four hours but, strangely, he'd stopped thinking of now. He was putting out embers on autopilot but the rest of his brain was moving forward.

Where did he go from here?

Before the fire, he'd thought he had almost reached the other side of a chasm of depression and self-blame. There'd been glimmers of light when he'd thought he could enjoy life again. 'You need to move on,' his shrink had advised him. 'You can't help Julie and together your grief will make you self-destruct.' Or maybe that wasn't what the shrink had advised him—maybe it was what the counselling sessions had made him accept for himself.

But now, working side by side, with Julie a constant presence as they beat out the spot fires still flaring up against the house, it was as if that thinking was revealed for what it was—a travesty. A lie. How could he move on? He still felt married. He still *was* married.

He'd fallen in love with his dot-point-maker, his Julie, eight years ago and that love was still there.

Maybe that was why he'd come back—drawn here because his heart had never left the place. And it wasn't just the kids.

It was his wife.

So… Twenty-four hours on and the mists were starting to clear.

Together your grief will make you self-destruct. It might be true, he conceded, but Julie chose that moment to thump a spark with a wet mop. 'Take that, you—' she grunted and swiped it again for good measure and he found himself smiling.

She was still under there—his Julie.

Together they'd self-destruct? Maybe they would, he conceded as he worked, but was it possible—was there even a chance?—that together they could find a way to heal?

It was time to get Amina and Danny and Luka out of the bunker.

It was dark, not because it was night—it was still mid-afternoon—but because the smoke was still all-enveloping. They'd need to keep watch, take it in turns to check for spot fires, but, for now, they entered the house together.

Rob was holding Amina's hand. He'd been worried

she'd trip over the mass of litter blasted across the yard. Danny was clinging to his mother's other side. Luka was pressing hard against his small master. The dog was limping a little but he wasn't about to leave the little boy.

Which left Julie bringing up the rear. She stood aside as Rob led them indoors and for some crazy reason she thought of the day Rob had brought her here to show her his plans. He'd laid out a tentative floor plan with string and markers on the soil. He'd shown her where the front door would be and then he'd swung her into his arms and lifted her across.

'Welcome to your home, my bride,' he'd told her and he'd set her down into the future hall and he'd kissed her with a passion that had left her breathless. 'Welcome to your Happy Ever After.'

Past history. Moving on. She followed them in and felt bleakness envelop her. The house was grey, dingy, appalling. There were no lights. She flicked the switch without hope and, of course, there was none.

'The cabling from the solar system must have melted,' Rob said, and then he gave a little-boy grin that was, in the circumstances, totally unexpected and totally endearing. 'But I have that covered. I knew the conduit was a weak spot when we built so the electrician's left me backup. I just need to unplug one lot and plug in another. The spare's in the garage, right next to my tool belt.'

And in the face of that grin it was impossible not to smile back. The grey lifted, just a little. Man with tool belt, practically chest-thumping…

He'd designed this house to withstand fire. Skilled with a tool belt or not, he had saved them.

'It might take a bit of fiddling,' Rob conceded, trying—unsuccessfully—to sound modest. 'And the smoke will be messing with it now. But even if it fails completely we have the generator for important things, like pumping water. We have the barbecue. We can manage.'

'If you're thinking of getting up on the roof, Superman…'

'When it cools a little. And I'll let you hold the ladder.' He offered it like he was offering diamonds and, weirdly, she wanted to laugh. Her world was somehow righting.

'Do you mind…if we stay?' Amina faltered and Julie hauled herself together even more. Amina had lost her home. She didn't know where her husband was and Julie knew she was fearful that he'd have been on the road trying to reach her. What was Julie fearful about? Nothing. Rob was safe, and even that shouldn't matter.

But it did. She looked at his smoke-stained face, his bloodshot eyes, his grin that she knew was assumed—she knew this man and she knew he was feeling as bleak as she was, but he was trying his best to cheer them up—and she thought: *no matter what we've been through, we have been through it.*

I know this man. The feeling was solid, a rock in a shifting world. Even if being together hurt so much she couldn't bear it, he still felt part of her.

'Of course you can stay.' She struggled to sound normal, struggled to sound like a friendly neighbour welcoming a friend. 'For as long as you like.'

'For as long as we must,' Rob amended. 'Amina, the roads will be blocked. There's no phone reception. I checked and the transmission towers are down.' He hesitated and looked suddenly nervous. 'When…when's your baby due?'

'Not for another four weeks. Henry works in the mines, two weeks on, two weeks off, but he's done six weeks in a row so he can get a long leave for the baby. He was flying in last night. He'll be frantic. I have to get a message to him.'

'I don't think we can do that,' Rob told her. 'The phones are out and the road is cut by fallen timber. It's over an hour's walk at the best of times down to the highway and frankly it's not safe to try. Burned trees will still be falling. I don't think I can walk in this heat and smoke.'

'I wouldn't want you to, but Henry…'

'He'll have stopped at the road blocks. He'll be forced to wait until the roads are cleared, but the worst of the fire's over. You'll see him soon.'

'But if the fire comes back…'

'It won't,' Rob told her. 'Even if there's a wind change, there's nothing left to burn.'

'But this house…'

'Is a fortress,' Julie told her. 'It's the house that Rob built. No fire dare challenge it.'

'He's amazing,' Amina managed as Rob headed out to do another mop and bucket round—they'd need to keep checking for hours, if not days. 'He's just…a hero.'

'He is.'

'You're so lucky…' And then Amina faltered, remembering. 'I mean… I can't…'

'I am lucky,' Julie told her. 'And yes, Rob's a hero.' And he was. Not her hero but a hero. 'But for now…for now, let's investigate the basics. We need to make this house liveable. It's Christmas tomorrow. Surely we can do something to celebrate.'

'But my Henry…'

'He'll come,' Julie said stoutly. 'And when he does, we need to have Christmas waiting for him.'

Rob made his way slowly round the house, inspecting everything. Every spark, every smouldering leaf or twig copped a mopful of water, but the threat was easing.

The smoke was easing a little. He could almost breathe.

He could almost think.

He'd saved Danny.

It should feel good and it did. He should feel lucky and he did. Strangely, though, he felt more than that. It was like a huge grey weight had been lifted from his shoulders.

Somehow he'd saved Danny. Danny would grow into a man because of what he'd achieved.

It didn't make the twins' death any easier to comprehend but somehow the knot of rage and desolation inside him had loosened a little.

Was it also because he'd held Julie last night? Lost himself in her body?

Julie.

'I wish she'd been able to save him, too,' he said out loud. Nothing and no one answered. It was like he was on Mars.

But Julie was here, right inside the door. And Amina and the kid he'd saved.

If he hadn't come, Julie might not have even made it to the bunker. Her eyes said maybe that wouldn't matter. Sometimes her eyes looked dead already.

How to fix that? How to break through?

He hadn't been able to four years ago. What was different now?

For the last four years he'd missed her with an ache in his gut that had never subsided. He'd learned to live with it. He'd even learned to have fun despite it, dating a couple of women this year, putting out tentative feelers, seeing if he could get back to some semblance of life. For his overtures to Julie had been met with blank rebuttal and there'd been nothing he could do to break through.

Had he tried hard enough? He hadn't, he conceded, because he'd known it was hopeless. He was part of her tragedy and she had to move on.

He'd accepted his marriage was over in everything but name.

So why had he come back here now? Was it really to save two fire engines? Or was it because he'd guessed Julie would be here?

One last hope…

If so, it had been subconscious, acting against the advice of his logic, his shrink, his new-found determination to look forward, to try and live.

But the thing was…Julie was here. She was here now, and it wasn't just the bleak, dead Julie. He could make this Julie smile again. He could reach her.

But every time he did, she closed off again.

No matter. She was still in there, in that house, and he wielded his mop with extra vigour because of it. His Julie was still Julie. She was behind layers of protection so deep he'd need a battering ram to knock them down, but hey, he'd saved a kid and his house had withstood a firestorm.

All he needed now was a battering ram and hope.

And a miracle?

Miracles were possible. They'd had two today. Why not hope for another?

The house was hot, stuffy and filled with smoke but compared to outside it seemed almost normal. It even felt normal until she hauled back the thick shutters and saw outside.

The once glorious view of the bushland was now devastation.

'I don't know what to do,' Amina whimpered and Julie thought: *neither do I.* But at least they were safe; Rob was outside in the heat making sure of it. The option of whimpering, too, was out of the question.

She looked at Amina and remembered how she'd felt

at the same stage in pregnancy. Amina wasn't carrying twins—at least she didn't think so—but this heat would be driving her to the edge, even without the added terrors of the fire.

'We have plenty of water in the underground tank,' she told her. 'And we have a generator running the pumps. If you like, you could have a bath.'

'A bath…' Amina looked at Julie like she'd offered gold. 'Really?'

'Really.'

'I'm not sure I could get in and out.' She gazed down at her bulk and even managed a smile. 'I used to describe it as a basketball. Now I think it's a small hippopotamus.'

'There are safety rails to help you in and out.'

'You put them in when you were pregnant?' It was a shy request, not one that could be snapped at.

'Yes.'

'You and Rob didn't come back here because this is where your boys lived?' Amina ventured, but it wasn't really a question. It was a statement; a discovery.

'Yes.' There was no other answer.

'Maybe I'd have felt the same if I'd lost Danny.' Danny was clinging to her side but he was looking round, interested, oblivious to the danger he'd been in mere hours before. 'Danny, will you come into the bathroom with me?'

But Danny was looking longingly out of the window. He was obviously aching for his adventure to continue, and the last thing Amina needed, Julie thought, was her four-year-old in the bathroom with her.

Luka had flopped on the floor. The big dog gave a gentle whine.

'I'll see to his pads,' Amina said but she couldn't disguise her exhaustion, or her desolation at postponing the promised bath.

'Tell you what,' Julie said. 'You go take a bath and Danny and I will take Luka into the laundry. There's a big shallow shower/bath in there. If he's like any golden retriever I know he'll like water, right?'

'He loves it.'

'Then he can stand under the shower for as long as he wants until we know his pads are completely clean. Then I'll find some burn salve for them. Danny, will you help me?'

'Give Luka a shower?' Danny ventured.

'That's the idea. You can get undressed and have a shower with him if you want.' And Julie's mind, unbidden, was taking her back, knowing what her boys loved best in the world. 'We could have fun.'

Fun... Where had that word come from? Julie McDowell didn't do fun.

'Will Rob help, too?' Danny asked shyly and she nodded.

'When he's stopped firefighting, maybe he will.'

'Rob's big.' There was already a touch of hero worship in the little boy's voice.

'Yes.'

'He made me safe. I was frightened and he made me safe.'

'He's good at that,' Julie managed, but she didn't know where to take it from there.

Once upon a time Rob had made her feel safe. Once upon a time she'd believed safe was possible.

Right now, that was what he was doing. Keeping them safe.

One day at a time, she thought. She'd been doing this for years, taking one day at a time. But now Rob was outside, keeping them safe, and the thought left her exposed.

One day at a time? Right now she was having trouble focusing on one *moment* at a time.

* * *

Rob did one final round of the house and decided that was it; he didn't have the strength to stay in the heat any longer. But the wind had died, there was no fire within two hundred yards of the house and even that was piles of ash, simmering to nothing. He could take a break. He headed up the veranda steps and was met by the sound of a child's laughter.

It stopped him dead in his tracks.

He was filthy. He was exhausted. All he wanted was to stand under a cold shower and then collapse, but the shower was in the laundry.

And someone was already splashing and shouting inside.

He could hear Julie laughing and, for some weird reason, the sound made him want to back away.

Coward, he told himself. He'd faced a bush fire and survived. How could laughter hurt so much? But it took a real effort to open the laundry door.

What met him was mess. Huge mess. The huge laundry shower-cum-bath had a base about a foot deep. It had been built to dump the twins in when they'd come in filthy from outside. The twins had filled it with their chaos and laughter and it was filled now.

More than filled.

Luka was sitting serenely in the middle of the base. The water was streaming over the big dog, and he had his head blissfully raised so the water could pour right over his eyes. Doggy heaven.

Danny had removed his clothes. He was using…one of the twins' boats?…to pour water over Luka's back. Every time he dumped a load, Luka turned and licked him, chin to forehead. Danny shrieked with laughter and scooped another load.

Julie was still fully dressed. She'd hauled off her boots and flannel overshirt but the rest was intact. Dressed or not, though, she was sitting on the edge of the tub, her feet were in the water and she was soaking. Water was streaming over her hair. She was still black but the black was now running in streaks. She looked like she didn't care.

She was helping Danny scoop water. She was laughing with Danny, hugging Luka.

Silly as a tin of worms...

Once upon a time Rob's dad had said that to him. Angus McDowell, Rob's father, was a Very Serious Man, a minister of religion, harsh and unyielding. He'd disapproved of Julie at first, though when Julie's business prowess had been proven he'd unbent towards her. But he'd visited once and listened to Julie playing with the twins at bathtime.

'She's spoiling those two lads. Listen to them. Silly as a tin of worms.'

Right now her hair was wet, the waves curling, twisting and spiralling. He'd loved her hair.

He loved her hair.

How had he managed without this woman for so long?

The same way he'd managed without his boys, he told himself harshly. One moment at a time. One step after another. Getting through each day, one by one.

Julie must feel the same. He'd seen the death of the light behind her eyes. Being together, their one-step-at-a-time rule had faltered. They could only go on if they didn't think, didn't let themselves remember.

But Julie wasn't dead now. She was very much alive. Her eyes were dancing with pleasure and her laughter was almost that of the Julie of years ago. Young. Free.

She turned and saw him and the laughter faded, just like that.

'Rob!' Danny said with satisfaction. 'You're all black. Julie says she doesn't have enough soap to get all the black off.'

'There's enough left.' Julie rose quickly—a little too quickly. Before he could stop himself he'd reached out and caught her. He held her arms as she stepped over the edge of the bath. She was soaking. She'd been using some sort of lemon soap, the one she'd always used, and suddenly he realised where that citrus scent came from. She smelled… She felt…

'You're not clean yet,' he managed and she smiled. She was only six inches away from him. He was holding her. He could just tug…

He didn't tug. This was Julie. She'd been laughing and the sight of him had stopped that laughter.

They'd destroy each other. They'd pretty much decided that, without ever speaking it out loud. Four years ago they'd walked away from each other for good reason.

How could you live with your own hurt when you saw it reflected in another's eyes, day after day? Moment after moment.

A miracle. He needed a miracle.

It's Christmas, he thought inconsequentially. *That's what I want for Christmas, Santa. I've saved Danny. We're safe and our house is safe, but I'm greedy. A third miracle. Please...*

'I'm clean apart from my clothes,' Julie managed, shaking her hair like a dog so that water sprayed over him. It hit his face, cool and delicious. Some hit his lips and he tasted it. Tasted Julie?

'I'll go change if you can take over here,' Julie said. 'Danny, is it okay if Rob comes under the water, too?'

'Yes,' Danny said. 'He's my friend. But you can both fit.'

'I need to find some clean clothes and something your

mum can wear,' Julie told him. 'And some dog food. And some food for us.'

'The freezer…'

'I've hooked it to the generator so I can save the solar power for important stuff,' she said and deliberately she tugged away from him. It hurt that she pulled back. He wanted to hold her. 'Like the lights on the Christmas tree.'

'So we have Christmas lights and there's enough to eat?' he asked, trying hard to concentrate on practicalities.

'If need be, we have enough to live on for weeks.'

'Will we stay here for weeks?' Danny asked and Rob saw a shadow cross Julie's face. It was an act then, he thought, laughing and playing with the child. The pain was still there. She'd managed to push it away while she'd helped Danny have fun but it was with her still. Every time she saw a child…

And every time she saw him. She glanced up at him and he saw the hurt, the bleakness and the same certainty that this was a transient, enforced connection. If they were to survive they had to move on.

He knew it for the truth. It was time it lost the power to hurt.

Miracles were thin on the ground. They'd already had two today. Was it too much to ask for just one more?

How long was frozen food safe? Where was the Internet when she needed it? Finally she decided to play safe. Using the outside barbecue—well, it had been outside but Rob had hauled it under the house during the fire so now it could be wheeled outside again—she boiled dried spaghetti and tipped over a can of spaghetti sauce. The use-by dates on both were well past, but she couldn't figure how they could go off.

'I reckon, come Armageddon, these suckers will survive,' she told Rob, tipping in the sauce.

'We might have to do something a bit more imaginative tomorrow,' Rob told her. Washed and dressed in clean jeans and T-shirt, he'd found her in the kitchen. He was now examining the contents of the freezer. 'Shall I take the turkey out?'

'Surely the roads will be open by tomorrow.'

'Don't count on it,' he said grimly. 'Jules, I've been listening to the radio and the news is horrendous. We're surrounded by miles of burned ground and the fire's ongoing. The authorities won't have the resources to get us out while they're still trying to protect communities facing the fire front.'

'Turkey it is, then,' she said, trying to make it sound light. As if being trapped here was no big deal.

As if the presence of this man she'd once known so well wasn't doing things to her head. And to her body.

She'd known him so well. She *knew* him so well.

One part of her wanted to turn away from the barbecue right now and tug him into her arms. To hold and be held. To feel what she used to take for granted.

Another part of her wanted to leave right now, hike the miles down the road away from the mountains. Sure, it would entail risks but staying close to this man held risks as well. Like remembering how much she wanted him. Like remembering how much giving your heart cost.

It had cost her everything. There was simply…nothing left.

'Can…can I help?' Amina stood at the doorway, Danny clinging by her side. She was dressed in a borrowed house robe of Julie's. She looked lost, bereft, and very, very pregnant.

'Put your feet up inside,' Rob said roughly and Julie

knew by his tone that he was as worried as she was about the girl. 'It's too hot out here already and Julie's cooking. Hot food!'

'You tell me where we can get sandwiches or salad and I'll open my purse,' Julie retorted. 'Sorry, Amina, it's spaghetti or nothing.'

'I'd like to see my house,' she said shyly and Julie winced.

'It's gone, Amina.'

'Burned,' Danny said. The adventure had gone out of the child. He looked scared.

'Yes, but we have this house,' Julie said. 'That's something. You can stay here for as long as you want.'

'My husband will be looking for us,' Amina whispered.

'If he comes next door the first place he'll look will be here.'

'Will Santa know to come here?' Danny asked. His dog was pressed by his side. He looked very small and very frightened. It was his mother's fear, Julie thought. He'd be able to feel it.

'Santa always knows where everyone is,' Rob said, squatting before Danny and scratching Luka's ears. It was intuitive, Julie thought. Danny might well recoil from a hug, but a hug to his dog was pretty much the same thing. 'I promise.'

'He's found us before,' Amina managed, but this time she couldn't stop a sob. 'I can't...we were just...'

'Where are you from?' Rob asked gently, still patting Luka.

'Sri Lanka. We left because of the fighting. My husband... He's a construction engineer. He had a good job; we had a nice house but we...things happened. We had to come here, but here he can't be an engineer. He has to retrain but it's so expensive to get his Australian accreditation. We're working so hard, trying to get the money so he can do the transition course. Meanwhile, I've been working as a cleaner.' She tilted her chin. 'I work for the firm that cleans this house. My job's good. We couldn't believe it when we were able to rent our house. We thought…this is heaven. But Henry has to work as a fly in, fly out miner. He'll be so worried right now and I'm scared he might have tried to get here. If he's been caught in the fire…'

Rob rose and took her hands. She was close to collapse, weak with terror.

'It won't have happened,' he said firmly, strongly, in a voice that Julie hadn't heard before. It was a tone that said: *don't mess with me; this is the truth and you'd better believe me.* 'They put road blocks in place last night. No one was allowed in. I was the last, and I had to talk hard to be let through. If your husband had come in before the blocks were in place, then he'd be here now. He can't have. He'll be stuck at the block or even further down the mountain. He'll be trying to get to you but he won't be permitted. He'll be safe.'

Danny was looking up at Rob as if he were the oracle on high. 'Papa's stuck down the mountain?'

'I imagine he's eating his dinner right now.'

'Where will he eat dinner?'

'The radio says a school has been opened at the foot of the mountains. Anyone who can't get home will be staying at the school.'

'Papa's at school?'

'Yes,' Rob said in that same voice that brooked no argument. 'Yes, he is. Eating dinner. Speaking of dinner… how's it coming along?'

'It's brilliant,' Julie said. 'Michelin three star, no less.'

'I don't doubt it,' Rob said, and grinned at her with the same Rob-grin that twisted her heart with pain and with pleasure. 'Do we have enough to give some to Luka?'

'If Luka eats spaghetti he'll get a very red moustache,' Julie said and Danny giggled.

And Julie smiled back at Rob—and saw the same pain and pleasure reflected in his eyes.

CHAPTER SIX

DANNY AND ROB chatted. It was their saving grace; otherwise their odd little dinner would have been eaten in miserable silence. Too much had happened for Julie to attempt to be social.

Amina was caught up in a pool of misery. Julie's heart went out to her but there was little she could do to help.

She pressed her into eating, with limited success, and worried more.

'When's your baby due?' she asked.

'The twentieth of January.' Amina motioned to Danny. 'We were still in the refugee camp when we had Danny. This was supposed to be so different.'

'It is different.'

'Refugees again,' Amina whispered. 'But not even together.'

'You will be soon,' Julie said stoutly, sending a fervent prayer upward. 'Meanwhile we have ice cream.'

'Ice cream!'

'It's an unopened container, not a hint of ice on it,' she said proudly. 'How's that for forethought? I must have pre-prepared, four years ago.'

There was an offer too good to refuse. They all ate ice cream and Julie was relieved to see Amina reach for seconds.

There was another carton at the base of the freezer. Maybe they could even eat ice cream for breakfast.

Breakfast… How long would they be trapped here?

'Now can I go next door?' Amina asked as the last of the ice cream disappeared.

Rob grimaced. 'You're sure you don't want me to check and report back?'

'I need to see.'

'Me too,' Danny said and his mother looked at him and nodded.

'Danny's seen a lot the world has thrown at us. And his father would expect him to be a man.'

Danny's chest visibly swelled.

Kids. They were all the same. Wanting to be grown-up. Wanting to protect their mum?

It should be the other way round. She should have been able to protect…

'Stop it, Jules,' Rob said in his boss-of-the-world voice, and she flinched. Stop it? How could she stop? It was as if the voices in her head were on permanent replay.

'We need to focus on Santa,' he told her, and his eyes sent her a message that belied his smile. 'Moving on.'

Move on. How could she ever? But here there was no choice. Amina was looking at her and so was Danny. Even Luka… No, actually, Luka was looking at the almost empty ice cream container in her hand.

Move on.

'Right,' she said and lowered the ice cream to possibly its most appreciative consumer. 'Danny, you're going to have to wash your dog's face. Spaghetti followed by chocolate ice cream is not a good look. Meanwhile, I'll see if I can find you some sturdy shoes, Amina, and I have a jogging suit that might fit over your bump. It's not the most gorgeous outfit you might like but it's sensible, and Sensible R Us. Let's get the end of this meal cleared up and then go see if the fire's left anything of your house.'

It hadn't left a thing.

A twisted, gnarled washing line. The skeleton of a washing machine. A mass of smouldering timbers and smashed tiles.

Amina stood weeping. Julie held her and Danny's hands as Rob, in his big boots, stomped over the ruins searching for… Anything.

Nothing.

He came back to them at last, his face bleak. 'Amina, I'm sorry.'

'We didn't have much,' Amina said, faltering. 'My sister…she was killed in the bombing. I had her photographs. That was what I most…' She swallowed. 'But we've lost so much before. I know we can face this too. As long as my Henry is safe.'

'That's a hell of a name for a Sri Lankan engineer,' Rob said and Amina managed a smile.

'My mother-in-law dreamed of her son being an Englishman.'

'Will Australian do instead?'

'It doesn't matter where we are—what we have. It's a long time since we dreamed of anything but our family being safe.'

And then she paused.

The silence after the roar of the fire had been almost eerie. The wind had dropped after the front had passed. There was still the crackle of fire, and occasionally there'd be a crash as fire-weakened timber fell, but there'd been little sound for hours.

Now they heard an engine, faint at first but growing closer.

Rob ushered his little group around Amina's burned car, around the still burning log that lay over their joint driveways and out onto the road. Rob was carrying Danny—much to Danny's disgust, but he had no sensible shoes. And if anyone was to carry him, it seemed okay that his hero should. Thus they stood, waiting, seeing what would emerge out of the smoky haze.

And when it came, inevitably, magically but far too late, it was a fire engine. Big, red, gorgeous.

Julie hadn't realised how tense she'd been until she saw the red of the engine, until she saw the smoke-blackened firefighters in their stained yellow suits. Here was contact with the outside world.

She had a sudden mad urge to climb on the back and hitch a ride, all the way back to Sydney, all the way back to the safety of her office, her ordered financial world.

Ha. As if this apparition was offering any such transport.

'Are you guys okay?' It was the driver, a grim-faced woman in her fifties, swinging out of the cab and facing them with apprehension.

'No casualties,' Rob told her. 'Apart from minor burns on our dog's feet. But we have burn cream. And ice cream. And one intact house.'

'Good for you.' The guys with her were surveying Amina's house and then looking towards their intact house with surprise. 'You managed to save it?'

'It saved itself. We hid in a bunker.'

'Bloody lucky. Can you stay here?'

'Amina's pregnant,' Rob said. 'And her husband will be going out of his mind not knowing if she's safe.'

The woman looked at Amina, noting Danny, noting everything, Julie thought. She had the feeling that this woman was used to making hard decisions.

'We'll put her on the list for evacuation,' she said. 'How pregnant are you?'

'Thirty-six weeks,' Amina whispered.

'No sign of labour?'

'N...no.'

'Then sorry, love, but that puts you down the list. We're radioing in casualties and using the chopper for evacuation, but the chopper has a list a mile long of people with burns, accidents from trying to outrun the fire or breathing problems. And it's a huge risk trying to take anyone out via the road. There's so much falling timber I'm risking my own team being here. Do you have water? Food?'

'We're okay,' Rob told her. 'We have solar power, generators, water tanks, freezers and a stocked pantry. We have plenty of uncontaminated water and more canned food than we know what to do with.'

'Amazing,' the woman told him. 'It sounds like you're luckier than some of the towns that have been in the fire line. We managed to save houses but they're left with no services. Meanwhile, there are houses further up the mountain that haven't been checked. Our job's to get through to them, give emergency assistance and detail evacuation needs for the choppers, but by emergency we're talking life-threatening. That's all we can do—we're stretched past our limits. But we will take your name and get it put up on the lists at the refuge centres to say you're safe,' she told Amina. 'That should reassure your husband. Meanwhile, stay as cool as you can and keep that baby on board.'

'But we have no way of contacting you if anything... happens,' Rob said urgently and the woman grimaced.

'I know and I'm sorry, but I'm making a call here. We'll get the road clear as soon as we can but that'll be late tomorrow at the earliest, and possibly longer. There's timber still actively burning on the roadside. It's no use driving anyone out if a tree's to fall on them, and that's a real risk. You have a house. Your job is to protect it a while longer and thank your lucky stars you're safe. Have as good a Christmas as you can under the circumstances—and make sure that baby stays where it is.'

They watched the fire truck make its cautious way to the next bend and disappear. All of them knew what they were likely to find. It was a subdued little party that picked its way through the rubble and back to the house.

Luka greeted them with dulled pleasure. His paws obviously hurt. Rob had put on burn cream and dressings. They were superficial burns, he reported, but they were obviously painful enough for the big dog to not want to bother his bandages.

Danny lay down on the floor with him, wrapped his arms around his pet's neck and burst into tears.

'My husband wanted a dog to protect us when he was away,' Amina volunteered, and she sounded close to tears herself. 'But Luka's turned into Danny's best friend. Today Luka almost killed him—and yet here I am, thanking everything that Danny still has him. I hope...I hope...'

And Julie knew what she was hoping. This woman had gone through war and refugee camps. She'd be thinking she was homeless once again. With a dog.

Once upon a time as a baby lawyer, Julie had visited a refugee camp. She couldn't remember seeing a single dog.

'It's okay, Amina,' she told her. 'If you've been renting next door, then you can just rent here instead. This place is empty.'

'But...' Rob said.

'We never use it.' Julie cast him an uncertain glance. 'We live...in other places. I know you have a lot to think about and this will be something you and your husband need to discuss together, but, right now, don't worry about accommodation. You can stay here for as long as you want.'

'But don't...don't *you* need to discuss it with your husband?' Amina asked, casting an uncertain glance at Rob.

Her husband. Rob. She glanced down at the wedding ring, still bright on her left hand. She still had a husband—and yet she hadn't made one decision with him for four years.

'Rob and I don't live together,' she said, and she couldn't stop the note of bleakness she could hear in her own words. 'We have separate lives, separate...homes. So I'm sure you agree, don't you, Rob. This place may as well be used.'

There was a moment's pause. Silence hung, and for a moment she didn't know how it could end. But then... 'It should be a home again,' Rob said. 'Julie and I can't make it one. It'd be great if you and Henry and your children could make it happy again.'

'No decisions yet,' Amina urged. 'Don't promise anything. But if we could... If Henry's safe—' She broke off again and choked on tears. 'But it's too soon for anything.'

Rob went off to check the perimeter with his mop and bucket again. They had a wide area of burned grass between them and any smouldering timber. The risk was pretty much over but still he checked.

Amina and Danny went to bed. There was a made-up guest room with a lovely big bed, but Danny had spotted the racing-car beds. That was where he wanted to sleep—so Amina tugged one racing car closer to the other and announced that she was sleeping there, with her son.

She was asleep almost as her head hit the pillow. Had she slept at all last night? Julie wondered. She thought again of past fighting and refugee camps and all this woman had gone through.

Danny was fast asleep too. He was sharing his car-bed with Luka. Julie stood in the doorway and looked at them, this little family who'd been so close to disaster.

Disaster was always so close…

Get over it, she told herself harshly. *Move on.* She needed work to distract herself. She needed legal problems to solve, paperwork to do—stuff that had to be done yesterday.

Rob was out playing fireman but there was no need for the two of them to be there. So what was she supposed to do? Go to bed? She wasn't tired or if she was her body wasn't admitting it. She felt weird, exposed, trapped. Standing in her children's bedroom watching others sleep in their beds… Knowing a man who was no longer her husband was out protecting the property…

What to do? What to do?

Christmas.

The answer came as she headed back down the hall. There in the sitting room was her Christmas tree. Was it only last night that she'd decorated it? Why?

And the answer came clear, obvious now as it hadn't been last night. Because Danny needed it. Because they all needed it?

'Will Santa know to come here?' Danny had asked and Rob had reassured him.

'Santa knows where everyone is.'

That had been a promise and it had to be kept. She wouldn't mind betting Danny would be the first awake in the morning. Right now there was a Christmas tree and nothing else.

Santa had no doubt kept a stash of gifts over at Amina's house, but there was nothing left there now except cinders. Amina had been too exhausted to think past tonight.

'So I'm Santa.' She said it out loud.

'Can I share?'

And Rob was in the doorway, looking at the tree. 'I thought of it while I mopped,' he told her. 'We need to play Father Christmas.'

They could. There was a stash from long ago…

If she could bear it.

Of course she could bear it. Did she make her decision based on emotional back story or the real, tomorrow needs of one small boy? What was the choice? There wasn't one. She glanced at Rob and saw he'd come to the same conclusion she had.

Without a word she headed into their bedroom. Rob followed.

She tugged the bottom drawer out from under the wardrobe, ready to climb—even as toddlers the twins had been expert in finding stuff they didn't want them to find. She put a foot on the first drawer and Rob took her by the waist, lifted her and set her aside.

'Climbing's men's work,' he said.

'Yeah?' Unbidden, came another memory. Their town house in the city. Their elderly neighbour knocking on the door one night.

'Please, my kitten's climbed up the elm outside. He can't get down. Will you help?'

The elm was vast, reaching out over the pavement to the street beyond. The kitten was maybe halfway up, mewing pitifully.

'Right,' Rob had said manfully, though Julie had known him well and heard the qualms behind the bravado.

'Let me call the fire brigade,' she'd said and he'd cast her a look of manly scorn.

'Stand aside, woman.'

Which meant twenty minutes later the kitten was safely back in her owner's arms—having decided she didn't like Rob reaching for her, so she'd headed down under her own steam. And Julie had finally called the fire department to help her husband down.

So now she choked, and Rob glowered, but he was laughing under his glower. 'You're supposed to have forgotten that,' he told her. 'Stupid cat.'

'It's worth remembering.'

'Isn't everything?' he asked obliquely and headed up his drawer-cum-staircase.

And then they really had to remember.

The Christmas-that-never-was was up there. Silently, Rob handed it down. There were glove puppets, a wooden railway set, Batman pyjamas. Colouring books and a blow-up paddling pool. A pile of Christmas wrapping and ties they'd been too busy to use until the last moment. The detritus of a family Christmas that had never made it.

Rob put one of the puppets on his too-big hand. It was a wombat. Its two front paws were his thumb and little finger. Its head had the other fingers stuffed into its insides.

The little head wobbled. 'What do you say, Mrs McDowell?' the little wombat demanded in a voice that sounded like a strangled Rob. 'You reckon we can give me to a little guy who needs me?'

'Yes.' But her voice was strained.

'I'm not real,' the little wombat said—via Rob. 'I'm just a bit of fake fur and some neat stitchery.'

'Of course.'

'But I represent the past.'

'Don't push it, Rob.' Why was the past threatening to rise up and choke her?

'I'm not pushing. I'm facing stuff myself. I've been facing stuff alone for so long…' Rob put down his wombat and picked up the Batman pyjamas. 'It hurts. Would it hurt more together than it does separately? That's a decision we need to make. Meanwhile, we bought these too big for the twins and Danny's tiny. These'll make him happy.'

She could hardly breathe. What was he suggesting? That he wanted to try again? 'I…I know that,' she managed but she was suddenly feeling as if she was in the bunker again, cowering, the outside threats closing in.

Dumb. Rob wasn't threatening. He was holding Batman pyjamas—and smiling at her as if he understood exactly how she felt.

I've been facing stuff alone for so long... She hadn't allowed herself to think about that. She hadn't been able to face his hurt as well as hers.

Guilty…and did she need to add *coward* to her list of failings as well?

'Would it have been easier if it all burned?' Rob asked gently and she flinched.

'Maybe. Maybe it would.'

'So why did you come?'

'You know why.'

'Because it's not over? Because they're still with us?' His voice was kind. 'Because we can't escape it; we're still a family?'

'We're not.'

'They're still with me,' he said, just as gently. 'Every waking moment, and often in my sleep as well, they're with me.'

'Yeah.'

'They're not in this stuff. They're in our hearts.'

'Rob, no.' The pain… She hadn't let herself think it. She hadn't let herself feel it. She'd worked and she'd worked and she'd pushed emotion away because it did her head in.

'Jules, it's been four years. The way I feel…'

'Don't!'

He looked at her for a long, steady moment and then he looked down at the wombat. And nodded. Moving on? 'But we can pack stuff up for Danny?'

'I…yes.'

'We need things for Amina as well.'

'I have…too many things.' She thought of her dressing table, stuffed with girly things collected through a lifetime. She thought of the house next door, a heap of smouldering ash. Sharing was a no-brainer; in fact Amina could have it all.

'Wrapping paper?' Rob demanded. The emotion was dissipating. Maybe he'd realised he'd taken her to an edge that terrified her.

'I have a desk full of it,' she told him, grateful to be back on firm ground.

'Always the organised one.' He hesitated. 'Stockings?'

She took a deep breath at that and the edge was suddenly close again. Yes, they had stockings. Four. Julie, Rob, Aiden, Christopher. Her mother had embroidered names on each.

But she could be practical. She could do this. 'I'll unpick the names,' she said.

'We can use pillowcases instead.'

'N…no. I'll unpick them.'

'I can help.' He hesitated. 'I need to head out and put a few pans of water around for the wildlife, and then I'm all yours. But, Jules…'

'Mmm?'

'When we're done playing Santa Claus…will you come to bed with me tonight?'

This was tearing her in two. If she could walk away now she would, she thought. She'd walk straight out of the door, onto the road down to the highway and out of here. But that wasn't possible and this man, the man with the eyes that saw everything there was to know, was looking at her. And he was smiling, but his smile had all her pain behind it, and all his too. They had shared ghosts. Somehow, Rob was moving past them. But for her… The ghosts held her in thrall and she was trapped.

But for this night, within the trap there was wriggle room. She'd remove names from Christmas stockings. She'd wrap her children's toys and address them to Danny. She'd even find the snorkel and flippers she had hidden up on the top of her wardrobe. She'd bought them for Rob because she loved the beach, she'd loved taking the boys there and she was…she had been…slowly persuading Rob of its delights.

Did he go to the beach now? What was he doing with his life?

Who knew, and after this night she'd stop wondering again. But on Christmas morning the ghosts would see her stuffing the snorkel and flippers in his stocking. He'd head out into the burned bush with his pails of water so animals wouldn't die and, while he did, she'd prepare him a Christmas.

And the ghosts would see her lie in his arms this night.

'Yes,' she whispered because the word seemed all she could manage. And then, because it was important, she tried for more. 'Yes, please, Rob. Tonight…tonight I'd like to sleep with you once more.'

Christmas morning. The first slivers of light were making their way through the shutters Rob had left closed because there was still fire danger. The air was thick with the smell of a charred landscape.

She was lying cocooned in Rob's arms and for this moment she wanted nothing else. The world could disappear. For this moment the pain had gone, she'd found her island and she was clinging for all she was worth.

He was some island. She stirred just a little, savouring the exquisite sensation of skin against skin—her skin against Rob's—and she felt him tense a little in response.

'Good, huh?'

He sounded smug. She'd forgotten that smugness.

She loved that smugness.

'Bit rusty,' she managed and he choked on laughter.

'Rusty? I'll show you rusty.' He swung up over the top of her, his dark eyes gleaming with delicious laughter. 'I've been saving myself for you for all this time...'

'There's been no one else?'

She shouldn't have asked. She saw the laughter fade, but the tenderness was there still.

'I did try,' he said. 'I thought I should move on. It was a disaster. You?'

'I didn't even try,' she whispered. 'I knew it wouldn't work.'

'So you were saving yourself for me too.'

'I was saving myself for nobody.'

'Well, that sounds a bit bleak. You know, Jules, maybe we should cut ourselves a little slack. Put bleakness behind us for a bit.'

'For today at least,' she conceded, and tried to smile back. 'Merry Christmas.'

'Merry Christmas to you, too,' he said, and the wickedness was back. 'You want me to give you your first present?'

'I...'

'Because I'm about to,' he said and his gorgeous muscular body, the body she'd loved with all her heart, lowered to hers.

She rose to meet him. Skin against skin. She took his

body into her arms and tugged him to her, around her, merging into the warmth and depth of him.

Merry Christmas.

The ghosts had backed off. For now there was only Rob, there was only this moment, there was only now.

They surfaced—who could say how much later? They were entwined in each other's bodies, sleepily content, loosely covered by a light cotton sheet. Which was just as well as they emerged to the sound of quiet but desperate sniffs.

Danny.

They rolled as one to look at the door, as they'd done so many times with the twins.

Danny was in the doorway, clutching Luka's collar. He was wearing a singlet and knickers. His hair was tousled, his eyes were still dazed with sleep but he was sniffing desperately, trying not to cry.

'Hey,' Rob said, hauling the sheet a little higher. 'Danny! What's up, mate?'

'Mama's crying,' Danny said. 'She's crying and crying and she won't stop.'

'That'll be because your house is burned and your dad's stuck down the mountain,' Rob said prosaically, as if this was the sort of thing that happened every day. 'I guess your dad won't be able to make it here for a while yet, so maybe it's up to us to cheer her up. What do you think might help?'

'I don't know,' Danny whispered. 'Me and Luka tried to hug her.'

'Hugs are good.' Rob sat up and Julie lay still and watched, trying not to be too conscious of Rob's naked chest, plus the fact that he was still naked under the sheet, and his body was still touching hers and every sense…

No. That was hardly fair because she was tuned to Danny.

She'd been able to juggle…everything when they were a family. She glanced at her watch. Eight o'clock. Four years ago she'd have been up by six, trying to fit in an hour of work before the twins woke. Even at weekends, the times they'd lain here together, they'd always been conscious of pressure.

Yeah, well, both of them had busy professional lives. Both of them thought…had thought…getting on was important.

'You know, hugs are great,' Rob was saying and he lay down again and hugged Julie, just to demonstrate. 'But there might be something better today. Did you remember today is Christmas?'

'Yes, but Mama said Santa won't be able to get through the burn,' Danny quavered. 'She says…Santa will have to wait.'

'I don't think Santa ever waits,' Rob said gravely. 'Why don't you go look under the Christmas tree while Julie and I get dressed? Then we'll go hug your mama and bring her to the tree too.'

'There might be presents?' Danny breathed.

'Santa's a clever old feller,' Rob told him. 'I don't think he'd let a little thing like a bush fire stop him, do you?'

'But Mama said…'

'Your mama was acting on incorrect information,' Rob told him. 'She doesn't know Australia like Julie and I do. Bush fires happen over Australian Christmases all the time. Santa's used to it. So go check, but no opening anything until we're all dressed and out there with you. Promise?'

'I promise.'

'Does Luka promise, too?'

And Danny giggled and Julie thought she did have senses for something—for someone—other than Rob.

To make a child smile at Christmas… It wasn't a bad feeling.

Actually, it was a great feeling. It drove the pain away as nothing else could.

And then she thought…it was like coming out of bleak fog into sunlight.

It was a sliver, the faintest streak of brilliance, but it was something that hadn't touched her for so long. She'd been grey for years, or sepia-toned, everything made two-dimensional, flat and dull.

Right now she was lying in Rob's arms and she was hearing Danny giggle. And it wasn't an echo of the twins. She wasn't thinking of the twins.

She was thinking this little boy had been born in a refugee camp. His mother had coped with coming from a war-torn country.

She'd wrapped the most beautiful alpaca shawl for Amina, in the softest rose and cream. She knew Amina would love it; she just knew.

And there was a wombat glove puppet just waiting to be opened.

'Go,' she ordered Danny, sitting up too, but hastily remembering to keep her sheet tucked around her. 'Check out the Christmas tree and see if Rob's right and Santa's been. I hope he's been for all of us. We'll be there in five minutes, and then we need to get your mama up and tell her things will be okay. And they will be okay, Danny. It's Christmas and Rob and I are here to make sure that you and your mama and Luka have a very good time.'

They did have a good time. Amina was teary but, washed and dressed in a frivolous bath robe Rob had once given Julie, ensconced in the most comfortable armchair in the living room, tears gave way to bemusement.

Julie had wrapped the sensible gifts, two or three each, nice things carefully chosen. Rob, however, had taken wrapping to extremes, deciding there was too much wrapping paper and it couldn't be wasted. So he'd hunted the house and wrapped silly things. As well as the scarf and a bracelet from Africa, Amina's stocking also contained a gift-wrapped hammer, nails, a grease gun—*'because you never know what'll need greasing'*, Rob told her—and a bottle of cleaning bleach. They made Amina gasp and then giggle.

'Santa thinks I might be a handyman?'

'Every house needs one,' Rob said gravely. 'In our house I wear the tool belt but Santa's not sexist.'

'My Henry's an engineer.'

'Then you get to share. Sharing a grease gun—that's real domestic harmony.'

Amina chuckled and held her grease gun like it was gold and they moved on.

Julie's stocking contained the nightdress she'd lusted after four years before and a voucher for a day spa, now long expired. *Whoops.*

'The girls at the spa gift-wrapped it for me four years ago,' Rob explained. 'How was I to know it had expired?' Then, 'No matter,' he said expansively. 'Santa will buy you another.'

He was like a bountiful genie, Julie thought, determined to make each of them happy.

He'd made her happy last night. Was it possible…? Did she have the courage…?

'You have another gift,' Rob reminded her and she hauled her thoughts back to now.

Her final gift was a wad of paper, fresh from their printer. Bemused, she flicked through it.

It was *Freezing—the Modern Woman's Survival Guide,*

plus a how-to manual extolling the virtues of ash in compost. He'd clearly got their printer to work while she'd gift-wrapped. He'd practically printed out a book.

She showed Amina and both women dissolved into laughter while Rob beamed benevolently.

'Never say I don't put thought into my gifts,' he told them and Julie held up the spa voucher.

'An out-of-date day spa?'

'They cancel each other out. I still rock.'

They chuckled again and then turned their attention to Danny.

Danny was simply entranced. He loved the pyjamas and his fire engine but most of all he loved the wombat puppet. Rob demonstrated. Danny watched and was smitten.

And so was Julie. She watched the two of them together and she thought: *I know why I fell in love with this man.*

I know why I love this man?

Was she brave enough to go there?

As well as snorkel and flippers—which Rob had received with open enjoyment before promising Danny that they could try them out in the bath later—Julie had given Rob a coat—a cord jacket. She remembered buying it for him all those years ago. She'd tried it on herself, rushing in her lunch hour, last-minute shopping. It had cost far more than she'd budgeted for but she'd imagined it on Rob, imagined holding him when he was wearing it, imagined how it'd look, faded and worn, years hence.

She should have given it to him four years ago. Now he shrugged himself into it and smiled across the room at her and she realised why she hadn't given it to him. Why she'd refused to have contact with him.

She was afraid of that smile.

Was she still? Tomorrow, would she…?

No. Tomorrow was for tomorrow. For now she needed

to watch Danny help Luka open a multi-wrapped gift that finally revealed a packet of biscuits scarily past their use-by date. Oatmeal gingernuts. 'They'll be the closest thing Santa could find to dog biscuits,' Rob told Danny.

'Doesn't Santa have dog biscuits at the North Pole?'

'I reckon he does,' Rob said gravely. 'But I think he'll have also seen all this burned bush and thought of all the animals out here who don't have much to eat. So he might have dropped his supply of dog biscuits out of his sleigh to help.'

'He's clever,' Danny said and Rob nodded.

'And kind.'

He's not the only one, Julie thought, and her heart twisted. Once upon a time this man had been her husband. If she could go back…

Turn back time? As if that was going to happen.

'Is it time to put the turkey on?' Rob asked and Julie glanced at him and thought *he's as tense as I am.* Making love didn't count, she thought, or it did, but all it showed was the same attraction was there that had always been there. And with it came the same propensity for heartbreak.

He was still wearing his jacket. He liked it. You could always tell with Rob. If he loved something, he loved it for ever. And she realised that might just count for her too. Whether she wanted that love or not.

Switch to practical. 'We still need to use the barbecue,' she said. 'We don't have enough electricity to use the oven.'

'That's us then,' Rob said, puffing his chest. 'Me and Danny. Barbecuing's men's work, hey, Dan?'

'Can my wombat help?'

'Sure he can.'

'I'm not sure what we can have with it,' Julie said. 'There doesn't seem to be a lot of salad in the fridge.'

'Let me look at what you have,' Amina said. 'I can cook.'

'Don't you need to rest?'

'I've had enough rest,' Amina declared. 'And I can't sleep. I need to know my husband's safe. I can't rest until we're all together.'

That's us shot then, Julie thought bleakly. For her family, together was never going to happen.

They ate a surprisingly delicious dinner—turkey with the burned-from-the-freezer bits chopped off, gravy made from a packet mix and couscous with nuts and dried fruit and dried herbs.

They had pudding, slices fried in the butter she'd bought with the bread, served with custard made from evaporated milk.

They pulled bon-bons. They wore silly hats. They told jokes.

But even Danny kept glancing out of the window. He was waiting for his father to appear.

So much could have happened. If he'd tried to reach them last night… All sorts of scenarios were flitting through Julie's mind and she didn't like any of them.

Once catastrophe struck, did you spend the rest of your life expecting it to happen again? Of course you did.

'He'll be fine.' Astonishingly, the reassurance came from Amina. Had she sensed how tense Julie was? 'What you said made sense. He'll be at the road block. And, as for the house… We've seen worse than this before. We'll survive.'

'Of course you will.'

'No, you have to believe it,' Amina said. 'Don't just say it. Believe it or you go mad.'

What had this woman gone through? She had no idea. She didn't want to even imagine.

'I'd like to do something for you,' Amina said shyly. 'If

you permit… In the bathroom I noticed a hair colour kit. Crimson. Is it yours?'

'Julie doesn't colour her hair,' Rob said, but Julie was remembering a day long ago, a momentary impulse.

She'd be a redhead for Christmas, she'd thought. Her boys would love it, or she thought they might. But of course she hadn't had time to go to a salon. On impulse she'd bought a do-it-yourself kit, then chickened out at the last minute—of course—and the kit had sat in the second bathroom since.

'I'm a hairdresser,' Amina said, even more shyly. 'In my country, that's what I do. Or did. My husband has to retrain here for engineering but there are no such requirements for hairdressing, and I know this product.' She gazed at Julie's hair with professional interest. 'Colour would look good, but I don't think all over. If you permit, I could give you highlights.'

'I don't think…'

'Jules,' Rob said, and she heard an undercurrent of steel, 'you'd look great with red highlights.'

She'd hardly touched her ash-blonde curls for four years. She tugged them into a knot for work; when they became too unruly to control she'd gone to the cheap walk-in hairdresser near work and she'd thought no more about it.

Even before the boys died… When had she last had time to think about what her hair looked like?

When she'd met Rob she'd had auburn highlights. He'd loved them. He'd played with her curls, running his long, strong fingers through them, massaging her scalp, kissing her as the touch of his fingers through her hair sent her wild…

Even then she hadn't arranged it herself. Her mother had organised it as a gift.

'I bought this voucher for you, pet. I know you don't

have time for the salon but you need to make a little time for yourself.'

Her parents were overseas now, having the holiday of a lifetime. They wouldn't be worried about her. They knew she'd be buried in her work.

They'd never imagine she'd be here. With time…

'I don't think…'

'Do it, Jules,' Rob said and she caught a note of steel in his voice. She looked at him uncertainly, and then at Amina, and she understood.

This wasn't about her. Rob wasn't pushing her because he wanted a wife…an ex-wife…with crimson highlights. He was pushing her because Amina needed to do something to keep her mind off her burned house and her missing husband. And she also needed to give something back.

She thought suddenly of the sympathy and kindness she'd received during the months after the boys' deaths and she remembered thinking, more than once: *I want to be the one giving sympathy. I want to give rather than take.*

Amina was a refugee. She would have been needing help for years. Now, this one thing…

'I'd love highlights,' she confessed and Amina smiled, really smiled, for the first time since she'd met her. It was a lovely smile, and it made Danny smile too.

She glanced at Rob and his stern face had relaxed.

Better to give than receive? Sometimes not. Her eyes caught Rob's and she knew he was thinking exactly the same thing.

He'd have been on the receiving end of sympathy too. And then she thought of all the things he'd tried to make her feel better—every way he could during those awful weeks in hospital, trying and trying, but every time she'd pushed him away.

'Don't get soppy on us,' Rob said, and she blinked and

he chuckled and put his arm around her and gave her a fast, hard hug. 'Right, Amina, we need a hair salon. Danny, I need your help. A chair in the bathroom, right? One that doesn't matter if it gets the odd red splash on it.'

He set them up, and then he disappeared. She caught a glimpse of him through the window, heading down to the creek, shovel over his shoulder.

She guessed what he'd be doing. He'd left water for wildlife, but there'd be animals too badly burned…

'He's a good man,' Amina said and she turned and Amina was watching her. 'You have a good husband.'

'We're not…together.'

'Because of your babies?'

'I…yes.'

'It happens,' Amina said softly. 'Dreadful things…they tear you apart or they pull you together. The choice is yours.'

'There's no choice,' she said, more harshly than she intended, but Danny was waiting in the bathroom eyeing the colouring kit with anticipation, and she could turn away and bite her lip and hope Amina didn't sense the surge of anger and resentment that her words engendered.

Get over it... It was never said, not in so many words, but, four years on, she knew she was pretty much regarded as cool and aloof. The adjectives were no longer seen as a symptom of loss—they simply described who she was.

And who she intended to be for the rest of her life?

Thinking ahead was too hard. But Rob was gone, off to do what he could for injured wildlife, and Danny was waiting in the bathroom and Amina was watching her with a gaze that said she saw almost too much.

Do something.

Back in the office, she'd be neck-deep in contracts.

It was Christmas Day.

Okay, back home, she'd have left her brother's place

after managing to stay polite all through Christmas dinner and now she'd be back in her apartment. Neck-deep in contracts.

But now…neck-deep in hair dye?

'Let's get this over with,' she muttered and Amina took a step back.

'You don't have to. If you don't want…'

She caught herself. If Rob came back and found her wallowing in self-pity, with her hair the same colour and Amina left alone…

See, there was the problem. With Rob around she couldn't wallow.

Maybe that was why she'd left him.

Maybe that was selfish. Maybe *grief* was selfish.

It was all too hard. She caught herself and forced a smile and then tried even harder. This time the smile was almost natural.

'Rob is a good man,' she conceded. 'But he needs a nicer woman than me. A happier one.'

'You can be happier if you try,' Amina told her.

'You can be happy if you have red hair,' Danny volunteered and she grinned at his little-boy answer to the problems of the world.

'Then give me red hair,' she said. 'Red hair is your mum's gift to me for Christmas, and if there's one thing Christmas needs it's gifts. Are you and Luka going to watch or are you going to play with your Christmas presents?'

'Me and Luka are going to watch,' Danny said, and he wiggled his glove puppet. 'And Wombat. Me and Luka and Wombat are going to watch you get happy.'

Almost as soon as they started, Julie realised that agreeing to this had been a mistake.

Putting a colour through her hair would have been a relatively easy task—simply applying the colour, leaving it to take and then washing it out again.

Amina, though, had different ideas. 'Not flat colour,' she said, just as flatly. 'You want highlights, gold and crimson. You'll look beautiful.'

Yeah, well, she might, but each highlight meant the application of colour to just a few strands of hair, then those strands wrapped in foil before Amina moved to the next strands.

It wasn't a job Amina could do sitting down. She also didn't intend to do a half-hearted job.

'If I put too much hair in each foil, then you'll have flat clumps of colour,' she told Julie as she protested. 'It won't look half as good. And I want some of them strong and some diluted.'

'But you shouldn't be on your feet.' She hadn't thought this through. Amina was eight months pregnant, she'd had one hell of a time and now she was struggling.

She looked exhausted. But…

'I need to do this,' Amina told her. 'Please…I want to. I need to do something.'

She did. Julie knew the worry about her husband was still hanging over her, plus the overwhelming grief of the devastation next door. But still…

'I don't want you to risk this baby,' she told her. 'Amina, this is madness.'

'It's not madness,' Amina said stubbornly. 'It's what I want to do. Sit still.'

So she sat, but she worried, and when Rob appeared as the last foil was done she felt a huge wash of relief. Not that there was anything Rob could do to help the situation but at least…at least he was here.

She'd missed him…

'Wow,' Rob said, stopping at the entrance to the bathroom and raising his brows in his grimy face. 'You look like a sputnik.'

'What's a sputnik?' Danny demanded.

'A spiky thing that floats round in space,' Rob told him. 'You think we should put Julie in a rocket launcher and send her to the moon?'

Danny giggled and Amina smiled and once again there was that lovely release of tension that only Rob seemed capable of producing. He was the best man to have in a crisis.

'Amina's exhausted, though,' Julie told him. 'She needs to sleep.'

'You need to keep those foils in for forty minutes,' Amina retorted. 'Then you need a full scalp massage to get the colour even and then a wash and condition. Then I'll rest.'

'Ah, but I'm back now,' Rob said, and Julie knew he could see the exhaustion on Amina's face. He'd have taken in her worry at a glance. 'And if anyone's going to massage my wife it's me. Forty minutes?' He glanced at his watch. 'Amina, I came to ask if there was anything precious, any jewellery, anything that might have survived the fire that you'd like us to search for. The radio's saying it may rain tonight, in which case the ash will turn to concrete. Sputnik and I could have a look now.'

Julie choked. *Sputnik?* She glanced in the mirror. She was wearing one of Rob's shirts, faded jeans, and her head was covered in silver spikes. Okay, yep. Sputnik.

'I could be a Christmas decoration instead,' she volunteered. 'One of those shiny spiky balls you put on top of the tree.'

'You'll be more help sifting through ash. I assume you can put a towel around the spikes—the wildlife has had enough scares for the time being without adding aliens to the mix. Amina, is that okay with you?'

'I will look,' Amina said but Rob caught her hands. He had great hands, Julie thought inconsequentially. He was holding Amina and Julie knew he was imparting strength, reassurance, determination. All those things...

He was a good man. Her husband?

'The ground's treacherous,' he told her. 'Your house is a pile of ash and rubble and parts of it are still very hot. Julie and I have the heavy boots we used to garden in, we have strong protective clothing and we're not carrying a baby. You need to take care of your little one, and of Danny. We won't stay over there for long—it's too hot—but we can do a superficial search. If you tell us where to look...'

'Our bedroom,' Amina told him, meeting his stern gaze, giving in to sense. 'The front bay window...you should see the outline. Our bed started two feet back from the window and was centred on it. The bed was six foot long. On either side of the bed was a bedside table. We each had a box...'

'Wood?' Rob asked without much hope.

'Tin.'

'Well, that's possible. Though don't get your hopes up too much; that fire was searing and tin melts. We'll have a look—but only if you try and get some rest. Danny, will you stand guard while your mum sleeps?'

'I want to help with the burn.'

'There'll be lots of time to help with the burn,' Rob said grimly. 'But, for now, you need to be in charge of your mother. Go lie down beside her, play with your toys while she sleeps, but if she tries to get up, then growl at her. Can you do that?'

Danny considered. 'Because of the baby?'

'Yes.'

'Papa says I have to look after her because of the baby.'

'Then you'll do what your papa asked?'

'Yes,' Danny said and then his voice faltered. 'I wish he'd come.'

'He will come,' Rob said in a voice that brooked no argument. 'He will come. I promise.'

CHAPTER SEVEN

'IT SHOULD HAVE been ours.' Julie stood in the midst of the devastation that was all that was left of Amina's house, she glanced across at their intact home and she felt ill.

'Fire doesn't make sense,' Rob told her, staring grimly round the ruin.

'No. And I understand that it was your design that saved it. But Amina's house was…a home.'

'Our place will be a home again. If we rent it out to them, Amina will make it one. I suspect she's been making homes in all sorts of places for a long time.'

'I know. Home's where the heart is,' Julie said bleakly. 'They all say it. If you only knew how much I hate that saying.'

'We're not here for self-pity, Jules,' Rob said, hauling her up with a start. He sounded angry, and maybe justifiably. This was no time to wallow. 'If it rains, then there'll be little chance of finding anything. Let's get to it.' He handed her a pair of leather gloves and a shovel. 'Watch your feet for anything hot. Sift in front of you before you put your feet down. Don't go near anywhere that looks unstable.'

There wasn't much that looked unstable. The house had collapsed in on itself. The roof was corrugated iron, but Rob must have been here before, because it had been hauled off site.

The bedroom. They could see the outline of the bay window.

'You focus on either side of where the bed would have been,' Rob told her. 'I'm doing a general search.'

What a way to spend Christmas afternoon. Overdressed, hot, struggling to breathe with the wafts of smoke still in the air, her hair in spikes, covered by a towel, squatting, sifting through layer upon layer of warm ash...

She found the first tin almost immediately. It had melted—of course it had—but it had held enough of its shape to recognise it for what it was.

Who knew what was inside? There was no time now to try and open it. She set it aside and moved to the other side of where the bed would have been and kept on searching.

And was stopped in her tracks by a whoop.

She looked up and Rob was standing at the rear of the house, where the laundry would have been. He'd been shovelling.

'Jules, come and see.'

She rose stiffly and made her way gingerly across the ruin.

It was a safe. Unmistakably it was a safe and it must be fireproof, judging by thc fact that it looked intact, even its paintwork almost unscathed.

'It must have been set in the floor,' Rob said. 'Look, it's still in some sort of frame. But I can get it out.'

'Do you think Amina knew it was there?'

'Who knows? But we'll take it next door. How goes the tin hunt?'

'One down.'

'Then let's find the other.' He grabbed her and gave her a hard unexpected hug. 'See, good things can happen. I just hope there's something inside that safe other than insurance papers.'

'Insurance papers would be good.'

'You and I both know that's not important. And we have five minutes to go before sputnik takes off. Tin, Jules, fetch.'

And, amazingly, they did fetch—two minutes later their search produced a tin box even more melted than the first. Three prizes. Rob brought the barrow from their yard, then they heaved the safe into it and carted it back. 'I feel like a pup with two tails,' Rob said.

Julie grinned and thought: *fun*.

That had been fun. She'd just had fun with Rob. How long since…?

She caught herself, a shaft of guilt hitting her blindside as it always did when she started forgetting. She had no right…

They parked their barrow on the veranda and went to check on Amina. She was fast asleep, as was Danny, curled up beside her. Luka was by their bedside, calmly watchful. The big dog looked up at them as if to say: *What's important enough to wake them up?*

Nothing was. But the foils had to come off.

'I can take them off myself,' Julie said, but dubiously, because in truth they were now overdue to come off and, by the time she took off every last one, the fine foils would be well overdone. What happened if you cooked your hair for too long? Did it fall out? She had no idea, and she had no intention of finding out.

'I'll take them out,' Rob said and looked ruefully down at himself. 'Your beautician, though, ma'am, is filthy.'

'In case you hadn't noticed, your client is filthy too. Can you imagine me popping into a high-class Sydney salon like this?'

'You'd set a new trend,' Rob told her, touching her foils with a grin. 'Smoked Sputnik. It'd take off like a bush fire.'

'Of course it would,' she lied. She'd reached the bathroom now and looked at the mirror. 'Ugh.'

'Let's get these things off then,' he said. 'Sit.'

So she sat on the little white bathroom stool, which promptly turned grey with soot. Rob stood behind her and she watched in the mirror as he slid each foil from her hair.

He worked swiftly, dextrously, intently. He was always like this on a job, she remembered. When he was focused on something he blocked out the world.

When he made love to her, the world might well not exist.

He was standing so close. He smelled of fire, of smoke, of burned eucalyptus. His fingers were in her hair, doing mundane things, removing foils, but it didn't feel mundane. It felt…it felt…

Too soon, the last of the foils was gone, heaped into the trash. Her hair was still spiky, looking very red. Actually, she wouldn't mind if it was green, she thought, as long as she could find an excuse to keep Rob here with her. To stretch out this moment.

'I can…' Her voice wobbled and she fought to steady it. 'I can go from here. I'll shower it off.'

'You need a full scalp massage to even the colour,' Rob told her, but his voice wasn't steady either. It was, however, stern. 'I'm Amina's underling. She's given us orders. The least we can do is obey.'

'I can do it by myself.'

'But you don't have to,' he said, and he bent and touched her forehead with his mouth. It was a feather touch, hardly a kiss, just a fleeting sensation, but it sent shivers through her whole body. 'For now, just give in and forget about facing things alone.'

So she gave in. Of course she did. She sat perfectly still while Rob massaged her scalp with his gorgeous, sensuous fingers and her every nerve ending reacted to him.

He was filthy, covered with smoke and ash. If you met this man on a dark night you'd scream and run, she thought, catching his reflection in the mirror in the split second she allowed herself to glance at him. For she couldn't watch. Feeling him was bad enough…or good enough…

Good was maybe too small a word. Her entire body was reacting to his touch. Any more and she'd turn and take him. She wanted…

'Conditioner,' Rob said, only the faintest tremor cutting through the prosaic word. 'Amina said conditioner.'

'It's in the shower.'

'Then I suggest,' he said, bending down so his lips were right against her ear, 'that we adjourn to the shower.'

'Rob…'

'Mmm?'

'N…nothing.'

'No objections?'

'We…we might lock the door first.'

'What an excellent idea,' he said approvingly. 'I have a practical wife. I always knew I had a practical wife. I'd just forgotten…'

And seemingly in one swift movement the door was locked and she was swept into his arms. He pushed the shower screen back with his elbow and deposited her inside.

It was a large shower. A gorgeous shower. They'd built it…well, they'd built it when they were in love.

It was wide enough for Rob to step inside with her and tug the glass screen closed after them.

'Clothes,' he said. 'Stat?'

'Stat?'

'That's what they say in hospitals in emergencies. Oxygen here, nurse, stat.'

'So we need clothes?'

'We don't need clothes. If this was a hospital and I was a doctor, that's what I'd be saying. Nurse, my wife needs her clothes removed. Stat.'

'Rob...'

'Yes?'

She looked at him and she thought she needed to say she wasn't his wife. She should say she didn't have the courage to take this further. She was too selfish, too armoured, too closed.

But he was inches away from her. He smelled of bush fire. His face was grimy and blackened. As was she.

The only part of her that wasn't grimy or blackened was her hair. Crimson droplets were dripping onto the white shower base, mixing with the ash.

How much colour had Amina put in? How had she trusted a woman she didn't know to colour her hair?

Rob was standing before her, holding her.

She trusted this man with all her heart, and that was the problem. She felt herself falling...

Where was her armour?

She'd find it tomorrow, she told herself. This was an extraordinary situation. This was a time out, pretend, a disaster-induced remarriage that would dissolve as soon as the rest of the world peered in. But for this moment she was stranded in this time, in this place...

In this shower.

And Rob was tugging her shirt up over her head and she was lifting her arms to help him. And then, as the shirt was tossed over the screen, as he turned his attention to her bra, she started to undo the buttons of his shirt.

Her hands were shaking.

He took her hands in his and held. Tight. Hard. Cupping her hands, completely enfolding them.

'There's no need for shaking, Jules. I'd never hurt you.'

'I might…hurt you.'

'I'm a big boy now,' he told her. 'I can take it.'

'Rob, I need to say…this is for now. I don't think…I still can't think…'

'Of course you can't.' He held her still. 'But for now, for this moment, let's take things as they come. Let our bodies remember why we fell in love. Let's start at the beginning and let things happen.'

And then he kissed her, and that kiss made her forget every other thing. Everything but Rob.

Water was streaming over them. Somehow they managed to stop, pull back, give themselves time to haul their clothes off and toss them out, a sodden, stained puddle to be dealt with later.

Everything could be dealt with later, Julie thought hazily as she turned back to her beautiful naked Rob. For now there was only Rob. There was only this moment.

Water was running in rivulets down his beautiful face, onto his chest, lower. He was wet and glistening and wonderful. His hands were on the small of her back, drawing her into him, and the feel of wet hands on wet skin was indescribably erotic.

For now there was no pain. There was no yesterday. There was only this man, this body. There was only this desire and the only moment that mattered was now.

'You think we should have a nap now, too?' Rob asked.

Somehow they were out of the shower, sated, satisfied, dazed.

Maybe she should make that almost satisfied, Julie thought. Rob was drying her. She was facing the mirror, watching him behind her. The feel of the towel was indescribably delicious.

He pressed her down onto the bathroom stool and started drying her hair. Gently. Wonderfully.

If she could die now, she'd float to heaven. She was floating already.

'If we go anywhere near the bed I can't be held responsible for what happens,' she managed and Rob chuckled. Oh, she remembered that chuckle. She'd forgotten how much she'd missed it.

How much else had she forgotten?

Had she wanted to forget…all of it?

'Maybe you're right. But maybe it's worth not being responsible,' Rob growled. 'But I want to see your hair dry first.'

Her hair. She'd had colour foils put in. Every woman in her right senses regarded the removing of colour foils with trepidation, hoping the colour would work. For some reason Julie had forgotten all about it.

'It looks good wet,' Rob said, stooping and kissing her behind her ear. 'Let's see it dry.'

She tried to look at it in the mirror. Yeah, well, that was a mistake. Rob was right behind her and he was naked. How was a woman to look at her hair when her hairdresser was…Rob?

'I…I can do it,' she tried but he was already hauling the hairdryer from the cabinet. This place was a time warp. Everything had simply been left. It had been stupid, but coming back here four years ago had been impossible. She'd simply abandoned everything…which meant she had a hairdryer.

And, stupid or not, that had its advantages, she decided, as Rob switched on the dryer and directed warm air at her hair. As did the solar panels he'd installed on the roof and the massive bank of power batteries under the house.

They had electricity, and every cent they'd paid for such a massive backup was worth it just for this moment. For the power of one hairdryer.

She couldn't move. Her body seemed more alive than she could remember. Every nerve was tingling, every sense was on fire but she couldn't move. She was paralysed by the touch of his hands, by the warmth of the dryer, by the way he lifted each curl and twisted and played with it as he dried it.

By the way he watched her in the mirror as he dried.

By the way he just…was.

He was lighting her body.

He was also lighting her hair. Good grief, her hair…

It was almost dry now, and the colours were impossible to ignore. They were part of the same magical fantasy that was this moment, but these colours weren't going to go away with the opening of the bathroom door.

What had happened?

She'd bought auburn highlights, but what Amina had done… She must have mixed them in uneven strengths, done something, woven magic…because what had happened *was* magic.

Her mousey-blonde hair was no longer remotely mouse. It was a shiny mass of gold and chestnut and auburn. It was like the glowing embers of a fire, flickering flames on a muted background.

Rob was lifting her curls, watching the light play on them as he made sure every strand was dry. Her hair felt as if it was their centre. Nothing else mattered.

If only nothing else mattered. If only they could move on from this moment, forgetting everything.

But she didn't want to forget. The thought slammed home and she saw Rob's eyes in the mirror and knew the thought had slammed into him almost simultaneously. They always had known what each other was thinking.

One mind. One body.

'Jules, we could try again,' he said softly, almost as if

talking to himself. 'We've done four years of hell. Does it have to continue?'

'I don't see how it can't.'

'We don't have to forget. Going forward together isn't a betrayal. Does it hurt, every time you look at me, because of what we had?'

'No. Yes!'

'I've seen a shrink. There I was, lying on a couch, telling all.' He smiled down at her and lifted a curl, then letting it drop. 'Actually, it was a chair. But the idea's the same. I'm shrunk.'

'And what did he…she…tell you?'

'She didn't tell me anything. She led me round and round in circles until I figured it out. But finally I did. Four people weren't killed that day, though they can be if we let them.'

'You can live…without them?'

'There's no choice, Jules,' he said, his voice suddenly rough. 'Look at us. It's Christmas, our fourth Christmas without them, yet it's all about two little boys who are no longer here. Out there is a little boy who's alive and who needs us to make him happy. We can help Amina be happy, at least for the day. We can do all sorts of things, make all sorts of people happy if we forget we're the walking dead.'

'I'm not…'

'No. You're not the walking dead. Look at your hair. This is fun hair, fantastic hair, the hair of a woman who wants to move forward. And look at your body. It's a woman's body, Jules, your body, and it gives you pleasure. It still can give you pleasure. Maybe it could even give you another child.'

'No!'

'Are you so closed?'

'Are you? You said you've been seeing other women?'

'I said I've been trying,' he said, and once again his fingers started drifting in her curls. 'The problem is they're not you.'

'You can't still love me.'

'I've never stopped.'

'But there's nothing left to love.' She was sounding desperate, negative, harsh. She'd built up so much armour and he'd penetrated it. It was cracking and she was fighting desperately to retain it. If it shattered…how could she risk such hurt again? She felt as if she was on the edge of an abyss, about to fall.

'Jump,' Rob said softly. 'I'll catch you.'

But she had to keep trying. She had to make him see. 'Rob, there are so many women out there. Undamaged. Women who could give you a family again.'

'Are you offering me up for public auction? I'm not available,' he said, more harshly still. 'Julie, remember the first time we came here? Deciding to camp? Me nobly giving you our only single air bed, then the rain at two in the morning and you refusing to move because you were warm and dry and floating?'

'I did move in the end.'

'Only because I tipped you off into six inches of water.'

'That wasn't exactly chivalrous.'

'Exactly. The thing is, Jules, that with you I've never felt the need to be chivalrous. What happens between us just…happens.'

'You did rescue the kitten…sort of.'

'That's what comes of playing the hero. You end up laughing.'

'I didn't laugh at you.'

'No,' he said and he stooped and took her hands in his. 'You laugh with me. Every time I laugh, I know you're laughing too. And every time I'm gutted it's the same.

That's what's tearing me apart the most. I've known, these last four years, that you haven't been laughing. Nor have you been gutted because I would have felt it. You've just been frozen. But I want you, Jules. I want my lovely, laughing Julie back again. We've lost so much. Do we have to lose everything?'

He was so close. His hands enfolded hers. It would be so easy to fall…

But it was easier to make love to him than what he was asking her now. She remembered that closeness. That feeling that she was part of him. That even when he drove her crazy she understood why, and she sort of got that she might be driving him crazy too.

They'd fought. Of course they'd fought. Understanding someone didn't mean you had to share a point of view and often they hadn't.

She'd loved fighting with him and often she hadn't actually minded losing. A triumphant Rob made her laugh.

But to start again…

Could she?

She so wanted to, but…but…

She was like the meat she had taken out from the freezer, she thought tangentially. On the surface she was defrosting but at her core there was still a deep knot of frozen.

If she could get out of here, get away from Rob, then that core would stay protected. Her outer layers could freeze again as well.

Was that what she wanted?

'Jules, try,' Rob said, drawing her into his arms and holding her. 'You can't waste all that hair on legal contracts. Waste it on me.'

'What do you think I'm doing now?'

'But long-term? After the fire.'

'I don't know.' The panic was suddenly back, all around

her—the panic that had overwhelmed her the first time she'd walked into the twins' empty bedroom, the panic that threatened to bring her down if she got close to anyone. The abyss was so close…

'I won't push you,' Rob said.

'So making love isn't pushing?'

'That wasn't me,' he said, almost sternly. 'It was both of us. You know you want me as much as I want you.'

'I want your body.'

'You want all of me. You want the part that wants to be part of you again. The part that wants to love you and demands you love me back.'

'Rob…I can't!' How could she stop this overwhelming feeling of terror? She wanted this man so much, but…but…

She had to make one last Herculean effort. One last try to stay…frozen.

'It's…time to get dressed,' she managed, and he nodded and lifted his fingers through her curls one last time.

'I guess,' he said ruefully, achingly reluctant. 'But let's try. Let the world in, my Julie. Let Amina see what her magic produced.'

'Only it's not magic,' she whispered. 'We can't cast a happy-ever-after spell.'

'We could try.'

'We could destroy each other.'

'More than we already have?' He sighed. 'But it's okay. Whatever you decide has to be okay. I *will not* push.' He kissed her once again, on the nape of her neck, and it was all she could do not to turn and take him into her arms and hold him and hold him and hold him. She didn't. The panic was too raw. The abyss too close.

But he was twisting a towel around his hips. It nearly killed her to see his nakedness disappear. If the world wasn't waiting…

Someone was banging on the front door. Luka started barking.

The world was indeed waiting. It was time to dress. It was time to move on.

Rob reached the front door first. He'd hauled jeans on and left it at that. Amina and Danny must be still asleep, or waking slowly, because only Luka was there, barking hysterically.

The knocking started again as he reached the hall, but for some reason his steps slowed.

He didn't want the world to enter?

Maybe there was a truck outside, emergency personnel offering to take them down the mountain, evacuate them to safety. The authorities would want everyone off the mountain. This place was self-sufficient but most homes were dependent on essential services. That first truck had been the precursor to many. The army could even have been called in, with instructions to enforce evacuation.

He didn't want to go.

Well, that was dumb. For a start, Amina desperately needed evacuation. It wasn't safe for an eight months pregnant woman to be here, with no guaranteed way out if she went into labour. With the ferocity of the burn and the amount of bushland right up to the edges of the roads, normal traffic would be impossible for weeks. So many burned trees, all threatening to fall… They needed to get out as soon as it was safe to go.

And yet…and yet…

And yet he didn't want to leave.

Maybe he could send Amina and Danny away and keep Julie here.

As his prisoner? That was another dumb thought. He couldn't keep her against her will, nor would he want to, but, even so, the thought was there. The last twenty-four hours had revealed his wife again. He knew she was still hurting. He knew that breaking down her armour required a miracle, and he also knew that once they were off the mountain, then that miracle couldn't happen. She'd retreat again into her world of finance and pain.

'She has to deal with it in her own time.' The words of his shrink had been firm. *'Rob, you've been wounded just as much as she has, but you're working through it. For now it's as much as you can do to heal yourself. You need to let Julie go.'*

But what if they could heal together? These last hours had shown him Julie was still there—the Julie he'd loved, the Julie he'd married.

But he couldn't lock her up. That wasn't the way of healing and he knew it.

What was? Holding her close? She'd let him do that. They'd made love, they'd remembered how their bodies had reacted to each other, yet it had achieved…nothing.

Could he keep trying? Dare he? These last years he'd achieved a measure of peace and acceptance. Would taking Julie to him open the floodgates again? Would watching her pain drive him back to the abyss? Only he knew how hard it had been to pull himself back to a point where he felt more or less at peace.

He knew what his shrink would say. *Move away and stay away. Leave the past in the past.*

Only the past was in their shared bedroom, with hair that glistened under his hands, with eyes that smiled at him with…hope? If he could find the strength… If, somehow, he could drag her to the other side of the nightmare…

Enough of the introspection. The knocking continued and he'd reached the door. He tugged it open, Luka launched himself straight out—and into the arms of a guy standing on the doorstep.

The man was shorter than Rob, and leaner. He looked in his forties, dark-skinned and filthy. He looked…haggard. His eyes were bloodshot and he hadn't shaved for a couple of days. He was leaning against the door jamb, breathing heavily, but as Luka launched himself forward he grabbed him and held him as if he was drowning.

He met Rob's eyes over Luka's great head, and his look was anguished.

'Amina?' It was scarcely a croak.

'Safe,' Rob said quickly. 'And Danny. They're both here. They're safe. You're Henry?' He had to be. No one but Amina's husband could say her name with the same mix of love and terror.

'Yes. I am. I went…next door. Oh, God, it's…'

'We got them here before the house went up,' Rob said, speaking quickly, cutting through Henry's obvious terror. 'They're tired but well. They're asleep now but they've been as worried about you as you seem to be about them. They're safe.'

The man's knees sagged. Rob grabbed the dog and hauled him back, then took Henry's elbows under his hands, holding him up. He looked beyond exhaustion.

'They're safe,' he said again. 'I promise. Happy Christmas, Henry. I know your house is burned and I'm sorry, but things can be replaced. People can't. Everything else can wait. For now, come in and see your wife.'

And Henry burst into tears.

After that things seemed to happen in a blur.

There was a whimper behind him. Rob turned and Amina was there, staring in incredulity. And then somehow she was in Rob's place, holding her husband, holding and holding. Weeping.

And then Danny, flying down the hall. 'Papa...' He was between them, a wriggling, excited bundle of joy. 'My Papa's come,' he yelled to anyone who'd listen and then he was between them, sandwiched, muffled but still yelling. 'Papa, our house burned and burned and Luka was lost and I was scared but Rob found me and then we hid in a little cave and we've been here for lots and lots and Santa came and we had turkey but we didn't have chocolates. Mama had them for us but they've been burned as well, but Mama says we can get some more. Papa, come and see my presents.'

Rob backed away and then Julie was beside him, in her gorgeous crimson robe with her gorgeous crimson hair, and she was sniffing. He took her hand and held and it felt...right.

They finally found themselves in the kitchen, watching Henry eat leftover Christmas lunch like he hadn't eaten for a week—but he still wasn't concentrating on the food. He kept looking from Amina to Danny and back again, like he couldn't get enough of them. Like he was seeing ghosts...

His plane last night, a later one than Rob's, had been diverted—landing in Melbourne instead of Sydney because of the smoke. He'd spent the night trying to get any information he could, going crazy because he couldn't contact anyone.

This morning he'd flown into Sydney at dawn, hired a car, hit the road blocks, left the car, dodged the road blocks and walked.

It didn't take any more than seeing his smoke-stained face and his bloodshot eyes to tell them how fraught that walk had been. And how terror had stayed with him every inch of the way.

But he was home. He had his family back again. Julie watched them with hungry eyes, and Rob watched Julie and thought that going back was a dream. A fantasy. He couldn't live with that empty hunger for ever.

'We've plenty of water. Go and take a bath,' he told Henry, and Danny brightened.

'Luka and I will help,' he announced and they disappeared towards the bathroom, with the sounds of splashing and laughter ensuing. Happy ever after…

'I'll go get dressed,' Julie said, sounding subdued, and Amina touched her hair.

'Beautiful.'

'Yes. Thank you.'

'Don't waste it,' Amina said sternly with a meaningful glance at Rob, and Julie flinched a little but managed a smile.

'I promise I won't wear a hat for months.'

Which wasn't what Amina had meant and they all knew it but it was enough for Julie to escape.

Which left Amina with Rob.

'You love her still,' she said, almost as if she was talking of something mundane, chatting about the weather, and Rob had to rerun the words in his mind for a bit before he could find an answer.

'Yes,' he said at last. 'But our grief threatened to destroy us. It's still destroying us.'

'You want…to try again?'

'I don't think we can.'

'It takes courage,' she whispered. 'So much courage. But you…you have courage to spare. You saved my son.'

'It takes more than courage to wake up to grief every morning of your life.'

'It's better than walking away,' she said softly. 'Walking away is the thing you do when all else fails. Walking away is the end.'

'Amina…'

'I shall cook dinner,' she announced, moving on. 'Food is good. Food is excellent. When all else fails, eat. I need to inspect this frozen-in-time kitchen of yours.'

'You need to rest.'

'I have rested,' she said. 'I have my husband back. My family is together and that's all that matters. We need to move on.'

Christmas dinner was a sort of Middle Eastern goulash made with leftover turkey, couscous, dried herbs, packet stock and raisins. It should have tasted weird—half the ingredients were well over their use-by dates—but it tasted delicious. The house had a formal dining room but no one was interested in using it. They squashed round the kitchen table meant for four, with Luka taking up most of the room underneath, and it felt right.

Home, Rob thought as he glanced at his dinner companions. That was what this felt like. Outside, the world was a bleak mess but here was food, security, togetherness.

Henry couldn't stop looking at Amina and Danny. From one to the other. It was like he was seeing a dream.

That was what looking at Julie felt like too, Rob thought. A dream. Something that could never be.

But still… Henry had made a quick, bleak foray across to the ruins of his house and came back grimly determined.

'We can build again,' he'd said. 'We've coped with worse than this.'

Building again… Could he and Julie? A building needed foundations, though, Rob thought, and their foundations hardly existed any more. At least, that was what Julie thought. She thought their foundations were a bed of pain, of nightmares. Could he ever break through to foundations that had been laid long before the twins were born?

Did he have the strength to try?

'You have our safe,' Henry said as the meal came to an end and anxiety was in his voice again. 'You said you managed to haul it out.'

'I did,' Rob told him. 'I'm not sure whether the contents have withstood the fire.'

'It's built to withstand an inferno. And the contents… it's not chocolate.'

'I'd like some chocolate,' Danny said wistfully, but there was ice cream. Honestly, wrapped containers might cope with a nuclear blast, Rob thought as they sliced through the layers of plastic to ice cream that looked almost perfect.

But Amina didn't want any. She was looking exhausted again. Julie was watching her with concern, and Rob picked up on it.

'You want to go back to bed?' he asked her. 'All of you. Henry's had a nightmare twenty-four hours and you've made us a feast of a Christmas dinner. You've earned some sleep.'

'I'm fine,' Amina said, wincing a little. 'I just have a backache. I need a cushion, that's all.'

In moments she had about four and they moved into the living room, settled in the comfortable lounge suite… wondering where to go from here.

He'd quite like to carry Julie back to the bedroom, Rob thought. It was Christmas night. He could think of gifts he'd like to give and receive…

But Danny had slept this afternoon, and he was wide awake now. He was zooming back and forth across the floor with his new fire truck. In Danny's eyes, Christmas was still happening. There was no way he was going calmly to bed, and that meant the adults had to stay up.

Henry was exhausted. He'd slumped into his chair, his face still grey with exhaustion and stress.

Amina also looked stressed. The effort of making dinner had been too much for her. She had no energy left.

Rob sank to the floor and started playing with Danny, forming a makeshift road for his fire engine, pretending the TV remote was a police car, conducting races, making the little boy laugh. Doing what he'd done before…

It nearly killed her. He was doing what she'd seen him do so many times, what she'd loved seeing him do.

Now he was playing with a child who wasn't his.

He was *getting over it*?

Get over it. How many times had those words been said to her? 'It'll take time but you will get over it. You will be able to start again.'

She knew she never would, but Rob just might. It had been a mistake, coming back here, she thought. Connecting with Rob again. Reminding themselves of what they'd once had.

It had hurt him, she thought. It had made him hope…

She should cut that hope off right now. There was no chance she could move on. The thought of having another child, of watching Rob romp with another baby… It hurt.

Happy Christmas, she thought bitterly. This was worse than the nothing Christmases she'd had for the last few years. Watching Rob play with a child who wasn't his.

She glanced up and saw Amina was watching her and, to her surprise, she saw her pain reflected in the other woman's eyes.

'Are you okay?' she asked. 'Amina…?'

'It's only the backache,' she said, but somehow Julie knew it wasn't. 'Henry, the safe… Could you check? I need to know.'

'I'll do it in the morning,' Henry said uneasily but Amina shook her head.

'I need to see now. The television...does it work?'

'We have enough power,' Rob told her. 'But there won't be reception.'

'We don't need reception. I just need to see...'

'Amina, it'll hurt,' Henry said.

'Yes, but I still need to see,' she said stubbornly. 'Henry, do this for me, please. I need to see that they're still there.'

Which explained why, ten minutes later, Rob and Henry were out on the veranda, staring at a fire-stained safe. The paint had peeled and charred, but essentially it looked okay.

'Do you want to open it in privacy?' Rob asked, but Henry shook his head.

'We have nothing of value. This holds our passports, our insurance—our house contents are insured, how fortunate is that?'

'Wise.'

'The last house we lost was insured too,' Henry said. 'But not for acts of war.'

'Henry...'

'No matter. This is better. But Amina wants her memories. Do you permit?'

He wasn't sure what was going on but, two minutes later, Henry had worked the still operational combination lock and was hauling out the contents.

Papers, documents...and a couple of USB sticks.

'I worried,' Henry said. 'They're plastic but they seem okay. It would break Amina's heart to lose these. Can we check them on your television?'

'Of course. Julie and I can go to bed if you want privacy.'

'If it's okay with you,' Henry said diffidently, 'it's better to share. I mean…Amina needs to…well, her history seems more real to her if she can share. Right now she's hurting. It would help…if you could watch. I know it'll be dull for you, other people's memories, but it might help. The way Amina's looking… Losing our house. Worrying about me. The baby… It's taken its toll.'

'Of course we can watch.' It was Julie in the doorway behind them. 'Anything that can help has to be okay by us.'

The television worked. The USB worked. Ten minutes later they were in Sri Lanka.

In Amina and Henry's past lives.

The files contained photographs—many, many photographs. Most were amateur snaps, taken at family celebrations, taken at home, a big, assorted group of people whose smiles and laughter reached out across distance and time.

And, as Julie watched her, the stress around Amina's eyes faded. She was introducing people as if they were here.

'This is my mother, Aisha, and my older sister Hannah. These two are my brothers. Haija is an architect like you, Rob. He designs offices, wonderful buildings. The last office he designed had a waterfall, three storeys high. It wasn't built, but, oh, if it had been… And here are my nieces and nephews. And Olivia…' She was weeping a little but smiling through tears as the photograph of a teenage girl appeared on the screen, laughing, mocking the camera, mischief apparent even from such a time and distance. 'My little sister Olivia. Oh, she is trouble. She'll be trouble still. Danny, you remember how I told you Olivia loves trains?' she demanded of her son. 'Olivia had a train set, a whole city. She started when she was a tiny child, wanting and wanting trains. "What are you interested in those for?" my father asked. "Trains are for boys." But Olivia wanted and wanted and finally he bought her a tiny train and a track, and then another. And then our father helped her build such a city. He built a platform she could raise to the roof on chains whenever my mother wanted the space for visitors. Look, here's a picture.'

And there they were—trains, recorded on video, tiny locomotives chugging through an Alpine village, with snow-covered trees and tiny figures, railway stations, tunnels, mountains, little plastic figures, a businessman in a bowler hat endlessly missing his train…

Danny was entranced but he'd obviously seen it before. 'Olivia's trains,' he said in satisfaction and he was right by the television, pointing to each train. 'This green one is her favourite. Mama's Papa gave it to her for her eighth birthday. Mama says when I am eight she'll try and find a train just like that for me. Isn't it lucky I'm not eight yet? If Mama had already found my train, it would have been burned.'

'Do you…still see them?' Rob asked cautiously.

Amina smiled sadly and shook her head. 'Our house was bombed. Accidentally, they said, but that's when Henry and I decided to come here. It's better here. No bombs.'

'Bush fires, though,' Rob said, trying for a smile and, amazingly, Amina smiled back at him, even as she put her hand to her obviously aching back.

'We can cope with what we have to cope with,' she said simply. She looked back at the television to where her sister was laughing at her father. Two little steam engines lay crashed on their side on the model track, obviously victims of a fake disaster. 'You get up and keep going,' she said simply. 'What choice is there?'

You can close down, Julie thought. *You can roll into a tight ball of controlled pain, unbending only to work.* That was what she'd done for four long years.

'Would you like to see our boys?' Rob asked and her eyes flew wide. What was he saying? Shock held her immobile and it was as if his voice was coming from the television, not from him. But, 'I'd like to show you our sons,' he was saying. 'They're not here either, but they're still in our hearts. It'd be great to share.'

No. No! She wanted to scream it but she couldn't.

'Would you like us to see them, Julie?' Amina asked shyly, tentatively, as if she guessed Julie's pain. As she must. She'd lost so much herself.

'We lost our boys in a car accident four years ago,' Rob told Henry. 'But it still feels like they're here.'

'But it hurts Julie?' Amina said. 'To talk about them? To see them? Is it better not?'

Yes, Julie thought. *Much better.* But then she looked at Rob, and with a shock she realised that his face said it wasn't better at all.

His expression told her that he longed to talk about them. He longed to show these strangers pictures of his sons, as they'd shown him pictures of their family.

'It's up to Jules, though,' Rob said. 'Julie, do you know where the disc is of their birthday?'

She did, but she didn't want to say. She never spoke of the boys. She never looked at their photographs. They were locked inside her, kept, hers. They were dead.

'Maybe not,' Amina said, still gently. 'If Julie doesn't want to share, that's her right.'

Share...share her boys... She wanted to say no. She wanted to scream it because the thought almost blindsided her. To talk about them...to say their names out loud...to act as if they still had a place in her life...

To see her boys on the screen…

'Jules?' Rob said gently and he crossed the room and stooped and touched her chin with his finger. 'Up to you, love. Share or not? No pressure.'

But it was pressure, she thought desperately, and it was as if the pressure had been building for years. The containment she'd held herself in was no longer holding.

To share her boys… To share her pain…

Rob's gaze was on her, calmly watchful. Waiting for the yay or nay.

No pressure.

Share… Share with this man.

A photo session, she thought. That was all he was asking. To see his kids as they'd been when they'd turned two. How hard was that?

'Don't do it if it hurts,' Amina whispered and Julie knew that it would hurt. But suddenly she knew that it'd hurt much more not to.

They were her boys. Hers and Rob's. And Rob was asking her to share memories, to sit in this room and look at photographs of their kids and let them come to life again, if only on the screen. To introduce them, to talk of them as Amina had talked of her family.

'I…I'll get it,' she said and Rob ran a finger the length of her cheek. His eyes said he did understand what he was asking, and yet he was still asking.

His gaze said he knew her hurt; he shared it. He shared…

She rose and she staggered a little, but Rob was beside her, giving her a swift, hard hug. 'I love that video,' he said but she knew he hadn't seen it for four years. It had been hidden, held here in limbo. Maybe it was time…

She couldn't think past that. She gave Rob a tight hug in return and went to fetch the disc.

* * *

And there they were. Her boys. It had been the most glorious birthday party, held here on the back lawn. All the family had been here—her parents, Rob's parents, their siblings, Rob's brother's kids, Rob's parents' dog, a muddle of family and chaos on the back lawn.

A brand-new paddling pool. Two little boys, gloriously happy, covered in the remains of birthday cake and ice cream, squealing with delight. Rob swinging them in circles, a twin under each arm.

Julie trying to reach Aiden across the pool, slipping and sprawling in the water. Julie lying in the pool in her jeans and T-shirt, the twins jumping on her, thinking she'd meant it, squealing with joy. Rob's laughter in the background. Julie laughing up at the camera, hugging her boys, then yelling at Rob's dad because the dog was using the distraction to investigate the picnic table.

The camera swivelled to the dog and the remains of the cake—and laughter and a dog zooming off into the bushes with half a cake in his mouth.

Family…

She'd thought she couldn't bear it. She'd thought she could never look at photographs again, but, instead of crying, instead of withering in pain, she found she was smiling. Laughing, even. When the dog took off with the cake they were all laughing.

'Luka wouldn't do that,' Danny decreed. 'Bad dog.'

'They look…like a wonderful family,' Amina said and Rob nodded.

'They are.'

They were. She'd never let them close. She'd seen her remaining family perfunctorily for the last four years, when she had to, and she'd never let anyone talk of the boys.

'Aiden and Christopher were…great.'

She said their names now out loud and it was like turning a key in a rusty lock. She hadn't said their names to anyone else since…

'They're the best kids,' Rob said, smiling. He was gripping her hand, she realised, and she hadn't even noticed when he'd taken it. 'They were here for such a short time, but the way they changed our lives… You know, in the far reaches of my head, they're still with me. When I get together with my parents and we talk about them, they're real. They're alive. I understand why you need your family tonight, Amina. For the same reason I need mine.'

Julie listened, and Rob's words left her stunned. His words left her in a limbo she didn't understand. Like an invitation to jump a crevice…but how could she?

The recording had come to an end. The last frame was of the twins sitting in their pool, beaming out at all of them. She wanted to reach out and touch them. She felt as if her skin was bursting. That she could look at her boys and laugh… That she could hold Rob's hand and remember how it had felt to be a family…

'Thank you for showing us,' Henry said, gravely now, and Julie thought that he knew. This man knew how much it hurt. He'd lost too, him and Amina, but now he was tugging his wife to her feet, holding her…moving on.

'We need to sleep,' he said. 'All of us. But thank you for giving us such a wonderful, magical Christmas. Thank you for saving my family, and thank you for sharing yours.'

They left.

Rob flicked the television off and the picture of their boys faded to nothing.

Without a word, Rob went out to the veranda. He stood at the rail and stared into the night and, after a moment's hesitation, Julie followed. The smouldering bushland gave no chance of starlight but, astonishingly, a few of the solar lights they'd installed along the garden paths still glowed. The light was faint but it was enough to show a couple of wallabies drinking deeply from the water basins Rob had left.

'How many did you put out?' Julie said inconsequentially. There were so many emotions coursing through her she had no hope of processing them.

'As many containers as I could find. I suspect our veranda was a refuge. There are droppings all over the south side. All sorts of droppings.'

'So we saved more than Amina and Danny and Luka.'

'I think we did. It's been one hell of a Christmas.' He hesitated. 'So…past Christmases…Julie, each Christmas, each birthday and so many times in between, I've tried to ring. You know how often, but I've always been sent straight through to voicemail. I finally accepted that you wanted no contact, but it hasn't stopped me thinking of you. I've thought of you and the boys every day. But at Christmas…for me it's been a day to get through the best way I can. But, Julie, how has it been for you? I rang your parents. The year after…they said you were with them but you didn't want to talk to me. The year after that they were away and I couldn't contact you.'

How to tell him what she'd been doing? The first year she'd been in hospital and Christmas had been a blur of pain and disbelief. The next her parents had persuaded her to spend with them.

Doug and Isabelle were lovely ex-hippy types, loving their garden, their books, their lives. They'd always been astonished by their only daughter's decision to go into law and finance, but they'd decreed anything she did was okay by them. Doug was a builder, Isabelle taught disadvantaged kids and they accepted everyone. They'd loved Rob and their grandsons but, after the car crash, they'd accepted Julie's decision that she didn't want to talk of them, ever.

But it had left a great hole. They were so careful to avoid it, and she was so conscious of their avoidance. That first Christmas with them had been appalling.

The next year she'd given them an Arctic cruise as a Christmas gift. They'd looked at her with sadness but with understanding and ever since then they'd travelled at Christmas.

And what had Julie been doing?

'I work at Christmas,' she said. 'I'm international. The finance sector hardly closes down.'

'You go into work?'

'I'm not that sad,' she snapped, though she remembered thinking if the entire building hadn't been closed and shut down over Christmas Day she might have. 'I have Christmas dinner with my brother. But I do take contracts home. It takes the pressure off the rest of the staff, knowing someone's willing to take responsibility for the urgent stuff. How about you?'

'That's terrible.'

'How about you?' she repeated and she made no attempt to block her anger. Yeah, Christmas was a nightmare. But he had no right to make her remember how much of a nightmare it normally was, so she wasn't about to let him off the hook. 'While I've been neck-deep in legal negotiations, what have you been doing?'

'To keep Santa at bay?'

'That's one way of looking at it.'

'I've skied.'

It was so out of left field that she blinked. 'What?'

'Skied,' he repeated.

'Where?'

'Aspen.'

She couldn't have been more astounded if he'd said he'd been to Mars. 'You hate the cold.'

'I hated the cold. I'm not that Rob any more.'

She thought about that for a moment while the stillness of the night intensified. The smell of the smoke was all-consuming but…it was okay. It was a mist around them, enveloping them in a weird kind of intimacy.

Rob in the snow at Christmas.

Without her.

Rob in a life without her.

It was odd, she thought numbly. She'd been in a sort of limbo since the accident, a weird, desolate space where time seemed to stand still. There was no future and no past, simply the piles of legal contracts she had in front of her. When she'd had her family, her work had been important. When she hadn't, her work was everything.

But, meanwhile, Rob had been doing…other stuff. Skiing in Aspen.

'Are you any good?' she asked inconsequentially and she heard him smile.

'At first, ludicrous. A couple of guys from work asked me to go with them. I spent my first time on the nursery slopes, watching three-year-olds zoom around me. But I've improved. I pretty much threw my heart and soul into it.'

'Even on Christmas Day?'

'On Christmas Day I pretty much have the slopes to myself. I ski my butt off, to the point where I sleep.'

'Without nightmares?'

'There are always nightmares, Jules,' he said gently. 'Always. But you learn to live around them.'

'But this Christmas—you didn't go to Aspen?'

'My clients finished the house to die for in the Adelaide Hills. They were having a Christmas Eve party. My sister asked me to join her tribe for Christmas today.

I'd decided…well, I'd decided it was time to stay home. Time to move on.'

Without me? She didn't say it. It was mean and unfair. She'd decided on this desolate existence. Rob was free to move on as best he could.

But…but…

He was right here, in front of her. Rob. Her beloved Rob, who she'd turned away from. She could have helped…

Or she could have destroyed him.

He reached out and touched her cheek, a feather touch, and the sensation sent shivers through her body. *Her Rob.*

'Hell, Julie, how do we move on from this?' His voice was grave. Compassionate. Loving?

'I don't know,' she whispered. 'I can't think how to escape this fog.'

There was a moment's hesitation and then his voice changed. 'Escape,' he said bitterly. 'Is that what you want? Do you think Amina was escaping by coming here?'

'I don't know.'

'Well, I do,' he said roughly, almost angrily. 'She wasn't escaping. She was regrouping. Figuring out how badly she and her family had been wounded, and how to survive. And look at her. After all she's been through, back she goes, to her memories, to talking about the ones she loves. You know why I wasn't going to Aspen this Christmas? Because I've finally figured it out. I've finally figured that's what I want, Jules. I want to be able to talk about Aiden and Christopher without hurting. Call it a Christmas list if you want, my Santa wish, but that wish has been with me for four years. Every day I wake up and I want the same thing. I want people to talk of Christopher and Aiden like Amina does of her family. I want to admit that Christopher bugged me when he whined for sweets. I want to remember that Aiden never wanted me to go the bathroom by myself. I want to be able to say that you sometimes took all the bedcovers…'

'I did not!'

'And the one time I got really pissed off and pinned them to my side of the bed you ripped them. You did, too.'

'Rob!'

'Don't sound so outraged.' But then he gave a rueful smile and shrugged. 'Actually, that's okay. Outrage is good. Anything's good apart from silence. Or fog. We've been living with silence for years. Does it have to go on for ever?'

'I'm…safe where I am.'

'Because no one talks about Aiden or Christopher? Or me. Do they talk about me, Julie, or am I as dead to you as the boys are?'

'If they did talk…it hurts.'

But he was still angry. Relentless. The gentle, compassionate Rob was gone. 'Do you remember the first time we climbed this mountain?' he demanded, and he grabbed her hand and hauled her round so she was facing out to where the smoke-shrouded mountain lay beyond the darkened bush. 'Mount Bundoon. You were so unfit. It was mean of me to make you walk, but you wanted to come.'

'I only did it because I was besotted with you.'

'And I only made you come because I wanted you to see. Because I knew it was worth it. Because I knew you'd think it was worth it.' His hand was still holding hers, firm and strong. 'So you struggled up the track and I helped you…'

'You pushed. You bullied!'

'So I did and you got blisters on blisters and we hadn't taken enough water and we were idiots.'

'And then we reached the top,' she said, remembering.

'Yeah,' he said in satisfaction and hauled her against

him. 'We reached the top and we looked out over the gorge and it's the most beautiful place in the whole world. Only gained through blisters.'

'Rob...'

'And what do you remember now?' he demanded, rough again. 'Blisters?'

'No.'

'So? Does my saying Aiden's name, Christopher's name, my name—does it hurt so much you can't reach the top? Because you know what I reckon, Jules? I reckon that saying Aiden's name and Christopher's, and talking of them to each other, that's the top. That's what we ought to aim for. If we could start loving the boys again...together...could we do that, Jules? Not just now? Not just for Christmas? For ever?'

And she wanted to. With every nerve in her body she wanted to.

'Do you know what I've done every Christmas?' he asked, gently now, holding her, but there was something implacable about his voice, something that said he was about to say something that would hurt. 'And every birthday. And so many times in between...I've taken that damned recording out and watched it. And you know what? I love it. I love that I have it. I love that my kids—and my Julie—can still make me smile.'

'You...you have it?' She was stammering. 'But tonight...I had to find the disc.'

'That's because tonight had to be your choice. I have a copy. Jules, I've made my choice. I'm living on, with my kids, with my memories and I've figured that's the way to survive. But you have to do your own figuring. Whether you want to continue blocking the past out for ever. Whether you want to let the memories back in. Or maybe...maybe whether you dare to move forward. With me or without. Julie, I still want you. You're still my wife. I still love you, but the rest…it's up to you.'

The night grew even more still. It was as if the world was holding its breath.

He was so close and he was holding her and he wanted her. All she had to do was sink into him and let him love her.

All she had to do was love in return.

But what did she have to give? It'd be all one way, she thought, her head spinning. Rob could say he loved her, he could say he still wanted her but it wasn't the Julie of now that he wanted. It was the Julie of years ago. The Julie she'd seen on replay. Today's Julie was like a husk, the shed skin of someone she had once been.

Rob deserved better.

She loved this man; she knew she did. But he deserved the old Julie and, confused or not, dizzy or not, she knew at some deep, basic level that she didn't have the energy to be that woman.

'Jules, you can,' he said urgently, as if he knew what she was thinking—how did he do that? How did he still have the skill?

How could she still know him when so much of her had died?

She wanted him, she ached for him, but it terrified her. Could she pretend to be the old Julie? she wondered. Could she fake being someone she used to be?

'Try for us,' Rob demanded, and his hands held her. He tugged her to him, and she felt…like someone was hauling the floor from under her feet.

Rob would catch her. Rob would always catch her.

She had to learn to catch herself.

'Maybe I should see the same shrink,' she managed. 'The one who's made you brave enough to start again.'

'The shrink didn't make me brave. That's all me.'

'I don't want…'

'That's just it. You have to want. You have to want more than to hide.'

'You can't make me,' she said, almost resentfully, and he nodded.

'I know I can't. But the alternative? Do you want to walk away? Once the road is reopened, once Christmas is over, do you want to go back to the life you've been existing in? Not living, existing. Is that what you want?'

'It's what I have to want.'

'It's not,' he said, really angry now. 'You can change. Ask Danny. His Christmas list was written months ago. Amina said he wanted a bike but he got a wombat instead and you know what? Now he thinks that's what he wanted all along.'

'You think I can be happy with second best? Life without our boys?'

'I think you can be happy. I think dying with them is a bloody waste.'

'There's no need…'

'To swear? No, I suppose not. There's no need to do anything. There's no need to even try. Okay, Jules, I'll back off.'

'Rob, I'm…'

'Don't you dare say you're sorry. I couldn't bear it.'

But there was nothing to say but sorry so she said nothing at all. She stood and looked down at her feet. She listened to the soft scuffles of the wallabies out in the garden. She thought…she thought…

'Please?'

And the outside world broke in. The one word was a harsh plea, reverberating through the stillness and it came from neither of them. She turned and so did Rob.

Henry was in the open doorway, his hands held out in entreaty.

'Please,' he said again. 'Can either of you…do either of you know…?'

'What?' Rob said. 'Henry, what's wrong?'

'It's Amina,' Henry stammered. 'She says the baby's coming.'

CHAPTER EIGHT

ALL THE WAY to the bedroom Julie hoped Henry might be mistaken. They reached the guest room, however, and one look told her that there could be no mistake about this. Amina was crouched by the bed, holding onto the bed post, clinging as if drowning. She swung round as Julie entered and her eyes were filled with panic.

'It can't come. It's too early. I can't…last time it was so… I can't do this.'

Right. Okay.

'And it's breech,' Amina moaned. 'It was supposed to turn; otherwise the doctor said I might need a Caesarean…'

Breech! A baby coming and breech! Things that might best have been known when the fire crew was here, Julie thought wildly. They'd had that one chance to get away from here. If they'd known they could have insisted on help, on helicopter evacuation. Amina would surely have been a priority. But now…it was nine o'clock on Christmas night and they'd already knocked back help. What was the chance of a passing ambulance? Or a passing anything?

They were trapped. Their cars were stuck in the garage. The tree that had fallen over the driveway was still there, huge and smouldering. It had taken Henry almost twelve hours to walk up from the road blocks and he'd risked his life doing so.

'The phone…' she said without much hope, and Rob shook his head.

'I checked half an hour ago.' He rechecked then, flipping it from his pocket. 'No reception. Zip. Jules, I'll start down the mountain by foot. I might find someone with a car.'

'I didn't see an occupied house all the way up the mountain.' Henry shook his head. 'The homes that aren't burned are all evacuated. Amina, can't you stop?'

Amina said something that made them all blink. Apparently stopping was not on the agenda.

'What's wrong with Mama?' It was Danny, standing in the hall in his new Batman pyjamas. The pyjamas Julie had bought for her sons. The pyjamas that she'd thought would make her feel…make her feel…

But there wasn't time for her to feel anything. Danny's voice echoed his father's fear. Amina looked close to hysterics. Someone had to do something—now.

She was a lawyer, Julie thought wildly. She didn't do babies.

But it seemed she had no choice. By the look of Amina, this baby was coming, ready or not.

Breech.

'You'll be fine,' she said with a whole lot more assurance than she was feeling. 'Rob, take Danny into the living room and turn on a good loud movie. He had a nap this afternoon; he won't be sleepy. Isn't that right, Danny?'

'But what's wrong with Mama?'

She took a deep breath and squatted beside the little boy. Behind her, Henry was kneeling by his wife—remonstrating? For heaven's sake—as if Amina could switch anything off. And Danny looked terrified.

And suddenly Julie was done with terror. *Enough.*

'Danny, your mama is having a baby,' she told him.

'There's nothing to worry about. There's nothing wrong, but I suspect this is a big baby and your mama will hurt a bit as she pushes it out.'

'How will she push it out?'

'Rob will tell you,' she said grandly, 'while he finds a movie for you to watch. Won't you, Rob?'

'Um…yeah?' He looked wild-eyed and suddenly Julie was fighting an insane desire to grin. A woman in labour or teaching a kid the facts of life—what a choice.

'And your papa and I will help your mama,' she added. But…

'No.' It was Amina, staring up at them, practically yelling. 'No,' she managed again, and this time it was milder. 'It's okay, Danny,' she managed, making a supreme effort to sound normal in the face of her son's fear. 'This is what happened when I had you. It's normal. Having babies hurts, but only like pulling a big splinter out.' *As if*, Julie thought. *Right.*

'But Papa's not going to stay here.' Amina's voice firmed, becoming almost threatening, and she looked up at Julie and her eyes pleaded. 'Last time…Henry fainted. I was having Danny and suddenly the midwives were fussing over Henry because he cut his head on the floor when he fell. Henry, I love you but I don't want you here. I want you to go away.'

Which left…Julie and Rob. They met each other's gaze and Julie's chaotic thoughts were exactly mirrored in Rob's eyes.

Big breath. No, make that deep breathing. A bit of Zen calm. Where was a nice safe monastery when she needed one?

'Give us a moment,' she said to Amina. 'Henry, no fainting yet. Help Amina into bed, then you and Danny can leave the baby delivering to us. We can do this, can't we, Rob?'

'I...'

'*You* won't faint on me,' she said in a voice of steel.

'I guess I won't,' Rob managed. 'If you say so—I guess I wouldn't dare.'

She propelled him out into the passage and closed the door. They stared at each other in a moment of mutual panic, while each of them fought for composure.

'We can't do this,' Rob said.

'We don't have a choice.'

'I don't have the first clue...'

'I've read a bit.' And she had. When she was having the twins, the dot-point part of her—she was a lawyer and an accountant after all, and research was her thing—had read everything she could get her hands on about childbirth. The fact that she'd forgotten every word the moment she went into labour was immaterial. She knew it all. In theory.

'You're a lawyer, Jules,' Rob managed. 'Not an obstetrician. All you know is law.'

And she thought suddenly, fleetingly: *that's not all I have to be.*

Why was it a revelation?

Weirdly, she was remembering the day she'd got the marks to get into law school. Her hippy parents had been baffled, but Julie had been elated. From that moment she'd been a lawyer.

Even when the twins were born...she'd loved Rob to bits and she'd adored her boys but she was always a lawyer. She'd had Rob bring files into hospital after she'd delivered, so she wouldn't fall behind.

All you know is law...

For the last four years law had been her cave, her hiding place. Her all. The night the boys were killed they'd been running late because of her work and Rob's work.

Rob had started skiing, she thought inconsequentially and then she thought that maybe it was time she did something different too. Like delivering babies?

The whole concept took a nanosecond to wash through her mind but, strangely, it settled her.

'We don't even have the Internet,' Rob groaned.

'I have books.'

'Books?'

'You know: things with pages. I bought every birth book I could get my hands on when the twins were due. They'll still be in the bookcase.'

'You intend to deliver a breech baby with one hand while you hold the book in the other?'

'That's where you come in, Rob McDowell,' she snapped. 'From this moment we're a united team. I want hot water, warm towels and a professional attitude.'

'I'm an architect!'

'Not tonight you're not,' she told him. 'It's still Christmas. You played Santa this morning. Now you need to put your midwife hat on and deliver again.'

She'd sounded calm enough when she'd talked to Rob but, as she stood in front of her small library of childbirth books, she felt the calm slip away.

What...? How...?

Steady, she told herself. *Think.* She stared at the myriad titles and tried to decide.

Not for the first time in her life, she blessed her memory. Read it once, forget it never. Obviously she couldn't remember every detail in these books—some parts she'd skimmed over fast. But the thing with childbirth, she'd figured, was that almost anyone could do it. Women had been doing it since time immemorial and they'd done it without the help of books. Ninety-nine times out of a hundred there were no problems; all the midwife had to do was encourage, support, catch and clean up.

But the one per cent…

Julie had become just a trifle obsessive in the last weeks of her pregnancy. She therefore had books with pictures of unthinkable outcomes. She remembered Rob had found her staring in horror at a picture of conjoined twins, and a mother who'd laboured for days before dying. *Extreme Complications of Pregnancy.* He'd taken that book straight to the shredder, but she had others.

Breech, she thought frantically, fingering one title after another. There were all sorts of complications with breech deliveries and she'd read them all.

But…but…

Ninety-nine per cent of babies are born normally, she told herself and she kept on thinking of past reading. *Breech is more likely to be a problem in first time mothers because the perineum is unproven.* Or words to that effect? She'd read that somewhere and she remembered thinking if her firstborn twin was breech it might be a problem, but if the book was right the second twin would be a piece of cake regardless.

'You're smiling!'

Rob had come into the living room and was staring at her in astonishment.

'No problem. We can do this.' And she hauled out one of the slimmest tomes on the shelf, almost a booklet, written by a midwife and not a doctor. It was well thumbed. She'd read it over and over because in the end it had been the most comforting.

She flicked until she found what she was looking for, and there were the words again. *If the breech is a second baby it's much less likely to require intervention.* But it did sound a warning. *Avoid home birth unless you're near good medical backup.*

There wasn't a lot of backup here. One architect, one lawyer, one fainting engineer and a four-year-old. Plus a first aid box containing sticking plasters, tweezers and antiseptic.

Breech... She flipped to the page she was looking for and her eyes widened. Rob looked over her shoulder and she felt him stiffen. 'My God...'

'We can do this.' *Steady,* she told herself. *If I don't stay calm, who will?* 'Look,' she said. 'We have step by step instructions with pictures. It's just like buying a desk and assembling it at home, following instructions. Besides, if we need to intervene, we can, but it says we probably won't need to. It's big on hands off.'

'But if we do? You know me and kit furniture—it always ends up with screws left over and one side wonkier than the other. And look what it says! If it's facing upward, head for hospital because...'

'There's no need to think like that,' she snapped. 'We need to stay positive. That means calm, Rob.' And she thought back, remembering. 'Forget the kit furniture analogy. Yes, you're a terrible carpenter but as a first time dad you were great. You are great. You need to be like you were with me, every step of the way. No matter how terrified I was, you were there saying how brave I was, how well I was doing, and you sounded so calm, so sure...'

'I wasn't in the least sure. I was a mess.'

'So you're a good actor. Put the act on again.'

'This isn't you we're talking about. Jules, I could do it when I had to.'

'Then you have to now.' She took a long, hard look at the diagrams, committing them to memory. Hoping to heaven she wouldn't need them. 'Amina has us. Rob, together we can do this.'

'Okay.' He took a deep breath while he literally squared his shoulders. 'If you say so, maybe we can.' Then suddenly he tugged her to him and hugged her, hard, and gave her a swift firm kiss. 'Maybe that's what I've been saying all along. Apart we're floundering. Together we might…'

'Be able to have a baby? Do you have those towels warming?' The kiss had left her flustered, but she regrouped fast.

'Yes, ma'am.'

'I'll need sterilised scissors.'

'I already thought of that. They're in a pot on the barbecue. So all we need is one baby.' He cupped her chin and smiled down at her. 'Okay, Dr McDowell, do you have your dot-point plan ready? I hope you do because we're in your hands.'

Breech births were supposed to be long. Weren't they? Surely they were supposed to take longer than normal labours, but no one seemed to have told Amina's baby that. When Rob and Julie returned to her room she was mid-contraction and one look at her told them both that this was some contraction. Surely a contraction shouldn't be as all-consuming if it was early labour.

Henry and Danny were looking appalled but Henry was looking even more appalled than his son. He'd fainted at Danny's birth, but then refugees did it tough, Rob thought, and who knew what the circumstances had been? Today he'd literally walked through fire to reach his family. He must be past exhaustion. He'd cut him some slack—and, besides, if Henry left with Danny, it would be Henry who'd have to explain childbirth to his son.

He put his hand on Henry's shoulder and gripped, hard.

'We can do this, mate,' he said. 'At least, Julie can and I'm here to assist. Julie suggested I take Danny into the living room and turn on a movie. If it's okay with Amina, how about you take my place? We have a pile of kids' movies. Pick a loud, exciting one and watch it until you both go to sleep. Hug Luka and know everything's okay. Danny, your mama's about to have a baby and she needs to be able to yell a bit while she does. It's okay, honest, most mamas yell when they have babies. So if you hear yelling, don't you worry. Snuggle up with your papa and Luka, and when you wake up in the morning I reckon your mama will have a baby to show you. Is that okay, Henry?'

'I'll stay,' Henry quavered. 'If you want me to, Amina…'

'Leave,' Amina ordered, easing back from the contraction enough to manage a weak smile at her husband and then her son. 'It's okay, sweetheart,' she told Danny. 'This baby has to push its way out and I have to squeeze and squeeze and it's easier for me if I can yell when I squeeze. Papa's going to show you a movie and Julie and Rob are going to stay with me to take care of the baby when it's born.'

'Can I come back and see it—when it's born?'

'Yes.'

'And will it be a boy?'

'I don't know,' Amina told him. 'But, Danny, take your papa away because I have to squeeze again and Papa doesn't like yelling. You look after Papa, okay?'

'And watch a movie?'

'Yes,' Amina managed through gritted teeth. Julie got behind Henry and practically propelled him and his son through the door and closed it behind them, and it was just as well because Amina was true to her word.

She yelled.

* * *

Hands off. Do not interfere unless you have to. That was the mantra the little book extolled and that was fine by Julie because there didn't seem to be an alternative.

She and Rob both washed, scrupulously on Julie's part, the way she'd seen it done on television. Rob looked at her with her arms held out, dripping, and gave a rueful chuckle. 'Waiting for a nurse to apply latex gloves?'

'The only gloves I have are the ones I use for the washing-up. I'm dripping dry,' she retorted and then another contraction hit and any thought of chuckling went out of the window.

'Hey,' Rob said, hauling a chair up by Amina's bedside. 'It's okay. Yell as much as you want. We're used to it. You should have heard Julie when she had the twins. I'd imagine you could have heard her in Sri Lanka.'

'But…but she knows…what to do? Your Julie?'

'My Julie knows what to do,' Rob told her, taking her hand. 'My Julie's awesome.'

And how was a woman to react to that? Julie felt her eyes well, but then Rob went on.

'My Julie's also efficient. She'll help you get through this faster than anyone I know. And if there's any mucking around she'll know who to sue. She's a fearsome woman, my Julie, so let's just put ourselves in her hands, Amina, love, and get this baby born.'

Which meant there was no time for welling eyes, no time for emotion. There was a baby to deliver.

By unspoken agreement, Rob stayed by Amina's side and did what a more together Henry should have done, while Julie stayed at the business end of the bed.

The instructions in her little booklet played over and over in her head, giving her a clear plan of action. How close? Julie had no clue. She couldn't see the baby yet but, with the power of these contractions, it surely wouldn't be long before she did.

She felt useless, but at the other end of the bed Rob was a lot more help.

'Come on, Amina, you can do this. Every contraction brings your baby closer. You're being terrific. Did anyone ever teach you how to breathe? You do it like this between contractions…' And he proceeded to demonstrate puffing as he'd learned years before in Julie's antenatal classes. 'It really works. Julie said so.'

Julie had said no such thing, she thought. She'd said a whole lot of things during her long labour but she couldn't remember saying anything complimentary about anything.

And Amina was in a similar mood. When Rob waited until the next contraction passed and then encouraged Amina to puff again, he got told where he could put his puffing.

'And it's breech,' she gasped. 'Julie doesn't know about breech.'

'Julie knows everything,' Rob declared. 'Memory like a bull elephant, my Julie. Tell us the King of Spain in 1703, Jules.'

'Philip Five,' Julie said absently.

'Name a deadly mushroom?'

'Conocybe? Death caps? How many do you want?'

'And tell me what's different about breech?'

'I might have to do a little rotating as the baby comes out,' Julie said, trying to sound as if it was no big deal.

'There you go, then,' Rob approved as Amina disappeared into another contraction. 'She knows it all. This'll be a piece of cake for our Julie.'

Only it wasn't. Rob had managed to calm Amina; there no longer seemed to be terror behind the pain, but there was certainly a fair bit of terror behind Julie's façade of competence.

One line in the little book stood out. *If the baby's presenting face up then there's no choice; it must be a Caesarean.*

Any minute now she'd know. *Dear God...*

Her mind was flying off at tangents as she waited. Was there any other option? They couldn't go for help. They couldn't ring anyone. For heaven's sake, they couldn't even light a fire and send out smoke signals. If it was face up...

'And my Julie always stays calm,' Rob said, and his voice was suddenly stern, cutting across the series of yelps Amina was making. 'That's what I love about her. That's why you're in such good hands, Amina. Are you sure you don't want to puff?'

Amina swore and slapped at his hand and a memory came back to Julie—she'd done exactly the same thing. She'd even bruised him. The day after the twins were born she'd looked at a blackening bruise on her husband's arm, and she'd also seen marks on his palm where her nails had dug in.

Her eyes met his and he smiled, a faint gentle smile that had her thinking...*memories can be good.* The remembrance of Rob's comfort. Her first sight of her babies.

The love...

Surely that love still deserved to live. Surely it shouldn't be put away for ever in the dusty recesses of her mind, locked away because letting it out hurt?

Surely Rob was right to relive those memories. To let them make him smile...

But then Amina gasped and struggled and Rob supported her as she tried to rise. She grasped her knees and she pushed.

Stage two. Stage two, stage two, stage two.

Face up, face down. *Please, please, please...*

There was a long, loaded pause and Amina actually puffed. But still she held her knees while the whole world seemed to hold its breath.

Another contraction. Another push.

Julie could see it. She could see…what? *What?*

A backside. A tiny bottom.

Face down. *Oh, God, face down. Thank you, thank you, thank you.* She glanced up at Rob and her relief must have shown in her face. He gave her a fast thumbs-up and then went back to holding, encouraging, being…Rob.

She loved him. She loved him with all her heart but now wasn't the time to get corny. Now was the time to try and deliver this baby.

Hands off. That was what the book said. *Breech babies will often deliver totally on their own.*

Please...

But they'd been lucky once. They couldn't ask for twice. Amina pushed, the baby's bottom slid out so far but as the contraction receded, so did the baby.

Over and over.

Exhaustion was starting to set in. Time for Dr Julie to take a hand? Did she dare?

Another glance at Rob, and his face was stern. He'd read the book over her shoulder, seen the pictures, figured what was expected now. His face said: *do it.*

So do it.

She'd set out what she'd need. Actually, she'd set out what she had. The book said if the head didn't come, then forceps might be required. She didn't actually have forceps or anything that could be usefully used instead.

Please don't let them be needed. It was a silent prayer said over and over.

Don't think forward. One step at a time. First she had to deliver the legs.

Dot-point number one. Carefully, she lubricated her fingers. One leg at a time. One leg…

Remember the pictures.

'Jules is about to help your baby out,' Rob said, his voice steady, calm, settling. 'Next push, Amina, go as far as you can and then hold. Puff, just like I said. Keep the pressure on.'

Next contraction… The baby's back slid out again. Deep breath and Julie felt along the tiny leg. What did the book say? *Manoeuvre your finger behind the knee and gently push upward. This causes the knee to flex. Hold the femur, splint it gently with your finger to prevent it breaking. This should allow the leg to…*

It did! It flopped out. *Oh, my…*

Calm. Next. Dot-point number two.

The other leg was easier. Now the baby could no longer recede. *Manoeuvre to the right position. Flex.*

Two legs delivered. She was almost delirious with hope. *Please…*

Dot-point number three. *Gently rotate the baby into the side position to allow delivery of the right arm.* Easier said than done but the illustrations had been clear. If only her hands weren't so slippery, but they had to be slippery.

'Fantastic, Jules,' Rob said. 'Fantastic, Amina. You're both doing great.'

She had the tiny body slightly rotated. Enough? It had to be. Her finger found the elbow, put her finger over the top, pressured gently, inexorably.

An arm. She'd delivered an arm. The dot-points were blurring, but she still had work to do. She was acting mostly on instinct, but thank God for the book. She'd write to the author. No, she'd send the author half her kingdom. All her kingdom.

She suddenly thought of the almost obscene amount of money she'd been earning these past years and thought…

And thought there was another arm to go and then the head, and the head was…

'Jules. We're doing great,' Rob growled and she glanced up at him and thought he'd seen the shiver of panic and he was grounding her again.

He'd always grounded her. She needed him.

Her hands held the tiny body, took a grip, lifted as the book said, thirty degrees so the left arm was in position for delivery. She twisted as the next contraction eased. The baby rotated like magic.

She found the elbow and pushed gently down. The left arm slithered out.

Now the head. *Please, God, the head.* She didn't have forceps. She wouldn't have the first clue what to do with forceps if she had them.

'Lift,' Rob snapped and he was echoing the book too. 'Come on, Jules, you know what the book says. Come on, Amina. Our baby's so close. We can do this.'

Our baby…

It sounded good. It sounded right.

'Next contraction, puff afterwards, ease off until Jules has the baby in position,' Rob urged Amina, and magically she did.

Amina was working so hard. Surely she could do the same.

She steadied. Waited. The next contraction passed. Amina puffed, Rob held her hand and murmured gentle words. 'Hold, Amina, hold, we're so close…'

Do it.

She held the baby, resting it on her right hand. She manoeuvred her hand so two fingers were on the side of the tiny jaw. With her other hand she put her middle finger on the back of the baby's head.

It sounded easy. It wasn't. She lifted the baby as high as she could, remembering the pictures, remembering…

So much sweat. She needed…she needed…

'You're doing great, Jules,' Rob said. 'Amina, your baby's so close. Maybe one more push. This is fantastic. Let's do this, people. Okay, Jules?'

'O…Okay.' She nodded. She'd forgotten how to breathe. *Please…*

'Okay, Amina, push,' Rob ordered and Amina pushed—and the next second Julie had a healthy, lusty, slippery bundle of baby girl in her arms.

She gasped and staggered but she had her. She had Amina's baby.

Safe. Delivered.

And seconds later a tiny girl was lying on her mother's tummy. Amina was sobbing with joy, and a new little life had begun.

After that things happened in a blur. Waiting for the afterbirth and checking it as the book had shown. Clearing up. Watching one tiny girl find her mother's breast. Ushering an awed and abashed Henry into the room, with Danny by his side.

Watching the happiness. Watching the little family cling. Watching the love and the pride, and then backing out into the night, their job done.

Julie reached the passage, leaned against the wall and sagged.

But she wasn't allowed to sag for long. Her husband had her in his arms. He held her and held her and held her, and she felt his heart beat against hers and she thought: *here is my home.*

Here is my family.

Here is my heart.

'Love, I need to check the boundaries again,' he said at last, ruefully, and she thought with a jolt: *fire.* She hadn't thought of the fire for hours. But of course he was right. There'd still be embers falling around them. They should have kept checking.

'We should have told Henry to check,' she managed.

'Do you think he would have even seen an ember? You take a shower. I'll be with you soon.'

'Rob…' she managed.

'Mmm?'

'I love you,' she whispered.

'I love you too, Dr McDowell.' He kissed her on the tip of the nose and then put her away. 'But then, I always have. All we need to do now is to figure some way forward. Think of it in the shower, my Jules. Think of me. Now, go get yourself clean again while I rid myself of my obstetric suit and put on my fireman's clothes. Figuring roles for ourselves… This day's thrown plenty at us. Think about it, Jules, love. What role do you want for the rest of your life?'

And he was gone, off to play fireman.

While Julie was left to think about it.

There was little to think about—and yet there was lots. She thought really fast while she let the water stream over her. Then she towelled dry, donned her robe and headed back out onto the veranda.

Rob was just finishing, heading up the steps with his bucket and mop.

'Not a single ember,' he announced triumphantly. 'Not

a spark. After today I doubt an ember would dare come close. Have I told you recently that we rock? If I didn't think Amina might be asleep already I'd puff out my chest and do a yodel worthy of Tarzan.'

'Riiiight…'

'It's true. In fact I feel a yodel coming on right this minute. But not here. Do you fancy wandering up the hill a little and yodelling with me?'

And it was such a crazy idea that she thought: *why not?* But then, she was in a robe and slippers and she should…

No. She shouldn't think of reasons not to. *Move forward.*

'That's something I need to hear,' she said and grinned. 'A Tarzan yodel… Wow.' She grabbed his mop, tossed it aside, took his hand and hauled him out into the night.

'Jules! I didn't mean…'

'To yodel? Rob McDowell, if you think I'm going through what we've gone through without listening to you yodel, you're very much mistaken.'

'What have I done?' But Rob was helpless in her hands as she hauled him round the back of the bunker, up through the rocks that formed the back of their property, along a burned out trail that led almost straight up—it was so rocky here that no trees grew, which made it safe from the remnants of fire—and out onto a rock platform where usually she could see almost all over the Blue Mountains.

She couldn't see the Blue Mountains tonight. The pall of smoke was still so thick she could hardly see the path, but the smoke was lifting a little. They could sometimes see a faint moon, with smoke drifting over, sending them from deep dark to a little sight and back again. It didn't matter, though. They weren't here to see the moon or the Blue Mountains. They were here…to yodel.

'Right,' Julie said as they reached the platform. 'Go ahead.'

'Really?'

'Was it all hot air? You never meant it?'

He chuckled. 'It won't be pretty.'

'I'm not interested in pretty!'

'Well, you asked for it.' And he breathed in, swelled, pummelled his chest—and yodelled.

It was a truly heroic yodel. It made Julie double with laughter. It made her feel…feel…as if she was thirteen years old again, in love for the first time and life was just beginning.

It was a true Tarzan yodel.

'You've practised,' she said accusingly. 'No one could make a yodel sound that good first try.'

'My therapist said I should let go my anger,' he told her. 'It started with standing in the shower and yelling at the soap. After a while I started experimenting elsewhere.'

'Moving on?'

'It's what you have to do.'

'Rob…'

'I know,' he said. 'You haven't. But you will. Try it yourself. Open your mouth and yell.' And he stood back and dared her with his eyes. He was laughing, with her, though, not at her. Daring her to laugh with him. Daring her to yodel?

And finally, amazingly, it felt as if she could. How long had it been since she'd felt this free? This alive? Maybe never. Even when they were courting, even when the twins were born, she'd always felt the constraints of work. The constraints of life. But now…

Rob's hands were exerting a gentle pressure but that pressure was no constraint. She was facing outward into the rest of the world.

She was facing outward into the rest of her life.

'Can you do it?' Rob asked, and he kissed the nape of her neck. 'Not that I doubt you. My wife can do anything.'

And she could. Or at least maybe she could.

Deep breath. Pummel a little.

Yodel.

And she was doing it, yodelling like a mad woman, and she took another breath and tried again and this time Rob joined her.

It was crazy. It was ridiculous.

It was fun.

'We've delivered a Christmas baby,' Rob managed as finally they ran out of puff, as finally they ran out of yodel. 'A new life. And we're learning Christmas yodelling duets! Is there nothing we're not capable of? Happy Christmas, Mrs McDowell, and, by the way, will you marry me? Again? Make our vows again? I know we're not divorced but it surely feels like we have been. Can we be a family? Can we take our past and live with it? Can we love what we've had, and love each other again for the rest of our lives?'

And the smoke suddenly cleared. Everything cleared. Rob was standing in front of her, he was holding her and the future was hers to grasp and to hold.

And in the end there was nothing to say except the most obvious response in the whole world.

'Why, yes, Mr McDowell,' she whispered. 'Happy Christmas, my love, and yes, I believe I will marry you again. I believe I will marry you—for ever.'

CHAPTER NINE

A RETAKING OF weddings vows shouldn't be as romantic as the first time around. That was what Julie's mother had read somewhere, but she watched her daughter marry for the second time and she thought: *what do 'they' know?*

People go into a second marriage with their eyes wide open, with all the knowledge of the trials and pitfalls of marriage behind them, and yet they choose to step forward again, and step forward with joy. Because they know what love is. Because they know that, despite the hassles and the day-to-day trivia, and sometimes despite the tragedy and the heartache, they know that love is worth it.

So Julie's mother held her husband's hand and watched her daughter retake her vows, and felt her heart swell with pride. They'd ached every step of the way with their daughter. They'd ached for their grandsons and for the hurt they'd known their son-in-law must be feeling. But in the end they'd stopped watching. Julie had driven them away, as she'd driven away most people in her life. But somehow one magical Christmas had brought healing.

It was almost Easter now. Julie had wanted to get on with their lives with no fuss, but Rob wasn't having any part of such a lame new beginning. 'I watch people have parties for their new homes,' he'd said. 'How much more important is this? We're having a party for our new lives.'

And they would be new lives. So much had changed.

They'd moved—Julie from her sterile apartment in Sydney, Rob from his bachelor pad in Adelaide—but they'd decided not to move back to the Blue Mountains. Amina and Henry were in desperate need of a house—*'and we need to move on,'* they'd told them.

Together they'd found a ramshackle weatherboard cottage on the beach just south of Sydney. They'd both abandoned their jobs for the duration and were tackling the house with energy and passion—if not skill. It might end up a bit wonky round the edges, but already it felt like home.

But... *Home. Home is where the heart is,* so somehow, some way, it felt right that their vows were being made back here. On the newly sprouting gardens around Amina and Henry's home in the Blue Mountains, where there was love in spades. Amina and Henry had been overjoyed when Rob and Julie had asked to have the ceremony here.

'Because your love brought us together again,' Julie had told Amina. 'You and Henry, with your courage and your love for each other.'

'You were together all the time,' Amina had whispered, holding her baby daughter close. 'You just didn't know it.'

Rob and Julie were now godparents. More. They were landlords and they were also sponsoring Henry through retraining. There'd be no more working in the mines. No more long absences. This family deserved to stay together.

As did Julie and Rob.

'I asked you this seven years ago,' the celebrant said, smiling mistily at them. She must have seen hundreds of weddings, but did she mist up for all of them? Surely not. 'But I can't tell you the joy it gives me to ask you again. Rob, do you take Julie—again—to be your lawful wedded wife, to love and to cherish, in sickness and in health, forsaking all others, for as long as you both shall live?'

'I do—and the rest,' Rob said softly, speaking to Julie and to Julie alone. 'Beyond the grave I'll love you. Love doesn't end with death. We both know that. Love keeps going and going and going, if only we let it. Will we let it? Will we let it, my love?'

'Yes, please,' Julie whispered, and then she, too, made her vows.

And Mr McDowell married Mrs McDowell—again—and the thing was done.

Christmas morning.

Julie woke early and listened to the sounds of the surf just below the house. She loved this time of day. Once upon a time she'd listened to galahs and cockatoos in the bush around their house. Now she listened to the sounds of the waves and the sandpipers and oystercatchers calling to each other as they hunted on the shore of a receding tide.

Only that wasn't right, she told herself. She'd never lain in bed and listened to the sounds of birds in the bush. She'd been too busy working. Too busy with her dot-points.

But now… They'd slowed, almost to a crawl. Her dot-points had grown fewer and fewer. Rob worked from home, his gorgeous house plans sprawled over his massive study at the rear of the house. Julie commuted to Sydney twice a week, and she, too, worked the rest of the time at home.

But they didn't work so much that they couldn't lie in bed and listen to the surf. And love each other. And start again.

She'd stop commuting soon, she thought in satisfaction. She could maybe still accept a little contract work, as long as it didn't mess with her life. With her love.

With her loves?

And, unbidden, her hand crept to her tummy, where her secret lay.

She couldn't wait a moment longer. She rolled over and kissed her husband, tenderly but firmly.

'Wake up,' she told him. 'It's Christmas.'

'So it is.' He woke with laughter, reaching for her, holding her, kissing her. 'Happy Christmas, wife.'

'Happy Christmas, husband.'

'I have the best Christmas gift for you,' he said, pushing himself up so he was smiling down at her with all the tenderness in the world. 'I bet you can't guess what it is.'

She choked on laughter. Last night he'd driven home late and on the roof rack of his car was a luridly wrapped Christmas present, complete with a huge Christmas bow. It was magnificently wrapped but all the wrapping in the world couldn't disguise the fact that it was a surfboard.

'I have no idea,' she lied. 'I can't wait.'

They'd come so far, she thought, as Rob gathered her into his arms. This year would be so different from the past. All their assorted family was coming for lunch, as were Amina and Henry and their children. For family came in all sorts of assorted sizes and shapes. It changed. Tragedies happened but so did joys. Christmas was full of memories, and each memory was to be treasured, used to shape the future with love and with hope and memories to come.

And dot-points, she thought suddenly. There were—what?—twenty people due for lunch. Loving aside, smugness aside, she had to get organised. Dot-point number one. Stuff the turkey.

But Rob was holding her—and she had her gift for him.

So: *soon*, she told her dot-point, and proceeded to indulge her husband. And herself.

'Do you want your present now?' she asked as they finally resurfaced, though she couldn't get her mind to be practical quite yet.

'I have everything I need right here.'

'Are you sure?'

'What more could a man want?'

She smiled. She smiled and she smiled. She'd been holding this secret for almost two weeks and it had almost killed her not to tell him, but now… She tugged away from his arms, then kissed him on the nose and settled on her back. And tugged his hand to her naked tummy.

She could scarcely feel it herself. Could he…? Would he…?

But he got it in one. She saw his eyes widen in shock. He was clever, her husband. He was loving and tender and wise. He was a terrible handyman—her kitchen shelves were a disaster and she was hoping her dad might stay on long enough to fix them—but a woman couldn't have everything.

Actually, she did. She did have everything. Her husband was looking down at her with awe and tenderness and love.

'Really?' he whispered.

'Really.'

And she saw him melt, just like that. A blaze of joy that took her breath away.

Joy… They had so much, and this baby was more. For it was true what they said: *love doesn't die*. The memories of Christopher and Aiden would stay with them for ever—tender, joyous, always mourned but an intrinsic part of her family. Their family. Hers and Rob's.

'Happy Christmas, Daddy,' she murmured and she kissed him long and hard. 'Happy Christmas, my love.'

'Do you suppose it might be twins again?' he breathed, awed beyond belief, and she smiled and smiled.

'Who knows? Whoever it is, we'll love them for ever.

Like I love you. Now, are you going to make love to me again or are you going to let me go? I hate to mention it but I have all these dot-points to attend to.'

'But here is your number one dot-point,' he said smugly, and gathered her into his arms yet again. 'The turkey can wait. Christmas can wait. Number one is us.'

* * * * *

“Damn it to hell, Rory...”

She stepped up nice and close. She smelled of that perfume she always wore, of roses and oranges and a hint of some dark spice. He’d always liked her scent. But now, tonight, it seduced him, made his head spin. She pulled her hand back.

Walker felt the loss of her touch as a blow, sharp and cruel.

But then she tipped up her sweet mouth to him.

It was the best offer he’d had in a very long time. And yet it felt all wrong. “I’m supposed to be looking out for you, not stealing kisses at bedtime.”

She took a soft, slow breath. “Because you’re my bodyguard.”

“That’s right.”

“Didn’t I try to warn you that being my bodyguard was not a good idea?”

Oranges. Spice. What would she taste like on his tongue? She really was killing him. “Uh, yeah. I believe that you did.”

“You should have listened to me.”

“Maybe so. Too late now, though.”

* * *

The Bravo Royales:
When it comes to love, Bravos rule!

A BRAVO CHRISTMAS WEDDING

BY

CHRISTINE RIMMER

Published in Great Britain 2014
by Mills & Boon, an imprint of Harlequin (UK) Limited,
Eton House, 18-24 Paradise Road, Richmond, Surrey, TW9 1SR

ISBN: 978-0-263-91340-8

23-1214

Harlequin (UK) Limited's policy is to use papers that are natural, renewable and recyclable products and made from wood grown in sustainable forests. The logging and manufacturing processes conform to the legal environmental regulations of the country of origin.

Printed and bound in Spain
by CPI, Barcelona

Christine Rimmer came to her profession the long way around. Before settling down to write about the magic of romance, she'd been everything from an actress to a salesclerk to a waitress. Now that she's finally found work that suits her perfectly, she insists she never had a problem keeping a job—she was merely gaining "life experience" for her future as a novelist. Christine is grateful not only for the joy she finds in writing, but for what waits when the day's work is through: a man she loves who loves her right back, and the privilege of watching their children grow and change day to day. She lives with her family in Oregon. Visit Christine at www.christinerimmer.com.

For my readers. I'm wishing you a beautiful,
richly blessed holiday season.

Chapter One

Strings had been pulled.

Aurora Bravo-Calabretti, Princess of Montedoro, knew this because Walker McKellan was waiting for her right there on the tarmac when the private jet her mother had insisted Rory use taxied in for a landing at the Denver airport.

Irritation at the sight of him—and at her mother, too—had her chewing her lower lip. God forbid she should be allowed to get off a plane and walk all the way to customs without some big, strong man watching over her, making sure she got there safely.

Tall and lean, wearing old jeans, battered boots and a heavy shearling coat, Walker had his arms folded across his broad chest, and he was leaning against his camo-green SUV. In the thin winter sunlight, he looked so American—a rancher fresh off the range, or maybe a mountain man taking a short break from wrestling grizzlies and taming bobcats. As frustrated as she was with the situation, Rory couldn't resist whipping out her trusty Nikon D700 and snapping several shots of him through a passenger window.

Walker was a great guy. Rory adored him. He'd been a very good friend to her over the seven-plus years she'd been visiting Colorado on a regular basis. People should not take advantage of their very good friends. Rory would never have done such a thing by choice.

But her mother, who usually had the sense to mind her own business, had gone over to the dark side for no comprehensible reason and taken advantage of Walker *for* her. And Walker had let Rory's mother do it.

The more Rory thought about that, the angrier she became with both of them—with her mother, for roping Walker into being responsible for her. And with Walker, too, for not allowing Rory to back out of the unfair arrangement gracefully.

She pulled on her coat, stuck her camera in her tote and headed for the exit, pausing to thank the flight steward and the pilots as she left.

When she started down the airstairs, Walker straightened from the SUV and strode toward her. "My favorite princess. Lookin' good." Those blue eyes with the manly crinkles at the corners swept over her red peacoat, long sweater and thick winter leggings tucked into a nice, warm pair of Sorel boots. He reached for a hug.

"Hey." She went into his arms for maybe half a second before ducking free.

His eyes narrowed briefly at her sullen greeting, but then he only asked, "Good trip?"

"It was fine," she said without even trying to sound as though she meant it. He gave her another swift, questioning glance. She ignored it. "There will be customs," she said. "But it should be quick."

A half an hour later, her luggage had been checked and loaded into the back of the SUV. They set out for the small town of Justice Creek, where her Bravo cousins lived.

As they sped down the interstate, he tried to get her

talking. He teased her about the number of suitcases she'd brought and then about how he planned to put her to work cooking and cleaning out at his ranch, the Bar-N. She returned brief responses and stared out her side window at the high, flat land rolling off toward the distant gray humps of the mountains.

Eventually he gave up, turned on the radio and hummed along in his slightly off-key baritone to country-western Christmas music.

Walker waited.

Her sulky act wouldn't last. Rory came at life full out, and nothing got her down for long.

He let her sit there and stew until they turned off the main highway onto the state road, heading northwest. When she still refused to snap out of it, he switched off the radio. "Come on. It's not all that bad."

She made a low, unhappy sound and slid him a grumpy glance. "Did you at least take the money she offered you?"

"I turned the money down."

A gasp of outrage. "Now, that's just wrong."

"She sent a big check anyway."

"Don't you dare send it back." Rory leveled a stern glance on him. "It's bad enough that you have to babysit me. No way are you doing it for free."

"I like babysitting you."

A scoffing noise escaped her. "The way you say that? Doesn't lift my spirits in the least. You know I hate it when you treat me like a baby."

"Whoa. Was *I* the one who called it babysitting?"

She let out a grouchy little grunting sound and stared straight ahead.

He kept after her. "What I mean is I like hanging

with you." When she only gave him more of the silent treatment, he added, "And it doesn't seem right to take money just for keeping an eye on you."

"But I don't *need* anyone keeping an eye on me. And what if some camper gets lost in the mountains?" He headed up the Justice Creek search-and-rescue team. "Or if there's a forest fire?" He also volunteered with the fire department during emergencies. "What are you going to do then?"

He shrugged. "Camping's more of a summer activity. And forest fires are down in the winter, too. But if something happens, we'll work it out."

Next, she tried threats. "I mean it, Walker. You put that check she sent you in the bank or I may never speak to you again."

Two could play that game. "Keep acting like this and I won't *care* if you never speak to me again—and I have to ask. Is it my fault your mother insists that you have security?"

"No, and I didn't say it was."

"So why are you blaming me?"

"Walker, I'm not *blaming* you."

"Then cut this crap the hell out."

"Great." She threw up both hands. "Now you're acting like you think you're my big brother. The last thing I need is one of those. I already have four, thank you very much."

Enough. "Okay, Rory. I've about had it. Knock it off."

She pinched up her full mouth. "See? What did I tell you? 'Knock it off.'" She faked a deep voice. "Just like a know-it-all, fatheaded, domineering big brother."

By then, she was really starting to get on his nerves.

"Fine. I give up. Sulk all the way to the Bar-N if that's your pleasure."

They subsided into mutually pissed-off silence. He didn't even bother to turn on the radio and pretend that her bad attitude didn't bug the hell out of him.

It took ten minutes of both of them staring out the windshield, acting as if the other wasn't there, before she couldn't take it anymore. She swiped off her red wool beanie and scraped her fingers back through her long brown hair. "I mean, the whole point of my coming alone was that I get to look out for myself. I'm an adult, but my mother won't stop thinking of me as the baby of the family. It's not right." She had the beanie in her lap and she was alternately twisting and smoothing it. "I really thought I was getting through to her, you know? She finally admitted that maybe, just possibly, my having a bodyguard everywhere I go outside Montedoro was overkill. Think about it. How many of us need that kind of security? It has to stop somewhere. I have eight siblings ahead of me in line for the throne, not to mention all my nieces and nephews, who are *also* ahead of me. I want to go where I need to go for my work." Rory was a talented photographer. "A normal life—it's all I'm asking for. I just don't need all that protecting. Not only is it unnecessary and a waste of money, it seriously cramps my style."

He suggested, "Look at it this way. It's a step. You *are* here without a bodyguard."

More scoffing sounds. "Because *you're* my bodyguard."

"We'll be spending a lot of time together, anyway. Isn't that what the best man and the maid of honor usually do?"

She blew out a hard breath and slumped her shoulders. "You're not going to cheer me up, Walker. Stop trying."

"Have it your way."

She said nothing. For about five minutes.

Then she shook her head. "I don't know..."

So far, she'd jumped his ass every time he tried to cheer her up, so he considered not trying again. But then, why prolong a stupid fight any longer than necessary? "Okay. I'll bite. You don't know what?"

"About Ryan and Clara getting married. I can't believe it's actually happening—and out of the blue this way. It's weird, seriously weird." His younger brother and her favorite Bravo cousin had surprised everyone just two weeks before with the news that they would tie the knot on the Saturday before Christmas. "I keep wondering what's *really* going on with them, you know?"

So, then. It looked as if she'd finished with the sulking. About time. He hid his grin of satisfaction. And then he thought about Clara and Ryan and he was frowning, too. "Yeah. Rye's been pretty cagey about the whole thing." Walker's brother had been claiming he was in love with Clara since high school. And Rye had proposed more than once in the past nine or ten years. Clara kept turning him down, saying how she loved him and always would, but not in *that* way.

"What changed all of a sudden?" Rory asked, her mind evidently moving on the same track as his. "And do you really think Ryan's ready to settle down?" Rye always claimed he loved Clara, but he hadn't exactly waited around, pining for a chance with her. He liked women and they liked him. The girlfriends never lasted long—a month, maybe two, and Ryan's latest ladylove would move on. A few more weeks would go by and he would turn up with someone new on his arm.

Walker said, "I don't know what changed. And I'm with you. I *hope* he's ready."

"It's just…not *like* Clara to suddenly decide Ryan's the guy for her after all these years of saying he's not. On the phone, she told me she was wrong before, that she really loves him and she knows they'll be happy together."

"She told me the same thing. She said she finally got smart and decided to marry her best friend."

Rory scrunched up her nose. "Well, I can see that. I guess…" And then she shook her head again. "No. I don't get it. If I can find the right moment, I'm going to try to talk to her some more, try to find out if she's sure about this."

"Better talk fast. It's two weeks until the wedding."

She dropped her head back and stared at the headliner. "Ugh. You're right. I don't want to make that kind of trouble. Ryan's always wanted to marry her, so no big surprise there. And Clara's no flake. She's strong and steady. If she's doing this, it must be what she wants."

They were climbing up into the mountains, the highway twisting through rocky moraine, pine-covered slopes rising to either side. Here and there, wide patches of snow from last week's storm caught the sunlight and sparkled like sequins on a pretty girl's white party dress.

"You want to stop at Clara's?" he asked as they began to descend into the Justice Creek Valley.

"It's after four." The sun had already slipped behind the mountains. "It'll be dark soon. Let's just go on to the ranch. I'll see her in the morning."

Rory admired the view as they approached the Bar-N. Nestled in its own beautiful, rolling valley with mountains all around, the Bar-N had been a working cattle ranch for five generations. The *N* stood for Noonan, which was Walker's mother's maiden name. The place had come down to Walker and Ryan from their mother, Darla, and their uncle, John Noonan. Four years ago, Ryan had sold his interest to Walker and moved into town.

Walker still kept a few horses, but the cattle were long gone. Nowadays, the Bar-N was a guest ranch. The homestead, in the center of the pretty little valley, contained a circle of well-maintained structures. Over the past couple of decades, Walker and his uncle before him had built five cozy cabins. There were also four full-size houses. The houses, constructed over the generations, had once served as homes for various members of the Noonan clan. Walker offered two of the houses, the cabins and the fully outfitted bunkhouse as vacation rentals.

Of weathered wood and natural stone, the main house had a wide front porch. Walker's German shorthaired pointer, Lonesome, and his black cat, Lucky Lady, were waiting for them when they arrived.

Rory laughed just at the sight of them. They were so cute, sitting patiently at the top of the steps, side by side. When Walker got out, the dog came running and the big black cat followed at a more sedate pace. He greeted them both with a gentle word and a quick touch of his hand. Then he started unloading her things.

Rory grabbed her tote and went to help, taking a suitcase in her free hand and following him into the house and up the stairs. He led her to a room in front. She hesitated on the threshold.

He set down the suitcases on the rag rug and turned to her. Rory met his eyes—and felt suddenly awkward and completely tongue-tied. Bizarre. She was *never* tongue-tied.

"There are hangers in the closet and I emptied out the bureau," he said. "I'll just get that last big bag for you." He eased around her and headed back toward the stairs again.

Once he was out of sight, Rory entered the room that would be hers for the next two weeks. It had a big window on the front-facing wall and a smaller one on the side wall. There was a nice, queen-size bed with a patchwork quilt, a heavy bureau of dark wood, a small closet and a bathroom.

The bathroom had two doors.

She opened the outer door and found herself staring across a short section of hallway into another bedroom, a small one with a bow window overlooking the backyard. Not Walker's room, she was reasonably sure.

Curiosity had its hooks in her. She zipped across the hall to have a quick look around that other room.

Definitely not Walker's. Walker liked things simple and spare—but this room was *too* spare, too tidy. Not a single item on the dresser or the nightstand that could be called personal.

She went back to the bathroom and stood frowning at her reflection in the mirror over the sink. Seven years of knowing Walker and this was the first time she'd been upstairs in his house. She wondered if this might be the only upstairs bath.

Would she and Walker be sharing? That could get awkward—well, for *her*, anyway. If Walker saw her naked, he'd probably just pat her on the head and tell her to get dressed before she caught a chill.

The front door opened downstairs. Rory shut the

outer door, ducked back into her bedroom and got busy putting her things away.

Walker appeared in the doorway to the hall. "Alva left dinner, so that's handled." The Colgins, Alva and her husband, Bud, helped out around the ranch and lived in the house directly across the front yard from Walker's. He rolled in the last bag. "Where do you want this?"

"Just leave it—anywhere's fine." Was she blushing? Her face felt a little too warm. Would he guess that she'd been snooping?

If he guessed, he didn't call her on it. "Hungry?"

"Starved. I'll finish unpacking and be right down."

He left and Rory continued putting stuff in drawers—until she heard his boots moving across the floor below. Then she shut the door to the hallway and zipped back into the bathroom.

She opened the medicine cabinet and the cabinet under the sink. There were the usual towels and washcloths. Also, bandage strips and a tube of antibacterial ointment, a bottle of aspirin long past its use-by date and a half-empty box of tampons.

Tampons left there by a girlfriend?

Walker with a girlfriend…

He didn't *have* girlfriends. Or rather, if he did, Rory had never met any of them.

He did have an ex-wife, Denise. Denise LeClair was tall, blonde and smoking hot—and long gone from Justice Creek.

Denise had moved to Colorado from Miami six years ago. She'd met Walker and it had been one of those thunderbolt moments for both of them. Or so everyone said. According to Rory's cousin Clara, Walker's ex-wife had sworn that she loved him madly and she only wanted to live her life at his side right there at the Bar-N.

One Rocky Mountain winter had obliterated that particular fantasy. They'd been married less than a year when Denise filed for divorce and headed back home to the Sunshine State, leaving Walker stunned at first, and later grim and grumpy.

Rory had actually met Denise only once, a few months after the wedding—and hated her on sight. And not because Denise was necessarily such an awful person…

Yes. All right. The embarrassing truth was that Rory had crushed on Walker from the first time she'd met him, seven years before. Even way back then, when she barely knew the guy, Rory'd had kind of a thing for him.

But it had never gone anywhere and it never would. There were issues, the debacle of Denise among them. True, they were all issues that could be overcome, if only Walker wanted to overcome them. But he didn't. And Rory accepted that.

Walker was her very good friend. End of story.

He seemed to have more or less got over Denise in the past couple of years. But there hadn't been anyone else for him since his marriage. He claimed that there never would be, that he was like his uncle John, a solitary type of man.

Rory stepped back and stared into the wide-open cabinets. Linens, bandage strips, ointment, aspirin. And the tampons. And four still-wrapped bars of plain soap. No men's toiletries.

So, then. Walker had his own bathroom. Mystery solved.

Rory sank to the edge of the tub. She felt like a balloon with all of the air let out, droopy with disappointment that she and Walker didn't have to share.

Bad. This was bad. She was long over that crush she used to have on him. Long past dreaming up possible situations where she might see him naked. She needed to pull it together.

For two weeks, she would be living here. Walker would provide the security her mother insisted she have. Nothing would happen between them. She would get through the days until the wedding without making a fool of herself. And then she would return to Montedoro and get on with her life.

Because she and Walker were friends. *Friends.* And nothing more. They were friends and she liked it that way.

She jumped to her feet and glared at herself in the mirror to punctuate the point.

And she ignored the tiny voice in her heart that said she did care, she'd *always* cared—and that was never going to change.

Chapter Two

"It's a little strange," Rory said when they sat at the table in the big farm-style kitchen, eating Alva Colgin's excellent elk stew with piping hot drop biscuits, which Walker had whipped up on the spot. "Staying here, in your house..."

He sipped his beer, the light from the mission-style fixture overhead bringing out auburn lights in his brown hair. "You have complaints?"

She split a biscuit in half. Steam curled up from the center. Those blue eyes of his were trained on her. She thought he seemed a little wary. "Relax," she told him. "No complaints. And I know I was a bitch before. Sorry. Over it."

He set down his beer. "Weird, how?"

"It's just not what we do, that's all." She'd always stayed at the Haltersham, Justice Creek's famous, supposedly haunted luxury hotel built by a local industrialist at the turn of the last century. "You know how we are..."

"How's that?" He forked up a bite of stew and arched an eyebrow at her.

Annoyance jabbed at her. Seriously? He didn't know how they were? With a great show of patience, she explained the obvious. "Well, we meet up at Ryan's bar." His brother owned and ran McKellan's, a popular neighborhood-style pub in town on Marmot Drive. "Or we hang out at Clara's house. Or we head up into the mountains." They both enjoyed hiking, camping and fishing. So did Clara and Ryan. The four of them had camped out together several times—just four good friends, nothing romantic going on. But now Clara and Ryan were getting married. And Rory was sleeping in Walker's house. "I've been here at the ranch maybe six times total in all the years we've known each other—and tonight is the first time I've seen the upstairs. Wouldn't you say that's a little bit weird?"

He was looking at her strangely. "You really don't want to stay here. That's what you're saying, right? That's why you've been so pissed off about having me handle your security."

Wonderful. Now she'd succeeded in making everything weirder. She set down half of the biscuit and picked up her butter knife. "No, Walker. That's not what I'm saying."

"It's not what you're used to, is it? Too far out in the sticks, no room service, iffy internet access."

"Not true. Wrong. It's beautiful here. And very comfortable. I promise you, I'm not complaining."

He went on as though she hadn't spoken. "I admit it's just easier for me, if you stay here at the ranch rather than the hotel. But if you want, we can—"

"Will you stop?"

"I want to work this out."

"There's nothing *to* work out. I just said it was a little weird, that's all. I was only…making conversation."

"Making conversation." His mouth had a grim set.

"Yes. I talk. You answer. I answer you back. Conversation. Ring a bell?"

He set down his fork. It made a sharp sound against the side of his plate. "Something is really bugging you. What?"

"Nothing," she baldly lied. "There's nothing."

But of course, there was.

It was the two doors to the bathroom. Because of those two doors, she'd thought about seeing him naked and that was not the kind of thing a girl was supposed to be thinking about her very good friend.

For years, they'd had everything worked out between them—for him, everything was *still* worked out.

But for her, well…he kind of had it right, though she would never admit it no matter how hard he pushed. She didn't really want to stay here—and not because it wasn't a luxury hotel.

Uh-uh. There was just something about staying in his house, something about having him as her bodyguard, something about Ryan and Clara suddenly getting married, something about everything changing from how it had always been. It had her mind going places it shouldn't go.

It had her heart aching for what it was never going to get.

He sat back in his chair, tipped his head sideways and studied her with a look that set her nerves on edge. "Whatever it is, you need to go ahead and tell me."

She played dumb. Because no way was she having the *I want to jump your bones, but hey, I get that you're just not that into me* conversation. Not tonight. Not ever again. "What *are* you talking about?"

"You *know* what I'm talking about."

Yes, she did. So what now? Truth or lie?

Lie, definitely. "No, really. There's nothing." She faked a yawn and hid it behind her hand.

He fell for it. "Tired?"

She lied some more. "Exhausted. It's—what? One in the morning in Montedoro. I'm just going to finish this amazing stew and go on up to my room..."

"You sure you're okay?"

"I am. Really. Just a little tired is all."

And that was it. He let it go.

After the meal, she helped him straighten up the kitchen. Then she went upstairs, had a nice bath and called Clara's house. Clara wasn't there, so Rory left a message saying she'd arrived safely after an uneventful flight and would see her in the morning for the final fittings. They were all—bride and bridesmaids—meeting at Wedding Belles Bridal on Central Street at ten.

Rory hung up and climbed into bed. She was certain she would lie there wide-awake for hours stewing over her inappropriate interest in her very good friend Walker. But she turned out the light and snuggled under that old quilt and smiled because the pillowcase smelled like starch and sunshine.

And the next thing she knew, thin winter sunlight was peeking between the white cotton curtains. She sat up and stretched and realized she felt great. Lucky Lady sat at the end of the bed, lazily licking her paw.

Rory beamed at the big black cat. All those weird emotional knots she'd tied herself up in the night before? Untied.

Honestly, if she still had a little bit of a crush on Walker, so what? She didn't have to get all eaten up over it. It just wasn't that big a deal.

* * *

Walker drove her into town. He found a parking space right on Central Street in front of Wedding Belles, under a streetlamp all done up for the holidays with an evergreen wreath covered in bright colored Christmas ornaments and crowned with a red bow.

Rory unhooked her seat belt. "I'll call you when we leave the shop."

He didn't fall for it. "I'll see you inside." He went to feed the meter.

Still hoping that maybe he'd give up and go hang with Ryan or something for a while, Rory entered the shop.

Wedding Belles was everything the name implied. Big, beautiful dresses in a delicious rainbow of colors hung on racks along the walls. More dresses tempted the buyer from freestanding displays. It was a truly girlie kind of place, and the final fitting was just supposed to be Clara and her attendants.

Best man not included.

Walker came in anyway. He assumed the bodyguard position, out of the way, near the door.

Clara was already there. She stood in the center of the shop, all in white, on a round white fitting platform in front of a silver-trimmed cheval mirror, her brown hair loose on her shoulders. She had her head tipped down at first, a pensive expression on her pretty face. Her dress was a gorgeous thing, with a layered organza skirt, three-quarter length lace sleeves and a fitted lace-and-beadwork bodice. Clara looked adorable in it. Another woman, probably the shop's owner, was busy fussing with the layers of fluffy organza hem.

As always, Rory had a camera with her. She whipped it out and snapped a few quick shots of the bride, who seemed lost in a world of her own, and the seamstress kneeling at her feet.

Clara looked up, her faraway expression vanishing as if it had never been. She beamed and held out her arms. "Rory!" The other woman stepped aside so Clara could hike up those acres of skirt and jump down from the platform for a hello hug.

Rory stuck her camera back in her tote and ran over to wrap her arms around her favorite cousin, who smelled of a light, flowery perfume—with just a hint of coffee and pancakes. Clara must have been at her restaurant, the Library Café, already that morning. "God," Rory said. "It's so good to see you." They grinned at each other.

Clara kissed her on the cheek and jumped back up on the platform. "This is Millie. She owns the place. Millie, my cousin Rory."

"Hey," said Rory. "We've met. Sort of." She'd talked to Millie on the phone a couple of times, giving the shopkeeper her size and measurements so her dress could be made up and ready for today.

The woman dipped a knee in a fair approximation of a curtsy. "Your Highness. I've been looking forward to meeting you in person. It's an honor."

Clara laughed. "Just call her Rory. She gets cranky when people treat her like a princess."

Millie gave Rory a questioning look.

And Rory said, "That's right. Just Rory."

"Fair enough. Rory." The shop owner straightened her pincushion bracelet and knelt again at Clara's hem.

Clara was watching Walker, who remained by the door. "I hate to break it to you, Walker. But this is a no-groomsmen-allowed kind of thing we're doing here."

He shrugged—and didn't budge. "You look beautiful, Clara. My brother's a lucky man."

"Thanks. You can go."

"Sorry. Can't do that. Pretend I'm not here." He stared out the window—on the lookout for kidnappers, no doubt.

Clara muttered to Rory, "What is going on with him?"

Rory grumbled, "My mother hired him to be my bodyguard for this trip."

Clara blinked. "No kidding."

Rory shook her head. "And as you can see, so far, he's taking his new job very seriously."

"I guess I should have noticed that you're minus security."

"Oh, but I'm not. I've got security. And his name is Walker. I'm staying out at the Bar-N, so he can protect me even when I'm sleeping." She gestured grandly toward the man in question. "Wherever I go, Walker goes."

"Hmm." Clara's green eyes gleamed and she pitched her voice even lower. "This could get interesting..."

"Don't even go there," Rory threatened. Clara knew too much. She was Rory's favorite cousin, after all. And a couple of times over the years Rory had just happened to mention that she had a sort of a thing for Walker. She really wished she'd kept her mouth shut—but both times there had been wine involved, and girls will be girls.

Clara flashed her a way-too-innocent smile. "Don't go *where*, exactly?"

Right then, the little bell over the door chimed, distracting Clara, so that Rory didn't have to answer any more of her annoying Walker-related questions. Elise Bravo and Tracy Winham breezed in.

Elise was Clara's sister and Tracy might as well have

been. When Tracy's parents died fifteen years ago, Elise and Clara's mother, Sondra, took Tracy into the family and raised her as a daughter. Together, Tracy and Elise owned Bravo Catering. The two were not only in the wedding party, they were handling the reception and providing all the food. They waved at Walker and hurried over to grab Rory in hugs of welcome.

The first thing out of Elise's mouth after "How are you?" was "Is there some reason Walker's lurking by the door?"

And Rory got to explain all over again about the bodyguard situation.

Then Joanna Bravo, Clara and Elise's half sister, arrived. Things started getting a little frosty about then.

Joanna hugged Rory, kissed Clara on the cheek and then said crisply, "Elise. Tracy." She gave them each a quick nod that seemed more a dismissal than a greeting.

And Elise said, "Clara, we really need to revisit the issue of the reception centerpieces."

Joanna, whom they all called Jody, spoke right up. "No, we don't."

Tracy popped in with, "Yes, we do."

Clara said softly, "Come on. We've been through this. Let's not go there again."

That shut the argument down momentarily.

But Rory knew they would definitely be going there again. If it hadn't been about the flowers, it would have been something else, because the Justice Creek Bravos shared a convoluted history.

Clara's father, Franklin Bravo, had raised two families at the same time: one with his heiress wife, Sondra Oldfield Bravo, and a second with his mistress, Willow

Mooney. All nine of his children—four by Sondra, five by Willow—had the last name Bravo.

When Sondra died, ten years ago, Frank Bravo had mourned at her funeral. And then, the next day, he'd married Willow and moved her and her two youngest children, Jody and Nell, into the family mansion, where Elise and Tracy still lived. Three years ago, Frank had died of a stroke. By then, there was only Willow, living alone in the big house that Frank had built with Oldfield money when he first made Sondra his bride.

Frank's five sons and four daughters by two different mothers were all adults now, all out on their own. Clara had told Rory more than once that they'd given up their childhood jealousies and resentments. Clara always saw the best in people and tried to think positive.

But maybe she should have thought twice before hiring Jody to do the flowers for the wedding—and Tracy and Elise to cater it.

As the caterers, Tracy and Elise thought *they* should be in charge of the reception flowers and should be answerable only to the bride. "We just want to be free to coordinate the look of your reception without having to check with Jody every minute and a half," groused Elise.

"We've already settled this." Jody pinched up her mouth and aimed her chin high. "*I'm* doing the flowers. *All* the flowers. It's as simple as that. And *I* will make sure that you get exactly what you want, Clara."

Rory moved around the edges of the room, snapping a bunch of pictures of them as they argued, feeling grateful for her camera, which gave her something to do so she could pretend to ignore the building animosity.

Tracy started in, "But the reception *needs* a consistent design. Elise and I really should be freed up to give that to you."

Clara pleaded, "Come on, guys. You all need to work together. Jody's doing the flowers. We've talked about this before and we've all discussed what I'm after." She glanced from a frowning Tracy to an unhappy Elise to a smug Joanna. "Jody will come up with something that works with your table design. I know it's all going to be just what I've hoped for."

Elise opened her mouth to give Clara more grief. But before she could get rolling, Nell Bravo, Willow's youngest, arrived.

Nell was one of those women who cause accidents just by walking down the street. She looked like a cross between the sultry singer Lana Del Rey and a Victoria's Secret model. Her long auburn hair was wonderfully windblown, her full lips painted fire-engine red and her enormous dark green eyes low and lazy. She wore a hot-pink angora sweater. Black leggings hugged her endless, shapely legs. The leggings ended in a pair of Carvela Scorpion biker boots.

Instead of harping at Clara again, Elise turned to the newcomer. "Nell. How nice that you finally decided to join us."

Nell's pillowy red upper lip twitched in a lazy sneer. "Don't start, Elise. I'm not putting up with your crap this morning." Nell glanced Rory's way and actually smiled. "Rory. Hey."

Rory peeled her camera off her face long enough to give Nell a hug. "Good to see you."

"Nellie, you look half-awake," Tracy remarked in full snark mode. "Have you been taking advantage of our permissive marijuana laws again?"

Nell smoothed her gorgeous hair with one languid stroke of her red-nailed hand. "It's a thought. I really should do *something* to relax when I know I'm going to have to put up with you and your evil twin here."

Elise sniffed. "Don't let her bother you, Trace. She was just born rude—and then badly brought up."

Nell covered a yawn. "Better rude and runnin' wild than the biggest bee-yatch in town."

Tracy and Elise gasped in outraged unison.

Rory had stopped taking pictures. Her gaze tracked toward the door and collided with Walker's. He was looking as worried as she felt. Elise and Tracy had been ganging up on Nell for as long as Rory could remember. And Nell had no trouble at all fighting back. The only question now was, how far would they go today? When they were teenagers, according to more than one source, the three of them used to go at it no-holds-barred, with lots of slapping and hair-pulling.

Poor Clara had begun to look frazzled. She patted the air with both hands. "Seriously, everyone. Could we all just take a deep breath—and will you put on the dresses so Millie can pin the hems and mark up any final alterations?"

Nell purposely turned her back on Tracy and Elise—and they did the same to her. Rory breathed a small sigh of relief. Nell said, "Millie, do I smell coffee? I would kill for a cup."

"Help yourself," said Millie. She had a table set up in the corner with a silver coffee service, cups, cream, sugar, everything—including a plate of tempting-looking muffins from the baker across the street.

"I love you," Nell told Millie in her husky bedroom voice as she filled one of the cups. Jody, who hadn't said a word since Nell entered the shop, had already poured herself a cup and taken a seat near the wall.

Clara tried again, "Put on your dresses, everyone, please. Millie's hung them in the dressing rooms." Millie had three dressing rooms. Clara pointed at the center one. "Rory, you're in there with me. Elise and Tracy on the left. Jody and Nell to the right." Assigning the dressing rooms was a smart move on Clara's part. It was one thing to try to pretend that her battling sisters had no issues with each other. But God knew what might happen if Nell ended up alone in a confined space with Tracy or Elise.

They went to their assigned rooms and put on their bridesmaids dresses, which were each a different style, but all floor-length and in a vivid eggplant-colored satin. Then they drank coffee and nibbled on muffins while taking turns getting up on the platform so that Millie could pin up the final alterations.

The process took until a little past noon. A few sharp remarks were tossed around. But on the whole, they all managed to behave themselves. By the end, Clara almost seemed relaxed.

After the fitting, Clara had lunch reservations for all of them at the Sylvan Inn. Everybody loved to eat at the inn. They had fabulous hammer steaks and wonderful crispy fried trout. The inn was a few minutes' drive southwest of town. Tracy and Elise said they would go together. Clara offered to drive everyone else.

Rory made a stab at getting Walker to allow her to go to lunch on her own.

He said, "Let Jody and Nell go together. I'll drive you and Clara. That way, if Jody or Nell gets into it with Elise and Tracy, there are viable escape options."

"Walker. You make it sound like a battle plan."

He grunted. "Because it is. More or less."

She wanted to argue that everything would be fine and he really didn't have to keep her in sight every minute of every day. But actually, knowing the Bravo sisters, it might *not* all be fine. And he seemed so determined to watch over her. It really was kind of sweet that he took the job of providing her security so seriously.

So she went back to her cousins and shared Walker's suggestion as to who should ride with whom—minus the part about battle plans and escape options. They all agreed Walker's way would be fine.

In Walker's SUV, Rory sat in the front seat next to him and Clara hopped in back. Once they were on the way, Clara said she wanted him to join them for lunch when they got to the inn.

He laughed. He really did have the greatest laugh, all deep and rough and sincere at the same time. "You'd probably make me sit between Nell and Elise."

And Rory kidded, "Well, you might as well make yourself useful. You can play referee."

"Not a chance. I'll just stay out of the way. You won't even know I'm there."

"Of course we'll know." Clara reached over the seat and poked at his shoulder.

Rory tried, "And it doesn't seem right for you not even to get some lunch in this deal."

But he just wouldn't go for it. "I'll get something later. Don't worry about me."

So she and Clara let it be.

At the inn, Walker had a private word with the hostess—no doubt to explain why he would be lurking and not eating. Then he took up a position near a window painted with a snowy Christmas scene. The spot was out of the way of the waiters and busmen, but with a clear line of sight to the table where Rory sat with her cousins. By then, they all knew that Walker was her stand-in bodyguard. Nell teased her about it and they both laughed.

Christmas favorites played softly in the background, and Clara had a bottle of champagne waiting on ice for them. It was nice. Festive. They each took a glass of bubbly, and Clara made a sweet little toast. She took a tiny sip and set the flute down and never touched it again. They ordered.

At first, it all seemed to go pretty well. At least everyone was civil. But then, shortly after the waitress brought their food, Tracy started in again about how she and Elise ought to be doing the reception flowers.

Jody said, "Oh, come on, Tracy. Give it up, already. It's been decided."

Elise scoffed, "That's what *you* think."

And then Nell said to no one in particular, "Because some people just can't stand not getting *everything* their way *all* of the time."

Tracy snapped, "Stay out of it, Nell. This has nothing to do with you."

"Come on, guys," Clara piped up hopefully. "Let it go. Let's have a nice lunch as a family. Please."

"Yeah, Clara." Nell mimed an eye roll so big, she almost fell over sideways. "Good luck with that."

"I'm not kidding," Elise muttered under her breath. "So freaking *rude*."

To which Nell replied with saccharine sweetness, "And what about you, Leesie? You're just a big ole plate of harpy with an extra-large helping of shrew on the side."

Elise glowered, teeth clenched. "Why you little—"

Clara cut her off. "Stop. This. Now." She sent a furious glare around the table. Clara never lost her temper, so to see her about ready to start kicking some sisterly butt shocked the rest of them so much they all fell silent.

Walker left his position by the window and started toward them, ready to intervene. Rory met his eyes and shook her head. There was nothing for him to do in this situation. Nothing for either of them to do, really.

He took her hint and went back to his observation point at the window.

And Clara's angry outburst actually seemed to have worked. They'd all picked up their forks and started eating again. Everyone but Clara. She sat there with her hands in her lap, sweat on her brow, her cheeks and lips much too pale.

Rory leaned close to her. "Are you all right?"

Clara gulped and nodded. "Fine, yes. Just fine…"

Clearly a complete lie. But Rory let it go. She feared that keeping after her might push her over whatever edge she seemed to be teetering on.

So they ate, mostly in silence. It was pretty awful. So bad that no one wanted anything off the famous Sylvan Inn dessert cart when the waitress wheeled it over. Tracy and Elise were the first to say they had to get going. They thanked Clara and left. Jody and Nell followed about two minutes later.

As soon as her two half sisters disappeared down the short hallway to the door, Clara shoved back her chair and leaped to her feet. "Be right back," she squeaked.

And then she clapped her hand over her mouth and sprinted toward the alcove that led to the restrooms.

For a moment, Rory just sat there gaping after her. Normally, Clara was hard to rattle. She took things in stride.

But she was certainly rattled now. And obviously about to toss what little she'd eaten of her hammer steak and cheesy potatoes.

Rory jumped up and went after her.

In the ladies' room, she found poor Clara bending over one of the toilets, the stall door left open in her rush to make it in time. She was already heaving.

"Oh, darling…" Rory edged into the best-friend position, gathering Clara's hair in her hands and holding it out of the way as everything came up.

Clara was still gagging, Rory rubbing her back and making soothing noises, when the outer door burst open. "Rory?" It was Walker.

Between heaves, Clara shouted, "Walker, out!"

Rory locked eyes with him. "I'm fine. Go."

"I'll be right out here if you—"

"Walker, go!" Clara choked out. He backed away.

"And don't let anyone in here," Rory added.

"Uh. Sure," he said, ducking out, the door shutting after him.

"It's all right, all right," Rory reassured Clara gently. "He's gone. It's just us…"

Clara heaved a couple more times and then stayed bent over the bowl, breathing carefully as they waited to see if there would be more.

Finally, Clara let out a slow, tired sigh. "I think that's it."

Rory hit the flush. They backed from the stall and

turned to the big mirror over the two sinks. Clara rinsed her mouth and her face. Rory was ready with the paper towels. Clara took them and blotted her cheeks. They'd left their purses at the table, so Clara smoothed her hair as best she could.

And then they ended up just standing there, staring into each other's eyes in the mirror.

Finally, Rory asked in a whisper, "Clara, what is going on?"

And Clara gave a tiny, sad little shrug. "I'm pregnant. Four months along."

Rory choked. "No…"

"Yeah."

"Shut the fridge door." Rory had already kind of figured it out. But it was still a surprise to hear Clara say it.

A weary little chuckle escaped Clara. "I haven't had morning sickness in a month. But today was too much." She pressed her hand against her belly, which was maybe slightly rounded, but only if you stared really hard. And even then, maybe not. "I might have to kill my sisters—all three of them. And Tracy, too."

Rory was still trying to get her mind around this startling bit of information. Clara. Pregnant. "So you actually had sex with Ryan?" The words just popped from her mouth of their own accord. She really hadn't meant to say them out loud. Clara winced and then looked stricken. And Rory felt so bad she started backpedaling like mad. "Well, I mean it's only that you always said you didn't see Ryan *that* way—but then, hey, what the hell?" She bopped her own forehead with the heel of her hand. "I mean, nobody can deny Ryan is hot. And you two *are* getting married, right? I mean, there's nothing to be surprised about, because even if there hadn't been a baby involved, you two would have had sex or be planning to have it. Because, well, sex *is* one of those things married people tend to do and—"

"Rory," Clara cut in softly.

Rory gulped. "Uh. Yeah?"

"You're just making it worse."

Rory let out a small whimper. "You're right. I am."

"Come here." Clara wrapped her arm around Rory's shoulders and drew her closer. Rory slid her hand around Clara's waist. They bent their heads to the side until they touched and they stared at each other in the mirror some more, both of them looking a little bit shell-shocked.

Finally, Rory said, "Four months? Seriously? You don't even look pregnant."

"I know." Clara did the pregnant-lady move, lovingly pressing her palm to her belly for the second time. "Not showing yet. I'll probably be like my mother. She once told me she would go for six months with nobody knowing. And then, all of a sudden…" Clara stretched her arm out in front of her. "Pop. Out to here. Like from one day to the next."

"God, Clara. Four *months*? Since August?"

Clara dropped her hand from Rory's shoulder, eased away and dampened a paper towel under the faucet. "Well, I didn't *know* until about five weeks later when I took the first test."

Rory couldn't help looking at her reproachfully. "You should have called me. You should have told me. I mean, who *have* you told?"

Clara blotted her flushed face with the wet towel. "Ryan."

"Only Ryan?"

Clara tossed the wet towel in the trash. "And he has

been wonderful. Right there for me, you know? Best friend a girl could have."

Best friend. Clara still talked about Ryan as a friend, a best buddy. She just didn't sound like a woman in love.

Rory turned so she was face-to-face with Clara and took her firmly by the shoulders. "Is everything all right, with you and Ryan?"

"Of course. It's wonderful. Couldn't be better."

"And the baby?"

Clara sighed. "No worries. Truly. The baby's fine. I've been to the doctor. Clean bill of health."

"Oh, my darling..." Rory gathered her close. Clara let out a little whimper and grabbed on. Tight. Rory murmured, "I'm here—you know that..." She rubbed Clara's back and stared at the row of toilet stalls without really seeing them.

Until she happened to catch a flicker of movement from the corner of her eye. One of the stall doors was closed. And the movement had occurred in that tiny sliver of space between the door and frame.

Rory paid attention then, her gaze tracking lower, to the opening between the bottom of the door and the black-and-white tile floor. No shoes or legs showing.

But then, there it was again: a shadow moving between the frame and the door.

Someone was standing on the stool, listening in.

Chapter Three

Rory let go of Clara and put a finger to her lips. Clara frowned at her, confused. So Rory turned her around and pointed at the stall.

Clara asked miserably, “Really?”

“Yeah. I think so.”

“Wonderful.” Clara marched right over there and tapped on the door. “Come on out. We know you’re in there.”

Below the door, a pair of black Dansko duty shoes and two black trouser legs lowered into sight.

The door swung inward. Rory recognized the face: one of the Sylvan Inn waitresses, though not the one who’d waited on their table.

Clara knew her. “Monique Hightower. What a surprise.” And not in a good way, considering Clara’s bleak tone. She said to Rory, “Monique and I went to Justice Creek High together.”

The waitress gave a sheepish giggle. “Hey, Clara.”

Clara didn’t smile. “How much did you hear?”

“Um, nothing?” Monique suggested hopefully.

“Liar.”

Monique giggled some more. “Well, all right. Everything. But I swear to you, Clara. I would never say a word about your private business to anyone.”

* * *

Walker stood in the parking lot, waiting, watching Clara and Rory, who whispered to each other about fifteen feet away.

After whatever had gone down in the ladies' room, Clara had settled up in the restaurant, and then Rory had asked him to give her and Clara a few more minutes alone. So there they stood, the two of them, between his SUV and a red pickup, both wrapped in heavy coats, their heads bent close together, their noses red from the cold winter air, talking a mile a minute, both of them intense, serious as hell.

Something very weird was going on. He wasn't sure he wanted to know what.

Finally, Rory hugged Clara and then raised her hand to signal him over. They all got in the SUV. He started the engine, turned the heater up and pulled out of the parking space.

Clara asked, "Can you let me out at the café?"

"Will do."

Neither of the women said a word during the short drive into town.

When Walker pulled to a stop in front of Clara's restaurant, she said, "Thanks, Walker. See you both tonight. Seven?" She'd invited him, Rory and Rye over for dinner, just like old times. Kind of.

"We'll be there," Rory promised.

"See you then," said Walker.

Clara got out, pushed the door shut and turned for the café.

He'd figured Rory would tell him what was going on as soon as they were alone.

But all she said was "I'll bet you're starving. Do you want to go in and get something to eat?"

"Naw. I'll get something at home." He headed for the Bar-N. Rory stared out the window, apparently lost in thought, through the whole drive.

At the ranch, she went straight upstairs to her room. He was kind of hungry, so he heated up some of last night's stew and ate it standing by the sink, staring out at the snow-covered mountains that rimmed the little valley where he'd lived all his life. He'd just put his bowl in the dishwasher when Rory appeared dressed in jeans and knee-high rawhide boots, carrying a camera as usual.

He asked, "What now?"

"I've never had a chance to get many pictures around the ranch. I'd like to take some shots of the horses and of the other houses and the cabins—and you don't have to go with me."

"I'll just get my hat and coat."

"Oh, come on. Take a break."

"I can't do that, ma'am." He laid on the cowboy drawl. "I take my bodyguardin' seriously—and do you really want me to keep that money your mother sent?"

"Of course I do."

"Then don't you think you'd better let me do the job?"

So they put on their winter gear and he followed her out. It was no hardship really, watching Rory. She was easy on the eyes, with that shining, thick sable hair and those pink cheeks and that look of interest she always wore. Rory found the everyday world completely fascinating. He watched her snap pictures of everything from a weathered porch rail to an old piece of harness someone had left on a fence post.

He thought about how she sometimes resented the

way being a princess hemmed her in, but even she would have to admit that her background had helped her in a highly competitive field. Because of who she was, she had a higher profile and an intriguing byline. Add that to her talent and drive: success. Her pictures had already appeared in *National Geographic* and a number of other nature, gardening and outdoor magazines.

The horses were waiting for them by the fence when they reached the corral. She took pictures of him petting them and feeding them some wrinkled apples he'd brought out from the house. They went into the stables. He mucked the main floor while she got more pictures. And then she put her camera in its case, hung it from a peg, picked up the other broom and worked alongside him.

She knew how to muck out a floor. One of her sisters was a world-famous horse breeder and Rory had grown up around horses.

They returned to the house at quarter after five to clean up. He was feeding Lucky and Lonesome when she came down at six-thirty, looking good in tight black jeans, tall black boots and a thick black sweater patterned across the top with white snowflakes.

On the way to Clara's, he couldn't resist asking, "So are you ever going to tell me what went on at the restaurant?"

She sent him a look—as if she was trying to figure out what he was talking about. Right.

He elaborated, "You remember. When Clara bolted to the ladies' room and chucked up her lunch and then yelled at me to get out and then you said not to let anyone in? And then eventually you two came out with Monique Hightower, who must have been in there with you the whole time? Yeah. That's what I'm talking about."

She coughed into her hand, a stall so obvious a toddler would have seen through it. "Clara got sick."

"Yeah. I figured that part out all by myself."

"I think it might have been the cheesy potatoes."

He sent her a speaking glance. One that said, *Give me a break*. "So, all right. You're not going to tell me."

She winced and slunk down in her seat a few inches and didn't even bother to try to deny that she'd lied.

He said, "You should know I'll find out eventually—whatever the hell it is."

Rory puffed out her cheeks with a hard breath. "I just don't know what to tell you."

"Clara swore you to secrecy, huh? Good luck with that. Because if Monique knows, everybody's going to know. Gossip is her life. She's been that way at least since high school."

"Yes. Well, Clara mentioned that—about Monique. But still. I don't know what to tell you. I mean—it's Clara's business, that's all." She sent him another pained glance. He took pity on her and left it at that.

For now, anyway.

Clara's house was around the block from her café, a sweet blue Victorian with maroon trim and a deep front porch. Rye greeted them at the door. He hugged Rory. And when he took Walker's hand and clapped him on the back with brotherly affection, his gaze slid away.

No doubt about it. Something was going on and it was not good.

Rye waited while they hung their coats on the hall tree. Then he led them through the dining room to the kitchen.

Clara stood at the counter tearing lettuce into a salad bowl. She greeted them with a too-broad smile. "Ryan, pour Rory some wine and get your brother a beer. I thought, since it's just us four, that we'd eat right here at the breakfast nook table."

While Clara pulled the meal together, they all stood at the counter, talking about the weather and the wedding, about Clara's out-of-control sisters and Walker's new job as Rory's bodyguard. Then they moved to the breakfast nook and sat down to eat.

On the surface, Walker thought, everything seemed okay. But it wasn't okay. The evening was just…off, somehow. Over the years, the four of them had hung out a lot. They always had a good time. That night should have been the same.

But Rory was too quiet. And both Clara and Ryan seemed tense and distracted. Clara had Rye pour her a glass of wine—and then never touched it. The food was terrific, as always at Clara's. But Clara ate no more than she drank. Maybe she really was sick.

But then why not call off the evening and take it easy?

Midway through the meal, she jumped up, just the way she had at the restaurant that afternoon. With a frantic, "Excuse me," she clapped her hand to her mouth and ran for the central hallway.

Rye and Rory jumped up and went after her.

A minute later, Rye returned by himself. He dropped back into his chair, those brown eyes of his full of worry, his charming smile no longer in evidence.

Walker had had enough. It was just too ridiculous to keep on pretending he hadn't guessed what was going on. "Clara's pregnant, right?"

Rye picked up his beer, knocked back half of it and set it down. "What makes you say that?"

"Damn it, Rye. Don't give me the limp leg on this. She threw up at lunchtime, too. In the restaurant toilet. Rory went in to help out. And whatever she and Rory said while they were in there, Monique Hightower heard, because she was in there with them—hiding in a stall, is my guess. If you were planning on keeping the news a secret, you need a new plan."

Rye swore under his breath—and busted to the truth at last. "We were trying to get through the wedding before we said anything. Clara's got enough to do, dealing with her crazy family and all."

"So she *is* pregnant?"

Ryan fiddled with the label on his beer bottle.

"Answer the question, Rye."

"Yeah." He lifted the beer and drank the rest down. "She's pregnant."

"And that's it…*that's* why you're getting married?"

"Hell, Walker. What kind of crap question is that?"

"Let me rephrase. Is that the *only* reason you're getting married?"

"Of course not."

Walker waited for Rye to say the rest. When Rye just sat there staring at his empty beer bottle, he prompted, "Because you're also in love with her?"

Rye scowled. "That's right and I always have been."

"So you're always saying."

"Because it's the truth—and why are you on my ass all of a sudden?"

It was a good question. Getting all up in Rye's face wasn't the answer to anything. "You're right. Sorry, man.

Just trying to figure out what's going on. I mean, you're stepping up, and that's a damn fine thing."

"What?" Rye bristled. "That surprises you—that I would step up?"

Walker looked him square in the eye. "Not in the least."

"Well, good." Rye settled back in his chair—and then stiffened at the sound of footsteps in the hallway. "They're coming back..."

The two women came in the way they'd gone out—through the great room. Rye got up, went to Clara and wrapped an arm around her shoulders. "You okay?"

She put on a smile and gave him a nod. They all three sat down again and Clara shot a glance at Walker. "Sorry. I've been queasy all day. Must be some minor stomach bug."

Walker just looked at her, steady on.

And Rye said, "It's not flying, Clara. He's figured out about the baby."

Clara drooped in her chair. "Oh, well." She reached back and rubbed her nape. "I have to admit, I'm starting to wonder why I even care who knows."

Walker reassured her. "Don't worry about me. I won't say a word."

And Clara actually laughed. "Yeah, there's Monique for that."

"Are you all right, really?" Walker asked her.

And Rory piped up with, "Do you want to lie down?"

Clara shook her head and picked up her fork. "All of a sudden, I'm starving." She started eating.

And she wasn't kidding about being hungry. They all watched her pack it away.

Rory said, "At least your appetite's back."

And Walker remembered his manners. "Congratulations, both of you."

Clara gave him a weary smile and then held out her hand to Rye. He clasped it, firmly.

After that, Walker started thinking that everything was good between his brother and Clara, that the two of them and the baby would have a great life. Rye got them each another beer and a little more wine for Rory and the conversation flowed. No more weird silences. They all laughed together, just like old times.

Yeah, Walker decided. Everything would be fine.

Rory was too quiet on the way back to the ranch. But it had been a long day with way too much drama. She was probably just beat.

Inside, they hung up their coats. He said good-night and turned for the stairs.

She reached out and pulled him back. "I need to talk to you."

He looked down at her slim fingers wrapped around his arm. She let go instantly, but somehow it seemed to him that he could still feel her woman's touch through the flannel of his sleeve.

Woman's touch? What the…?

He shook it off.

It was just strange, that was all. To be there in his house alone with her at night—and to know that she wouldn't be leaving in an hour or two for her suite at the Haltersham Hotel. That they would both go upstairs to bed. And in the morning, at breakfast, she would be there, at his table.

And wait a minute. Why should that suddenly strike him as strange—not to mention, vaguely dangerous?

But it doesn't, he argued with himself. They were friends and he was looking after her. Nothing strange or dangerous about that.

She asked, "Are things seeming weirder and weirder with Clara and Ryan, or is it just me?"

He didn't really want to talk about Clara and Ryan—not now that he had it all comfortable and straight in his mind. Talking about it would only raise doubts.

No need for those.

But then she tipped her head to the side, her dark hair tumbling down her shoulder. "No response, huh?" Her sweet brown eyes were so sad. "Okay, then." She tried to sound cheerful, with only minimal success. "Never mind. See you in the morning."

He couldn't just leave her standing there. "Hold on." Lonesome was whining at the front door. He went over and opened it. The dog wiggled in, thrilled to see him. He scratched him behind the ears as Lucky came in behind him.

The cat went straight to Rory, and Rory picked her up and buried her face in the silky black fur. She asked, "Well?"

"Come on." He turned for the great room at the back of the house, the dog at his heels. "You want something? Coffee?"

Still holding Lucky, she followed. "No, just to talk."

He stopped by the couch. She put the cat down and dropped to the cushions. He went and turned on the fire, which he'd converted to gas two years before. The cat and the dog both sat by the hearth, side by side. When he went back to her, she'd lifted her right foot to tug off her tall black boot.

"Here," he said. A boot like that was easier for someone else to get off. "Let me."

"Thanks." She stuck out her foot in his direction.

He moved around the end of the coffee table, took the boot by the toe and the heel, eased it right off and handed it to her. She tucked it under the end table and offered the other one. He slid that one off, too. And then he stood there, above her, boot in hand, staring at her socks. They were bright red with little white snowmen on them. Cute. He had the most bizarre urge to bend down and wrap his hand around her ankle, to take off that red snowman sock, to run his palm over the shape of her bare heel, to stroke his hand up the back of her slim, strong calf…

He was losing it. No doubt about it.

"Here." She took the left boot from him, stuck it under the table with the right one and patted the sofa cushion beside her. Apparently, she had no clue as to his sudden burning desire to put his hands on her naked skin.

And that was good. Excellent. He sat down next to her.

She turned toward him and drew her knees up to the side. "There's tension between them—and not the sexy kind. Did you notice?"

Tension between who?

Right. Rye and Clara. And he *had* noticed. "Yeah, but only until Clara finally busted to the truth about the baby. After that, everything seemed just like it used to be."

She flipped a big hank of silky hair back over her shoulder. "Exactly." He thought about reaching out, running his hand down that long swath of dark hair, feeling the texture of it against his palm, maybe bringing it to his face, sucking in the scent of it, rubbing it over his mouth. "Walker?"

He blinked at her, feeling dazed. "Huh?"

Her pretty dark brows had drawn together. "You still with me here?"

"Uh. Yeah. Of course I am. You said things were tense with Clara and Ryan. I said that by the end of the night, it was just like it used to be."

"Walker. Think about it. 'Like it used to be' is that they were friends. *We* were friends, the four of us."

He wasn't following. Her shining hair and soft pink lips weren't helping, either. "Yeah. We were friends. And we still are."

"But I mean, with Clara and Ryan now, shouldn't there be *more*?" She paused, as though waiting for him to speak. He had nothing. She forged on. "I do understand that with a baby coming, marriage might be an option. But is it really the right option for them? Lots of people have babies now without thinking they need a wedding first. I can't help but wonder why the two of them are racing to the altar—and seriously, I…well, I don't know how to say this, but…"

He knew he shouldn't ask. "Say what?"

"Well, frankly, I just can't picture Clara and Ryan having sex."

Through the haze of ridiculous lust that seemed to have taken hold of him, he felt a definite stab of annoyance—with the direction of this uncomfortable conversation in general, and with Rory in particular. "Just because you can't picture it doesn't mean it didn't happen."

"It's only…" She stared off into the fire.

"What?" he demanded.

And she finally turned and looked at him. "I don't *feel* it between them."

"What do you mean? Because they're friends, is that what you're saying? You can't picture two lifelong friends suddenly deciding there's more than friendship between them?"

"Well, no."

"No?"

"I mean, yes. I *could* picture that, picture friends becoming lovers."

Why were they talking about this? "So what's the problem?"

"It's just that Clara and Ryan, they're not…*that* way with each other."

"You're overcomplicating it."

"No. I don't think so."

"Yeah. You are. She's a woman. He's a man. They're together a lot—you know, being *friends* and all. It happens. I don't see anything all that surprising about any of it. And as for them getting married, well, Rye's a stand-up guy and Clara's having his baby. And he was only a baby when our loser of a dad took off never to be heard from again. He's always sworn no kid of his will grow up without him. He just wants to do the right thing."

"But that's what I'm saying. Maybe for Clara and Ryan, it just *isn't* the right thing. They're great together, as pals. But as husband and wife? I'm not seeing it. And you know how Ryan is."

"Now you're going to start talking trash about my brother?"

She flinched and sat back away from him. "Whoa. Where did that come from?"

He glared at her, feeling agitated, angry at her and knowing he really had no right to be, all stirred up over her snowman socks and her shining hair, every last nerve on edge. "What exactly do you mean, 'how Ryan is'?"

"Walker." Her voice was careful now. "It's not talking trash about Ryan to say the truth about him."

"Right. The truth. That he's a dog, right? That it's one woman after another with him."

"I did not say that."

"It's what you meant, Rory. You know it is."

"I *meant* that he likes women. In a casual kind of way. He's a great guy, but he's also a player. Will he really be capable of settling down? Especially with Clara, who doesn't seem all that thrilled to be marrying him?"

Okay. Now she was just plain pissing him off. "What are you saying? You think Clara's too good for Rye, is that it?"

"No, I most definitely am *not* saying that." Now *she* was getting pissed. She always sounded more like a princess when she was mad, everything clear and clipped and so damn superior.

"It sure does sound like it to me." He got up so fast she let out a gasp of surprise.

"Walker, what…?"

He glared down at her, with her shining eyes and her silky hair and those damn cute snowman socks with all that bare skin underneath them. "I've had about enough."

She gaped up at him, bewildered. "But—"

"Good night." And he turned on his heel and got the hell out of there.

Chapter Four

Walker felt like about ten kinds of idiot by the time he was halfway up the stairs. But he just kept on going to the top and onward, along the upper hallway to his room across from hers.

Inside, he shoved the door shut and headed for the bathroom, where he stripped off his clothes and took a cold shower. He stood under the icy spray, shivering, wondering when it was, exactly, that he and his rational mind had parted company.

But then, he *knew* when it was: the moment he saw those snowman socks. He'd looked at those socks and they'd taken him somewhere he never planned to go—not with Rory. Uh-uh. She was his *friend*, for God's sake. And too young for him. And about a thousand miles out of his league.

And was that what had happened with Clara and Rye, then? Some kind of snowman-sock moment, when everything changed and they ended up in bed together, resulting in Clara's pregnancy, making it necessary for Rye to step up, messing with their friendship—and worse, with their lives and the lives of an innocent kid.

No way was he letting that happen to him and Rory.

He turned off the freezing water and groped for a towel, rubbing down swiftly with it and then wrapping it around his waist. And then just standing there in the middle of the bathroom, staring into space, thinking…

It was both really great and damn confusing, having Rory around all the time. Great because he liked her so much and she was low-maintenance, ready to help out, flexible and fun. Confusing because he wasn't used to having someone else in the house round the clock, not for years, not since Denise walked out on him. He wasn't used to it, and he couldn't afford to *get* used to it.

Rory would be gone in a couple of weeks. She was leaving right after the wedding. Her brother Max was getting married in Montedoro a few days after Rye and Clara.

She would go. And he would be alone again. That was just how it was—how he wanted it.

And was any of what was eating at him her fault?

Absolutely not.

She was probably calling her mother about now, asking to have a real bodyguard sent ASAP so that she could move back to the Haltersham, where nobody jumped down her throat just for saying what was on her mind.

He dropped the towel and reached for his jeans.

When he opened his bedroom door and stuck out his head, Lonesome was there waiting on the threshold. The dog eased around him and headed for his favorite spot on the rug by the bed.

Walker stared at Rory's bedroom door, which was shut. It had been open before.

She must have come upstairs.

He stepped across the hall and tapped on the door. And then he waited, more certain with each second that passed that she was in there packing her bags, getting ready to get the hell away from him. He was just lifting his hand to knock a second time when the door swung inward, and there she was.

In a white terry-cloth robe with her hair piled up loosely and the smell of steam and flowers rising from her skin.

"Uh," he said.

She looked so sweet and smelled so good…and whoa. He should have thought twice before knocking on her bedroom door in the middle of the night.

And then her soft lips curled upward in a slow smile, and that cute dimple tucked itself into her round cheek. Pow. Like getting hit in the chest with a big ole ball of wonderful, watching her smile. It was bad, worse than seeing her snowman socks, to be standing there staring at her fresh from a bath.

She said, "Ready to apologize for being such a jackass?"

He nodded and made himself get on with it. "That's right. I'm sorry." It came out gruff, not smooth and regretful as he meant it. But it was the best he could do at the moment, given the smell of her and the sweet, pink smoothness of her skin that he was having a real hard time not reaching out and touching. "I'm sorry for being a complete douche bag."

She smiled wider. "Why, yes. You *were* quite the douche."

"You've got on your princess voice."

"Excuse me?"

"When you're pissed off, you always sound…" What in hell was he babbling about? "Never mind. And you didn't *have* to agree, you know? You could tell me I wasn't *that* bad."

"I just call it like I see it."

He folded his arms across his chest and leaned against the door frame. Better. With his arms folded, he was less likely to do something stupid like try to touch her, and leaning against the door frame made him almost believe he felt easy and casual. He said, "Well, this is the deal. The real truth is, I'm a little worried about Rye and Clara, too."

Her bright, hard smile turned softer. "Yeah. I kind of thought that you were."

"I don't think there's much we can do about it, though."

She stared up at him, so earnest now, so sweet. "It's just good to know I'm not the only one who's got doubts about this wedding."

He thought back over the evening at Clara's. "A couple of times tonight, they seemed…I don't know, good together, tight with each other."

She nodded. "Like when I brought her back into the kitchen after she got sick, when Ryan jumped up and went to her. He put his arm around her and asked her if she was all right…"

"Yeah, then. And also when she took his hand, a little later, at the table."

"So you're thinking it could be that we're worried for nothing?"

"It's possible."

She nodded again. "Yeah. You're right. And I really, truly, did not mean to be insulting to Ryan. He's a great guy and I love him."

"I know that you do." *Say good-night,* warned the voice of reason inside his head. He peeled himself off the door frame. "Well…"

She gave a little chuckle and the sound made a hot pass along his nerve endings, tempting him to want things he had to keep remembering he was never going to get. “I know,” she said softly. “It’s late. And there’s Rocky Mountain Christmas in town tomorrow.”

“How could I forget?” All the local crafters and clubs set up booths in the town hall. Then at night, there was a Christmas show put on by the schoolkids in the newly renovated Cascade Theater. He used to go to it every year. But about a decade ago, he’d realized that when you’d been to one Rocky Mountain Christmas, you’d pretty much been to them all. “I take it we’re going.”

“Oh, yes, we are.”

Say good-night, you fool. Do it now. “’Night, Rory.”

“’Night, Walker.” She stepped back and shut the door.

He stood there for several seconds before turning away, staring at that closed door, arms wrapped extra tight across his chest, his pulse hard and hungry in his own ears.

In the morning before dawn, Rory got up and splashed cold water on her face. She put on a pair of comfy long johns and thick wool socks. Over the long johns, she wore jeans and a warm shirt. She pulled on sturdy boots. And then she put on her heavy jacket and a watch cap. Grabbing her winter riding gloves, she went out to help Walker and Bud Colgin with the horses.

An hour later, Bud went back to his house. Rory and Walker tacked up a couple of the horses and rode out toward the mountains as the sun was coming up. It was great, just the two of them and the horses in the freezing winter dawn, with Lonesome trailing along in their wake.

They got back to the house at a little after nine, both of them really hungry. He fried eggs and bacon. She made the coffee and toasted the bread.

"This isn't bad at all," she told him when they sat down to eat.

He grunted. "What isn't bad?"

"This. Ranch life. When I move to Justice Creek, I might just get my own spread."

"Princess Aurora, Colorado rancher?" Was he making fun of her? If so, at least he was doing it good-naturedly.

"Smile when you say that."

He ate a piece of bacon and played along. "So, you planning on running cattle, too?"

"Just a few horses. I want a big, old house and a dog and a cat. Kind of like the Bar-N. But with chickens." She sipped her coffee. "Yeah. I see my ranch with chickens."

He shook his head. "What about your career as a world-famous photographer."

"I can do more than one thing, you know. I'm guessing I could fit fiddling with my cameras in somewhere between grooming the horses and feeding the chickens."

He mopped up the last of his eggs with the toast. "You're never really going to move to Justice Creek." He kept his eyes focused on his plate when he said that.

She studied his bent head, his broad shoulders, those strong, tanned hands of his. "My sister Genevra? She's a year older than me. Married an English earl last May. They live at his giant country house, Hartmore, in Derbyshire."

He lifted his head and looked at her then, those eyes so blue—and so guarded. "I know who Genevra is.

And what has she got to do with your moving to Justice Creek?"

"Genny loves Hartmore. She says that from the first time we visited there, when we were small, she knew it was meant to be her home. Justice Creek is like that for me."

He pushed back his chair and picked up his plate. "Winters are long and cold."

"Is that supposed to be news to me? Because guess what? It's not."

He carried the plate to the sink, set it down and turned to face her. "It's fun for a couple weeks. You can call the ice-cold mornings brisk, get all excited over a few snow flurries. But wait till the snow is piled past the windowsills. You'll be dreaming of Montedoro by about February."

"So then I'll get on a plane and visit Montedoro."

He folded his arms across his chest the way he'd done the night before, when he came to her bedroom door to apologize. And he muttered gruffly, "You make it all sound so simple."

"Well, maybe for me it is simple. I like Justice Creek—scratch that. I *love* Justice Creek. And I've been thinking about moving here for a long time."

"You never mentioned it to me."

"I think about a lot of things I don't mention to you." Oh, did she ever. "And are we about to have another argument? Because if we are, I think we should just…not."

He stared down at his boots. A small smile curved his wonderful mouth. "I think you're right."

She decided to take that at face value. "Great, then."

And she rose and helped him clean up the kitchen, all the time wondering what was going on with him. There was that argument last night. He really had seemed angry with her, though at least he'd had the grace to apologize later. And then just now, getting all hostile when she said she might make a home in Justice Creek.

Did he have some problem with her moving there? Maybe they should talk about that...

"Hey." He bent to put the frying pan away in a low cupboard.

She hung up the dish towel. "Yeah?"

"You really are considering moving here?"

"Yes, I am. You probably ought to start getting used to the idea."

"I'll work on it."

"Is something bothering you, Walker?"

He closed the cupboard door and straightened. "Not a thing."

She didn't believe him. But she left it at that.

Walker took Rory into town at a little before noon. After acting like a jerk at breakfast, he'd promised himself he wouldn't act like one again.

He was determined not to let this sudden yen for her screw everything up. So what if he suddenly had a burning desire to put his hands all over her? He would keep that desire strictly under control. No more acting edgy around her. No more getting into arguments with her over things that never would have bothered him before.

If she was moving to Justice Creek, terrific. More power to her. And if she had her doubts about how things would work out between Rye and Clara, well, he had his doubts, too, and it was nothing to pick a fight over.

He would keep it fun and casual and everything would be fine.

Every year in downtown Justice Creek, right after Thanksgiving, the Chamber of Commerce crew not only hung wreaths from the streetlights, they also strung party lights from all the trees. They kept them on round the clock until the day after New Year's. Even in daylight, the lights made everything seem a little magical and a lot festive. Outside speakers played Christmas tunes and people strolled from store to store, carrying bags full of gifts and goodies.

As they made their way down Central Street, Rory took a lot of pictures and wanted to go into every single shop. She seemed happy, just to be there, on the crowded street with all the other Christmas shoppers. And even if Walker had seen more Rocky Mountain Christmases than he cared to remember, somehow, it was better, to be there with her.

After they'd visited each and every shop on Central, they entered the town hall, which was jam-packed, upstairs and down, with craft, club and food booths and a whole bunch of shoppers. Rory took more pictures and bought a lot of handmade ornaments.

By the time they got out of there, even she was ready for a break. So they carried her packages to the SUV, which he'd left in the parking lot behind Ryan's pub.

"How about a beer?" he asked.

"Sure."

They went into McKellan's, which was just about as packed as the town hall had been. They got lucky, though, and found stools at the long mahogany bar, where they ordered pints and burgers. Rye was there. He waved at them in greeting and went back to expediting food orders.

Rory took a sip of her beer, wiped the foam mustache off her upper lip and asked, "So when do you put up your Christmas tree?"

He grunted. "That is assuming I *have* a Christmas tree."

"I knew it." She gave him a sideways look. "You're a total Scrooge."

"Am not."

"Are so."

"I could have a Christmas tree," he offered limply.

"Oh, yes, you could. And you *are*."

It all came way too clear to him then. "All that Christmas crap you bought...?"

"Yep. All for you. Say 'thank you, Rory.'"

He thought it over and wondered out loud, "Why do I not feel more grateful?"

"As I said. Total Scrooge. But I've decided to help you with that."

"Uh-oh."

"You do have at least a few lights and decorations, right? Up in the attic, maybe? Stuff that Denise bought or your mom had in the olden days?"

"Denise wasn't big on Christmas. She put a bunch of shiny balls in a bowl, I think. And strung some fake garland around. And I don't even remember what happened to that stuff—and look over there, by the front entrance, the twelve-foot tree covered in old-fashioned ornaments and bubble lights?"

She turned to look where he pointed, next to the hostess stand, just inside the vestibule. "It's beautiful."

"Those decorations were my mom's. I gave them all to Rye when he opened this place. He uses them every year."

She faced him again and she kind of glowed at him,

brimming with good feelings and Christmas cheer. "Be right back." She grabbed her camera from the big purse she'd been toting around and wove her way through the packed tables to take a bunch of shots of the tree.

By the time she slid up onto her stool again, their burgers had arrived. They dug in.

While they ate, she told him how it was going to be. "After we've eaten, we're going back to the town hall to pick up more ornaments. Then we'll visit that big shopping center on West Central to get the lights and everything else we'll need. Fake tree or real one?"

"I get to choose?"

"Don't give me attitude."

He couldn't help chuckling. "Yes, ma'am. Real, please."

"Excellent. Finish up. We have a lot of work to do."

It went the way she wanted it to go.

They returned to the town hall, where she made a lot of Christmas craft booth owners very happy. They saw two of her cousins, Willow's oldest son, Carter Bravo, and Sondra's second-born, Jamie Bravo. She stopped and chatted with them. Both men said they were just leaving. They had that dazed look men get when confronted by too much knickknacky stuff all in one place. As a matter of fact, Walker figured he probably had that look himself.

He carried the bags while she shopped the craft booths for the second time that day, after which they put the stuff in the SUV and headed for the shopping center, where she bought a tree stand, a sparkly green-and-red tree skirt, way too many lights and a bunch of other junk he didn't need. Things like little ceramic snowmen and Christmas candles, a music-box tree that played "Silent Night" as it slowly turned, a set of three mercury glass angels and four stockings to hang on the chimney—for him, for her, for Lucky and for Lonesome.

It was a little after five when she said they could head back to the ranch.

"You mean we don't have to go to the Christmas show at the Cascade Theater?"

"Maybe next year."

He put on a hangdog look. "I was really looking forward to that Christmas show."

She elbowed him in the ribs. "Don't push your luck, mister—I do want to check on Clara first, though, before we go. She'll probably be home by now." Clara's café closed at four.

So Rory called Clara. It turned out she was just finishing up at the café. So they went over there and Clara let them in. She gave Walker a cup of coffee, and he waited at the counter while the women went back in the kitchen and whispered together.

"She says she's fine," Rory told him doubtfully on the way home. "But she looks tired. I'm worried about her. I told her to call me if she needs anything."

"She'll be okay," he said, and hoped he was right.

She made a low sound in response to that, a sound that might have meant anything.

At the ranch, they carried all the Christmas crap inside and piled it up by the window in the great room, where she planned to put the tree. Then they changed to work clothes and went out to tend to the horses.

Alva had left a roast chicken and potatoes waiting in the oven for them. When they came back inside, they ate. Rory talked about the tree they were going out to chop down together after chores and breakfast the next morning.

He looked at her across the table as she chattered away between bites of chicken and potatoes and he thought about that first summer she'd come to Colorado.

She'd been just eighteen, eager to meet the Justice Creek branch of her father's family, to hike the Rockies and take a bunch of pictures of the Wild, Wild West. Walker's first impression of her was of those big golden-brown eyes and that wide, dimpled smile.

Back then, before the kidnapping of one of her brothers in the Middle East, her family had been less security-conscious, and Rory had been allowed to travel on her own. She went around in jeans and T-shirts, a pack strapped to her back. If he hadn't been told she was a princess, he never would have guessed. She'd seemed 100 percent American to him. A great kid, he'd thought. Friendly and not the least pretentious.

She was still the same, down-to-earth and easy to be with. But a kid? Uh-uh. Not anymore.

After they cleared off the table, they watched a movie—a comedy that wasn't really all that funny. They sat together on the sofa. Twice, he caught himself in the act of stretching his arm across the sofa back and hooking it around her shoulders to pull her closer to him.

Both times, he hauled his arm back to his side of the sofa where it belonged and wondered what the hell was the matter with him. It would be way too easy to get used to this—to having her with him all of the time. Even though he made grim faces over all this Christmas crap she insisted on, he was actually kind of enjoying himself. Rory had a way of putting a whole new light on an ordinary day.

He really needed to keep some perspective on the situation. He needed not to let himself forget that they were friends and that was all. And nothing else was going to happen.

Nothing. Zero. Zip. Snowman socks be damned.

The movie ended. He knew this because the credits came on suddenly. He blinked at the TV and realized he didn't even remember what the damn thing had been about.

He grabbed the remote and turned everything off.

She said good-night and went up to bed.

And he just sat there, Lonesome at his feet, wondering why he couldn't stop thinking about her, couldn't stop wanting to get up and follow the fresh, tempting scent of her up the stairs, to knock on her door and grab her in his arms and kiss her senseless, to strip off all her clothes and sweep her high in his arms, to carry her to the bed and keep her there, naked, all night long.

And maybe for a while in the morning, too.

He got up, turned off the fire and the lights and went upstairs, Lonesome right behind him. He did not knock on her door, but went straight to his own room, where a long, ice-cold shower was waiting.

The next morning at breakfast she told him she'd had an idea.

He stared across the table at her and almost said, *You want to have sex with me? Because if you do, there is no way I'll be able to say no to you.*

She said, "Walker. You should see your face."

He reached up and rubbed his palm along his jaw. "I shaved. Did I miss a spot?"

She chuckled at him and the sound kind of curled

around him, all cute and soft and tempting and reminding him of sex—because all of a sudden, everything she did reminded him of sex. "I mean your expression," she said. "You look kind of dazed. Did you have a rough night?"

He pretended to have to think that over. "You know, now you mention it, I was awake kind of late. Thinking."

"About?"

Crap. Walked right into that one. "You know, I don't really remember what, exactly, I was thinking about..."

She sipped her coffee, ate a bite of her toast. "You seem...I don't know. Different, somehow. Kind of vague and unfocused. Maybe you're coming down with something."

Lust. He had it. A really bad case of it. Was it incurable? It sure felt as if it might be. "No. Just a little tired, that's all."

She pushed back her chair. He watched her come around the table to him, wishing she wouldn't, so glad that she was. She stepped right up beside him and put her cool, smooth hand on his forehead. "You don't feel hot."

Oh, he was hot, all right. Burning like a house afire. He stared at the soft, amazing curves of her breasts, which just happened to be at his eye level. She smelled of coffee and toast, with a hint of spice and flowers. And he had to hold himself very still to keep from lurching forward and burying his face right between those beautiful breasts he really shouldn't be gaping at. "I told you, I'm fine."

She sighed and shrugged and went back to her chair.

Somehow, he managed to just sit there and let her go. When she started eating again, he picked up his fork and concentrated on his sausage and eggs.

After a few minutes of silence between them, he began to feel that he should say something. If he didn't, she'd be starting in again about how he must be getting sick. He asked, "So are we going out to cut that tree down this morning?" He dared a glance in her direction.

She got up again, carried her coffee mug to the counter and refilled it. She wore faded, snug jeans. He stared at her backside. By God, it was fine. And then she turned around and held up the pot to him. He remembered to shift his gaze upward, and he was pretty sure she didn't guess that he'd been staring at her ass. "More coffee?"

If she came and stood beside him again and he had to smell her and look at her up close, he wouldn't be responsible for what he might do next. "Uh, no. I'm fine, thanks."

She put the pot back and returned to her chair. "So anyway, I was thinking a party. A tree-decorating party."

Between this sudden bad case of burning desire for her and two nights without sleep, it took him a minute or two to process. "A party. Here, at the house?"

"Yes." She beamed, so pleased with herself.

"I don't have parties. You know that."

She sat back in her chair. "Yes, Walker. I do know. You're a solitary man, a loner and all that."

He scowled at her. It felt kind of good. If he got mad at her, he might forget for a little while how much he suddenly wanted to get her naked in his bed. "Are you making fun of me?"

"A little, I guess." All light and playful. Those amazing bronze eyes full of teasing and fun. God. She was killing him. And then the playfulness faded. She got serious, all sweet and soft and hopeful, which was somehow every bit as exciting as her teasing smiles had been.

"I was just thinking how much fun it would be. We've got that party at Ryan's bar on Saturday." Clara and Ryan had decided to combine their bachelor and bachelorette parties. All of Rory's crazy cousins would be there Saturday night, and a bunch of other people, too. "So maybe Thursday then, for the tree-decorating party? That gives us a few days to invite everybody and organize things. We could hold off on getting the tree until Wednesday. That way it'll be nice and fresh. We can invite Clara and Ryan. And any other friends you can think of. We'll have hot cider and cocoa. And we'll string popcorn and sing Christmas carols while we do this house up right for the holidays."

He stared at her and realized he would probably do just about anything she asked of him. Walk on hot coals maybe, or throw himself off a cliff. And he probably always would have done just about anything she wanted. But before he would have done it fondly, because she was his friend. Now he would do it with a blazing fire inside.

How had this happened to him? He just didn't get it. Feeling like this over a woman was dangerous for him. Look what had happened with Denise.

No way could he take going through that kind of hell again.

She said, "Well? What do you think?"

And he said lamely, "You make it sound really great."

"Is that yes, then? We can have the party?"

"Hell, Rory. Sure. You want it, you got it."

Chapter Five

The minute breakfast was over, she called Clara.

Willing the bulge in his jeans to go down, Walker cleared off and loaded the dishwasher while she talked to her cousin. By tuning her out and concentrating on scraping plates and wiping counters, he got better control of himself and was feeling almost normal when she hung up.

He turned around and she was sitting there, staring out the window, her phone on the table in front of her, looking thoughtful. "What?" he asked. "Clara won't come to your party?"

She looked at him. Bam. A thrill shot all through him, just from that simple glance. *Get a grip, idiot.* "It's *your* party, Mr. Grinch," she teased. "And of course she'll come. She thinks it's a great idea. She asked me to invite her sisters. All three of them—and Tracy, too."

He folded his arms across his chest, leaned back against the counter and shook his head. "You thought she wouldn't? Come on, you don't want to have a party and not invite all your cousins."

She sank back in her chair. "But you saw how it was Friday. We'll be lucky if they don't kill each other."

"They need to learn to get along—before the wedding, if possible."

"Yeah. I know you're right…" She stared out the window some more.

He watched her, thinking he was doing okay for the moment, acting reasonably normal, keeping the wood down. "It's going to be fine, Rory. You'll see."

She looked at him again. Ka-pow. Bad as before, like a lightning bolt to the solar plexus. But he took it. He could do this. It was bound to get better, the yearning easier to ignore the longer he worked at it. "Well, all right, then." A smile curved those beautiful lips he was never going to kiss. "I'll call the family. You can call Ryan. Who else?"

He named off a few friends and said he would call them. And then he went to his study at the front of the house and made his calls while she made hers.

Later, they went riding. That worked for him, getting outside. It was easier to keep from making a move on her when they were on horseback out under the wide Colorado sky.

Back at the compound, he told her he had some work to do at one of the guesthouses. This time of year, he didn't have many guests. He made improvements and performed routine maintenance so he'd be ready for the busy season.

She went along with him to the empty house across the yard, bringing her laptop so she could catch up on her correspondence and do some editing and organizing of the million and one pictures she'd taken since she arrived. The water was off there. He'd drained the pipes so they wouldn't freeze. But he turned on the propane heat and the place got warm pretty fast.

That went okay, he thought. It wasn't all that hard to control his burning lust when she sat in an upstairs bedroom with her computer while he tore out the tile across the hallway in the bathroom.

By dinnertime, he was patting himself on the back. He could do this. He could get through the days until the wedding, do his job watching over her without laying a hand on her. One day, one hour, one minute at a time. That was how any sane man dealt with temptation.

And he did get through it—through Monday and Tuesday. Wednesday, they took his uncle's old pickup and went out to find a tree. They cut down a beauty, brought it back in the bed of the truck, hauled it inside and put it up on the stand in front of the picture window in the great room. The whole house smelled of evergreen.

Not bad at all.

They loaded up a bunch of Christmas music on the PC in his study and then she insisted they go into town to buy some decent speakers for it. Back at the ranch, she went over to Alva's place and talked her into helping bake stuff and make candy for the party. All the rest of the day the house smelled of fudge and divinity and Christmas cookies.

He probably shouldn't let himself get used to it, to having her around all the time. To the way she lit up a room and filled it with laughter and the smell of cookies.

But hell. It was Christmastime, right? And he was kind of getting into it, into the Christmas spirit, into the actual fact that he was having a party at his house. It was something he hadn't done in years. Not since his mom used to throw birthday parties for him and Ryan when they were growing up.

He decided he was ready for it—to have some friends over and have a good time.

By nine Thursday evening, the house was full of Bravos and their dates and his lifelong friends from school. Christmas music filled the air. There were cookies and candy set out on the kitchen island and the coffee table, and chips and dip and popcorn, too. Everyone had a cup of cider or cocoa or something stronger.

It was going pretty well, Walker thought. They had the lights strung on the tree and had moved on to hanging the ornaments. The men were mostly just standing around, drinking beer and talking work and sports, leaving the women to do the decorating. But everybody seemed to be having a good time, and that was the point.

Walker felt a happy glow of good feeling, all sentimental and mushy. Ordinarily, he wasn't real big on sentimentality. But this was good, having the house full of people. He liked that it was Christmas, though for years he'd hardly noticed when the holidays came around. He liked that, thanks to Rory, he had an actual Christmas tree by the window and three mercury glass angels decorating his coffee table. And every time he glanced at her in her red sweater and jeans and knee-high boots, he had the most excellent feeling of simple, perfect contentment.

That night, for some reason, raging lust for her didn't seem to be a problem for him. He just felt glad. Glad that she was there, in his house, wearing a red sweater, her long hair loose and shiny on her shoulders, a happy smile on her beautiful face.

Even her cousins seemed to be caught up in the spirit of good cheer. They all got along—at first.

Then, around ten-thirty, Tracy and Elise got into it with Jody. It was the same argument they'd had that day at the bridal shop, about who would arrange the flowers for the reception. But Rory stepped right in and reminded them that this was a party, not another chance to argue over who got to run what. That shut them up.

Ryan had brought vodka and Kahlúa for Black Russians. Tracy and Elise started drinking those. So did Nell. They didn't seem to be drinking too much, really. And Rye was always careful when he brought booze. As a bar owner, he knew how to keep an eye on people and not to overserve.

But he must not have been watching Nell closely enough. Around midnight, she jumped up from her chair by the tree, pushed aside the two guys who were trying to make time with her and marched over to Clara, who was helping Rory decorate the mantel with greenery, glittery Christmas ornaments and strings of multicolored lights.

Nell tapped Clara on the shoulder.

Clara turned around. "Nell? What—"

Nell grabbed her hand. "Clara, I just have to tell you..."

Clara smiled cautiously. "Yeah?"

"That I like you. I *love* you. I always did. You're a good person. And I'm glad you're my sister—or, I mean, half of one, anyway."

Clara's smile bloomed wide then. "Well, Nell. I'm glad, too."

"And I was just sitting over there in that chair by the tree, listening to a couple of guys I am not going out with tell me how great they are, but really just thinking about our family and getting all teary-eyed, you know? Thinking that it's completely cool, the way you made us all your bridesmaids, me and Jody *and* those two bitches who drive me insane but who *are* my sisters—even Tracy, who's not even blood to me, but still...I mean, we are family, aren't we? We're all family and we need to learn to get along."

Clara kind of gaped at her for a second. And then she nodded. "You're right, Nell. We're family and we need to remember that. We need to cherish that."

Nell let out a big, gusty sigh. "Oh, yeah. Truth." She pressed her hand to her chest and her big eyes brimmed with fat tears. "I love you, Clara." And then she reached out and yanked Clara close. "Oh, I love you, honey. I do..."

"Um, me, too." Clara hugged Nell back. "I love you, too, Nell..."

"Yes!" Nell took Clara by the shoulders, held her away and stared at her intently for a long count of ten. Then she swiped at the tears on her cheeks, tossed her long auburn hair and announced at full volume, "And don't you let all that crap Monique Hightower is blabbing all over town bother you one bit. Any kid would be lucky to be raised by you. You're gonna be a great mother."

By then, everyone at the party had stopped to watch. Even the Christmas music seemed to have hit a pause. Rye was the only one moving. He was weaving through the crowd in the kitchen, headed for Clara's side.

Rory tried, "Uh, Nell. How about some coffee?"

Nell ignored her. She grabbed Clara's hand again. "You know what I'm sayin'? Tell me you know."

By then, Tracy and Elise had stopped merely staring with their mouths hanging open. They were making outraged noises and moving as a unit toward Clara and Nell.

Rory moved to intercept them. "Stay out of it, you two."

Tracy scowled at her, and Elise made a harrumphing sound. But they did stop in their tracks.

And Clara actually seemed fine with what Nell was laying on her. "Yeah," she said softly. "Oh, Nellie, I know exactly what you're saying. And thank you."

Rye reached her side then. "Everything okay here?"

Clara nodded. "Fine, Ryan. Really."

Nell swiped at the makeup and tears running down her cheeks and turned a defiant glance Rye's way. "Ryan, you're a great guy."

"Uh, thanks."

She sniffled. "But how many times have you asked Clara to marry you?"

"Uh…"

"And how many times did she turn you down?"

"Uh…"

"Several. Am I right?"

"Well, Nell, I really don't think that's any of your busi…"

She swung up a hand at him, palm out, and Rye stopped in midword. "Hold that thought. Like, forever." Then she turned those huge, mascara-smeared eyes back on Clara again. "Like I said, I do love you, Clara. And I just want you to be *sure*, you know? Just 'cause you're pregnant doesn't mean you have to marry the guy. I mean, consider my mother—not that anybody really wants to. Because, hey. We all know what people say about her." She shrugged. "Unattractive things. Gold digger. Home wrecker. And worse. And Dad *couldn't* marry her, I mean, being married to *your* mom and all. What were they thinking—Dad, your mom, my mom? I'll never understand what they thought they were doing. Why my mom never had the integrity and good sense to walk away—or at least practice a little contraception, for cryin' out loud. It was wacked, and we all know it. And now, my mom's the only one left with any real insight into that whole sad, weird situation. Not that she'll ever explain herself. Willow Mooney Bravo plays it cagey at all times. I mean, to keep having Dad's babies, one after another, at about the same rate as your mama across town? It makes no sense. And what about *your* mama? Why did she even stay with him?"

Clara frowned. "I think she—"

"Never mind." Nell patted her shoulder fondly. "It doesn't matter."

"But—"

"And what was I saying…? Oh, yeah. I got it. My mom had all five of us long before she married dear old Dad, who was still married to *your* mom. And look at us." She flapped a hand back behind her, probably to indicate Garrett and Carter, two of her three full brothers, who stood over by the kitchen island; and Jody, who sat on the sofa with some guy from Denver. "We're doin' just fine. Yeah, we might have had a little more trouble in school, might have had to bust a few heads now and then, you know, keep the smack talkers under control. But a good fight makes you stronger—a good fight shows you what you're made of." She lifted her arm, shoved her sweater up past her elbow and flexed her biceps, which was tattooed with flowers and dragonflies. "Look at that. You don't want to be messin' with that…" She clapped her other hand over the muscle in question—and that struck her as funny for some reason. She started laughing. She laughed so hard she staggered on those dagger-heeled boots of hers.

But Clara, who really did seem to be taking it all in stride, caught her and gently helped her to sit down on the hearth. "No more Black Russians for you, Nellie."

Nell kept laughing. She started to fall sideways. Clara put her arm around her and pulled her close.

"Whoa," moaned Nell. "Has anyone noticed that the room is goin' round and round?"

And Elise chose that moment to make her big move. "Really, this is just too much." She zipped around Rory and descended on Nell. "You are disgusting."

Clara shot her a warning glance. "Elise. Just don't."

And Nell rested her head on Clara's shoulder and sighed. "Yeah, Leesie, put a sock in it, why don't you?"

Tracy zipped around Rory's other side. "Don't listen to her, Elise. As usual, she's out of control."

And then, out of nowhere, Jody leaped up from the sofa. "Why can't you two just leave poor Nell alone?"

Elise gasped. She and Tracy whirled from Nell to Jody. They both opened their mouths to light into her at once.

But Nell beat them to it. "You just shut your mouth, Joanna Louise. I don't need you defending me. It's about a decade too late for that now. Where were you when Dad married Mom and we had to move in with them? Did you have my back then?"

Jody gulped. "Well, I… Actually, it was just that I…"

"Hah!" crowed Nell. "See what I mean? You got nothin'."

Jody huffed, "It so happens, *dear* little Nell, that I had a lot going on at the time and I—"

"Don't even bother with the excuses. We both know what you did. You kept your head down and moved out of that house as quick as you could and left me behind for them to torture." And with that, she shot upright, wobbled a little on her high-heeled boots, and then somehow managed to draw herself up straight. "I learned to fight my own battles, thank you very much. So don't even imagine I suddenly need support from you." And with that, she tossed her hair one more time, aimed her chin high and stalked from the room.

The only sounds were her footsteps walking away—and Elmo and Patsy singing "Grandma Got Run Over by a Reindeer."

Finally, Rory said kind of reverently, "I think she's going upstairs."

And everybody strained to listen.

Yep. No doubt about it. Nell's boot heels echoed on the stairs.

Clara stood. "I'll just go and make sure she's all right." And she went after Nell.

Tracy turned to Elise. "I think we should go, too." Elise nodded—and they followed after Clara.

That left Jody, standing there next to the guy from Denver, looking kind of stricken—until, with a sad little sob, she took off after Tracy and Elise.

Walker went over, clapped his brother on the shoulder and asked, "You all right, man?"

Rye let out a hard breath. "Hangin' in."

"Hey. Sometimes that's about the best you can do. Beer?"

"Good call."

So they each got a beer. Rory turned up the music and everyone seemed happy enough to go back to partying and decorating, letting the Bravo sisters deal with their issues in private upstairs.

The five women came down about an hour later. They all seemed pretty subdued. Clara whispered to Rory, who led them all to the kitchen area and whipped them up hot cocoa.

It was a good choice, the cocoa, Walker thought. Rory made it using her brother Damien's special recipe, which involved chopping bars of quality bittersweet chocolate, then whisking the bits into heated milk, adding brown sugar and a dash of sea salt. Walker had sampled that cocoa in the past. Killer. Each of the women took a cup. They sipped and talked together quietly.

Walker sat by the fire with Rye, nursing his beer, watching them. Once he saw Elise pat Nell on the shoulder. And Nell chuckled at something Jody said.

Rye leaned toward Walker and spoke out of the side of his mouth. "Damned if it doesn't look like they're all getting along. What do you think?"

Walker suggested, "A Christmas miracle?"

Rye raised his beer. "I'll drink to that."

Rory stood by the stairs, which were now festively twined with lighted garland, watching as Walker locked up.

It was two-thirty Friday morning, a light snow was falling and the last guest—that guy from Denver—had finally said goodbye.

When Walker turned to her, she asked, "Hot chocolate?"

He looked at her sideways. "Your brother's special recipe?"

"That's the one."

"You're on. I'll turn off the music."

She grinned at him. "Meet you in the kitchen."

While she made the cocoa, he turned off the lamps and the rustic chandelier in the great room, leaving only the tree lights, the lights on the mantel and the light of the fire. Then he joined her in the kitchen area.

She poured them each a mugful of chocolate. "Let's go sit by the fire."

He followed her over there. They sat down together and he sipped from his mug. "Good," he said approvingly. He had a milk-froth mustache.

She watched him lick it off and couldn't help picturing herself leaning close and helping him with that. But then, that wasn't who they were, and she'd been doing pretty well at just enjoying this time with him, not letting her imagination and her secret yearnings run away with her.

Now and then in the past few days, she'd had the feeling that something wasn't right with him. He would get too quiet—and he tended to stand around with his arms crossed over his chest, as if he felt threatened or something.

But she'd let it be, whatever it was. She figured if he wanted to talk to her about it, he would.

Tonight, though—both during the party and right now—he seemed relaxed. Happy, even.

Which was pretty surprising, given the Bravo sisters' outrageous behavior.

He said, "The party was a great idea. I had a really good time."

"You did? I was kind of thinking you'd never forgive me for roping you into it."

"Forgive you? Uh-uh. Seriously, I enjoyed myself."

"Even when my crazy cousins started yelling at each other?"

And he laughed. He did have the nicest, deepest, warmest laugh. "Even then."

"You sure?"

"Absolutely—and did anyone give you the story on what happened upstairs?"

Clara had, actually. "What? You want the dirty details?"

"Yes, I do. And I'm not ashamed to say so."

She sipped her cocoa and stared at the tree.

Until he nudged her with his elbow. "Come on. The dirt. Out with it."

"Hmm. Well, let's see… There was crying. Clara said they *all* cried. Then Nell started in about all the awful things Elise and Tracy did to her when they had to live together after Sondra died and Willow married Frank."

"What things?"

"Well, Tracy and Elise lured Nell down to the basement. Somehow, they managed to tic her to a support beam down there. Then they left her there for hours in the dark—after Tracy had whispered to her that the basement just happened to be infested with black widow spiders."

"Whoa."

"Yeah. And once they rigged a bucket full of water dyed with blue food coloring so it came down on her head when she entered her bedroom."

"My God."

"But then Nell ended up confessing that she'd pulled a few stunts on them, too—stole their stuff, booby-trapped the bathroom with marbles on the floor and put oil-based paint in their body lotion. And then they all started crying again. And Jody apologized for not being there for Nell. And Tracy and Elise said they were sorry for all the bad stuff they did to Nell. And Nell admitted that she'd got her licks in, too. After that there was hugging and declarations of sisterly solidarity."

"Wow. So Clara actually did it."

"What?"

"Got her sisters to pull together, to put all the old crap aside."

"You know, I guess she kind of did."

"Color me impressed." His blue eyes held hers. She felt a glow all through her, just to have him looking at her in that warm and open way. The past few days, he really had been distant—and too cautious around her, somehow. But he wasn't distant now. He said, "And it was something special, having the old homestead filled with light and music and people having a good time."

"Some of them were seriously misbehaving people," she reminded him. "And there was more yelling than laughing."

"Naw. Overall, I'd say the laughing won out. And who cares about a few tense moments? It was a good time—and now the house is all lit up for Christmas."

"And you actually admit that you like it?"

"I do, yeah. A lot."

Well now, that made her feel a bit dewy-eyed. She'd kind of worried he might be annoyed at her for pushing him into throwing the party. But he didn't seem to be—far from it. "Good," she said, and realized she was staring at him a little too adoringly. So she lowered her gaze, lifted her cup and took a sip.

He said, "You know, it's been…really good, having you here."

"Yeah?" She exercised great care to sound merely friendly and interested—rather than ready to jump in his lap and snog the poor man silly.

"Yeah. You're kind of helping me to see…" He let

the sentence wander off unfinished and stared off toward the tree.

She really wanted to know what he'd started to say. So she dared put her hand on his bare arm, below where he'd rolled the cuff of his wool shirt. His skin was so warm, dusted with gold hair and corded with lean muscle beneath. He blinked and glanced down at where she touched him.

She pulled her hand back, cleared her throat and prompted, "Helping you see what?"

He stared down into his mug, as though something really interesting was floating around in there. "I guess…"

Look at me, Walker. Please. Look at me.

And it was almost as though he heard her. Because he looked up and into her eyes, and he gave her the most beautiful, sad smile. "You're making me see how, after Denise left me, I kind of shut down. I stopped putting in the effort to get out and be with people. So I've been thinking that when you leave, I'm going to make a point of being more social."

When you leave...

Oh, but she didn't want to leave. Not ever. She wanted to stay right here, with him, at the Bar-N.

Also, at that moment, she wanted to break down and cry.

Snap out of it, Rory. He had his life, she had hers. They were the best of friends and would remain so. End of story.

"That's good," she said. "I'm glad." And somehow, she managed to sound upbeat and sincere.

Walker had to wonder: Was he giving himself away?

It had happened again, just now, when he looked up from his cocoa and into her eyes again.

Ka-pow! A strike right to the core of him. He wanted to drop the mug and wrap his arms across his chest in self-defense—or wait, scratch that. He wanted to drop the mug and wrap his arms around *her.*

God. She was so beautiful, her hair shining in the firelight, her eyes more gold than brown. And her mouth…soft. Pliable.

What would it feel like under his?

What would she do if he grabbed her and kissed her? Slap his face?

Or kiss him right back?

Oh, come on. No chance of that.

She was young and beautiful—not to mention a princess for real. She could have any guy just by crooking a finger. No way was she ever going to decide to settle down on the Bar-N with her good buddy Walker.

And he wasn't up for the forever thing anyway, wasn't willing to go there again.

But, damn, what he wouldn't give for one night with her…

He wanted her, ached for her. So much. Enough that he was almost willing to blow off his responsibility to her as her bodyguard—and her friend. Enough that he'd started asking himself if there could be any chance at all she might go for a one-night stand.

Or wait. One night wouldn't do it. He needed more than that.

A Christmas love affair.

Yeah. Just the two of them, sharing his bed—and the sofa, the kitchen table, that rag rug, right there by the fireplace…

And any other available surface they happened to stumble on.

He wanted that; he burned for that: to be her lover for the week and two days left until Rye married Clara and Rory left him to return to Montedoro.

But she'd never go for it. Long, wet kisses and getting naked together and having sex all over the house wasn't what they were about—though once, five years ago, not long after Denise messed him over, Rory *had* made a move on him.

He stared off toward the glowing lights of the Christmas tree and remembered.

It had happened in August…

They'd been camping with Clara and Ryan up in the national forest near a local scenic attraction called Ice Castle Falls. In the early morning, before breakfast, they left Rye and Clara at camp and hiked the rest of the way to the summit, just the two of them. From the summit, it wasn't far down to the falls. When they reached them, they stood at the top for a little while, admiring the rush and roar of the water rolling off the cliff face, churning and foaming as it dropped to the rocks below. Rory took some pictures. Then she put her camera away and they began the climb down the rocks toward the base of the falls, moving closer to the water as they went. They got soaking wet.

Dripping and laughing, they stopped on a small ledge and looked up. The view from there took your breath, that long tumble of white water falling from the cliffs above to pound the rocks below.

He'd said something—about the hike, about the falls?—he didn't remember what anymore.

And he'd glanced over at her beside him on that ledge.

Her face was wet, her hair clinging to her soft cheeks. And she'd had this look, so sweet and hopeful. And he remembered that he'd felt a sudden tightness in his chest at the sight of her staring at him that way.

"Oh, Walker..." She'd whispered his name, so quietly he could hardly hear it under the roaring of the falls.

And then she turned all the way toward him. She reached out and grabbed his shoulders and then she was falling—right into his arms. He'd caught her, pulled her close to him, felt her body, so slim and strong and soft in all the right places, pressed up good and tight to his, felt the promise of her—of what might be between them.

She lifted that soft mouth of hers and her eyes drifted closed.

And for a second or two, a moment suspended between one heartbeat and the next, he almost just went ahead and took what she offered him.

But that second passed. And she must have felt his resistance, must have known he was trying to figure out how to gently pull away.

She opened her eyes.

And he said her name, regretfully. "Rory. Rory, I..."

And she shut her eyes again. "Oh, God. Bad idea, huh?"

He'd babbled out some lame little speech, about how he was tempted, but he didn't want to take a chance of ruining their friendship. She hadn't believed him. She shoved at his shoulders and he let her go.

The words she said next remained burned in his brain: "Hey. Fine. I get it. You're my friend. My good buddy. And you can dress it up with all kinds of polite excuses, but the plain truth is, you're just not that into me."

"Rory, I—"

"Don't, okay? Just don't."

"But you have to know how much I care about you and—"

"Stop." She put two fingers against his lips. "I get it. Enough said." And with that, she backed away from him, crouching, lowering her legs over the side of the ledge, climbing down…

"Walker?"

He blinked and turned to look at her, sitting there beside him at 3:00 a.m. on that snowy night. "Yeah?"

"You seem a million miles away."

"Sorry. Just thinking…"

"About?"

He hesitated, stuck in that narrow space between a safe lie and the dangerous truth—but then he didn't have to make the choice.

Because she said, "Never mind. It's late." She took his empty mug from him. "Time for bed."

He watched her carry the mugs to the sink, wishing he had just gone ahead and told her how much he wanted her, how he couldn't stop thinking about what her mouth would taste like, wondering how the fresh, clean scent of her body would change, growing musky, when she was aroused. About how it would feel to have her beneath him, calling his name. He thought of those impossible things, and he thought of the girl she'd been five years ago.

And of the woman she was now.

She'd been so right. He never should have agreed to be her bodyguard. A week's worth of constant proximity had broken him down, until she was all that he thought of, day and night.

If he had any sense, he'd call it off now. Tell her to have her mother send a soldier to look after her.

But he wasn't going to do that. Uh-uh. It felt too damn good to suffer this much.

He felt burned by her, branded. He needed her there with him, needed to be able to look at her and fantasize about what it might be like if he did make a move, if the miracle happened and she said yes.

The rules he'd established between them—the bedrock of friendship and trust? Those rules were dissolving, like shaved chocolate in hot milk. And he was finding he didn't even care.

He just wanted this time with her, whether he ever crossed the line with her or not.

When she came back to him, he was on his feet, switching off the fire.

"Good night," she said.

"'Night, Rory." He waited until she'd disappeared down the hallway to the stairs before turning off the rest of the lights.

Rory needed to talk to someone she trusted.

So when she got to her room, she called her sister Genevra in England. It was a little after 10:00 a.m. there.

Genny answered on the second ring. "Rory, hey. Aren't you in Justice Creek?"

"Yeah. Staying out at Walker's ranch. Mother hired him to be my bodyguard."

"What time is it there?"

"After three in the morning."

"Shouldn't you be in bed?"

"Spoken like a very pregnant old married lady."

"Oh, stop. I'm only a year older than you."

"Are you in the middle of something?"

"Not a thing—what's up?"

Rory almost didn't want to say it, because it felt as if saying it out loud might make it suddenly only a trick of her overactive imagination.

And how to describe it? That moment when he'd glanced up from his mug of cocoa—and she *knew*.

All at once, it all came together. She got what was going on with him—the faraway looks, the muscular arms folded protectively across his broad chest, the constant feeling that he was keeping something back.

Oh, God, yes. She'd seen it. She *knew* it. It was right there in his eyes.

She knew that look. After all, she'd spent years trying to hide looks like that from *him*. She ought to know them when she saw them.

There was heat in that look. And hopefulness. And fear, too.

Fear of giving in. Of giving over.

Of the very large chance that it would only lead to rejection—and possibly the end of a wonderful friendship.

"Rory? You still on the line?"

"Still here." She went ahead and said it. "I think Walker almost tried to kiss me tonight."

Genny gasped sharply. "Seriously?"

"Uh-huh. He's been acting strangely for days now. You know, avoiding eye contact, staring off into space, acting closed off. I couldn't figure out what was up with him. But tonight, well, there was something in the way he looked at me. I just knew. It all came clear."

"Do you *want* him to kiss you?"

"Oh, yeah. I do. I really do."

"But I thought that you and he were just good friends."

"Yeah. Exactly," she said glumly. And then she brightened. "But after tonight, I can't help thinking that everything could be about to change."

"And then what?"

"Genny. Come on. One day at a time and all that. If I think about what will happen later, I'll probably get cold feet. I'd rather just see where this goes—and you're too quiet. What? Say it, whatever you're thinking."

"Well, the truth is, I was thinking about Rafe and me." Rafael DeValery was her husband, the earl.

Rory laughed. "Go ahead. Make it all about you."

"Rafe and I were friends, too."

"I remember. Since you were what, five?"

"That's right. And the first time I kissed him...*really* kissed him?"

Rory felt suddenly breathless. "Yeah...?"

"A revelation."

"Oh, I love that!"

"But, Rory, I shouldn't encourage you. It's dangerous. You could lose what you have with him. Rafe and I almost did."

"But you *didn't.* You're so happy. I mean, look at you now."

"Well, yes. We have it all—I know that we do. And I am grateful for every day, every hour, every moment at his side."

"And do you ever regret taking that chance, sharing that first real kiss?"

"Not on your life. Even last spring, when things were the toughest...never."

"I knew you would say that."

Genny was quiet. Then, "When will you talk to him about how you feel?"

"Did I ever tell you that I tried to kiss him once, years ago?"

"No. I had no idea..."

"He turned me down. He said he was tempted, but I was too young for him and had my whole life ahead of me, that I was a real-life princess and he was only an ordinary guy who couldn't even make his marriage work—and what else? Oh, yeah. He said he would never do anything to threaten our friendship."

Genny made a pained sound. "Ouch."

"Yeah. It was awful. Practically damaged me for life."

"I'll bet."

"But now it's his turn to suffer. I mean, I know it's petty of me, but I'm feeling just a little bit smug."

"Don't make him suffer *too* much."

"I won't."

"What will you do?"

"Nothing. I'm thinking it's about time *he* made the first move."

Chapter Six

Walker didn't sleep any better in what was left of that night than he had the night before.

At daylight, when he got up to take care of the horses, Rory was downstairs waiting for him, dressed in jeans, work boots and a heavy sweater, looking fresh and rested and so damn beautiful he wanted to grab her and…unwrap her.

Yeah. Best Christmas present ever. Rory, wearing nothing but a tempting smile. Once he had her stark naked, her clothes strewn across the stairs, he would lift her high in his arms and carry her back to the tangled bed he'd just crawled out of.

"Thought you'd never get up," she teased, and flashed him a dimpled grin that tied the rock-hard knot of hungry desire even tighter inside him.

God. She would kill him. He'd curl up into a husk of frustrated longing and blow away on the winter wind without ever so much as laying a hand on her. "It's pretty cold out. Why don't you stay in, get the coffee going?"

"Not a chance." She took her heavy quilted jacket from the hall tree. "Let's get to work."

They went out into the predawn darkness. The snow had stopped, leaving a few inches of icy flakes on the ground to crunch beneath their boots as they crossed the yard.

By the time they finished in the stables, the sun was coming up. "How about a ride?" she asked. "Just a short one, before breakfast..."

So they tacked up and rode out, taking a trail he knew up into the hills above the Bar-N. A half hour or so after they left the stables, they reached Lookout Point, an outcropping with a great view of the Bar-N below.

As always, she had a camera with her. They dismounted. She changed lenses and followed him out onto the point. They gazed down at the circle of buildings. Alva and Bud still burned wood. A trail of smoke spiraled up from their chimney. The pines, the land and the rooftops were all dusted with sparkling new snow. She shot several pictures. And then she lowered her camera and simply took in the view.

"Such a pretty scene," she said, her breath emerging in a white vapor trail. "You're a lucky man, Walker." She slanted him a happy glance that took hold of his heart and wouldn't let go. "The Bar-N is something special. And you've made good choices, fixing up the houses and the cabins, making it as comfortable for visitors as it is beautiful to stand up here and admire."

He was admiring, all right. But not the Bar-N. "So it's been okay for you, staying here?"

Her smile bloomed wider, and the hand around his heart squeezed a little harder. The pain was delicious. Somehow, the more it made him burn to look at her, the better he felt, the more acutely alive—and the more terrified that he was headed for disaster.

She said, "I'm loving every minute. Believe me."

He wanted to reach for her, to feel her stiffen in

surprise—and then melt into his arms. To capture her lips. They would be cold at first from the icy air, but then swiftly growing warmer. "I'm glad you're here."

"Yeah?" So sweet. So hopeful. Reminding him of that long-ago August morning at Ice Castle Falls.

"Yeah." Somewhere far overhead, a bird cawed.

"Crow," she told him softly, though he already knew. Her eyes were the strangest electric-bronze color right then. He watched her gaze moving—from his eyes to his mouth, and back again.

It was right then, as he watched those amber eyes tracking, that he got the message loud and clear: she knew exactly what was happening with him. She had him figured out.

"Damn it, Rory." The two words came out sounding rough, dangerous as rocks tumbling down a mountain, picking up bigger and bigger boulders as they rolled, becoming a full-out landslide. "You *know*."

She caught her plump lower lip between her teeth, and he wanted to growl at her, *Let me do that.* And then she nodded. Her mouth trembled a little. It was almost a smile. But not quite.

He demanded, "How long have you known?"

She hitched up her pretty pointed chin. "You don't have to growl at me."

He growled again, "How long?"

She hesitated. For a second he thought she would refuse to answer him. But then she said, "Since last night, after the party. When we were having that last cup of cocoa by the fire…"

"I'm that obvious, huh?" He swore under his breath and didn't know whether to feel humiliated that he was behaving like a desperate kid with a first big crush, or relieved that she finally knew and they could move on from here—to where, exactly, he had no idea.

"Not obvious. Honestly. It was cumulative. You've been acting strange for days."

He reached out, clasped her arm in the quilted jacket, felt the softness, the firmness, the slender bones beneath. "Tell me..." The words ran out.

She looked down at his gloved hand, and then back up into his eyes. It burned, that look she gave him. Burned so good. Seared him where he stood. "Tell you...what?"

"Tell me what I told you five years ago. To forget about it, that it's a bad idea."

Her eyes sparked with defiance. "You can tell yourself that. No reason I need to do it, too." She eased her arm free of his grip. "Let's get back, get some breakfast."

He swiped off his hat and stood there, lost in the sight of her, as she put her camera away and mounted up. Once she was in the saddle, he only wanted to drag her back down off that horse and into his waiting arms.

She patted the gelding's neck and then bent low to whisper some soothing word that had the horse chuffing softly and twitching his ear. Lucky damn animal. "You coming, or not?"

With a muttered oath, he shoved his hat on his head and got back on his horse.

All that day she treated him the same as she always had—with warmth and fondness and easy smiles. She never said a word about those few minutes at Lookout Point, when she'd admitted that she was onto him, that she knew the desperate, hungry way he'd started thinking of her. She just went on as always, helping with breakfast, pitching in to clean up after the party, working on her laptop for a couple of hours. And then riding into town with him for groceries and to pick up a few things at the hardware store.

It was driving him crazy, to feel this way and know that she knew. But then again, well, it had been driving him crazy *before* he knew that she knew. So what was the difference, really? Either way, he'd lost his mind.

He needed to make a move of some kind, but all the possible moves seemed like bad ones. There were no safe choices. He felt frozen in place.

Somehow, he got through that day.

They returned home from town. Alva had left pork chops, lemon rice and mixed vegetables waiting in the oven. They dished up and sat down.

He looked across the table at her and she glanced up and into his eyes—and it was too much. He couldn't go on trying to ignore the heat and confusion all tangled up inside him. "Have I ruined everything?"

She set down her fork. "You have to stop being so hard on yourself. You have not ruined anything. Whatever happens, it will be all right."

"How can you know that?"

She actually chuckled. "Well, I *don't* know. Not really. But I was raised in a happy family where things always seem to work out in the end, so I'm going with that. Things will work out."

"My family wasn't so happy. My dad took off when Rye was only a baby."

"I know," she said gently. He'd told her all about it one night in the forest, camped out under the stars. "And your mother spent the rest of her life waiting for him."

"She...had it so bad for him. And she never got over it. It was like a disease with her. I always promised myself I would never be like that, pining for someone who'd been nothing but bad for me."

Rory knew what came next. "And then there was Denise, who did you wrong, who swore to love you forever and then left you cold."

"So I guess I don't have the same happy outlook as you."

She jumped right to his defense. "That's not true. Most of the time, you're a pretty upbeat guy."

"Not about this. Not about..." *Love.* The word was there, a threat and a promise inside his head and heart. He didn't let it out. "I don't want to lose you, to lose what we have."

She tipped her head to the side, thinking that over. "I don't want to lose you, either. But things change, you know? Between people, over time. You can't stop that. You can't make time stand still. We might...grow closer together. Or we might grow apart. But denying what you're feeling right now is not going to somehow magically keep our friendship all safe and tidy and just the way it's always been."

"What are *you* feeling?"

She only looked at him for a very long time. "Not fair," she said finally. And he knew she was right. He'd turned her down once. And he was the one who'd started this now. It was his job to step up, make his move.

Or let it go.

"Hey," she spoke softly.

"Yeah?"

"Eat your pork chop before it gets cold."

The night before had been a long one and Saturday night was the party at Rye's bar. So they both decided to turn in early. He switched off the fire and the lights.

She followed him up the stairs and along the hall to their two bedroom doors, across from each other. He turned to tell her good-night, and then, out of nowhere, she offered him her hand.

He took it, fast, before he could convince himself that he shouldn't. Wrapping his fingers around her softer, cooler ones, he felt the heat within him, coiling deep down. "Damn it to hell, Rory…"

She stepped up nice and close. She smelled of that perfume she always wore, of roses and oranges and a hint of some dark spice. He'd always liked her scent. But now, tonight, it seduced him, made his head spin. She pulled her hand back.

He felt the loss of her touch as a blow, sharp and cruel.

But then she tipped up her sweet mouth to him.

It was the best offer he'd had in a very long time. And yet it felt all wrong. "I'm supposed to be looking out for you, not stealing kisses at bedtime."

She took a soft, slow breath. "Because you're my bodyguard."

"That's right."

"Didn't I try to warn you that being my bodyguard was not a good idea?"

Oranges. Spice. What would she taste like, on his tongue? She really was killing him. "Uh, yeah. I believe that you did."

"You should have listened to me."

"Maybe so. Too late now, though."

"Is it?" She lifted a hand and laid it, flat, on his chest. His heart started booming. He was sure she could feel it bonging away in there, yet more proof of what she did to him.

And then, very slowly, she closed her slender fingers

into a fist, taking his shirt with it, and then pulling him down to her, until you couldn't fit so much as a feather between his mouth and hers.

It was too much. With a low, needful sound, he gave in, lowering his head that fraction more and touching those waiting lips with his.

Petal-soft and perfect, those lips of hers. She sighed. He let himself fall into her—but slowly, with care. It was his first real taste of her, in all the years of knowing her.

It might very well be his last. He was determined to savor it, to savor *her*.

She offered only her mouth to him and kept her fist, still clenching his shirt, between them. She didn't let her body sway to his.

He accepted those terms, even approved of them. It was important to him that they go no further than this.

This.

God, *this*…

He brushed his lips back and forth across her slightly parted ones. Sweet as sugar, tender as a breath, she stunned him with pleasure. He nipped her plump lower lip and she moaned—a tiny sound, inaudible, really.

Oh, but he heard it. His arms ached to draw her in—but no. He kept them at his sides.

Slowly, he settled his mouth more firmly on hers. He dipped his tongue in. So good, the taste of her. She swirled her tongue around his, teasing him, inviting him.

He moaned, a deeper sound, one that betrayed how close he was to losing control, to reaching out and hauling her close to him.

And that was when she let go of his shirt and stepped away.

He longed to grab her back. But there was his obligation, the contract he'd made with her mother, a promise to take care of her. It was a whole different kind of taking care of her to climb into her bed—not the kind her mother had intended, that was for sure.

So in the end, he only said, "'Night, Rory."

"'Night," she whispered, taking another step backward. Now she was fully past the threshold, into her bedroom. Slowly, she closed the door, those bronze eyes, shadowed to deep brown now, holding his until he lost sight of her and found himself standing there in the upper hallway.

Alone.

As soon as she shut the door between them, Rory turned and sagged against it.

Enough.

Yes, it had been fun, at first, to torment him a little. After all the years of keeping her feelings in check, giving him a little taste of his own medicine had been very, very sweet.

But Walker took his commitments so seriously. He didn't want to want her—at least, not now, while he had a responsibility as her protector.

Knowing him, he probably didn't want to want her, period. There were those issues they would have to get past. But they couldn't even begin to tackle the issues now, not as long as he was her bodyguard.

She had to do something about that. And she intended to.

As soon as it was morning in Montedoro.

She took a bath. Then she let Lucky in, got in bed and read half of a mystery novel on her laptop, with the cat curled up next to her. When she grew tired of reading, she played video games and fiddled with some of the shots she'd taken. Way too slowly, the hours crawled by.

At 1:00 a.m.—nine, in Montedoro—she picked up her phone and called her mother's cell.

Adrienne Bravo-Calabretti, Sovereign Princess of Montedoro, answered on the first ring. "Aurora, darling. Hello."

"Good morning, Mother."

A pause, then cautiously, "Isn't it very late there?"

"It's just one."

"Are you well?"

Rory got down to it. "This isn't working out, having Walker as my bodyguard."

"How so?"

"Can't you just take my word for it? Please."

Silence. "Are you angry with me, my darling?"

"Well, yes. I guess I am, a little."

"Why?"

"Oh, please."

"Oh, please?" her mother echoed. "That tells me nothing. What does that mean?"

"You're making me feel like a bratty child, Mother."

"Darling, I can't *make* you feel anything. Your feelings are all your own."

Rory slumped against the pillows and took a long, slow breath.

Her mother spoke again. "I really do like your friend Walker so much." Her mother and her father had met him in person just once, four years ago, when they came to Justice Creek for a visit—and to check out the place Rory seemed to want to spend so much time. "Is he… not taking care of you?"

Rory wanted to pitch her laptop across the room. "Of

course he's taking care of me. He hardly lets me out of his sight. He's the most responsible man I've ever known."

"Then what is the problem?"

"I don't want to go into it. It's personal."

That elicited a longer-than-ever pause from her mother. Finally, "Fair enough. I'll have Marcus send a replacement." Commandant Marcus Desmarais was Rory's sister Rhia's husband. He ran the Covert Command Unit, the elite Montedoran fighting force from which the family's bodyguards were chosen.

"No replacement," Rory said flatly.

"Oh, but, darling, we've talked about this and—"

"Yes, we have. And you haven't listened. I promise, if I go somewhere dangerous, I will take security. But Justice Creek is not Afghanistan. I don't need a bodyguard—not here. I truly don't. I want my freedom, Mother. I *need* it. You have to let go and give it to me."

Another brief pause then, "All right," her mother said wearily.

Rory's mouth dropped open. "Did I hear you correctly? Did you just say 'all right'—as in, no bodyguard?"

"Yes, I did. You're very insistent, darling. And your father and I have been talking about it. He says I'm holding on too tightly."

"You think?" But she said it affectionately.

"You are my baby, the last of my brood."

Rory chuckled. "You make us sound like puppies."

Her mother's answering laugh warmed her. "I love you, Aurora Eugenia."

"Oh, Mother. And I love you."

* * *

Walker went downstairs an hour earlier than usual Saturday morning. He was hoping to steal a little time on his own before Rory came down and filled up his world.

He got lucky. She wasn't down yet. Technically, as her bodyguard, he shouldn't leave the house without her. But he needed to get outside, in the open, to clear his head of the scent of her, to clear his mind and his heart, too.

So he piled on the outerwear and left the house, Lonesome trailing after him. He went straight to the stables. He tended the horses, Bud joining him after a while and helping him finish up. Once that chore was handled, Bud returned to his house. Walker went and stood in the yard and stared up at the dark, star-thick sky and took long, deep breaths.

One week until the wedding. And after the wedding, Rory would go. He just needed to get through that week without doing anything too stupid, needed to remember that he had a job to do, a responsibility he'd taken on. He'd made a contract with her mother, the sovereign princess, and he needed to keep that in the front of his mind.

One week. And then she would go…

God. He was a basket case. She was driving him wild and he needed her to go—but he didn't know how he would stand it once she left.

She had him spinning in circles. The last day or two, he was getting to kind of despise himself. Somehow, he'd turned into a steaming pile of tortured feelings—not like any kind of man at all.

That was the thing about him. Deep down, he was just like his mother. Darla Noonan McKellan spent her whole life loving a man who'd left her and their children without a backward glance. And Walker? He'd never learned how to want a woman in moderation. When he fell, it was like jumping off a mountain, a surrender of all control, so that all he could do was plummet helplessly to the rocks below.

Time to go in, time to face Rory again and find some way to get through this day. And the next one, and the one after that.

As he started for the front steps, he noticed that the light was on in the entry. He'd turned it off when he went out. She must be up, waiting. Wondering why he hadn't come down. His heart raced as if he'd run a marathon and his palms, in his heavy gloves, were sweating.

Easy, man. Take a deep breath and suck it the hell up.

He mounted the porch steps and went in, Lonesome bumping in behind him, sliding around him, heading straight for the kitchen and his food bowl. She was sitting on the bottom stair, long dark hair pulled back in a ponytail, wearing jeans, work boots and a thermal T with a flannel shirt over it, looking like every rancher's fantasy of the perfect woman: hot as the Yellowstone caldera and ready to work.

She stood. "I was wondering where you were." He noticed then that she had her cell phone in her hand. "Hold on, Mother."

He didn't think he liked this. "What's going on?"

She held out the phone. "My mother would like to talk to you."

His heart dropped to his boots. It felt like an ambush, somehow. But what could he do? He took the phone. "Your Highness?"

That smooth, cultured voice said, "Hello, Walker.

My daughter tells me you're doing a wonderful job as her bodyguard."

"Well, uh, thank you, ma'am."

"But she's also finally convinced me that she needs her independence and that it's time I gave up being overly protective of her."

"Ah," he said idiotically, because she'd stopped talking and it seemed like his turn to make some sort of sound.

"So I'm relieving you of duty, as of right now. Rory wants a chance to take care of herself. I'm giving it to her."

Did that mean she was going, leaving his house? Of course it did. If she didn't have to have him watching over her, she could go to the Haltersham, order up room service and visit the spa. She could rent her own vehicle and go where she wanted, when she wanted, without him stuck to her side like a burr on a saddle blanket.

His gut churned. He turned away, so that she couldn't see his face until he got better control of his damn, wimpy emotions.

"Walker?" Rory's mother asked.

"Yes, ma'am?"

"You *will* cash that check that I sent you. You may consider that at my command."

"Uh, yes, ma'am. All right, then."

"Merry Christmas, Walker."

"Thank you, ma'am. Same to you."

"I hope we'll be seeing you in Montedoro someday soon."

Why the hell would he ever go to Montedoro? But his mouth was on autopilot. "Yes, ma'am. One of these days, I'd like that very much." He made himself turn back to

Rory, but he refused to meet her eyes as he handed her the phone.

She took it. "Thanks, Mother… Yes, it's all arranged. I'll be there, as promised, the day after Clara's wedding. My love to everyone. Yes, right. Goodbye…" She disconnected the call.

He stood locked in place, staring at her as she gazed steadily back at him. And then he made himself move. He took off his gloves, stuck them in the pocket of his heavy jacket and hung it on the coat tree. Then he dropped to the stairs and pulled off his dirty boots. He carried the boots to the door, pulled it open and tossed them out onto the porch.

When he shut the door and turned back around, she was still standing in the same spot near the foot of the stairs, still holding her phone.

Might as well get on with it. "So. You all packed and ready to go?"

She puffed out her lips with a heavy breath. "You're angry with me."

Damn straight he was angry. "I'm guessing you're moving to the Haltersham, then?"

"One of us had to do *something*, Walker. You're making yourself crazy, you know? And you're making me crazy, too."

The fact that she happened to be right didn't ease the storm inside him one bit. "Just tell me what you want from me."

"I want you to admit that it wasn't working out, to stop blaming me for putting an end to it."

"Are we going to stand here and flap our jaws all morning?"

"Walker…" She reached out. Her finger brushed his

sleeve. He wanted to grab hold and never let go. Instead, he stepped back, out of her reach. "You know you're being a complete jerk about this." She said it gently. Regretfully.

He didn't need her damn gentleness. "Look. Do you want some breakfast before you go?"

"The horses—"

"I took care of them. Breakfast?"

"Sure."

Rory felt her temper rising to meet his.

But she refused to give in to it. She just stuck her phone in her pocket and followed him to the kitchen, where he fed Lonesome and Lucky and then they worked side by side without a word, putting the breakfast on the table.

They took their chairs across from each other and ate in a deep and burning silence. That meal zipped by lightning fast. She knocked back the last of her coffee, picked up her plate and carried it to the counter, bending to scrape off the last bite of sausage and eggs into the compost bin under the sink.

His chair dragged the floor. "Leave it," he said. "Get your stuff together."

That did it. Carefully, she set the plate on the counter. And then she turned to confront him. He stopped midway between the table and the sink as she caught his hooded gaze and held it. "It's fine if you're mad. I think you're overreacting, but that kind of seems to be your style the last few days." She waited for him to say something. Anything. But she got nothing. "All right. I probably should have told you that I was going to try again to get through to my mother on the bodyguard issue. I apologize for not telling you."

He just stood there in his stocking feet, holding his plate and his cup, wearing that cold-eyed, granite-jawed expression that made her want to pick up her own plate again—and hurl it at him.

She tried one more time. "Look at it this way. Now, if you want to kiss me, you can just do it. No more conflict of interest. Not on that front, at least."

"Go on," he said, gesturing toward the central hallway with his empty mug. "Get your things."

"I'm getting pretty fed up with you, Walker."

But he only stood there, waiting for her to go.

So, fine, then. She would give him exactly what he was waiting for.

Walker felt like an ass and a half. Probably because he was being one.

And he kept being one, as he loaded her luggage into the SUV and drove her to town.

At the Haltersham, he pulled in at the wide front portico. The mountains loomed, gorgeous, craggy, snow-capped, behind the white, red-roofed hotel.

A porter appeared as if by magic, rolling a brass luggage trolley.

The porter opened her door for her. "Your Highness. So good to have you with us again."

"Hello, Jacob. How are you?" She pressed some bills into his hand and, beaming, he rolled the trolley to the back of the vehicle. Walker beeped the rear door open and the unloading began.

Rory picked up the giant bag at her feet and started to swing her legs to the ground.

He couldn't quite let her go like that. "You need anything, you call me."

She froze. But she refused to turn her sweet face to him. "Thanks for the ride. I'll see you tonight."

He remained seriously pissed at her—for reasons he knew made no sense at all.

So he just sat there behind the wheel, and she got out and shut the door. He watched her walk up the wide front steps, drank in the gentle sway of her hips and the way the thin winter sunlight brought out bronze lights in her dark hair. By the time the porter finished loading his cart and shut the hatch in back, she'd already disappeared through the wide lobby doors.

Walker started the engine and got out of there.

Chapter Seven

After Rory checked in and got settled in her suite, she called the concierge and they got her a nice little 4x4 from that car rental place on Sweetwater Way. She went downstairs and they had the car there waiting and the paperwork ready.

Before noon, she had both her room and her ride. They always treated her right at the Haltersham.

Unlike some people she could mention.

It was pretty depressing the way things had gone with Walker. Never, in all the years she'd known him, had he behaved the way he had that morning.

She went back upstairs for a while and fiddled on her laptop. Around one, she decided to go to Clara's café for lunch and see if that might cheer her up a little.

In the five years that Clara had been running it, the Library Café had become a Justice Creek landmark. The place was spare, streamlined and yet comfortable, the tan-and-coffee-colored walls hung with art by local artists. There were lots of windows and great mountain views. Every table had a pendant light above it, the glass shades in swirling, bright patterns, no two the same. In the center of the dining area, a cast-iron spiral staircase led up to a second dining level, which was open to the main floor.

One wall was all mahogany bookcases, accessible from both floors, every shelf packed. You could read while you ate—or take a book home with you if it caught your fancy. Nobody policed the books. People took them and brought them back when they were finished. Customers regularly brought in boxes full of well-used volumes to donate, so those shelves never went bare.

And the food? Clara served all-organic beef and free-range chicken from the Rising Sun Ranch in Wyoming, which was jointly owned by three Bravo cousins. The lamb and pork were organic, too. As much as possible, she ordered her produce from local farms. She offered craft beer and wonderful, reasonably priced Northwest wines. And then there were the desserts. The café had its own pastry chef, Martine Brown. Martine had been called a genius by more than one famous foodie.

The place was packed for Saturday lunch, but the waitresses all knew Rory. She got a deuce in a nice, cozy corner.

Clara came by for a hug. "Apple-smoked BLT with avocado?"

"You read my mind."

"And to drink?"

"Just water."

"You got it. I'll be back when I get a minute—and wait, where's your favorite bodyguard?"

"Don't ask."

Clara frowned. "I'm not liking the sound of that."

"I'm at the Haltersham as of this morning."

"What? I want to hear everything." Clara hugged her again. "We'll talk…"

"Go. I know you're swamped."

So Clara rushed off to expedite orders, and Rory

browsed the bookshelves and had lunch. She hung around after, waiting for Clara. By three, the place had started to clear out, and at four Clara turned the Closed sign on. It took another half hour for all the customers to leave and a half hour after that for Clara to finish closing up. Rory waited for her.

At a little after five, they walked around the corner to Clara's house together.

Once they were inside and Clara had her shoes off and her feet up, Rory started to feel a little guilty. "I should go, let you rest. I'll bet you're beat. And there's still the party tonight."

Clara waved a hand. "But I don't have to go in until afternoon tomorrow. Renee always has my back." Renee Beauchamp was Clara's head waitress and manager.

"But really, Clara. How are you feeling?"

"Better, to tell you the truth. I don't know what made me think it would be a good idea to keep the baby a secret. Now it's out I feel calmer about everything." She did seem more relaxed. But Rory still didn't get what was really going on with Clara and Ryan. She had a feeling that Nell had nailed the real issue in her Black Russian-fueled rant Thursday night.

At some point, Lord knew why, Ryan and Clara had ended up in bed together, with classic consequences. When the stick turned blue, they had settled on the classic solution. But "classic" wasn't always the right way to go.

She was trying to figure out a graceful way to broach that subject, when Clara said, "Now, talk. What is going on with you and Walker?"

And she really, really did want to talk about Walker.

So she gave Clara a quick rundown of the situation,

including Walker's sudden, rather tortured romantic interest in her—and the fact that she'd finally convinced her mother she could go without a bodyguard. "So I made my mother fire him first thing this morning."

Clara blinked. "Whoa. You mean, you're not interested in getting anything going with him, after all?"

"Of course I'm interested. I've been crushing on the guy since I was eighteen years old."

"So, then, why fire him and move to the Haltersham?"

"Clara. He was never going to make a move on me when he felt responsible for me as my bodyguard. I wanted to—I don't know—free him up, I guess, to remove a barrier that was holding him back. I just wanted him to give the two of us a chance."

"But your plan backfired."

"Oh, yeah. What I actually did was seriously piss him off. Maybe his pride? Maybe he's thinking that *I* think… Oh, God. As if I *know* what he's thinking. Because I don't."

"Give him a day or two. He'll come around."

"Oh, I hope so. I've never seen him like this."

"Well, there's tonight, right? You'll be there. He'll be there. Try to talk to him. Work it out."

"I tried this morning. Repeatedly."

"That's so weird. Walker's usually the most reasonable guy in the room."

"Not lately. Not with me."

"That's too bad—but it could be a good sign."

"A good sign of what?"

"That he's so crazy for you, he can't think straight."

Rory gave her a patient look. "I'm just worried I'll never get him to talk to me."

"Then maybe you should forget about talking—for

tonight, anyway. You'll be dressed to seduce. Go with that."

"Right," Rory replied with zero enthusiasm.

Clara insisted, "You *will* be dressed to seduce."

"Is that an order?"

"You bet it is. It's a bachelorette party, after all. I want to see short skirts and do-me shoes on all of my bridesmaids."

"Hold it. There's a *dress* code for the party tonight?"

"Damn right."

"Oh, come on, Clara. Is that even fair?"

"Who ever told you life was going to be fair? Are you trying to tell me you don't have a short skirt and killer heels?"

"Of course I do."

"Then wear them—and look at it this way. If he won't work it out with you, you can at least drive him mad with desire."

"You haven't been listening to me. Driving him mad with desire has not worked out for me so far. Right now, I would prefer that he would just talk to me."

Clara sighed. "Sorry, honey. Sometimes a girl has to take what she can get."

The party started at nine in the upstairs bar at McKellan's.

"Rory!" Ryan greeted her at the top of the stairs. They shared a hug. And then he swept out an arm. "What do you think? I had my crew go for a combination holiday and bachelor party theme."

"Perfect," she replied, as he turned to greet the next guest.

Actually, it looked more like New Year's—with shiny

streamers everywhere, laser party lights and champagne on ice. The upper room was already packed with people, the DJ on the corner stage spinning rock-and-roll Christmas tunes.

Clara appeared out of the crowd and handed her a flute full of champagne. "Love that sparkly bronze top. And the skirt is barely decent, which is amazing. And those shoes…?" They were Valentino, lace-wrapped leather with crystal accents and five-inch heels. "Perfect." She leaned close again. "He won't know what hit him. The Mack truck effect."

Rory's pulse accelerated. "Is he here?"

"Not yet."

A sad thought occurred to her. "He *is* coming, right?"

"He'd better."

Ryan appeared again, stepping in next to Clara, who sent him a strange, tight little smile. Ryan's mouth barely twitched in response. He asked Rory, "By the way, where's my brother?"

Rory really didn't feel like explaining all that right then. So she only shrugged. "Not a clue."

He kept after her. "But I don't get it. I thought he was supposed to be your bodyguard."

Clara muttered, "Didn't she just tell you she doesn't know where he is?"

Ryan looked bewildered. "But I was only—"

"Come on." Clara grabbed his hand. "The DJ's playing our song. We need to dance."

"'Walking 'Round in Women's Underwear' is our song? Clara, what the hell? I just—"

"Shut up and dance." And she waltzed him into the crowd, where he couldn't ask Rory any more depressing questions.

Rory stared after them, torn between worrying about how they were getting along and feeling glum about Walker.

But then Nell grabbed her and spun her around. "God, you look hot. If you weren't my cousin, I think I'd try to have sex with you."

Rory couldn't help grinning. "You are looking stunningly doable yourself."

"Well, I try." Nell wore a jaw-dropping strapless red minidress that clung to every beautiful curve.

"Rory!" The other cousins crowded around.

Rory greeted them with hugs and air kisses. They all seemed to be having a great time—and getting along, too, which was the best news of all.

Everyone had got the bachelorette dress code memo. They wore short skirts and skimpy party tops and shoes made to drive a man insane. They led her to the buffet, which included all kinds of snacks and finger foods. And for dessert, a red-and-green corset cake decorated with ribbons that looked like holly. Also cupcakes in Christmas colors topped with miniature frosting G-strings, bras and leather-looking studded jockstraps.

Rory ate a little and danced a little and tried not to be disappointed that Walker had probably stayed away from his own brother's bachelor party in order to avoid seeing her.

At eleven, with a big "Ho-ho-ho!" Santa arrived. He carried a giant green Santa bag over one muscular shoulder. Everyone whistled and applauded, clearing a path for him.

He jumped up on the bar and whipped packages out of the bag, tossing them out over the crowd. They all laughed and ripped them open. There were feather boas, candy G-strings and a pink drink cozy that said She's Finally Picked One—and more.

Once his Santa bag was empty, he threw that over his shoulder. A bartender caught it. And then everybody cheered as the DJ started playing music clearly meant to strip to.

And Santa did. He was down to his big black boots and a red satin thong when Mrs. Santa appeared, in a white wig with wire-rim glasses, wearing an awful baggy green dress and granny boots.

Two helpful guys hoisted her up on the bar and everyone, including Santa, clapped and shouted encouragements as the missus got out of everything but the boots, a green G-string, a red bra—and the wig and granny glasses. She was in excellent shape under that ugly green dress.

"The penis candy isn't half bad," said the unforgettable voice she'd been waiting to hear all night. He was standing right behind her.

Her heart did the happy dance, and she told it to knock it off as she turned to Walker. "All of a sudden, you're speaking to me?"

His eyes burned into hers. And he said, low and rough and for her ears alone, "How'd you get so damn beautiful?" He held out the bag of X-rated candy. "Help yourself."

She was way too glad to see him. Her mouth tried to smile. She didn't let it. "No, thank you."

He dropped the bag on the nearest table and grabbed her hand, those big, rough fingers wrapping tight around hers, sending excited shivers surging across her skin. "Let's find someplace quiet."

She didn't say no. How could she?

He turned and led her through the crowd toward the stairs to the main floor. Ryan, behind the bar mixing up a row of pretty pink drinks, spotted him and called his name.

Walker gave him a wave and kept moving, across the upper floor and down the stairs, where it was just as packed as upstairs, but with the regular Saturday-night crowd. She followed, but hanging back a little, making him work for it after the way he'd treated her that morning.

"Where are we going?" she called to him as he pulled her along.

"This way," he said, which told her nothing. He led her under an arch at the end of the bar and down a short hallway to a pair of swinging doors. He pushed through them into the kitchen.

"Walker, hey!" The cooks aimed a wave in his direction and went back to their work.

He pulled her through another door and they were in the storage rooms. He led her past metal shelves stacked with restaurant supplies and food to the door to Ryan's office. It was locked.

"Stay right here," he commanded. "I mean it, Rory. Don't try to run away." And he went back the way they'd come.

She leaned against the door and wondered why she'd let him drag her down here and if he would have to go all the way back upstairs and find Ryan to let them in. But then he reappeared just a minute or two after leaving her. He held up a key. Apparently, he knew where to find one downstairs. She straightened from the door and stood dangerously close to him, all too aware of the warmth of him and the clean scents of soap and aftershave that clung to his skin. He wore plain dark slacks, a black dress shirt and his best pair of tooled boots.

And, well, she ought to keep in mind how pissed off she was at him. But she couldn't help it. Gladness filled her heart, just to be standing beside him.

He opened the door and gestured her in. Her pulse ratcheting higher again, she went in first.

The office was nothing fancy. Ryan had a wide oak desk, a couple of file cabinets, three chairs, a sofa and a sad-looking rubber plant near the lone window. Walker followed her in and closed the door behind him, locking them into the functional space.

She backed to the desk and faced off against him. "All right. It's quiet. Talk."

He didn't. Not for several never-ending seconds during which he just stared at her. When he did speak, he said thickly, "Those shoes are just plain bad. And that skirt, that itty-bitty shirt that shines the same color as your eyes? Cruel, Rory. Heartless."

A flush of pleasure warmed her cheeks. She scowled really hard so he wouldn't know his flattery was getting to her. "Blame Clara. Her party, her dress code—and are you going to apologize to me for the way you acted this morning, or not?"

He looked down at his good boots. "You're driving me out of my mind, okay?"

Triumph flared through her at the admission. She tamped it down. This was about more than her feminine ego. "So. You're attracted to me now, and that's somehow my fault?"

"I didn't say that."

She perched on the edge of the desk. "Well, yeah. You pretty much did."

He flashed her a hot glance—and then stared at his boots some more. In the silence between them, the pounding beat of the music overhead seemed to grow louder.

And then at last, he spoke again. "I had it set in my mind, that's all. That somehow I would get through the wedding without letting things get out of hand between us, that you would go home and I would…I don't know, get over you and move on, I guess. All without getting in too deep, without getting hurt—or hurting you. And then you changed everything up without warning, calling your mother, talking her into letting you go off on your own."

It didn't really make sense to her. "But then, why wouldn't you be happy to have me out of your house, out of the bed in the room across from yours? Why wouldn't you be happy that I reduced the, er, temptation?"

His head shot up and he pinned her with a look. "You don't get it."

"Isn't that what I just said?"

"And now you're going to expect me to explain," he muttered in a weary tone.

"That is exactly what I expect."

He slanted her a narrow-eyed look. "You're getting that princess tone, you know that? Like you rule the world?"

That stung. "I don't need this." She straightened to go. "You're blocking the door."

He put up both hands. "Stay. Please." He did seem contrite.

"Oh, Walker." She ached inside. For both of them. "You're going to need to tell me something that will make me want to stay."

And he said, "It's just not easy. I don't know where

to start." She only watched him, waiting. And eventually, he did try again. "Once I started seeing you differently, once I started wanting you, having you with me all the time was torture…" He folded his arms across his chest then, in that defensive posture she'd been seeing so much of lately.

Cautiously, reminding herself not to get comfortable, she sat on the desk again. "So I'll ask one more time, why not be glad, then, that I moved to the Haltersham?"

"Because I didn't want you to go!" The words were hot with frustration. He took a moment—to rein himself in? Whatever. When he spoke again, his voice was gentler. "Because it was torture, but it was…good, too. Real good. You and me together, round the clock. Even at night alone in my bed, I knew you were there, right across the hall. I got to have you near me, see you smile, ride out with you in the mornings after we finished with the horses, sit across from you at dinner, watch a movie with you, just the two of us, side by side on the couch. Yeah, it was just about killing me, not to put my hands on you. But it was also my reward." He uncrossed those big arms and lifted a hand to rub the back of his neck. "Damn. Is that pitiful?"

"No," she whispered, and she meant it.

He grunted. "Sounds pretty pitiful to me."

She crossed her legs and rotated her ankle in her lacy, sparkly shoe, watched those blue eyes of his flare with heat as she did it. "You're telling me that you didn't want me to go, that you liked having me at the ranch, even though it was difficult for you, that just being with me, even with all the usual barriers in place, was enough for you?"

He tipped his head back and stared at the ceiling, as

though seeking help from above. "That is exactly what I'm telling you."

"But see, Walker, that's just us being together in the way that we've always been. Just being friends, keeping a certain physical distance. But with this new excitement between us..."

He dragged in a slow breath. "What about it?"

"It's *not* enough for me."

His eyes were on her again, laser-focused. And then, gruffly, he admitted, "It's not enough for me, either."

She let out a groan. "So, then, what in the world are we arguing about?"

Obstinate as ever, he muttered, "If we took it further, it wouldn't turn out well."

"How can you be sure of that?"

"Wake up, Rory. You're a princess. I'm no prince."

She leveled her coldest look on him then. "Do not give me that. So my mother rules a country. I'm not my mother. Being a princess is not a problem for me."

"It is for me."

"It doesn't have to be. It's just an artificial reason you've always held on to, like your being eleven years older than me. Just one of those fake reasons you're giving yourself so you won't have to take the next step with me."

"You've got me turned around in circles."

"Right. And you keep saying you love that."

"Rory, you *matter* to me. And we've got something special between us. I don't want to take a chance of wrecking it."

"But, Walker, you've said it yourself. Everything between us has changed. In that sense, it's already wrecked."

"Don't say that."

"Don't say the truth? Sorry, but there's no going back. And I don't *want* to go back."

"You're braver than I am." He said it in a rough whisper as the rock-and-roll Christmas music pounded overhead. "You always have been."

Was she? Not really. "You think I'm not scared—to lose what we've always had? Wrong. I just don't see any going back now, that's all." *Because I've been dealing with this wanting since the day I first saw you,* she thought, but lacked the courage to say.

It seemed she'd spent most of their friendship getting all torn up over him, then getting over him and moving on—only to realize at some later point that the wanting hadn't gone away at all. She'd just managed to pretend for a while that it had.

And if she were as brave as he seemed to think, she'd open her mouth and tell him right now that she'd been wanting him for seven years.

But she didn't. She wasn't that brave. And she just wasn't ready to give him that kind of power over her.

He was watching her now, his focus absolute. A hungry wolf on the hunt, a hawk sighting the kill. How long had she waited for him to look at her in just this way—waited without really admitting to herself that she was waiting?

Too long.

She loved it, that look. So hungry and so hot. His blue gaze willed her to cross the distance between them and come to him.

She longed with her whole heart to do just that. But at some point, he had to do the reaching, to make the move. He had to be the one to come to her and he had to make that choice on his own.

He knew it, too. “You’re not coming over here.” Slowly, she shook her head. “You’re going to make *me* do it.”

“Uh-uh. You’re going to choose to do it.” *Or not to do it,* a knowing voice in her head taunted. She steeled her heart against that voice. Now was not the time for doubt.

He wanted her. And she’d made it more than clear that she was willing. He *would* come for her.

He said something so low that she couldn’t quite make out the word. Something thick and dangerous and dark. And then, at last, he straightened from the door.

And he came for her.

She turned her mouth into his palm and bit the pad of his thumb, sending a sharp burst of pleasure racing along the nerves there, making him groan again. "I'm willing," she said, her voice smoky and low. "But not exactly prepared."

"Now you mention it, neither am I." He hadn't thought to bring a condom, hadn't known how it would go with her, hadn't dreamed he would need one—not right now, not here.

And come to think of it, no way. Not here. Not across his brother's scarred-up desk in the back of McKellan's. Not for their first time.

"Rory." He brushed his hands down the satiny sweep of her hair. Because he could. Because this was happening. She wanted it and he wanted it and there was just no stopping it now. He might as well enjoy every second for as long as it lasted. So that later, if their friendship imploded in the aftermath of this unexpected five-alarm fire between them, well, at least he'd have some scorching memories to keep him company at night.

"Oh, Walker…"

"Not here." He leaned closer, pressed his rough cheek to her smooth one, allowed himself to get lost again, just a little, in the feel and the scent of her. "It shouldn't be here…"

She sighed. "You're right. I know you are."

Someone knocked at the door. "Walker?" It was Rye. "Rory? You in there?"

Walker pressed his forehead to hers again and whispered, "Caught in the act."

She chuckled. And then she called out, "Yes, we're here!"

The doorknob jiggled. "Why's the door locked?"

Walker held her gaze. "Should I let him in?"

"Well, it is his office, after all."

Rye jiggled the knob again. "Come on, you guys."

"He's not going away," she said.

"Right." Reluctantly, he let her go and went to open the door. "What?"

Rye regarded him, narrow-eyed. "What's going on in here?"

"If I told you, you wouldn't believe it."

Rye craned around him and asked Rory, "Everything okay?"

"Everything is just perfect," she replied in that husky, womanly tone that put Walker's poor body on high alert all over again.

Rye clapped him on the shoulder. "I was beginning to wonder if you would show."

"Wouldn't miss it."

"And then you got here—and disappeared again."

"I'm right here. Ready to party."

"You?" Rye scoffed. "Party? I'll believe it when I see it."

Rory stepped up close, taking Walker's arm and pressing herself into his side, a more-than-friends move that had Rye's eyes widening. Overhead, the DJ was still on the job. Walker could just make out Chuck Berry crooning "Merry Christmas, Baby." She squeezed his arm and he gave her a look that probably revealed more than Rye needed to know.

"I want to dance," she said, head tipped up to him, a knowing smile on those lips he couldn't wait to kiss again.

Whcn he looked back at Rye, his brother's mouth was hanging open, his gaze darting from Rory to Walker and back again. Finally, Rye found his voice. "Well, okay, then. The night is young. Come on back upstairs."

Rory would never forget that night. Whatever happened in the end between her and Walker, Clara and Ryan's joint bachelor party at McKellan's would be a memory to treasure.

She led Walker out onto the dance floor and melted into his arms. It wasn't the first time she'd danced with him—far from it. But it was the first time dancing with him had ever felt like this. Sexy and intimate and heavy with the promise of what was to come.

She knew people were staring, most of them probably as stunned as Rye had been at the sight of two longtime good buddies suddenly discovering a whole new dimension to their relationship. Rory had no doubt the rumors were flying, just as they had when Clara and Ryan decided to get married.

But this, with her and Walker, was a whole different thing than with Clara and Ryan. She doubted people were talking about how it wasn't *that* way between them. Because, well, as of tonight, it most definitely *was* that way. Exactly that way.

And Rory could not have cared less who knew it.

Oh, they didn't get flagrant. Walker wasn't the kind of man to get flagrant in public. But all she had to do was look up into those hungry blue eyes of his, feel the way he held her in those hard arms—just a little too close. Listen to his voice when he whispered in her ear.

Yeah. It was happening. It was *that* way between them.

For a while, they played pool in the back room. And then they danced some more.

Ryan had mistletoe tacked up in every doorway. Walker danced her under a big sprig of it during a slow song about a lonely girl waiting for Santa to bring her the man of her dreams. And then he lowered his mouth to hers and kissed her, a kiss that was long and soft and so very sweet.

Now, there was a moment, one she wouldn't soon forget.

"Come home with me tonight." He kissed the words onto her lips.

She twined her arms behind his neck. "I thought you'd never ask."

Ruefully, he whispered, "I need to spend a little time with Rye first."

She nodded. "Being the only groomsman and all…"

He left her to find his brother. She joined her cousins, who seemed to be having a great time. Wonder of wonders, they were also still getting along.

"Something's up with Rye," Walker said when he rejoined her an hour later. They'd found a little corner table where the light was extra dim and they were more or less alone to whisper together and steal a kiss or two. "He's only pretending to have a good time."

"Did he tell you that?"

"He didn't have to. I was six when he was born. I used to change his diapers. I have a lot of experience at reading his moods. If something's bugging him, I can tell."

"Did you ask him what was wrong?"

"I did. And I got complete denial. Told me he's happy, the luckiest man alive."

She mentioned the strained glances between Ryan and Clara earlier that night. "I'll try to get some time alone with Clara—maybe tomorrow. See if I can get her to open up a little."

"And then what?" he asked just a little bit bleakly.

She put up both hands. "Hey. I'm winging it here..."

He leaned in close. "Your eyes are deep brown in the shadows like this..."

She touched his cheek, in that sexy hollow just below his cheekbone, and then she traced the shape of his ear. "Are you changing the subject on me?" It came out all breathless, with a little hitch at the end.

He eased a hand under her hair and cupped the nape of her neck. She loved that, the cherishing way he touched her, the roughness of his palm against her skin. "So tell me. Was there something you planned to do about Clara and Rye tonight?"

She stared into his shadowed eyes and all she could think of was that soon, she would go home with him, to his house at the Bar-N and, at last, to his bed—and what was the question?

Right. About Clara and Ryan. "What *can* I do tonight?"

"Exactly." He pulled her closer. His breath was warm across her cheek. And then he kissed her.

And after that, there was just the two of them, sharing kisses in the corner, getting up a few minutes later to dance some more.

The party finally broke up at a little before three.

By then, she was aching to be alone with him. He offered to go with her to the Haltersham. But she knew that Lonesome and Lucky would be waiting at the ranch. And the horses would need tending within the next few hours.

"Not the Haltersham," she told him. "The Bar-N. I'll follow you."

Still in her party clothes and her vintage ankle-length

black velvet evening coat, she climbed in behind the wheel of her rented 4x4 and she followed him home.

When they got there, they went up the front steps together. In the entry, they stopped for a kiss—a long, slow one—as Lonesome waited a few feet away. Lucky, on the stairs, meowed once in protest, impatient for the humans to stop fondling each other and come up to bed.

Walker helped her out of her velvet coat, shrugged out of his and hung them both on the hall tree. "You want anything? Coffee?"

"Yes, I do want something. But coffee's not it."

"Good," he said gruffly.

They went up the stairs with their arms around each other, Lucky leading the way and Lonesome taking up the rear. For the first time, when they reached the end of the upper hall, she didn't have to say good-night and turn for the other door.

In his room, he pushed a dimmer switch on the wall. The room brightened to a soft glow. Lucky jumped up on a comfortable chair by the front window and Lonesome stretched out at the foot of the bed. Walker took her in his arms again.

But she pressed her hands against his chest. "This is the first time I've ever been in your bedroom."

He bent close. "And?"

"I just want to look around for a moment."

He traced a finger down the outside of her arm, causing a chaos of sensation to spread in ripples across her skin. "You want a tour? It will be short."

"Give it to me anyway." She bit his earlobe. And loved that he couldn't control a rough gasp when she did it.

So he let go of her and stepped away. She wanted to reach out and grab him back.

But she made herself wait as he gestured around the large, simple room. "Chair. Chair with cat. Steamer trunk my great-great-grandmother Aislinn O'Meara brought with her from Ireland. Lodgepole bed. Matching bed stands. Twin bureaus made by my great-uncle Stanley. Fireplace." He went over and turned it on. Cheery flames licked the artificial logs within. He turned and pointed at the inner door. "Master bath through there, walk-in closet beyond."

"It's just how I pictured it." And it was. Rustic and comfortable, the bed linens thick and inviting, in red, brown and tan with blue accents. "Beautiful."

He returned to her and tipped up her chin with a finger. "It's just a room. *You're* what's beautiful."

All at once, she was trembling. "I can't believe I'm here with you."

He pulled her close again, warming her with his body that was so big and strong and easy to lean against. He took her face between his hands, brushed a kiss between her brows. "Reservations?"

She met those blue eyes steadily. "Not a one."

"All right, then." He put those wonderful capable hands around her waist and lifted her. And she did what came naturally, wrapping her legs around him, hooking her ankles at the small of his back. Her skirt rode up. Way up. He stroked his hands downward to cradle her bare thighs and they groaned in unison.

She lowered her mouth to his and kissed him, spearing her tongue into the heat and wetness beyond his parted lips, rocking her hips to him, feeling him growing hard through the layers of their clothing.

He carried her like that to the bed and laid her down across it. She released him, resting back on her elbows.

For a long, delicious moment, they simply looked at each other. And then he lowered his head again and started kissing his way down her throat, between her breasts—and lower.

His lips burned a path over her tiny, bunched-up skirt and along the inside of her right thigh, rousing goose bumps as he went, making her moan with anticipation and pleasure. When he reached the inside of her ankle, he stopped kissing her and got busy taking off her shoe, undoing the tiny buckle, sliding it off, dropping it to the rug and going to work on the other one.

By the time he had the second shoe off, impatience got the better of her. No way could she just lie there while he slowly unwrapped her. She sprang into action, scooting to a sitting position.

"Come back here," he ordered, rough and low.

Laughing, she went up to her knees and reached for him.

And he reached for her. And after that, it was all a hot, lovely tangle of legs and arms and ragged breathing as they unbuttoned and unhooked, as they tugged and kissed and fondled, working together to get mutually naked, their clothing flying every which way.

At the end of all that frantic undressing, when he finally got his second boot and sock off, they just sat there, facing each other, staring. He looked so good without a stitch on, everything hard and honed in that lean, cut way of a ranching man. The crisp almost-golden trail of hair in the center of his chest led down to where he was hard and ready for her.

His eyes were indigo—and shining. "I think I forgot how to breathe, just looking at you."

She offered, "Merry Christmas to us."

He held out his hand to her.

She took it, going up to her knees again, moving close and then closer still, until he wrapped both arms good and tight around her. It felt so good, his hard chest to her soft breasts, belly to belly, skin to skin.

He kissed her, lingering and deep.

And then he was guiding her down to the bed again, stretching out beside her, his hands roaming over her, learning all the secrets of her body. She returned his caresses, memorizing every hard, muscled inch of him, so strong and hot and male.

He kissed her everywhere, taking the longest time over her breasts, and then nipping at her belly, dipping his tongue into her navel. And moving downward from there.

He stayed there, low down, for a very long time, kissing her, working his own special magic on her wet, eager woman's flesh.

She clutched his head in her hands as he played with her.

And she came. And then she came again.

And then she couldn't take it anymore. Her body shimmered in afterglow, and she still wanted everything, all of him, every beautiful, hard inch.

Now.

She reached down between them and wrapped her fingers around him.

He caught her wrist, muttered darkly, "I won't…make it if you do that, not this first time with you."

And she stared up at him, into those ocean-blue eyes. "Then don't make me wait for you anymore."

He needed no further urging, was already reaching for the bedside drawer. He pulled out a strip of condoms and tore one off. She watched him, memorized the heat and tension in his dear face as he disposed of the wrapper and rolled the condom carefully down over his thick, ready length.

And then she was reaching for him again, pulling him to her, gripping his broad shoulders, caressing his muscular arms. He came down to cover her with a deep groan, settling between her legs, rising up on his arms to keep from crushing her.

She wrapped her legs around him.

And at last, he sank into her. He did it so slowly, his face above her flushed, concentrated.

It felt…just right, as she had always known it would. So right, in fact, that she could almost forgive him for taking so long to get here with her. So right, that for this glorious moment she hardly remembered that she'd given up on *ever* getting here.

Right now, tonight, it all seemed perfectly inevitable to her, as clear as the road to a known destination. As though she'd been born to be here, on this ranch outside Justice Creek, Colorado, in this very bedroom, with this particular man.

As though her body already knew him, welcomed him to her after waiting for so long.

She thought all those things, at once.

And then she let all that go.

So that there was only the feel of him within her, filling her up so completely, pushing deep. Until there was only her eager body taking him, rising with him, the press of his hard chest to her soft breasts, the way his arms closed around her, claiming her and cherishing her, both at once.

His breath and her breath, mingled. One.

Rising and falling, together.

She cried out as the end swept over her, a climax harder and longer than the two times before. She lifted her body, straining toward him.

He pressed in deep, arms tight around her, throwing his head back, groaning her name.

Chapter Nine

Curled up together, they slept for a little while. The bed was big and comfortable and she felt right at home, spooned in the cradle of his hard arms and long, hair-roughened legs.

She woke when the alarm went off. He tried to slip out of the bed. “Walker?”

He smoothed her hair on the pillow, pressed a kiss to her temple. “Shh. Just the horses. I won’t be long.”

She tried to sit up. “I’ll come. I’ll help.”

“Wearing what? Those naughty shoes and that tiny little scrap of a skirt?”

“I’ll bet the horses wouldn’t complain.”

He chuckled as he gently pushed her back down and pulled the blankets up around her. “Keep the bed warm. Give me something to look forward to.”

She gave in and snuggled down. “Don’t be long…”

“I won’t. I promise.” He breathed the words against her cheek, and then he was gone.

She woke again, briefly, when he slid back under the sheets with her. “God. You’re freezing…”

He gathered her in, wrapping those fine arms around her. She shivered at first, but he quickly grew warm again. He kissed the curve of her shoulder, smoothed his hand over her hair. “Sleep.”

And she did.

The next time she woke, he was standing over her wearing a season-appropriate red-and-green flannel robe.

She squinted up at him. "I smell coffee."

"Right here." He gestured at the tray on the bed stand. It held an insulated carafe, two cups, and cream and sugar.

She sat up. "Am I in heaven?"

"Just my bed." He handed her a full mug.

She sipped. It was so good. Plus, there was the way he looked at her, all the magic of last night warming his eyes. "I think I like here," she told him softly. "In your bed."

He smiled then, a real smile, warm as the look in his eyes. "That's what I like to hear."

She glanced toward the bedside clock—and then did a double take. "Noon? Seriously?"

He shrugged. "Hey. We didn't get to sleep until five or so."

"And you were up an hour later. Did you get any rest at all?"

"Rory, don't fuss. I'm fine." He dragged one of the two comfy chairs to the bedside, took his own full mug and sat down, hoisting his bare feet up onto the bed beside her. "So, then. Today you're checking out of the hotel and moving back in here."

It was not a question. And that pleased her no end. "Yes, I am."

"Good. You're only here for one more week. I want you with me, until you go."

She cradled her mug carefully against the covers and longed to suggest that it didn't have to end when she left. He could come with her, to Montedoro, for Max's wedding and for Christmas. She *wanted* him to come.

But no. They'd only been together—*really* together—since last night. She should give him a few days, at least, before she tried to drag him home to meet the family.

He was watching her face. "You're wrinkling your forehead. Why?"

She took another lovely sip. "I am not wrinkling my forehead. I am thinking."

"About?"

"Nothing you need to know." And he didn't. Not right at the moment, anyway.

He sipped his coffee and bumped her thigh with his bare foot. "Fair enough." And then he just looked at her. For a long, lovely time.

Until she scooted over and patted the empty space beside her. "I'm getting so lonely in here all by myself..."

His blue eyes got lower and lazier and he made a tsking sound, his tongue against his teeth. "If I climb in there with you, I may never get back out. And I have tile to install and drywall I really should get going on."

She set her mug back on the tray and lifted the covers to beckon him in. "It's Sunday. You know, the day of rest?" A low groan escaped him, so she lifted the covers a fraction higher.

"Rory. You're killin' me here."

She only smiled.

Apparently, the smile did the trick. He got up and put his mug down next to hers. Then he untied the flannel sash of his robe and let the robe drop to the rug.

She smiled even wider. "Don't worry," she whispered, as he came down to her and wrapped his arms around her. "We can make this quick..."

But of course, they didn't. They took their sweet time and it was glorious.

Around two, they got up, went to the kitchen and whipped up a big breakfast of pancakes, sausage and eggs. After that, they both showered—using separate bathrooms so they wouldn't be tempted to start fooling around again.

She put on her clothes from the night before. He was waiting for her in the upper hall. They walked downstairs again together. He held her velvet coat for her. She slipped her arms into the sleeves.

He wrapped it around her. "I'll come with you into town." He kissed the words into the crook of her neck.

A low chuckle escaped her. "What about the drywall?"

"God, you smell so good." He nibbled on her neck. "The drywall can wait."

"Uh-uh." She turned in his arms and fiddled with the collar of his heavy shirt. "Go to work. I'll be fine."

He started buttoning her coat for her. "Let me guess. You want to stop at Clara's."

"You're right. I'm going to try to get a little time with her, if she's around. Be back by six or so at the latest?"

He kissed her long and slow. And then, with obvious reluctance, he let her go.

At the Haltersham, Rory changed into jeans, a soft sweater and warm boots. Then she packed up her stuff. With all her things in the 4x4 at four-thirty in the afternoon, she called Clara, who was at home and said she should come on over.

Clara made coffee for Rory and poured apple juice for herself. They sat at the table in the breakfast nook and Clara said, "Let me guess. You went home with Walker last night."

Rory grinned. She couldn't help it. "Oh, yeah. And I just now checked out of the Haltersham."

"Going back out to the ranch, huh?"

"Yes, I am. And I will be there until after the wedding. Is everybody talking?"

"After last night? Oh, you'd better believe it."

Rory had to know. "What are they saying?"

"Just that you two are smokin' hot together, and who knew, after all these years?"

Rory leaned across the table toward her favorite cousin. "You know what *I* say?"

Clara did know. "'About damn time.'"

They laughed together, and Rory confessed, "I'd begun to think it was never going to happen."

"Well, love looks good on you."

Love. Rory winced at the enormity of that one little word and felt driven to clarify. "I wouldn't call it love, exactly. I mean, we just, well, it's all so new. And who knows where it's going?"

Clara reached across and clasped her hand. "All right, fine. Forget the *L* word for now. The point is you look amazing. You've got that glow, the one that says there's a special man in your life and you're completely blissed out about it."

Rory made a low sound of agreement. "I *am* blissed out. No doubt on that score. I'm wild for Walker and, what do you know, the day has actually come that he's wild for me."

"Oh, honey..." Out of nowhere, Clara's face crumpled. Her eyes brimmed with moisture.

"Clara?" Rory cried. She jumped up and darted around to Clara's side of the table.

Clara swiped at her eyes. "I just don't know what's the matter with me."

Rory knelt by her chair and took both her hands. "What is it? What's happened?"

Clara dashed at her eyes again, but the tears kept coming. "You just look so happy, that's all, to want a special guy and be wanted right back. And…I'm an idiot—an idiot who needs a tissue."

Rory got the box from the windowsill. "Here you go."

Clara took it and blew her nose and waved Rory back to her seat. "Go on. Drink your coffee before it gets cold."

Rory returned to her chair. But then she had to ask, "Is this about you and Ryan? I thought things seemed a little tense between you two last night."

Clara's eyes brimmed again. But then she fell back on the usual denials. "No. Of course not. Ryan and I are great. Solid."

"Clara. Come on. Whatever it is, you can tell me—you know that."

Clara rested an elbow on the table and put her hand over her mouth—as if she needed to keep any dangerous words from getting out. Above that hand, her red-rimmed eyes met Rory's. And then shifted away. Finally, with a weary sigh, she lowered her hand and drew in a slow, shaky breath. "I'm sorry. It's only pregnant-lady hormones—that's all."

Rory knew damn well there was more. "Clara. I love you so much. And I just don't believe you."

"Well, you should." Clara sniffed. "Because it's hormones, really. Hormones, that's all—and please, don't say anything to Walker about my getting all weepy on you today. Don't say anything to anybody, for that matter."

"I won't say a word. But if you ever want to talk about it—"

"Rory. How many ways can I say it? I'm happy for you and I'm feeling emotional. It's no big deal."

Walker was sitting on his front porch, Lonesome on one side, Lucky on the other, waiting for her, when Rory got back to the ranch that evening. Her heart just lifted right up at the sight of him, as if someone had suddenly filled it full of helium.

Lonesome trailed in his wake as he came out to meet her. She pushed open the door. He reached right in and took hold of her hand, causing lovely shivers to course across her skin, setting a thousand butterflies loose in her belly.

"I thought you'd never get here." He pulled her out of the driver's seat and into his arms for a hello kiss that went on for the longest, loveliest time. When he finally lifted his head, he said, "Dinner's in the oven. Let's get your things inside."

They carried everything in and she unpacked. By seven, they were sitting down to a dinner of Alva's excellent pot roast with root vegetables.

He asked, "So what did Clara have to say?"

Rory longed to tell him everything. But she *had* made Clara a promise. So she told the truth—just not all of it. "Not much. She says she's fine and happy and she and Ryan are solid."

His fork stopped halfway to his mouth. "And you believed her?"

"Does it matter what I believe? That's her story, and she made it painfully clear she's sticking to it."

"I don't like it."

"Neither do I," she confessed sadly. "But what can we do about it?"

"Not a thing that I can figure out." He stuck the bite of pot roast in his mouth and chewed with a worried frown.

They ate in silence for a while. She fretted about Clara and Ryan and figured that he was probably doing the same.

Then he said, "Rye warned me off Denise—did I tell you?"

She sat up straighter. "Of course not. You never talk to me about Denise."

He shrugged. "All I'm saying is that I had to make that mistake for myself. Maybe this, with him and Clara, is the same—not a mistake, necessarily, but something they have to work through for themselves."

She longed to know more about Denise. So she asked, without really expecting him to answer, "What did Ryan say to you about Denise?"

And then, wonder of wonders, he actually told her, "That she wasn't a stayer. Rye said she had the bright lights and the big city in her blood and before long she'd be headed back to where she came from. He said that hanging with me out here at the ranch was just a temporary thrill for her, that it would get old for her fast."

Rory winced. "Harsh."

"Yeah, well. The truth is that way sometimes—not that I believed him. I believed *her.* She'd sworn she would love me forever. I told Rye he was just jealous, because I'd found what every man dreams of. He called me a fool. And I called him a coward, said he was scared to find a good woman who loved him and settle down, scared of being left like dear old dad left our mom." He let out a low rumble of laughter. It wasn't a happy sound.

"And then what happened?"

"Then he punched me in the jaw and I punched him back, after which I helped him to his feet and we agreed to disagree." He broke a hunk of bread off the sourdough loaf in the middle of the table. "You didn't really want to hear all that, now, did you?"

She stared at him straight on. "Yes, Walker. I did want to hear it. I know that everything's changing between us, after last night. But I'm still your friend and I always will be, no matter what."

"You say that now."

"Because it's true. No matter what happens, even if it turns out for some reason that I never see you again, in my heart I will still be your friend and I want to hear anything you want to tell me about yourself."

He sopped up gravy with the bread and ate it, eyes focused on his plate. Finally, he muttered, "I *was* a fool."

"No, you weren't."

He scoffed. "Now, just how do you figure that?"

"You loved her. You gave yourself to that love. Even if it didn't work out, that's a beautiful thing. How sad and gray life would be without love, without surrender to something that's bigger than we are."

"Spoken like a princess from a large, happy family."

"I am that, and I don't deny it."

"Life doesn't always work out like you think, Rory. It's not all some big, romantic fantasy."

She put down her fork and asked him quietly, "Where are we going with this?"

He sat so still across the table, just staring at her.

"Last night, this morning. It's been like some dream. Magic time, you know? You and me. I never knew that it could be like this. So hot. And cozy and comfortable, too."

Warmth stole through her. Okay, he might be fighting it. But he *was* in this with her, in deep and loving it, same as she was. Softly, she asked him, "Good?"

"Better than good." His voice was just a little bit ragged.

"Oh, Walker." She leaned toward him. "It's good for me, too."

He sat back. "We can't… We just need to keep our heads, I think." He said it gruffly and somehow tenderly, too.

She was the one scoffing then. "Keep our heads? Wrong. The whole point is that we're out of our minds and loving every minute of it."

Walker watched her shining face across the table. He shouldn't have mentioned Denise.

Denise was too sharp a reminder of all the things that don't turn out the way you dream they might. He and Rory had found something special together. They had a week, if he didn't blow it before then.

A week of her beautiful face across from him at meals, of her fine body in his arms at night. Of her laughter and her tender sighs. A week of heaven.

Why not enjoy every minute of it?

Yeah, there would be a price. A high one. That was just how life went. But for a week with her, he would pay it and try to remember, when the time came, to pay it gladly.

He teased, "How can you make insanity sound so right?"

"Because this *is* right," she insisted. "And I'm so glad it's happening." She picked up her water glass and raised it high. "To right here and right now."

He grabbed his own glass and tapped it to hers. "Here and now, Rory."

The rest of the evening was about as perfect as an evening can get.

After dinner, they sat on the sofa by the light of the Christmas tree. He watched some TV, and she fiddled on her laptop, editing pictures, then going online to check out information on wilderness trails and look up the weather forecast.

Eventually, she put her laptop away and he turned off the TV. They shared a kiss that led to another kiss, each one longer and hotter than the one before. He kept thinking they should probably take it upstairs.

But somehow, they ended up naked on the rug in front of the fire. At the last possible second, as he rose up over her, he remembered. "Condom." He groaned the word.

"Uh-oh," she said, and started laughing.

"I can't believe I almost forgot the condom…" With another groan, he rolled away from her. She lay there beside him without a stitch on, still laughing. He sent her a dark look. "You think this is funny?"

"I do, yes." And then she grabbed his hand, pulled him to his feet—and turned off the fire. She dragged him over to the tree and flipped the switch on it, too. Finally, she led him, dazed and stumbling, to the front hall.

"Wait," he said when they reached the stairs.

"Oh, but I don't want to wait." Her face was flushed, those golden eyes gleaming.

"Come here." He scooped her high in his arms.

"Oh!" she cried, and then pressed her tender hand against his cheek. "Careful…"

"You say that," he accused. "But look at us. This isn't careful, not in the least. If we were being careful—"

She put two fingers against his lips. "Shh. Kiss me. It will be all right."

He didn't believe her—but he kissed her anyway. How could he resist? He captured her mouth and carried her up the stairs.

In the bedroom, he took her straight to the side of the bed. He went on kissing her as he slowly let her down to the rug.

She pushed at his shoulders. "Wait."

"I thought you didn't want to wait." But he did as she commanded, watching her, a dumb-ass grin on his face, as she folded back the covers and took a condom from the drawer.

"There." She looked so pleased with herself. And so incredibly beautiful, her hair loose and wild on her shoulders, mouth swollen from kissing him, breasts so tempting, the nipples drawn tight, begging for his touch. "Lie down," she commanded. "On your back, please."

At that moment, she could have told him to go jump out the window, and he would have done it without hesitation. He stretched out on the bed and she came down beside him, curling her soft, knowing hand around him, and then lowering her head.

She took him in, her silky, wet mouth surrounding him, her long hair brushing against his belly. It felt so far beyond good, he almost lost it right then.

But somehow he held out, held on, as she worked her will and her sweet, open mouth on him.

She was so right, he decided. No reason at all to think of what would happen later. Here and now. Nothing like it. Every minute with her a gift. She was Christmas come early, and he planned to unwrap her over and over, every chance he got.

When she finally rolled the condom down on him, he stared up at her, completely in her power. And just about ready to explode.

She straddled him. And then, so slowly, she lowered her body onto him, taking him in by measured degrees, her eyes locked with his. "Good?" she asked in a teasing, breathless whisper.

"Better than good."

She bent over him, her curling dark hair falling, tickling his chest, soft as silk across his throat.

A kiss, an endless one. She moaned into his mouth, and he gave that moan back to her as she rode him. Lifting up to a sitting position again, she pressed her soft hands to his chest, sought his eyes and held them—at first.

But then, as it went on and on, she let her eyes droop shut and her head fall back. A few moments later, she cried out her release.

He took her hips in his two hands and pulled her down flush against him, so he could feel her pleasure pulsing around him.

She murmured something under her breath, so low and husky that he couldn't make out the words.

And he rolled them then, taking her under him, rising up on his hands, rocking into her and then going still.

Waiting.

Until her eyes opened, glowing golden and misty,

full of joy and wonder. "Oh, Walker… Merry Christmas, Walker."

He started to speak, but all that came out was a moan. What man could form words at a time like this? He hovered way too close to the brink. There was only her body, so tight and wet around him, only those eyes of hers, gazing up at him, inviting him to drown in her.

She lifted her hands and braced them on his shoulders. "Yes, Walker. Now…"

That did it. That set him free. He let his body take over, let his own head fall back. He moved in her hard and fast. She met every thrust. The end came roaring at him, rolling through him in a long, deep, endless wave.

She pulled him down to her. Wrapping those smooth arms and strong legs good and tight around him, she whispered soft, tender things as his climax faded slowly to sweet afterglow.

The alarm rang as usual, before dawn.

He reached over, gave it a whack to silence it and automatically started to push back the covers.

"Wait," said the woman beside him.

"Horses," he grumbled.

"I know." Her soft hand on his shoulder. So good, that simple touch. And the warmth of her beside him? Best Christmas present ever. "But talk to me," she coaxed in a whisper. "Just for a minute, please."

He switched on the lamp and rolled back to look at her, all rumpled and squinty-eyed and impossibly fine. "What?"

"I have an idea."

"Horses first. Then coffee."

She laughed at that. "No, really. I've been lying here thinking…"

"Thinking before horses and coffee? You know that's not normal, right?"

She nudged at him playfully. "Listen."

"Fine." He wrapped an arm around her, snugging her sleek, warm body nice and close to him. Now, this was a feeling without compare: Rory naked in his arms so early in the morning it still kind of felt like the middle of the night. "Go for it."

She shifted just enough to kiss the bulge of his shoulder. "Today, could you take a break from whatever needs doing at the houses and cabins? I want you to hike with me up to Ice Castle Falls. I was thinking we could go after breakfast. You know, pack a lunch and just go on foot. I looked it up online last night."

"Oh, did you?"

"Mmm-hmm." She idly stroked his arm. "There's a trailhead that takes off right here at the ranch." He knew that trailhead. They'd gone in from the other side and come down the falls from above, that summer they camped near there. She went on, "That trail is what—six or seven miles round-trip?"

He made a low sound. "That sounds about right."

"And there hasn't been a lot of snow yet, so it should be pretty easy going."

"I know that trail well."

She gazed up at him from under her lashes. "I kind of figured you did."

"And it's only in that last half mile or so that the going gets steep and rocky."

"So we could definitely be back by early afternoon."

Ice Castle Falls. Where she'd almost kissed him five years ago. "Why Ice Castle Falls?"

She was thinking about that summer morning, too. He could see it in her eyes. "It's been cold, but not snowing a lot. And there's no snow predicted today or tomorrow. Perfect conditions. The falls should be frozen, but not all mucked up with snow. Castles of ice. I want to get some shots of that."

"So it's just the pictures you want, huh?"

She snuggled even closer and shyly confessed, "Maybe I'd like to make a few new memories."

"I knew it." He tried really hard not to smile.

"Do not give me that smug look."

He nuzzled her ear. "You're using your princess voice again."

She shoved at his shoulder. "Let me go."

He held on. "Wait."

She stopped shoving. "Then tell me something good."

He told her the truth. "I did want to kiss you that day."

Her sweet mouth trembled. She tucked her head beneath his chin and mumbled against his chest, "You just didn't want to kiss me *enough*."

"Hey."

She came out of hiding and met his eyes again. "I know you have work you need to do, but—"

"Are you kidding? Work can wait. Whatever you want, if it's in my power, I'm giving it to you."

Rory's phone rang as they were cooking breakfast. She checked the display. It was her sister Genny.

Walker said, "Take it. I'll deal with the food."

She answered the call and her sister said, "Have you been online today?"

You didn't grow up a Bravo-Calabretti without dreading the question Genny had just asked. "Oh, God. How bad is it?"

"Not that bad, really."

"Right," Rory replied doubtfully. "Hold on." She went and got her laptop from the coffee table in the living area. Genny rattled off a couple of royal-watching blogs and celebrity news websites as Rory carried the computer back to the table and opened it up. "I swear I never spotted a thing. And I've usually got a radar for the paps—and tell me, honestly, is it bad?"

"Mostly, you look fabulous. Love those Valentino sandals with the lace and rhinestones."

"The Valentino sandals. That means it must have been Saturday night, right? Some creep was taking pictures at the bachelorette party—wait." She got on the first site Genny had mentioned. The headline was the usual drivel: Her Highness Takes a Cowboy—For the Night. It was followed by a series of pictures of her and Walker. Dancing. Playing pool. And cuddling in the corner. "You think mother's seen these?"

"Mother sees everything."

Too true. Her Sovereign Highness's secretary had an assistant whose main job was to keep on top of tabloid stories that needed managing.

Walker sent her a questioning glance from over at the stove and dread curled through her. She waved a hand at him and shrugged, trying to look lighthearted and unconcerned.

He was a very private sort of man. Twice before this, the paparazzi had taken shots of the two of them together—strolling down Central Street on a warm summer day four years ago. And sitting together last year in Clara's café.

He hadn't liked that some stranger had been stalking them just to get shots of the two of them walking side by side or drinking coffee in a restaurant. He would like it even less now that the shots were of them smooching and slow dancing.

"Um, scroll down to the bottom," Genny suggested sheepishly.

Rory did. And there it was: a shot of her in her long velvet coat, zero makeup and the telltale Valentino do-me shoes, getting out of her little rental 4x4 in front of the Haltersham yesterday afternoon.

They'd caught her in her walk of shame.

Chapter Ten

Rory let out a groan. “Lovely.”

That did it. Walker turned down the fire under the bacon and came to see what the groaning was about.

What was there to do but turn the laptop his way and let him scroll through the pictures for himself?

Genny said, “Well, the good news, clearly, is that you and Walker have moved on to the next level.”

“And the bad news, clearly, is that everybody in the world knows it.”

Walker had apparently seen enough. He swiveled the laptop back toward her and returned to the stove.

“It’s really not that awful,” Genny pointed out. “You’re perfectly decent in that long coat. I just wanted to clue you in.”

“Thanks. And you’re right,” Rory replied. “Better to hear the news from someone who loves me.”

They chatted for a couple of minutes more.

When Rory hung up, she shut the laptop and carried it back to the living area. The coffee was finished brewing, so she poured them each a cup. “Shall I start the toast?”

“That would be great.”

They finished the breakfast preparations in silence, which freaked her out a little. Was he going to want to call it off with her, now he'd got a dose of how mortifyingly public her private life could be?

He brought the food to the table and she carried over the plate of toast. They sat down to eat. More dead silence as she forked up eggs and crunched her bacon and tried to think of a way to convince him that it really wasn't so bad. You just needed to have the right attitude toward it all, just get on with your life and not let it bother you. Much.

Then he said, "Look. If you want to call it off now, you know I'll understand."

She hard-swallowed the bite of egg that seemed to have got stuck in her throat, and then sipped her coffee to get it to go the rest of the way down. "Ahem. Are you saying that *you* want to call it off?"

His eyes flashed blue fire. "Hell, no."

Suddenly she could breathe again. "You're sure?"

"Yeah. Those sneaky, wimpy-assed bastards don't get to mess up what we've got going. Not as far as I'm concerned. But you didn't answer my question."

"Oh, Walker, no. Of course I don't want to call it off. No way."

His bleak expression softened. "You should know that I'm going to be on the lookout for those scum-suckers now. And if I catch one in the act, someone could lose a camera."

"I'll consider myself warned—but I'll tell you from experience that it's better just to pretend they're not there. Walk on by, you know?"

"You want me to walk on by, I'll try. No promises, though."

She gazed at him across the table, light-headed with

relief that he didn't plan to call it off. "Well. We're okay, then, huh?"

He nodded. "Eat your breakfast." He said it gently. Even tenderly. "Ice Castle Falls is waiting."

Pure happiness cascaded through her.

But then her phone rang again. She glanced at the display.

Walker guessed. "Her Highness Adrienne?"

"'Fraid so." She answered it. "Hello, Mother."

"Good afternoon, darling—or I guess, from your perspective, I should say good morning."

Might as well get right down to it. "I suppose you've seen the pictures."

"I have." A pause, and then with real concern, "Are you all right?"

"Yes." Across the table, Walker was looking tense again. She sent him a bright, relaxed smile to reassure him. "Walker and I are just fine."

"Are you staying back at his ranch again, then?"

"Yes, I am. It's beautiful here. Cold, crisp and clear—and you're taking this very well."

"Why wouldn't I? I'm a bright woman, my darling. I run a country. A very small country, but still..."

What was she hinting at now? "Just say it, Mother. Please?"

Her Sovereign Highness Adrienne played it cool, as always. "Your father was a little upset. Fathers get that way, even in the twenty-first century. But I've settled him down. And I'm so happy, my darling, to see you finally getting your heart's desire."

Her heart's desire...

Rory took a moment to let that sink in. It could only mean one thing.

"Darling? Are you still there?"

Rory pulled it together and faked a breezy tone. "And I thought I'd been so careful not to give myself away."

"I *am* your mother," Adrienne said, as if that explained everything.

And wait a minute. If Adrienne knew that Rory had a thing for Walker, then what did that say about Adrienne's roping him into bodyguard duty? Until that moment, it hadn't even occurred to Rory that her mother might have set Walker up to look after her with more than her protection in mind.

"We'll have to talk about all of that when I get back to Montedoro," she replied.

"Yes, darling. I feel certain that we will. And I always look forward to speaking openly and frankly with you."

Hah. "Mother, I really do have to go now. We're in the middle of breakfast."

"I understand. Have a fabulous time, darling. Enjoy every minute. Life flies by so quickly. The best parts deserve to be savored."

"Thanks."

"My fondest regards to Walker."

"I'll tell him, yes." She hung up. "My mother sends her regards." And as she had no idea what to say next, she grabbed her fork and concentrated on her plate.

Walker asked, "She's not ready to kill me?"

"Absolutely not. My mother is a civilized woman who respects the private lives of her fully grown children." *Well, mostly, she does.*

"But your dad wants my head on a pike—am I right?"

"Of course not." *Not anymore, anyway.* "My father thinks the world of you." She ate a bite of toast, and the last bite of bacon.

He watched her, narrow-eyed. And he wasn't finished with the questions. "What did you mean when you said that you were careful not to give yourself away?"

"Er, just that my mother thinks she knows everything."

He looked at her doubtfully. "And you and your mother will have to talk about all of *what*, when you get home?"

She slanted him a teasing look. "You really shouldn't listen in on my phone conversations."

He grunted. "You do know that when you want privacy for a call, you need to leave the room, right?"

But if she'd left the room, he would have known for certain that they were talking about him. "You're right. And it was nothing, really." Okay, yeah. Total lie. But she just wasn't ready to go into how she'd been dreaming for years that someday he would look at her the way he looked at her now.

And to sit here and talk about how her mother might very well have been matchmaking them when she hired him as her bodyguard?

Maybe later, if things continued to go well.

Or maybe never. Time would tell.

"She's not upset, then, about the pictures?"

"No, Walker, not at all."

"I just don't get that."

Rory rose, got the coffeepot and refilled their mugs. Then she carried the pot back to the warming plate and took her seat across from him again. "My mother's lived her whole life in the spotlight. You might think it would make her self-centered, or give her an unrealistic idea of what matters. Not true. She's learned to keep a certain perspective. She focuses on what really counts in any given situation. And she rarely gets upset over what shows up in print and online. If she finds what she sees to be truly offensive, she takes steps to achieve damage control. And if she feels that one of us needs a good talking-to, she'll do that—always with kindness and a certain gentle grace. But most of the time, she simply refuses to give small-minded people any power over her. And she expects the rest of us in the family to do the same."

He was watching her in the strangest way, a bemused smile on that ruggedly handsome, so-American face. "You're always complaining that she drives you crazy."

"She does. About some things. She's more controlling with me than with the others, because I'm her baby. But the truth is, deep down where it matters, I pretty much admire the hell out of her."

Walker might have been a fool now and then in his life. But he was no idiot.

He knew that Her Highness Adrienne had said a lot more than Rory had told him. But from the way she was taking it, he didn't think any of it was all that bad, so he left it alone.

They finished their breakfast, filled a pair of day packs with the things they would need for the hike and bundled up well. He grabbed his satellite phone, which he took with him as a matter of course anywhere there would be iffy cell phone reception.

It was a clear morning, the temperature in the mid-teens. Lonesome panted and whined to go with them, and Walker was tempted to take him along. But pets weren't permitted on the hiking trails in Rocky Mountain Park, and though a good portion of the trail wound through Bar-N land, the last mile or so and the falls themselves were in the park. Walker ordered the dog into the house and they stopped at the Colgins' place briefly to tell them where they were headed and when they'd be back.

From the homestead, they crossed a wide meadow, and moved into the shadow of tall pines for maybe a quarter of a mile. From there, they emerged into open meadow again. As they walked along, Rory got out her favorite camera, switched lenses and snapped several shots of the rugged granite cliffs surrounding them.

It was easy going most of the way, patches of ice and snow sparkling here and there in the winter sun. They spotted a bull elk grazing in the long shadow of a ponderosa pine. He ambled off at the sight of them, but not before Rory snapped several pictures.

At the fork in the trail on the edge of the meadow, they moved onto park land and started gaining elevation, working harder as they climbed, entering thick ponderosa forest. It grew colder, with more snow on the ground and some danger of slipping on patches of ice. Rory put her camera away as they focused on the climb.

But then they reached a grove of winter-bare, white-barked aspens. At that elevation, about fifteen hundred feet above the meadow where the trail forked, there was maybe a foot of snow on the ground, white around the white tree trunks. The trail, snow tramped away by hikers and horses, wound through them.

He turned to Rory. "I know you want shots of this."

The pom-pom on her red hat bounced with her eager nod. "I love the tree trunk shadows against the white..."

So he waited as she took the pictures, and smiled when she got lucky and captured several shots of a fox on the move, zigzagging through the tree trunks, leaving delicate paw prints in the snow behind him.

She lowered her camera and stared off in the direction the fox had gone. "What's that, way over there?" She was pointing west, away from the trail, beyond where the aspens petered out, toward the darkness of the surrounding pines. "Do you see it? It looks like a red tin roof…"

He nodded. "It's a cabin, on Bar-N land, though barely. That lower trail we left at the edge of the meadow curves around to it. My great-grandfather built it. Rye and I still use it now and then, for a hunting base, and to get away from everything. It's basic. No power, no running water."

She grinned. "I want to see it. Let's take a little detour."

He pointed at the gunmetal clouds bubbling up over the peaks to the north of them. "On the way down, if the weather holds."

"But there's no storm predicted."

"And there probably won't be one. But just in case, we ought to keep our eyes on the prize. You do want those pictures of the frozen falls, don't you?"

"You know I do." She gave him one of those looks, full of their shared history.

"Then let's keep moving."

She packed up her camera and they went on through the aspen grove, moving roughly north into pine forest again. They reached the creek, frozen on the surface, the current bubbling along under a gleaming crust of ice. The trail followed the creek, makeshift log bridges crossing it, then crossing back.

Finally, they reached the narrow ravine that led up to the falls. From there, they had to climb the rocks, a steep ascent, and tight, the frozen creek to their left, the water beneath making soft chuckling sounds as it rushed below the ice.

She went up first; he took the rear.

In no time, they were climbing that last jut of rock and coming onto the small platform of boulders at the base of the falls. He followed her up there.

Fists on her hips, she stared at the frozen columns of water, jagged and gleaming, looking very much like castles of ice. "Fabulous. I want to get some shots here, and then can we work our way up to the top and I'll get some views looking down?"

The clouds were closing in. They had that heavy look that promised snow—no matter what the weather services had said. Still, it wasn't that far back to the ranch. Even if it started snowing, they could make it home pretty fast if they needed to.

"Go ahead. Take all the pictures you want."

"I will. But first…"

He knew that gleam in her eyes. He teased, "Lunch?"

She pointed at a ledge about ten feet up from them. It was a smaller ledge than the one they stood on now, a ledge even closer to the towers of frozen water. "That ledge look familiar?"

He knew it. "It's where I almost kissed you."

She made a distinctly unprincesslike snorting sound. "Uh-uh. Where *I* tried to kiss *you*. And you turned me down."

He faked a scowl. "What is this you're planning? Some kind of sick romantic revenge?"

She pretended to think it over, tapping her gloved finger against the tip of her chin. "Hmm. You know what? Sick romantic revenge is exactly what is happening here. We're going up to that ledge and you're going to kiss me like you mean it."

"So young to be so bitter."

She stepped in closer and tipped that angel's face up to him. "Are you telling me no?"

"I wouldn't dare."

"Good answer." Her bronze eyes glowed.

And those lips of hers were too tempting to resist. He swooped down fast and captured them. Cold. But so soft. She made a noise of playful outrage and pushed at his chest.

He didn't let go. Instead, he wrapped a hand around the back of her head and held her where he wanted her.

And he kept on kissing her, slowly deepening the contact, until she wasn't pushing him away anymore. Uh-uh. Her gloved hands slid up the straps of his pack to curl around the nape of his neck.

Once they got to that point, he really didn't want to let her go. He could have stood there, kissing her on that ledge, forever.

But he felt the first snowflakes as they landed on his cheeks and forehead.

They broke the kiss to look up at the steadily darkening sky and the occasional snowflake lightly drifting down. "Okay," he said. "We should get going. It's probably no big deal, but there's no sense in playing chicken with winter weather."

She gave a moan of protest. "Snow was not in my plan, not today."

"You still want a kiss on that upper ledge, let's go."

"Don't get bossy, mister. I'm running this show."

He gave her his best look of infinite patience. "The upper ledge? Or not?"

"The upper ledge. Definitely."

It took only a minute to get up there. He went first and she gave him her hand. He pulled her onto the ledge. She eased her pack off her shoulders and set it away from the edge.

He took his off, too, and put it down next to hers.

Then he took her into his arms.

Rory gazed up at him, watched the snowflakes catching on his eyebrows. They caught on her eyelashes, too, sharply cold. And on her lips. She licked one off. Delicious.

What a great moment. They stood right next to the frozen falls, so close that there were fat icicles hanging from the jut of rock above them and ice, like a froth of lace, on the cliff face to either side.

She confessed happily, "I never thought this would happen, you and me, here again together—only this time, *really* together."

His fine mouth quirked in the start of a smile. And then he grew more serious. "God. You are beautiful. And yeah. It's good, to be here like this with you."

The wind came up then, icy cold, whistling as it swirled against the rocky cliffside. The thickening snowflakes spun around them. His straight, manly nose was red and his eyes were so blue.

And like an echo on the whistling wind, she heard her mother's voice.

"I'm so happy, my darling, to see you finally getting your heart's desire..."

And it was like a switch tripping, snapping her out of self-imposed darkness and into the blinding light of pure truth. She couldn't stop herself from knowing, couldn't deny the basic longing in her heart for one second more.

She loved him. She was *in* love with Walker.

He must have caught some hint of the sudden chaos within her. He frowned. "Rory, what? What's the matter?"

Oh, she did long to tell him. But how would he take it? After the debacle of Denise, the *L* word was the scariest one of all for him.

What if he freaked?

"Rory." He searched her face, looking for clues to what was happening inside her. "What…?"

And she pulled it together, sliding her arms up to encircle his neck. "There's nothing." She gave a little laugh, just to show him that this was not the least serious, just more lovely fun and games between two very good friends-become-lovers. "Kiss me."

And right then, as she let her eyes drift closed and he lowered his mouth to hers, there was the strangest crack of sound, like a pistol shot.

She opened her eyes and glanced up just in time to see a large chunk of ice as it hurtled downward onto her head.

Chapter Eleven

Everything happened in a blur.

She ducked back to try to avoid getting hit on the top of her head, but only succeeded in taking the blow on the forehead instead. That hurt. And the tipping backward? Maybe not so smart. She lost her balance and toppled off the ledge.

Or she would have, if Walker hadn't grabbed her and pulled her back just in time. There was this stunned, numb moment. She gaped up at him, whispered, "Oops."

About then, shock kind of took over. She felt herself crumpling and closed her eyes with a groan.

A second or two later, when she opened them again, she was still on the ledge, but out from under the overhang. Walker had come down with her. She had her head on his knees and he was bending over her, taking off his heavy gloves. "Rory. Can you hear me?"

She blinked up at him. "Wha…?" Her head stung and throbbed simultaneously. She reached up to touch it.

He caught her gloved hand before she could. "There's blood. It's messy. Plus, we want to avoid contaminating the wound." He guided her hand back down and she let him do it. "I've got a first aid kit in my pack," he said, his voice so calm and slow. "But before that, I need to know, do *you* know what happened to you?"

She blinked up at him. Now that he'd mentioned it, she could feel the warmth of the blood, dripping down her temples into her cap and her hair. The snow was getting thicker, the flakes churning out of the cloud-darkened sky.

"Rory? You with me?"

"Uh, yeah. Yeah, I'm okay. And I get it. You want to know if I know what happened because you're checking for signs of a concussion."

He almost smiled then. The white lines of strain around his mouth eased a little. He reached for his pack, pulled it next to them and unzipped a compartment. "So. You remember?"

"You were just about to kiss me. I heard a loud crack. And I saw this giant icicle coming down."

"Got you right on the forehead."

"I noticed. Believe me." And not only was she on her back and bleeding, she hadn't got her kiss. She'd really, really wanted that kiss.

And no pictures, either. What a bust.

He eased off her wool cap and carefully brushed her hair away from her face. Then he took out the kit and unzipped it. He cleaned his hands with an antiseptic towelette. Then he went to work cleaning *her*. His touch was swift and gentle as he began dressing the wound, using those little strips to close the edges. He kept up with the questions as he opened the bandages. "Do you feel sick to your stomach, or nauseated?"

"No. Really. I'm okay—I mean, my head hurts. But isn't that to be expected?"

"Foggy thoughts?"

"None. All my thoughts are crystal clear."

"Woozy?"

"I swear, Walker. I'm fine—well, other than the gash on my head and the blood in my hair and the kiss and the pictures I'm unlikely to get now. All that's not so great."

"There." He slipped the bloody wipes and gauze into a baggie, stuffed it in his pack and closed up the kit.

"Done, then?"

"Bandaging you? Yes."

"Help me up."

"Wait. Are you sure you're ready for that?"

"You know that you're beginning to sound like somebody's psychiatrist, right?"

He actually grinned then. "Sense of humor. Excellent sign."

She shivered a little. The snow swirled around them. "Give me my hat back. My ears are getting cold."

"It's a little bloody."

"Better than nothing."

"Hold still, then." Carefully, cradling her head in his big, soothing hand, he eased the hat on. "There. Now look directly up at me." She blew out a slow breath, blinked away a random snowflake and stared into his eyes. He leaned in closer. "Your pupils seem fine." Reaching in the pack again, he pulled out his sat phone.

She caught his hand before he could use it. "You're overreacting."

"Oh, I don't think so."

"I'm okay, Walker. And I'm the one in the best position to know that."

"You're flat on your back with a gash on your head."

"Gash, yes. Flat on my back..." She popped to a sitting position. "No."

"Whoa." He tried to ease her back down.

She slapped his hands away. "See?" She gestured dramatically with a wide sweep of both arms. "Not dizzy. Clearheaded. A-okay."

"Head trauma is nothing to fool with." He pulled out the phone's antenna.

She caught his hand again. "I can climb down this waterfall and I can hike to wherever we need to go. It's an easy walk back to the ranch. There's no big danger here. And if you call for help, then what? We wait here until they mobilize? How long will that take? How much will it cost?"

"Why are you worried about the cost?"

"Because I'm not some idiot who gets in trouble in the forest and just whips out a phone to summon the troops. It's wasteful and irresponsible and I will not do it if it's not needed."

He had that look, as if he really wouldn't mind strangling her. "Yes, Your Highness," he muttered through clenched teeth.

"Thank you." The snow just kept coming down harder. "Let's get started before the storm gets any worse."

He clasped her shoulder through her thick down jacket. "Rory. Seriously? You're sure you're all right?"

"Yes, Walker. I honestly do know how I feel. And I'm okay. Plus, what do you know, I have the captain of the Justice Creek search-and-rescue team right here beside me—to patch me up and help me through any rough spots."

He scowled at her. "You do seem in complete control of your faculties—and as bossy as ever."

"So, then. May we go?"

He grumbled about her princess voice and then made her promise that if she felt the least bit dizzy, disoriented or sick to her stomach, she would cop to it immediately. Then he put his gloves back on, put the phone in a pocket of his jacket and helped her to her feet.

More solicitous questioning. Was she dizzy *now*? Did she feel the least bit unsteady? What about her stomach? Did she think she might vomit?

As the snow began to collect on the trees and the cliff ledges, she reassured him yet again. Yes, the cut on her forehead stung a little and there was a slight ache from the icicle blow, but she felt strong and capable. "Now, let's go."

They shouldered their packs. He descended to the lower ledge first and then waited as she came down, ready to catch her if she fell.

She did not.

They proceeded to the base of the falls without incident and then began climbing back down the ravine.

When they got to the trail, he insisted on yet another discussion of her mental state and level of pain. She knew he was worried and just being careful, so she suppressed her impatience and honestly answered every one of his questions.

They set out again, with her in the lead. That way he could watch her for any sign she wasn't as fit as she kept insisting she was. Both times, he called a halt when they reached the creek crossings and took the lead, then waited on the other side as she came to him. Then he put her in the lead again.

She kept a lid on her irritation at all his coddling. After all, he was just trying to watch out for her. But she really did know her own body and mind. Yeah, the cut on her forehead throbbed a little, but it was definitely bearable.

The real problem was the snow. It was piling up fast on the trail, the wind getting stronger, actually approaching blizzard conditions. How could the weather services have got it so wrong?

They forged on, heads bent to the wind.

It wasn't too long before they entered the aspen grove. The storm had reached pretty close to whiteout level by then. She wasn't surprised when he stopped her and pointed to the west, into the pines, off the trail.

"The cabin?" she shouted against the wind.

He nodded. "I'll lead! It's not far! Put a hand on my shoulder. Follow close!"

She moved in behind him and did as he instructed. Now he would know that she remained upright and moving—and they wouldn't get separated, even if they couldn't see three feet in front of their faces.

He led her off the trail, where the new snow formed a thickening blanket over the old. It was a hard slog, every step an effort, with the blowing snow in their faces and the foot and a half of it already piled up on the ground.

The going got a little easier when they reached the pines. The thick layers of branches overhead slowed the wind and trapped the snow. He came to a trail and they followed it—not far. A couple hundred feet. And then, at last, the cabin loomed before them, a red-roofed shadow, rising out of the storm.

It was small, probably only one room inside, with shutters blocking the two windows flanking the door. No porch to speak of, just an overhang of tin roof above the entrance. Two rough steps led up to the door. He took her right to the door and up the steps, then turned and clasped her shoulders, guiding her in under the overhang, where she was somewhat protected from the storm. About then she noticed the padlock on the door.

Snow crusted his eyelashes beneath the fur trim of his trapper hat. His eyes were bluer than ever beneath the rim of white and full of concern for her. "Okay?"

"Doing great."

"We used to leave the place open, but it was vandalized twice. So we lock it up. There's a key hidden around back. Wait here." He left her.

She huddled in the doorway, shivering a little, hoping he would come back fast and leave her no time to stand there and worry that he might somehow get lost while he was out of her sight—a ridiculous fear, and she knew it. The man was a wilderness expert and these woods were his home.

Two minutes—three, max—and he appeared from around the side of the building, forging through the thickening blanket of snow. He came up the stairs. She scooted over a little so he could get to the padlock and open the door.

She went in first. He hooked the padlock back on the hasp, came in behind her and shut the door.

It was just as cold in there as it had been outside, but minus the wind and the snow. Also, with the windows covered, she couldn't see a thing.

He came and slid her pack off her shoulders, dropping it to the floor. "Come on. Sit down here..." He guided her backward to a rocking chair.

She wanted to argue that she could help with whatever needed doing. But then she kept remembering that worried look on his face when he left her for the key. This was his cabin. He would know what to do. Better if she just sat down and let him do it, let him get a fire going in that woodstove she'd spotted briefly before he shut the door.

The rocking chair creaked as Rory eased herself down onto the button-tucked pillow.

He came down with her, putting his big hands on the chair arms. She felt his warm breath across her cold face. "Okay?"

"Absolutely."

His mouth brushed hers, so sweetly. Too briefly.

I love you, Walker. The words like a promise inside her head. *You are my heart's desire.*

"You're being much too agreeable," he said.

She actually chuckled, holding her love gleefully inside herself, so precious, brand-new. "Don't expect that to last."

A half an hour later, they had a fire in the stove and Walker had taken down the shutters. From the spring out back, he'd filled a big pan and a heavy teapot and put them on the stovetop to boil. He even had a pair of kerosene lanterns stored there at the cabin and several bottles of fuel, so if they had to stay the night, there would be light.

They sat in the two ladder-back chairs at the battered gateleg table together eating some of the lunch they'd brought. There were three sandwiches, apples, granola bars, bottled water and a big plastic bag of trail mix. Right now, they were sharing a chicken sandwich and munching on the apples. The rest, they were saving. Just in case they were stuck at the cabin for a day or two more.

"Definitely basic," she said, glancing around at the stove and the ancient horsehair sofa, the rocker, the little section of counter, the sink with a drain but no faucet. Rows of open shelves were stacked with a few mismatched dishes, bowls and scratched glassware.

On a side wall, stairs climbed to a sleeping loft. And a second door at the back led directly into an attached woodshed and storage area, with a second door to the outside beyond that.

He glanced at his watch, which was the same cheap and trusty Timex Expedition he'd been wearing the day she first met him, more than seven years ago now. "It's a little past two. Looks like we're going to be staying the night. I'm hoping the storm will blow over by tomorrow. Guessing we'll get a couple feet of snow, at least. I can call Bud and he'll bring us some snowshoes when the storm ends."

"Sounds like a plan." Her forehead throbbed, a minor ache, but irritating. Instinctively, she lifted a hand to touch the bandage—but stopped herself in time.

Twin lines formed between his straight brows. "Is it hurting?"

"A little—but I swear to you, Walker. No dizziness, foggy thinking or urge to vomit."

"I have acetaminophen you can take."

"Later. I'm fine." There was a mirror on one of the shelves over the sink. She'd dared to look in it once he got the shutters off the windows. Not pretty. A white bandage with now-dried blood seeping through it covered most of her forehead. Purple bruises had inched into her eyebrows below the bandage, and she had a definite suspicion that by tomorrow, she would be sporting a matched pair of black eyes.

A muscle twitched in his jaw. "It's my damn fault."

"What *are* you talking about?"

"I should have paid attention to that ice on the ledge above us." His wonderful mouth twisted. "We shouldn't have been standing right under it. But I was too wrapped up in kissing you…"

"And I was all wrapped up in kissing *you*. And that is exactly what we *should* have been doing. Because when you kiss someone, the kiss is *all* you should be thinking about. Otherwise, why even bother?"

"I should have been looking out for you."

"Walker, stop it. I mean it."

"It's the truth."

"Oh, please. It was one of those things that happen, that's all. Like locking your keys in the house or a sudden, unexpected snowstorm. Crap happens. You deal with it. Which is exactly what we are doing now." She glanced around again, at the funky sofa and the stairs leading up to the sleeping loft. "Besides, it's kind of romantic. Stranded together in a snowstorm, just the two of us." She put on her best sex-kitten purr. "You can change my bandage for me. And when the water gets hot, I'll give you a sponge bath."

He groaned, and clearly not from passion. "Does anything ever get you down?"

"Sure. But not for long."

His expression softened. "You are something really special—and I mean beyond your being an actual real-life princess and all." And then he reached across the table.

Rory reached back. Their fingers met and twined in the middle.

I love you, Walker. Love you, love you...

It sounded so good inside her head. It sounded right. She was just about to go ahead and say it.

But then, with his other hand, he grabbed his phone, which he'd set on the edge of the table. "I've got to try to get hold of Bud. He'll call Rye for me. And then you can call Clara. You can have Clara call your mother."

She pulled her hand from his. "Walker." Now she was the one groaning. "Talk about a mood killer."

He wiggled his fingers. "Give me your hand back. Do it now." She made a face at him, but then she did put her hand in his again. He wrapped his fingers around hers and rubbed his thumb across her knuckles, bringing a little thrill of happiness to curl around her heart. "There'll be time for romance once we let everyone know where we are."

She laughed. "Right. In between your checking my pupils, changing my bandage and monitoring my vital signs."

His gaze was tinged with reproach. "I'm just trying to keep us safe."

How could she fault him for that? "Thank you—and fine. Let's make those calls."

He called Bud, who promised not only to look after the animals, but also to call Ryan and tell him what was going on. As soon as the weather cleared, he would come with the snowshoes.

The phone was the kind that kept a thirty-hour charge and could get reception in the most remote places, but tended to drop calls in the middle of conversations due to the movement of the satellites it accessed. Rory had to call Clara twice to tell her all she needed to know—which did not include the part about the gash on her head. Clara agreed to call Rory's mother and explain that she and Walker were waiting out a sudden snowstorm in a cozy mountain cabin a few miles from Walker's house and out of cell phone reach for a day or two.

When she hung up, Walker was watching her accusingly. "You didn't say a word about your injury."

"That's right. If Clara doesn't know, I don't have to ask her to lie to my mother for me."

"Your mother has a right to—"

"Don't even get started. What my mother doesn't know won't hurt her. I am going to be fine, and if she knows I'm stuck in a blizzard with a big bandage on my head, she's only going to worry—and just possibly decide she's got to fly to my rescue. No, thanks."

"I don't like lying to your mother."

"But you haven't lied to her. And neither have I, really. I've just…omitted a detail or two."

"Princess voice," he muttered.

She stood. "And now, if you don't mind, I need to use that little hut with the half-moon on the door." The outhouse was twenty paces from the exit outside the attached woodshed lean-to.

Of course, he insisted on going out with her. "First aid precaution. You don't want to be alone for twenty-four hours after a head injury."

She'd taken more than one first aid course and knew he was right. So she didn't even argue. They put their coats back on and went out into the storm again, trudging the short distance through the drifts together. He did let her go in alone, but he waited for her beside the outhouse door.

Back in the cabin, they peeled off their coats and washed their hands using the water they'd warmed on the stove. He wouldn't let her disturb her bandage, but he did help her clean the dried blood from her temples and her hair. Once that was done, she didn't look quite so grisly. She rinsed out her wool cap and set it close to the stove to dry.

After that, came the waiting. He found an old pack of cards and they played gin rummy. By four, it was still snowing. They lit the lamps.

At six, they had dinner. Rory had scoured the shelves and discovered an old canister full of Lipton tea bags, so they drank hot tea with their half sandwiches.

"The rest of the evening should be spectacular," he said wryly. "More gin rummy. And did you notice that shelf full of ancient magazines and old paperbacks by John le Carré and Louis L'Amour?"

"I did." She blew on her tea and then sipped. "My father's a big fan of Louis L'Amour. I might give old Louis a try."

He studied her for a minute. "You're bored to death, right?"

"No," she said, and meant it. "Do I look like I'm bored?"

He shook his head. "No. I guess you don't."

Silence. The words rose in her throat, begging to be said. *I love you, Walker.* But she swallowed them down yet again.

She ate the rest of her half sandwich and thought about seducing him. Fat chance. No way would he let his guard down that much. He seemed to feel honor bound to watch her constantly for signs of incipient mental deterioration caused by her injury—for which he'd decided to blame himself.

So, then. If he wouldn't make love with her and she couldn't quite get her mouth around the *L* word, at least they could talk about something that mattered.

So she asked, "Did you ever bring Denise here?"

His eyes widened. Classic are-you-kidding expression. "To this cabin?" At her nod, he said, "Never." And he actually chuckled. "You have no idea how much she would have hated it."

"Well, I don't hate it. But then, I'm not Denise."

She had to give him credit. He got the message. And he didn't get defensive about it. "No, you're not."

"Not in any way."

"Nope. Not the least little bit."

She sipped more tea and batted her eyelashes. "Denise was way hot. Are you saying I'm not?—and wait." She pointed at her forehead. "Don't answer that until the bandage comes off and the bruises fade."

Of course, he answered anyway. "You *are* hot. Very. Even with a bloody bandage on your forehead."

"Well, okay. I may keep you around, after all." They'd both finished their meager meal. She pushed her chair back. "Bring your tea. Let's sit on the sofa. We'll have a nice chat."

"A chat about…?"

"You'll see."

He eyed her with caution—but he did rise and follow her over there, where they sat side by side and put their mugs on the rough-hewn low table in front of them.

She'd taken off her boots earlier. Now she turned toward him and drew up her knees to the side. "I want you to talk to me about Denise."

He looked slightly pained. "And this is a good idea… why?"

"Because you almost never talk about her. And I want to understand…" She didn't know exactly how to finish.

"I don't know, whatever you want to tell me. Whatever you want to say about her."

"You're serious?" He searched her face.

"Yeah."

Walker watched Rory's battered face. The bruises had spread below the delicate ridge of her brow. But her eyes were as clear and focused as ever. He was pretty sure she was going to be fine.

No thanks to him. He would never forgive himself for not taking better care of her back at the falls.

"Walker?"

"Huh?"

"Just talk about Denise a little. Whatever you want to say."

"Nothing?" he suggested hopefully.

But Rory only waited.

He gave in. "She… What can I say? The first night I met her, at that bar where Rye used to work before he opened McKellan's, she swore she loved it here in the mountains. She went home to the ranch with me that first night. The next morning, she said how much she loved it there, that it would really be something, to live there with me, forever. I believed her. I was gone, gone, gone.

"But as soon as we were married, she changed it all up. Suddenly, she was all about sunshine and palm trees. She would drag around the house in her robe all day. She cried all the time. We started fighting a lot. She laid down the law. She wanted to go home, and she wanted me to come with her, to relocate. I refused. I'm not a Florida kind of guy. But more than that, I kept remembering that Rye had warned me she wasn't for real. I felt I'd been played, you know?"

She made a small sound, encouraging. Understanding. "I can see how you would feel that way."

He plowed on. "She packed up and left. Said she'd send the divorce papers. In spite of how bad it had been by the end, I missed her. I really was gone on her and the feeling hadn't died yet. I started rethinking the situation, started trying to see her side of it."

"Which was?"

"She *was* my wife. I loved her. And I owed it to her, owed it to what we had together, to try harder to make it work. Instead of blaming her for playing me, I tried to see it through her eyes. I told myself she *hadn't* been working me, that she really had thought she wanted a life on the ranch with me, but then, once she was living the life she'd been so sure she wanted, she'd realized she'd been wrong. Honest mistake. I started thinking that maybe I ought to give Florida a chance."

She stared at him, wide-eyed. "Wow. You. Living in Miami. Not really picturing that."

"Yeah, well. Rye told me not to go, that he'd seen Denise coming a mile away, that she was one of those women who's all sweet and easygoing at first. It's only later a guy learns that it's *her* way or forget it. I didn't believe him. I decided to go to Florida to try to work it out with her."

"I never knew you went to Florida."

"I told Rye. No one else. It was a short trip."

"So…what happened?"

He touched her cheek. So soft. And he smoothed her long brown hair. Because it felt good. Everything about Rory felt good. Better. Richer. Fuller than with any other woman he'd ever known—better even than the best times with Denise. "Rory. It's enough. You already know that it didn't work out."

"Walker. *Tell* me."

"It's not a good story."

"Please. I want to know."

"Why?"

She gave him one of those looks. Patient and maybe a little put out at him. "Because it's about you and you matter to me."

"So are you going to tell me about all your other boyfriends?"

She didn't bat an eye. "Absolutely, if that's what you want from me."

Did he? Want to know about her and some other guy? What for? It would only make him long to start rearranging somebody's face. "You still seeing any of them?"

"No. Of course not."

"Carrying a torch for any of them?"

"No."

He couldn't help smirking. "I'll let you know when I'm ready to hear all about them."

"Wonderful." She waited, undeterred.

He grunted. "Why are you looking at me like that?"

"I'm waiting for you to tell me what happened when you went after Denise in Miami."

"Crap."

"Still waiting."

He gave in and told her the rest. "A week and a half after she left me, I called Denise. Said we needed to talk, that I was flying to Miami. She seemed glad to hear from me. Hopeful. Sweet. She picked me up at the airport and took me to her apartment, which it turned out she'd had before she came to Colorado. She'd only sublet it for the year she was gone. She said how happy she was to see me. I told her I was willing to try Florida. For her. Things got intimate. Then her boyfriend showed up."

Rory gasped. "Wait. What boyfriend?"

"The guy she'd been with before she came to Colorado. She'd gotten back with him."

"No way."

"Oh, yeah. It was pretty bad. Turned out, when I called and said I was coming to see her, she'd dumped him all over again. Poor guy was wrecked. Tears running down his face, he swore that the past week and a half had been the happiest of his life."

"Week and a half?" Rory squeaked. "But didn't you say it was a week and a half since she left *you*?"

"Yeah. I did the math, too. Meanwhile, the other guy was beside himself—begging her not to leave him, threatening to kick my teeth in. She finally got rid of him and then she started telling me how that guy was nothing, and she was so glad I'd finally realized that with her, in Miami, was where I was meant to be. She had it all planned. Back then, Rye and I were still co-owners of the Bar-N. She wanted me to sell my half—to Rye or to whoever was willing to pay the money. And then she and I would use the profit to buy a small business right there in Miami, maybe a Subway franchise, maybe a discount liquor store."

"Oh, Walker." She took his hand, wove her fingers with his. "I'm just not seeing you with a Subway franchise."

"Exactly. That was what really did it, really ended it with her and me. Not her walking out on me, not her getting back with that poor sucker the day she got off the plane from Colorado. It was when she said I should sell my half of the Bar-N."

"You would never do that." She said it quietly, but with absolute conviction.

"That's right. And that was when I finally understood that it was never going to work with her. I still wanted her, still believed that I loved her. That was hard, still being so far gone on her when I didn't even *like* her anymore. Rye had been right about her. And I'd completely misread her. We had nothing in common, really. It was chemistry. That's all we had. And it was wild and sweet for a little while, but we never should have gotten married. I was a complete idiot to think it was ever going to work. Learned my lesson on that one."

"What lesson?" she asked kind of breathlessly.

"Never should have gotten married. Never doing it again."

She pulled her hand free of his. "Hold on. Just because it didn't work with Denise doesn't mean—"

"Yeah, it does."

"Oh, you are so wrong."

"Look. My father left my mother when I was six years old. She waited her whole life for him to come back. The day she died, she was still waiting. She died saying his name. That's delusional. I just don't get marriage. It's like some foreign language to me. I've got no experience of how to be married, of what makes a marriage work. And selfishly speaking, it took me too damn long to get past what happened with Denise. I don't want to go through that again."

"But you don't *have* to go through that again. Not if you choose someone who wouldn't tell you lies, someone more suited to you, someone who really does love exactly the kind of life that you do…" Her voice trailed off. But her eyes held the strangest look. A pleading, vulnerable sort of look.

And it was right then, by that look in her eyes, that he finally began to realize there was more going on here than he was picking up.

He asked carefully, "You mean someone who isn't lying when she says she wants the same things I want out of life?"

"Well, yeah." Beneath the blood-spotted white bandage, she gazed at him so hopefully.

And that did it. He might be thick as a post when it came to love and the female mind. But Rory, well, she was different. Not only his lover, but his friend in the basic, best sense of the word. He *knew* her in ways he'd never known another woman. He could read her. And as much as he understood any woman, he understood her.

And he knew what he saw in those big brown eyes of hers.

She thinks she's in love with me.

And damned if she wasn't trying to find a way to tell him so.

Love. Uh-uh. He was no good for that. Not good *at* it. She deserved so much better.

He had to make her see that the whole love thing with him was never going to work. And he needed to do that before she said anything she would later regret. He grunted. "Get real. What happens when I mess that up, too?"

"But you won't."

"Yeah, I will."

"Oh, Walker, don't you see? That's the point. It's really pretty simple. If you choose the right person and both of you are honest and true to each other. If you work hard, together, to *make* it work—"

"Uh-uh. I'm a lot better off not trying to do something I've got no clue how to do. And so is any poor woman who might be crazy enough to think it's a good idea to take me on."

"But—"

"There are no buts. Not about this."

A gasp of outrage escaped her. "Of course there are buts. Love is like anything else in life. If you don't know how, you learn. You get better as you go along."

"Maybe for some people. Not for me."

"But—"

"Not going to happen, Rory. Not going there. Not ever again. I've got a good life and I like it just the way it is."

Rory got the picture. She got it crystal clear.

He *knew*.

He knew that she was in love with him. He got that she was trying to find a way to tell him so.

He knew. He got it. And he didn't want to hear it.

That hurt worse than a giant icicle to the head. She longed to launch herself at him, beat on his broad chest and yell at him for being a pigheaded fool who didn't know the greatest thing in the world when it was staring him in the face.

But she didn't yell or pound his chest.

She just sat there and glared at him and tried to decide…

Did she intend to tell him, anyway? Was she going to say it out loud, that she loved him and wanted him, wanted to live her life with him, right here in Colorado, at the Bar-N?

Was she going to offer everything? Her love, her life, her beating heart? Was she going to hold out all she had to him and have him refuse her outright, anyway?

And after he'd tried so hard to save her the trouble, to salvage her pride?

She considered herself a brave person.

But you know what?

Not tonight.

"Okay." She pasted on a smile. "I get it."

"Rory…" His voice had changed, gone deep and roughly tender. Now he'd got through to her, he wanted to soothe her, to make her feel better.

Well, there was no making her feel better. Not about this. "You'll never fall in love again and you'll die a single man. Have I got that right?"

"Damn it, Rory." He reached for her.

She showed him the hand. "Right?"

And he was forced to say it. "Yeah. That's right."

It hurt. Hurt as much as the first time he'd said it. She wondered when the hurt would fade. She hoped it would be soon.

But so far that evening, the things that she'd hoped for had not come true.

Chapter Twelve

They shared the bed in the loft that night.

But Rory stayed on her side. And Walker didn't even try to wrap himself around her.

He woke her every couple of hours, as the first aid manuals instructed, to make certain she was still showing no symptoms of complications from the blow to her head. She sat up when he lit the lamp, let him look in her eyes and answered his questions.

And then she turned over and pretended he wasn't there.

By daylight, the storm had played itself out. Bud showed up a little after eight with the snowshoes. They locked up the cabin and slogged back to the homestead, where the house was all ready for Christmas and just the sight of the tree and the mantel and the mercury glass angels made her want to burst into tears. She tried not to look at them while she called her mother and Clara to let them know she'd returned safely to the ranch house.

The snowplows had been hard at work. They'd cleared the road to town. Walker insisted on taking her in to the hospital. The doctors ran a few tests, rebandaged the wound and told her she was going to be fine. She would have a thin scar, which she might want to see a plastic surgeon about later.

She asked if it was safe for her to drive and be on her own now.

The doctor assured her that it was.

Back at the ranch again, she hugged Lucky and petted Lonesome and then went upstairs to pack.

Walker followed her up there and stood in the doorway looking manly and grim. "So you're leaving, just like that?"

She dropped a stack of panties into an open suitcase and turned to him. "Do you want me to stay?"

"Of course I do."

"And just pretend that nothing happened last night? Seriously? That's really what you want?"

He braced his shoulder against the door frame, wrapped his arms across his chest and studied his boots.

"Great answer," shc muttered, and went to get her bras from the bureau.

"I knew this was going to happen," he said in a low, unhappy rumble. "I knew it from the first."

Oh, she wanted to throw that stack of bras at him. But she restrained herself. Barely. "Okay, Walker. You were right. It's ended in a big mess, just like you predicted. Does that make you feel better?"

He pushed off the doorway and entered the room. "It makes me feel like crap." He grabbed her arm.

She let out a low cry—and it wasn't from outrage. It felt good, to have his hand on her again. Too damn good. Now that she'd been his lover at last, how would she bear her life without his touch?

She dropped the bras into the suitcase and turned to face him. Her heart was a caged thing, beating frantic and ragged at the walls of her chest. He pulled her closer.

And she let him.

And then his arms were around her and…

She couldn't do it, couldn't make herself push him away. She lifted her mouth to his and he took it.

They stood there, by the open suitcase, kissing so hard and deep, just eating each other up. She never wanted to stop.

She wanted to shove the suitcase off the bed and pull him down onto it with her; to get lost in his big, strong body, in his beautiful kisses, in the wonder he could work with those rough and tender hands.

But where would that get them—except right back around to last night again?

She broke the kiss, pressing her hands to his chest to keep him from swooping down and claiming her lips again. "I need some time alone, okay? I need some time to think."

He took her face between his hands. His eyes were desperate. Wild. "This is worse. Worse than with Denise. How the hell can that be?"

"Walker." She took his wrists in either hand. "You have to let me go now."

"Tell me that you'll be okay. Tell me that…" He seemed to run out of words.

"Walker. Let me go."

That finally got through to him. He dropped his cradling hands from her face and stepped away. "I'll…carry your things down. As soon as you're packed." And then he turned on his heel and left her alone.

She went back to the Haltersham.

Once she'd checked in, she called Clara, who came right over.

Rory opened the door and Clara cried, "My God, Rory. What happened to you?"

"An icicle fell on me and then Walker said he could never love me." She burst into tears.

Clara held out her arms. Rory went into them gratefully. She cried for a long time.

And then she told Clara everything.

Clara asked, "So what are you going to do about it?"

Rory had to admit that she didn't know yet. "I just want to get through these next few days and the wedding."

"And after that?"

She only shrugged. "I meant what I said. I really don't know."

The next day Rory picked up her dress at Wedding Belles. Millie gasped at the sight of her.

"I'm thinking a whole lot of makeup," Rory told the dressmaker hopefully. "That might hide the black eyes. But then, there's still the ugly bandage..."

The dressmaker had her wait and hemmed a large square of the same eggplant satin as the dress. Then Millie showed her how to wear the makeshift scarf so it covered the bandage.

It wasn't great, but it was better than nothing.

Friday arrived. Her sister Genny called her early in the morning to tell her that she had a new nephew. They'd named him Tommy. Mother and son were back home at Hartmore and doing fine. Genny sounded so happy, perfectly content with the earl she loved and their new baby. She had the life she'd always dreamed of at last. When she asked about Walker, Rory just didn't feel like going into it all again, so she told her sister about the accident at the falls and being stranded in the cabin overnight and left out the part about how she and Walker were through. She would tell Genny later, when the hurt wasn't so fresh.

Afternoon rolled around and with it the rehearsal and rehearsal dinner. Her cousins fussed over her and swore that she didn't look bad at all. They continued to behave themselves. No scenes, not a single snarky comment.

Things between Clara and Ryan still didn't seem right. They were way too polite to each other, hardly touching at all and avoiding eye contact. Rory felt awful just watching them together. Since the night at the cabin, she'd been so wrapped up in her own misery, she'd hardly given a second thought to Clara and the mysterious, ongoing trouble between her and Ryan.

And then Walker showed up. One look in his eyes and Rory's poor heart broke all over again. After that, he tried not to glance her way. She tried not to look at him, either. But she did. And she caught him looking back more than once. She knew that look.

Hungry. Aching. He looked just like the way she felt.

But somehow, they got through it. When the dinner was over, he and Ryan left together. His leaving didn't help. Now, instead of hungry and aching, she just felt empty and sad.

The rest of them lingered over dessert. When the evening finally broke up, she tried to get Clara alone, hoping to maybe talk about Ryan a little. But there was a last-minute issue with the reception, something about the menu. Clara went off with Elise and Tracy to deal with that.

Rory returned to the hotel alone. She watched a couple of back-to-back Christmas specials hoping all the good cheer might lift her spirits. Didn't really happen. She gave up and went to bed.

The next morning, Clara's wedding day, the sun was shining. Maybe that was a good sign. Rory called Clara, but got voice mail. She left a brief message. "It's me. Call me back." Then she ordered room service. Her cell rang as she glumly poked at her eggs Benedict. She assumed it must be Clara.

But no.

"Hello, darling," her mother said.

Rory almost burst into tears on the spot. But she held it together somehow and rattled off a lame excuse about how she couldn't talk right now, with the wedding and all.

Adrienne said patiently, "I called Walker's ranch first, assuming you would be there. Walker told me you're back at the hotel. I am getting the distinct impression that all is not well."

"I just… I'll be back in Montedoro tomorrow night. And I don't want to go into it all now."

"I'm here. You know that. Anything you need."

Rory blinked away another spurt of unwanted tears. "I know. Thank you. I love you and I have to go now." She hung up before she started sobbing like a baby.

Clara didn't call. Rory texted her twice. Finally, she got a text back.

Swamped. CU @ the wedding. Limo @ 1:00

Swamped with what? More last-minute menu snafus? Or maybe Clara just didn't feel like listening to Rory moan over Walker. But that made no sense. Clara was always ready with a shoulder to cry on. She supported friends and family no matter how annoying their various personal issues might become.

Chances were, Clara just didn't want to talk about Ryan and she'd guessed that Rory intended to go there again.

What more could Rory do?

She called down to the hotel spa. They could take her right away. She had a hot rock massage and a mani-pedi. And then she went back to her suite, showered, troweled on the makeup, tied the eggplant scarf over her bandage the way Millie had shown her and put on her maid of honor dress.

At one on the dot, the limo arrived. Her cousins—all but Clara—were already inside. Nell handed her a flute of champagne and they toasted to love and forever-after. Rory had her cameras ready. She got some fun shots as they laughed and chatted, everyone getting along, not a single discouraging word. They sailed happily down Central Street, which was chockablock with Christmas shoppers.

The driver stopped in front of the big white church on Elk Street. They piled out, lifted their satin skirts and raced up the wide church steps, shivering, all of them eager to get in out of the cold. Clara was waiting for them, looking absolutely gorgeous in her snow-white lace-and-beadwork dress. There were hugs and good wishes and a sentimental tear or two. Rory took more pictures, the candid kind that Clara liked the best.

At two-fifteen, they grabbed their purple-calla-lily-and-white-rose bouquets and took their places. The wedding march began. One by one, the cousins headed down the aisle. Rory followed last before Clara, her stomach twisting a little at the sight of Walker in a good black suit, his face bleak and his eyes that heartbreaker blue, flanking Ryan at the altar.

Rory reached the others. She took her place on the left, closest to the waiting minister.

A breath-held pause and then Clara appeared, a vision in organza and lace, her sweet face barely visible beneath her veil. When she reached Ryan's side, she handed her bouquet to Rory and the ceremony began.

Rory watched the bride and groom and took great care never once to glance in the best man's direction. She was concentrating so hard on not looking at Walker, she really wasn't paying very close attention to the deep, solemn voice of the minister or the mostly familiar words of the traditional marriage ceremony.

Did the minister even ask the classic question about whether there was any reason the bride and groom should not be joined in holy matrimony? Rory couldn't have said.

She only knew that in the middle of her trying so hard not to look at Walker, Clara suddenly burst out with, "No. No, really. This is no good," and threw back her veil.

An audible gasp went up from the guests. The minister sputtered, "Well, but...I must say, this is highly unusual."

Someone let out a cry of surprise and an elderly voice demanded, "What is it? What's happened? What's gone wrong?"

And Ryan said, "Clara. It's okay. Really. I want to—"

"Shh," she said gently, and took both his hands. "You are the best friend any woman could have. But I can't do this to you. I can't do this to myself, or my baby. It just isn't right."

Someone whispered way too loudly, "I told you she was pregnant."

And someone else hissed, "Shush."

And Clara said to Ryan, "I know you've only tried to help me, to do what you could for me. And I do love you for it, but this, you and me married, it just isn't who we are. It isn't going to work."

There were more whispers, followed by more shushing.

Clara turned her head toward the pews. Chin high, she looked out over the sanctuary full of her wedding guests. "Ryan's not my baby's father, in case you all just have to know. The father is not in the picture and Ryan couldn't stand the thought of my child growing up without a dad. So he proposed. And I was weak and needy and said yes."

More gasps and whispers.

Clara turned back to Ryan. "I should have called it off long before now."

He searched her face. "Clara. My God. What can I say?"

"You don't have to say anything. You're not up for this. Neither am I. We both know I'm right. I can see in your eyes that you know. I've been seeing it for weeks now. You're my dearest friend and always will be. But marriage? Uh-uh. That's just not us." Clara's voice broke then. A small sniffle escaped her. "I want my friend back. Please."

"Aw, Clara…" Ryan let go of her hands, but only so that he could wrap his arms around her. For a moment, they just stood there, holding each other tight. And then he asked quietly, "Are you sure?"

She tipped her head back and met his waiting eyes. "Oh, Ryan. Yes. I am."

* * *

Walker wasn't exactly in a partying mood. But he wanted to support Clara and Rye, who had decided to hold the reception anyway.

The venue was the old Masonic Hall and most everybody came. They enjoyed Bravo Catering's excellent buffet, took advantage of the open bar and filled up the dance floor when the DJ took the stage. It was actually a great party, everybody said.

Walker did manage to get Rye aside for a few minutes before they served the big purple-and-white cake decorated with real purple flowers. Rye confessed that after being raised without a dad, he couldn't stand to think that Clara's child would have to grow up fatherless, too. Clara would never tell him who the dad was or why the hell the guy wasn't around.

"It went all wrong, though," Rye said. "The closer we got to the altar, the more strained things got between us. It wasn't going to work out with us. I wanted to give that baby a daddy. But even I can see that I'm not the one to do that. Calling it off was for the best."

Walker clapped him on the back. "I'm glad you're okay with the way it's turned out."

And then Rye asked, "So what's up with you and Rory?"

Walker lied with zero remorse. "I've got no idea what you're talking about."

"Not ready to discuss it yet, huh?"

"Discuss what?"

It was Rye's turn to clap *him* on the back. "You know I'm here for you, man, the minute you're ready to get honest about this."

For the rest of the evening, Walker mostly tried to

stay away from Rory, who had managed to look absolutely beautiful in spite of all the makeup she'd piled on to disguise those two serious shiners and the weird purple thing she had tied around her head. It wasn't easy, watching her dance with a bunch of other guys, knowing that she was leaving tomorrow and it was just possible she would never speak to him again.

He lasted until pretty late in the evening without bothering her. And then the DJ started playing a slow, romantic holiday song.

And he couldn't take it. He walked up behind her, grabbed her hand and led her out onto the floor.

Yeah, he half expected her to jerk away, maybe slap his face, or just turn and stalk off. He wouldn't have blamed her for an instant if she did any of those things.

But she only followed after him and then let him wrap his yearning arms around her. They danced. He breathed in the spice and sweetness of her, memorized all over again the softness and the strength of her, wondered how the hell he was going to get through the night without her. And the day after that. And the one after that.

He saw the future reeling out before him, an endless chain of emptiness—without her there to brighten the days and light up the nights.

That dance flew by so damn fast. It was over and he hadn't said a word to her, just held her and *breathed* her and somehow managed not to beg her never to go.

She spoke at last. "The dance is over. You need to let me go now."

Some desperate voice way down inside him cried out, *Never.* "Let me take you to the airport tomorrow."

"Walker. It's not a good idea."

"I know." He pulled her just a little closer, pressed

his rough cheek to her soft one, whispered prayerfully, "Let me take you."

"Walker..."

He cast about wildly for some convincing argument, some way to get her to see that he needed to do that, needed to see her on her way.

But then she made arguments unnecessary. Because she gave in. "I have to leave the hotel at seven in the morning."

"Seven. I'll be waiting for you right outside the lobby doors."

She nodded. "All right, then." And she stepped from the circle of his arms and left him standing there.

Rory and Clara stole a few minutes alone. They shared a pink tuck-and-roll sofa in the ladies' lounge.

"You're all right, then?" Rory asked her favorite cousin.

Clara drew in a breath and let it out slowly. "Yeah. Yeah, I really am." They were both leaning back against the cushions. Clara turned and grinned at her. "I have to say—only you could pull off that do-rag you're wearing."

Rory put on her princess voice. "This is no do-rag. It's an artfully tied handmade scarf. Scarves are quite the thing this year."

"Oh. Right. I knew that—and I saw you dancing with Walker."

So much for the lighthearted mood. "He's taking me to the airport tomorrow."

"Excellent."

"Not really. Clara, everything I told you the other day

still stands. He wants me, yeah. But he doesn't want love. He doesn't want *us*. It's not going to happen."

"Give him time."

Rory just shook her head. And then she leaned closer to her cousin and asked, "If Ryan's not the dad, then who?"

Clara sighed again. "I just… I can't talk about it now."

Rory longed to keep after her. But Clara didn't want that. And Rory tried to respect the wishes of her friends. "When you're ready to talk about it, you know I'll be there."

Rory half hoped that maybe Walker wouldn't show up to drive her to the airport, after all. The more she stewed over the situation, the more she dreaded the hour-and-a-half ride to Denver, just the two of them.

But then, she knew he would be there. Walker might not be willing to love again, or to marry. But when he made a promise, he kept it.

He was there in his SUV, waiting, when Jacob, the porter, wheeled out the luggage cart piled with her bags. Walker got out and helped get everything loaded.

Rory handed over a tip. And Jacob gave her a great big smile. "Thank you, Your Highness. Come and stay with us again soon."

She promised that she would and got in on the passenger side.

They set out. For the first twenty miles or so, she waited with a knot in her stomach, dreading whatever Walker planned to say.

But then he didn't say anything. A light snow was falling. The sun was a slightly brighter smudge behind the cloud cover, slowly lifting above the mountains.

He turned on the radio. Christmas music filled the empty space between them. Apparently, he had no big goodbye speech planned. It was just what he'd said it would be: a ride to the airport, nothing more. Just Walker being Walker, needing to finish what he'd started, to see her safely to the plane.

Rory levered her seat back and closed her eyes.

When she woke, the snow had stopped and the mountains were behind them. He'd turned off the radio.

"You looked so sweet and peaceful sleeping," he said on a gruff husk of breath.

She didn't say anything. She didn't know what to say.

In no time, they reached the airfield where the private planes took off. The family jet was waiting. One of those motorized carts idled right there at curbside, complete with driver, ready to load her luggage onto the plane.

Walker opened the hatch and the guy went to work.

Rory stayed in her seat, reluctant to get out. Once she did, it would truly be over. There would be nothing left but to say goodbye and walk away. It was tearing her up inside, like leaving him all over again, just to get out of his car.

He didn't move, either, not at first. They sat there, side by side, staring out the windshield—together, and so far apart.

And then, so suddenly that she had to swallow a gasp, he leaned on his door and jumped out. Still, she sat there, chewing her lower lip a little, as he came around to her door and pulled it open. The cold outside air swirled in, making her shiver.

He held out his hand. She took it.

And the second his warm fingers touched her cool ones, she knew what she had to do.

She swung her legs down to the blacktop. Once she stood on solid ground, it took only a single step forward to rest her hands against his heart.

"Rory..." He growled her name, eyes like a storm at sea.

"Shh." And she went on tiptoe and pressed her lips to his.

He froze for a second, and then he grabbed her good and hard. The kiss went deep. She reveled in it, drinking it in, determined to remember everything, the taste of his mouth, the buttery softness of his shearling jacket against her palms, the low groan he couldn't hold back.

"Rory..." He lifted that wonderful mouth much too soon.

She pressed a finger to his lips. "Are you listening?"

"My God. What?" He looked at her as though he would never let her go. But she knew the truth. His fear of what she offered was greater than his need.

She told him anyway. "I love you, Walker McKellan. I'm in love with you and only you." Now he just looked stunned. She rubbed her thumbs across his fleece collar and added cheerfully, "There. I've said it. Now there's no doubt about it. I've said the dreaded *L* word right to your face. And you can never pretend I didn't say it, never try to tell yourself that you didn't know for certain what was in my heart."

Chapter Thirteen

Walker watched her walk away.

As soon as she was out of sight, he got back in the SUV and went home to the ranch.

But going home was no good. Everything there reminded him of her. Lucky and Lonesome kept watching him mournfully. As if they wished they could speak human so they could ask him right out where she'd gone.

And what was it about that perfume of hers? Somehow it seemed to linger in the air. He kept thinking he smelled it—and then when he would sniff again…?

Gone.

How had he let this happen? He was supposed to know better. He was too damn much like his mother, the kind who fell so hard he hardly knew how to get back up on his feet again.

Somehow, in the time she'd stayed with him, she'd put her mark on everything. He had nothing left that didn't have her in it. His sofa, the hearth, the kitchen table, his bed…everything. All of it. Every stick of furniture he owned.

And the damn Christmas crap. What was he supposed to do about that? He couldn't bear to see it now. He wanted to chuck it all out a window, get rid of everything she'd touched.

But then there was the house itself. She'd filled up every room with her laughter and her passion and her flat-out love of life. No way to get the echoes of her out of there, except to strike a match and burn it to the ground.

He went out to the stables, thinking he'd ride up into the mountains. But then he just stood there staring blankly as the horses whickered softly in greeting, remembering the way she would get up early every morning to help with the animals, the way she pitched in around the place, always ready to work.

By noon, he'd had enough of wandering numbly from the house to the stables and back to the house again. He grabbed his keys and headed for town.

He decided he'd have lunch at Rye's place. And maybe a beer—or ten. Might as well get good and drunk. He seemed to be incapable of doing anything constructive.

When he got to McKellan's Rye took one look at him and declared, "It's about enough, big brother. We have to talk." Rye led him to the back and into his office. He shut the door.

Walker stared glumly at Rye's battered desk, remembering Rory perched on the edge of it the night of the bachelorette party, wearing a skirt the size of a postage stamp and those shoes that could give a man a heart attack. He remembered how he couldn't stop himself from kissing her, how they'd come so close to taking it all the way. Right there. On that very desk…

He shook his head. She was gone. But she was everywhere. There was no escaping the sweet, unbearable memories of her.

"You're a mess," Rye said. "Sit down before you fall down."

Walker didn't even bother to lie and say he was fine. He just backed up and dropped into one of the chairs.

Rye waited several seconds. When Walker just sat there, Rye asked, "So what happened?"

"Rory said she loves me. She said she's *in* love with me."

"And that's bad?"

"I didn't want her to say it. I tried to keep her from saying it. But she said it anyway."

Rye dropped into the chair behind the desk and swung his boots up onto the desktop. "Okay, I don't get it. This is not adding up. She says she's in love with you and you're acting like she took a shotgun to your heart."

"Because she did. She…got to me. Got to me deep. You know how I am, Rye. Kind of like Mom was. I fall too hard and I end up getting messed over. I'm better off on my own."

Rye made a snorting sound. "I will agree that you're better off on your own than with that crafty bitch Denise, yeah. But better off without Rory? Are you out of your mind? Rory's the real deal. If she says she loves you, you know it's the truth."

"She's too good for me. She grew up in a palace. Come on. I have to get real here. No way can it last."

"So?"

"So I'll end up like Mom, dragging around half-alive, waiting my whole life for her to come back."

"Kind of like what you're doing now?"

"I'm *not* waiting for Rory to come back." He said it a little louder than he meant to—or maybe a lot louder.

Loud enough that Rye put up both hands like a robbery victim at gunpoint. "Okay, okay. Whatever you say."

Walker muttered, "I did catch myself thinking of burning the house down."

"Totally healthy reaction to thwarted love, no doubt about it."

"I'm not thwarted. She didn't thwart me. She said that she *loves* me."

"Oh, right. I get it. The thwarting is something you're doing all on your own."

He gave his brother a look of deadly warning. "Don't mock me, Rye."

"I'm not mocking you. I'm just telling you what you need to hear. Because it's too late for you. You're so gone on her, you can't see straight. You're outta control. I know how you hate that, how you need to be on top of every little thing. But with love, well, there's nothing to do but give in to it."

"How the hell do you know so much about love all of a sudden?"

Rye shrugged. "I tend bar. You learn a lot about what makes people tick tending bar. Eventually I'm hoping to apply what I've learned to my own life. Hasn't happened yet, but I'm workin' on it—and where was I? Oh, yeah. There's a point in every love affair where a man can turn and walk away clean. You are way past that point, big brother. Right now, the only sensible thing for you to do is to get your ass to Montedoro and pray to heaven she takes you back."

"I'm not going to Montedoro. What's a guy like me going to do in Montedoro?"

Rye only looked at him, shaking his head.

"You *were* matchmaking, weren't you, Mother?" Rory purposely made the question into something of an accusation. Sometimes, with her mother, the only way to go was on the offensive.

Adrienne sat on the long velvet sofa in her private office at the palace. She sipped oolong from a beautiful old Sevres teacup. Wincing a little, she eyed the bandage on Rory's forehead. "Tell me you had that looked at."

"I did, yes. And I'm taking proper care of it—and answer my question. Were you matchmaking?"

A slight smile curved her beautiful mother's still-full lips. "Yes, I suppose I was. I really like Walker, and I thought the two of you would make a fine couple."

"You hardly know him. You spent maybe three hours in his presence that time you and Papa came to Colorado."

"I have a great sense for people. I knew instantly that he was a good man, a man of strength and integrity. And then there was the fact that you've been in love with him for years. You would hardly love a man who wasn't worthy."

Rory set her teacup on the low table between them. "It wasn't love, for all those years. Not exactly, anyway. And I really, really thought that nobody knew."

"Oh, my darling. Forgive me. But I *am* your mother. And sometimes a mother just knows." She patted the space beside her on the sofa.

Rory gave in to her need for comfort. She got up, went around the low table and sat down. With a shaky little sigh, she laid her head on her mother's Chanel-clad shoulder. "It didn't work out. And it hurts so damn much."

Her mother smoothed her hair and pressed a kiss against her temple, at the edge of the bandage. "Sometimes the best ones have a hard time surrendering."

"You say that as if there's still some hope. Seriously. There's not."

Her mother made a tsking sound. "It's not like you to give in so easily, my darling."

"But I haven't given in easily. Believe me, I haven't. I've waited years for him. I've offered him everything—my heart, my future, my two capable hands. At some point, he's got to start offering back. That hasn't happened. And he's given me no reason to believe that it ever will."

Two days before Christmas, His Serene Highness Maximilian Bravo-Calabretti, heir to the Montedoran throne, married Texas-born Yolanda Vasquez, former nanny and budding novelist. There were two ceremonies, one religious and one of state.

Rory attended both. It did her heart good to see her oldest brother happy at last, after losing his first wife in a tragic accident. Yolanda, whom they all called Lani, wore a cream silk day suit for the ceremony of state and a gorgeous white gown with a lace-and-beadwork train for the religious ceremony.

That night, people celebrated through all of Montedoro. There were parties in the grand casino, Casino d'Ambre, with twenty giant Christmas trees blazing bright in the area of exclusive shops called the Triangle d'Or. Every café and restaurant through all ten wards was packed with revelers.

In the Prince's Palace, on its rocky promontory above the Mediterranean, Her Sovereign Highness Adrienne and her beloved husband, Prince Evan, held a wedding gala. The guests filled the heated tents erected in the gardens, where dinner was served on the finest china, beneath a fantasy of party lights, to the glow of a thousand crystal candlesticks.

After the meal, everyone made their way up to the ballroom. Lani's father, an English professor from the Fort Worth area, led her out onto the floor for the first dance. As tradition dictated, Max cut in. The father surrendered his daughter to her prince.

Rory stood on the sidelines in a floor-length strapless gown of gold metallic lace, a matching scarf tied artfully over the bandage on her forehead. She sipped champagne, happy for her brother and his bride in spite of the sadness that dragged on her heart.

She visited with her sisters Alice and Rhiannon, both of whom were married now—just like Max and Rule and Alexander and Damien, like Arabella and Genny, too. Genny was the only one of Rory's siblings who hadn't made it to the wedding, having given birth to little Tommy such a short time before.

For Rory, it felt more than a little lonely, to be the only one still single of the nine of them. Especially now, after her two magical, impossible, beautiful, frustrating weeks with Walker at home in Justice Creek.

Home.

She felt the tears rise and gulped them down. She loved Montedoro and she always would. But Colorado was her home and no matter how hard it was going to be to have to see Walker now and then, around town, she would not give up the home of her heart. One day she *would* have a place of her own in Justice Creek.

Alice and Rhia wanted to hear all about her adventures in the Rockies. She told them of the view from Lookout Point and the beauty of Ice Castle Falls. And she described what it was like to spend a snowy night stranded in a tiny cabin in the piney woods.

But then their husbands came to claim them. The men greeted Rory warmly and took their wives off to dance.

Rory watched them, her heart so full.

"Don't turn around," said a deep, rough voice behind her.

She couldn't breathe, couldn't move. Hope was rising, undeniable. She bit her lip and froze in place.

He touched her then. She felt his rough, warm, knowing finger. He traced a light path across the bare skin between her shoulder blades. Heat flared across her skin. But still, she didn't turn to look.

Didn't dare.

Couldn't bear to know if this was real. Or just a sweet hallucination brought on by her stubborn, yearning heart, a heart that simply couldn't bear to accept defeat.

He leaned closer. She felt the warmth and height of him behind her. The scent of him came to her. Woodsy, clean. All man. "You are so beautiful," he said. "So fine. So completely outside the boundaries of my wildest dreams. I didn't want to want you, Rory. It seemed… way too dangerous. And to love you? Complete insanity. You're so much braver and bolder than I am. I can't hope to live up to you."

"Walker." There. She'd done it. Said his name right out loud.

And he was still there. She could feel him, still real and warm and solid, standing right behind her. "I should have said I love you that day at the airport," he told her. "I should have dropped to my knees and begged you to marry me."

Oh, God. Real. He was really there, no doubt about it now. No trick. No fantasy. Real.

She asked, "Is there…some reason you told me not to turn around?"

"Do you want to walk away from me?"

"Are you insane? Of course not."

"Because if you do, just go, just don't even look at me. Don't even…" His voice broke. A low oath escaped him. And then his hands were on her, clasping her bare shoulders tight. Heat sizzled through her. His touch felt so good. "Never mind." The words came out in a sandpaper whisper. "Forget I said that. Don't walk away from me. Oh, God, Rory. Please…" And he pulled her back against his tall, hard body and pressed his cheek to hers. "I love you. I see that now. There's no going back. I want a chance with you. I don't care how long it lasts, where we end up. I just want…a chance, okay?"

She couldn't take it anymore. She turned in his arms, put her palms flat against his broad chest and stared up into his beloved grim face. "How did you get here?"

"Well, they have these machines called airplanes…"

She wanted to punch him. And she wanted to grab him to her and never, ever let him go. Or maybe both. "Very funny."

He wore the same good dark suit he'd worn to Clara and Ryan's almost wedding and he looked at her with eyes full of love. "I have an actual engraved invitation," he told her. "It came by courier to the ranch yesterday morning."

She knew then. "Let me guess. My mother sent it."

He nodded. "I had to scramble for flights."

"What? My mother didn't send a family jet for you?"

"She offered in the little note that came with the invitation. It said to call her and she would take care of transportation."

"But you didn't call her."

"It seemed the least I could do, to book my own damn flight."

"You're too proud, Walker."

He shrugged. "I ended up with a damn stopover in London that lasted half a lifetime. I started to wonder if I would even make it here tonight."

"But you did." She gazed up at him. She would never get enough of that, of just looking at him, of being held in his arms.

"Tell me now," he said, his tone gone desperate. "Have I blown it completely? Is there any way that you might be willing to try again?"

Her brother Damien danced by, his wife, Lucy, in his arms. Her brother Alex came right after with his wife, Liliana.

She said, "I think you should dance with me."

He blinked. "Dance…?"

She put one hand on his shoulder and held the other up for him to take. "Dance."

He led her onto the floor and took her in his arms. As they swayed and turned beneath the dazzling light of the world-famous Empire-style gold-and-crystal chandeliers, she said, "You would have to learn to trust me. To trust what we have together."

"Yes," he said. "I see that. I do. And I do trust you, Rory. I believe in you."

"And I believe in you. I do, Walker. You are my heart's desire."

"Rory…" They had somehow stopped dancing. They swayed together in the middle of the ballroom floor.

The other couples seemed unfazed. They simply danced around them. He asked again, “Another chance? You and me?”

“I love you, Walker.”

“I can’t believe it. I think you just said yes.”

“I have it all figured out,” she told him. “How it’s going to be. We’ll take it slow, okay? We won’t be rushing anything.”

He suddenly looked stricken. “Are you saying you already know that you’ll never marry me?”

“Oh, I will definitely marry you. No worries on that score.”

“Whew. You scared me there for a minute.”

“Kiss me, Walker.”

“Right here? In the middle of the dance floor?”

“Kiss me. Now.”

And he lowered his lips to hers.

Epilogue

Later that night, after they retired to her palace apartment and celebrated their reunion in the most intimate way, Walker proposed properly, on his knees, wearing nothing, offering her a beautiful cushion-cut diamond engagement ring.

She accepted, joyfully.

Walker remained with her at the palace for Christmas and New Year's. On the second of January, they flew home to Justice Creek, stopping off on the way for a few days with Genny, Rafe and little Tommy in Derbyshire, England.

In February, after the wound on Rory's forehead had healed to a thin, red scar, they hiked back to Ice Castle Falls. The falls were still frozen. Rory got some great pictures. And on that same fateful ledge where he'd turned her down all those summers before, Walker took her in his arms and kissed her slow and sweet and deep.

From there, they went to the cabin in the woods. They took the shutters off the windows, built a fire against the cold and climbed the stairs to the sleeping loft with their arms around each other. The old iron bed up there was a creaky one. Neither of them cared.

In March, Rory accepted an assignment to photograph the birds of the coastal marshes in Virginia's Chincoteague National Wildlife Refuge. They left the Colgins in charge at the ranch and Walker went with her. For three weeks, they camped out. It was rugged and isolated and absolutely wonderful.

After they returned, Clara had her baby and found her own heart's desire.

Summer came and with it peak season at the Bar-N. Guests filled the houses, the cabins and the bunkhouse. Rory helped out around the place and studied up on raising chickens. There were a lot of options and she wanted to get it right. She settled on pasturing, which included a movable fence, an electric energizer to keep the birds in and the predators out, and a portable chicken house. The chickens had a safe, movable area that contained grass, bugs, sunshine and fresh air. By September, she had two dozen happy, healthy birds.

Walker said, "I didn't believe you really meant it when you claimed you wanted chickens."

She went and sat on his lap and whispered, "Next, I want a rooster. I want to raise my own chicks."

"A rooster, huh?" He stood up suddenly, taking her with him.

She laughed in surprise. "Walker, what…?"

"Come on upstairs." He nuzzled her neck. "We can talk it over in bed."

He carried her up to their bedroom and made slow, delicious love to her in the middle of the afternoon. The rooster was temporarily forgotten. Rory didn't mind.

For Thanksgiving, Rory and Walker flew to Montedoro. They visited her family and attended the traditional Prince's Thanksgiving Bazaar and the annual Thanksgiving Ball.

Christmastime, they spent at home in Justice Creek. She dragged him to Rocky Mountain Christmas again, and they bought more "Christmas crap," as he so fondly called it.

That evening at home, she said, "I want a tree-decorating party, same as last year. It's going to be an annual tradition with us."

He scooped her high in his arms. "We can talk about it upstairs." And he carried her to their bed, where he took off all her clothes and kept her awake late doing lovely, naughty things. The tree-decorating party discussion? Didn't happen.

But really, what more was there to say? Rory wanted the party and Walker did, too, though he kind of enjoyed playing Scrooge about it. The next day, they invited friends and family to come and help them make the ranch house ready for the holidays. Everyone had a great time and they all agreed it should be an annual affair.

Rory's parents arrived on December 20. And on Christmas Eve at two in the afternoon, in a tiny log church surrounded by the snow-covered peaks of the Rockies, Rory stood at the altar with Walker at her side.

His voice shook just a little when he said, "I do."

He slid the platinum band on her finger to join the engagement ring he'd given her the year before. And then he took her in his arms and he kissed her so tenderly.

"Merry Christmas, Your Highness," he whispered.

"Forever and always," she answered.

"And that," he said gruffly, "is the only Christmas present I'm ever going to need."

* * * * *

MILLS & BOON®

Exciting new titles coming next month

With over 100 new titles available every month, find out what exciting romances lie ahead next month.

Visit

www.millsandboon.co.uk/comingsoon

to find out more!